MEDUSA GONE

A Novel

by WYATT TREMBLAY

Raspberry Press

For information contact:
wyattsworld@me.com
http://www.wyattsworld.ca

Cover front and back design by Maja Hampson

Print ISBN: 978-1-7780881-4-8
Published by Raspberry Press
www.raspberrypress.ca

First Edition: June 2022

For Bonnie, who believed.

PROLOGUE

THE MIGHTY TITAN WAS DYING.

Globules of dark red blood were spinning lazily in and out of the limited field of vision he had with the one eye he was able to open. The crimson blobs oozing from the various wounds in his body looked oddly animated, rolling, and spinning as they reflected starlight, sunlight, and Earthlight, some smashing into each other, forming larger glistening irregular balls, while others twisted and careened like bumper cars at a carnival. He'd rarely ever seen his own blood, his skin was remarkably impervious to the elements of the universe. Still, the grievous wounds that his enemy had inflicted over their hour-long battle above the Earth had wounded him in ways he hadn't thought possible.

"How?" his mind begged.

The simple question was unable to find the proper motor neurones to reach his broken, swollen mouth to form the word.

His great strength, its once immeasurable power was ebbing out along with his blood, apparently as easily as the grains of sand slipping between the fingers of a hand. Had he ever truly contemplated his death? He'd thought upon it once or twice before The Event, but he'd been far younger then and had only just begun his journey as the Mighty Titan. That was more than a century ago, and the possibility of his death hadn't been a consideration, not really. He wouldn't live forever, that much had been obvious as his body had aged, but slowly, the remarkable energy within him had extended his life well past the human average and perhaps would do so for another hundred years.

Since The Event, he'd always been hyper-aware of every cell in his body, and he could feel with certainty that his wounds wouldn't heal in time to avert a complete neurological or cardiac failure. The deep rips, cuts, and tears, alarmingly devastating, reached down to a sub-molecular level. His mind had assessed the damage, and what had been done to him would certainly be irreversible if he couldn't flee. Yet escape seemed improbable at the moment, as it appeared his power was so weakened that he had little control over what he could do with it. If he'd been able to return to the security of the Fortress, his power would regenerate and repair his body over time, but no, it was too late now.

He'd failed. He'd failed the Earth and its noble people.

Somewhere close above him, he heard a shrill laugh. It was Magus, giddy with his unexpected win no doubt, mocking him with the impending victory. The grating sound pierced the near-death fog of Titan's mind and he wished he could turn and face Magus, but his power was weaker than he'd ever thought possible.

He was adrift, looking down upon the Earth, over which their epic battle had taken place, the last of their many, many confrontations it would appear. The coast of Scotland, its night sky bathed in the innocence of wispy moon-glow-tinged clouds, was only recognizable far beneath him because of his familiarity with his cherished blue planet, and because it was his family's, the Mackenzie's, ancestral home. He hadn't remained in the Scottish Highlands after The Event, and perhaps he should have, but when Hunter MacKenzie was miraculously transformed and he willingly took upon himself the role of the defender of the helpless and the weak as the Mighty Titan, the universe became his broader home, and the League became his family.

Yet here was Earth, the home of this childhood, beautiful and more dazzling with its diversity of life than any planet he'd ever seen, and he'd seen many. Some were gas giants inhabited by amoeba-like spectral creatures, while others were tiny ocean moons, teaming with intelligent life. Yes, life was everywhere in the galaxy, existing on every imaginable and unimaginable planet, but none were quite like Earth. It wasn't entirely a shame that this would be his last moment, but he regretted that he'd never see this view again.

A brutally strong hand punched through the normally near-impenetrable energy that protected Titan from the elements and laws of physics of the universe, and from the attacks of his enemies. Magus gripped his shoulder, squeezing without mercy.

Hunter cried in anguish. He'd never felt such intense and invasive pain. His cells had ignored the savage heat of the sun's corona, he'd flown through the sky-splitting fury of the lightning storms of Jupiter with barely a tickle to tell him of their awesome power, but what Magus had done to him was undeniable and unbelievable. His worst foe, his greatest enemy, had defeated Earth's greatest superhero, and now he was about to die.

"I know what you're thinking," said his adversary's voice, hot and putrid, grating across his left ear, washing over his bruised cheek. "How? How did Magus defeat the all-powerful Mighty Titan?"

"I. Don't. Care."

The words bubbled from his bloodied throat. It was a lie. He wanted to know what Magus had done to him, and how.

Magus laughed again and drove a thumb deeper into the gruesome and gaping wound that dissected Titan's shoulder, leaving his left arm useless, powerless. The Mighty Titan clenched his teeth and used what little strength he could muster to force the pain to the back of his awareness. He would die, but he wouldn't give Magus the satisfaction of enjoying this moment.

Hands roughly grabbed Titan's shoulders and he was quickly flipped over, revealing Magus hovering just over him, his face filled with a triumphant grin.

"Oh, I do so love this moment," he gloated.

He pushed back and rose up above Titan before dropping down heavily to stand on his enemy's mid-torso, one booted foot resting on his abdomen, the other over the flaming 'T' that emblazoned his chest.

Titan cried out in pain, his blurred vision seeing the black boot of his nemesis resting on the flaming 'T.' The bold letter was the colour of the glow of a red giant star and was embraced by stylized flames of translucent blue. It was a symbol recognized across the Earth and on dozens of other inhabited planets. It would never be seen as a symbol of hope again and Titan felt a moment of something he'd only occasionally felt. Sorrow, he felt deep sorrow.

The moon, an ever-silent observer wrapped in the starry curtain of space, shone brightly down over Magus's right shoulder. Titan squinted, his eyes hurting from the glare. Neither Luna nor Sol had ever hurt his eyes before, so he shifted his head slightly, putting the reflected glare of the sun behind his enemy's scarred face. These were the scars he'd given him as they'd battled over the decades.

Magus snorted and stomped a foot hard against Titan's chest. Magus shouldn't have been able to wound him like this, but Titan was injured beyond what he thought possible. His nostrils flared, as his broken body struggled to control the sudden assault of pain from the heavy boot.

"Thomas. Stop," Titan gasped.

Magus squatted down and grabbed Titan by the edge of his shattered mask, yanking his head forward.

"Do not call me by that pathetic name, ever. I am Magus the Magnificent, Magus the Glorious, I am Magus your death."

Titan groaned in agony, bursts of light, pelting his vision like a hundred tiny meteorites. He pushed the shadow of death away and looked at the angry face of his longtime foe.

"You were once Thomas Stewart. You were once a compassionate human being."

"Bah!" Magus scoffed as he stood up, his booted feet pressing painfully into Hunter's midsection. "Human? You mean human weakness, that's what you mean. Weakness is for pains in the asses like you, Hunter. Do-gooders, interferers, you know nothing of greatness, of my greatness. Thomas is dead, he was weak. I am the Magnificent Magus."

He laughed riotously, and sneered down at Titan, then suddenly dropped, to straddle his midsection, slapping both hands palm down hard over the 'T.'

"Aren't you the least bit curious? Don't you want to know how I defeated you?"

"No," Hunter sputtered, as waves of pain lashed through his chest, penetrating deep into his being.

"Oh, yes you do. I know you. You're such a terrible liar. You do want to know. I can see it in your eyes, well, your one eye."

Laughing, he pushed the shattered remains of Hunter's mask up over his head, flicking it away into the cold of space just beyond the glistening bubble of energy that surrounded them both. Magus's deathly cool eyes focused on his foe's face.

"See, you do want to know!"

"How?" said Titan, forcing the question through the shattered teeth of his mouth.

"My piece de resistance," Magus misspoke, laughing at his own mangled use of the phrase.

He'd never been that educated or articulate, just insanely intelligent, and with enough crazed imagination to have devised a way to kill the planet's strongest hero in the span of but a few hours. It shouldn't have been possible, yet here he was, defeated.

Magus reached around and thrust his hand into a thigh pocket of Titan's armoured suit, extracting a black disc not much larger than the palm of his gloved hand.

"I slipped it into your suit earlier, as we tussled out there near the Moon," he said, then laughed, lowering the object toward Titan's face so he could see it clearly.

The device had an inky blackness to it that was more devoid of light than any of the darkest, most distant corners of the universe Titan had ever travelled to. It was almost indiscernible, like trying to see a black object against a black background. As Magus slowly turned it, like a coin in his hand, Titan saw that its surface was etched with unusual markings, hieroglyphs perhaps, that glowed with a faint blue tinge, just enough to make the markings visible. He'd seen a similar device before, in the hands of Gloria, just before she had died.

"You had no idea, did you?" he said wistfully, as he slowly turned the object over in his gloved hand. "Every time you used your power to strike me, you were striking yourself."

Titan suddenly felt foolish, not a feeling he was accustomed to. He was the Mighty Titan. He was far more powerful than Magus. He'd been so assured of this, of his own prowess, of his own strength, that he hadn't once imagined that Magus could defeat him. His arrogance had left him open and vulnerable.

"Medusa and I searched the galaxy for this substance, my dear Titan."

"Gloria," Hunter groaned, painfully.

"What's that?" Magus sneered, his eyes narrowing to flaming slits. "How dare you speak her name?"

He leaned in closer to growl in Titan's ear.

"She's Medusa to you. You aren't worthy to speak her beautiful name, nor are you worthy of the death you're about to taste!"

Titan twisted under the pressure of Magus's weight, but his spine wouldn't cooperate.

"You poisoned her mind," he said, sucking a breath in harshly. "With your promise of ultimate power."

Magus laughed.

"Oh, my sad, sad foe, she was much more powerful than either of us. She didn't need me to make her more powerful. She needed me to guide her to the full potential of that power. She was my greatest student!"

He chortled.

"She found the discs on an ocean planet, days before you killed her! That's how I knew they existed, those fish creatures told me she had taken one of them with her. And then you killed her. How dare you!"

Hunter shook his head, despite the shocking pain that came with the movement.

"No! I didn't kill her. It was your madness that killed her. You pushed her in your quest for ultimate power. You drove her to despair."

His mind flashed to many years earlier, to thoughts of Gloria, alone, a tiny figure in a high orbit above the ocean planet of Rathmus II, with her long, thick hair, always woven into dozens of braids that flowed out from the crown of her head, undulating around her face as she held two palm-sized discs in her gloved hands. Hunter saw this as he zoomed in with the power of his vision, and noted that the devices were intensely black, almost indiscernible from the darkness of space. Gloria, the formidable Medusa, was laughing uncontrollably, her mind ravaged, he believed, by Magus's manic claims of greatness and the promise of power beyond anything in the universe. She hadn't sensed Titan's approach until he was almost upon her. Only then did their eyes meet and for a moment the world returned to a time when he'd thought, perhaps foolishly, that they could have been on the same side of justice. Yet then, as suddenly as it had come, the thought vanished.

Medusa smiled and winked at him as if they were old friends exchanging a greeting in passing. The gesture was peculiar and unsettling to him. He'd never wished to be her enemy. He'd long thought that he could save her from the influence of Magus, but that wish had never transpired. Then she pulled off her gloves and pushed the discs together between her two palms. Space itself began to fold and ripple around her hands, as she funnelled her energy into the devices. Within seconds, a sparkling sphere of energy formed around her hands, pulsing and expanding to quickly envelop her torso, before finally swelling and engulfing her entire body.

Her face grimaced. He thought she was in pain, so he shifted to within a metre of her, reaching out for her hands to pull them apart, to save her, but the bubble of energy that had formed around her, from whatever the devices were doing, violently repelled him. He quickly recovered a dozen metres away then turned to watch in horror as her body began to modulate, slipping in and out of focus. He called her name, forcing the energy from his voice toward her, and she opened her eyes, turning her head, looking for him. Their eyes met, and she smiled sadly at him. It was a strange, odd smile, as her tears flowed like rivers down her cheeks, their glittering trails reflecting the light from the planet's distant star. Her eyes then grew terribly wide as she sucked in her breath, every muscle in her neck and face taut.

Then she screamed.

The sound exploded from deep within her, smashing out through the energy field that held her, traversing the distance between them in the near vacuum of space to smash into his own energy field. It was a horrible, soul-wrenching cry, like nothing Titan had ever heard, and one he'd never forget.

Then, Medusa's energy burst from within her. The familiar writhing dark cloud pushed out through every cell of her body in a mess of twisting tendrils, like the arms of an octopus reaching out in every direction. Then they pulled back in violently, erupted back out then pulled in again, before flinging outward and whipping around her body and back in through her two clasped hands. Finally, the dark arms of her power exploded violently outward in a jagged starburst, some of the angry tendrils almost reaching Titan. They paused at their apexes, dozens of vibrating arms shimmering with their destructive power as if grasping for something just out of reach. Her face turned to his again, her blue eyes streaming blood from burst capillaries. She seemed so sad, he'd thought. Then the outstretched tendrils unfroze and imploded with blinding speed back into her hands, causing such an intensely bright flare that even Titan had to squint. Her terrible cries immediately stopped, and the deafening silence of outer space collapsed in around him. When he looked to where she was, he watched her body break apart into millions of particles of glimmering energy that quickly faded away, like sparks from a campfire disappearing into the night sky, leaving the empty shell of her costume.

He'd thought of her death every day since then.

"You killed her," his enemy snarled, as he held the black object close to Titan's face. "You killed the only person who loved me, who truly accepted my greatness. She found the Black Energy. She found it and you killed her!"

Magus pushed the disc against the skin of Titan's cheek, causing excruciating pain as cells wrenched violently away from their natural electrical bonds, pulled apart by an incredible force. It hurt like hell.

Magus leaned in closer to watch the effect.

"Yes, you killed her, but now the Black Energy shall take away your pathetic life."

Titan almost laughed, but it was requiring all the strength he could muster to hold the claws of eternity at bay. Magus had always been a melodramatic megalomaniac.

"Not much of a name," Titan managed to groan.

"It doesn't need to be, you visionless putz. Whether I call it the Black Energy or a child's brick, it's how I defeated you and why you're about to die."

Magus tapped Titan sharply on the side of his beaten head with the weapon. Extraordinary explosions of pain pounded the hero's body.

"How?"

Magus laughed, holding the disc close to his own eyes as he slowly turned it in his hand.

"You know, my old foe, when you killed Gloria, I thought for sure you'd taken the discs she'd found, but now I see you're more a fool than I thought. You lost your one chance to destroy me."

Magus looked down into Titan's face.

"Oh, I see you're wondering how this little thing can cause you so much pain."

He tapped the side of Titan's head again, relishing in the discomfort he could see it caused his enemy.

"Perhaps this is the strongest, most efficient, most powerful energy-absorbing substance in the universe," he said, his laughter rising to a screech. "I don't know, really. The fishy scientists I took them from are all dead!"

He touched two fingers to his chin.

"All dead. What a terrible, sad, sad accident." He threw his arms wide. "Who cares how it works? All I know is that I have four of these little objects, and they consume every bit of energy they come in physical contact with. Why, when I first handled them, they gave me a great deal of pain, until my superior genius figured out how to handle them."

He lowered the object close to Titan's face again and laughed, the sound chilling.

"While you were pummelling me with all those blasts moments ago, you were actually orchestrating your own defeat!"

His voice rose in an excited, gleeful pitch.

"Every hit on me was a much more powerful hit on your powers," he said, his hands arched above his head in a show of triumph. "Ironic, isn't it? Your own almighty, all-powerful strength has killed you."

"Why doesn't it affect you?" Titan struggled to say.

"Why not me?" Magus echoed, tilting his head to one side, as he smiled.

Magus clasped the disc between the fingers of his two gloved hands, gazing into its impenetrable blackness with something close to affection.

"Platinum. Woven platinum. Black Energy has no effect on it. The cases those creatures were keeping them in are made of platinum. Amazing, really, something this deliciously powerful has no effect on this simple element."

Titan felt a sharp moment of hope. Magus's arrogance had always been his undoing. He never knew when to shut up. Titan closed his eyes and focused, drawing every last bit of strength and resolve from every last cell of his body. He'd always been able to do that, to feel the powerful energy coursing through the very fabric of his being. This time, and the feeling frightened him, there was almost nothing left to draw upon, but he focused, narrowed the flow of his energy to his left shoulder, to the damage inflicted by Magus. The dead, broken cells awoke, and began to knit, to repair themselves. But it was slow work, bringing life back to dead flesh, and he was too weak to do much more than this.

Magus continued to gloat in the pleasure of his victory, to boast of his crushing blow to Earth's greatest hero, and Hunter continued to channel his last remaining strength into one concentrated plan of action.

It was suicide, but it would also end Magus's life, something he'd been loath to do for more than a century.

"Ah, yes," Magus continued to gloat, "so brilliant, is it not? Medusa knew if we could harness this magnificent power, we'd be the most formidable …"

Then the Mighty Titan, Earth's greatest superhero, launched his final attack against his greatest enemy.

As fast as he was able, which was considerably faster than any healthy human, Titan reached up with his right hand and grabbed Magus's gloved hand that held the disc, while simultaneously yanking the glove from Magus's other hand with his own left. The sudden demand on his damaged left shoulder brought searing, fiery pain. The muscles screamed in protest, as newly knitted tissue tore afresh and cells exploded, but the arm held together, obeying the task he'd commanded it to fulfill. Not bothering to look for a reaction, he grasped Magus's now bare hand and forced both their hands against the energy-absorbing black disc still clasped within Magus's gloved hand. His enemy never had the chance to resist. Black energy connected with Magus's flesh, its insatiable need for power clawing through Magus's hand into Titan's own.

"What? No! You fool! You'll kill us both!" Magus bellowed as he struggled to pull away.

Titan could see the sudden fear in his enemy's eyes, and he laughed, despite the almost unbearable spasms of agony that coursed through his entire being. Magus was not known for his thoughtful planning. Titan pushed their two hands together with even more resolve, drawing on the deepest reserves of his power, pulling energy from every cell, every molecule, every particle of his body. Magus resisted, tried to pull their hands apart, slammed his knees viciously and repeatedly into Titan's ribs, then twisted, pulled, and yanked, but Titan was singular, focused, and he and his power had only one purpose now.

Magus drew on his own power, trying, Titan supposed, to blast their hands apart, but the device just pulled Magus's energy into itself as if it was a black hole, mercilessly pulling in any and all energies touching it.

Titan closed his eyes and focused. Don't let go of his hand, he commanded himself, don't let go, and his hands, his arms, and his damaged shoulder obeyed. The universe slowed, and his breathing pulled into focus, in, out, in, out. And Magus struggled, screamed, head-butted Titan, and pulled and wrenched with all his might, but Titan didn't concede to the pain. His power, the mysterious almost sentient energy that had infused his body as a young man during The Event, grew, pulsed, and rose to the challenge, fighting for this one moment, this one final moment of battle.

Titan opened his eyes, pushing past the compulsion to keep them shut. He wanted to see his own death and that of Magus. Sparks, like tiny shooting stars, began to erupt from within their hands, finding spaces of release around their glowing fingers. The smell of burning flesh enveloped them both, as the black disc reacted to this convergence of powerful energies. A light as intense as Sol flashed and rapidly expanded, consuming both men, and far below, in Edinburgh and all of Scotland, people would talk for weeks of an explosion overhead of such brilliance and magnitude that night became day for the briefest of moments. Footage of the burst from CCTV cameras and from stargazers with their telescopes trained overhead in the direction of the explosion would play again and again on televisions and digital devices, while scientists and news commentators would ponder what it had been, on what had occurred at the edge of space over Scotland to have caused such a violent explosion.

Hunter McKenzie, the Mighty Titan, was aware of Magus' screams, which matched his own. The pain was so complete, so thorough, that he could no longer contain himself and his own anguish poured from within him in shocking torrents. He could feel every molecule of his once powerful body rend itself apart. Still, even then he knew he'd made the right decision. He might cease to exist, but all of the worlds that had suffered under the hands of Magus would finally be free of him. In the end, after all the times he could have rid the universe of the scourge that was Thomas Stewart, Magus, this final act was worth the sacrifice.

He closed his eyes one final time, as his cells were being consumed, absorbed by the mysterious device. As the blackness behind his eyes turned into a brilliant white, Titan thought of the young man he'd once been, so long ago.

How odd, he thought, that his last thoughts would be of the awkward young man who had no idea who he would become.

Then it was over, and everything became nothing.

ONE

"Prepare to die, cretinous vermin!"

SOMETHING HAD GONE TERRIBLY WRONG, that much was obvious, as he seemed to be without a body. Still, Magus gloated, Titan was dead. However, it seemed he might also be dead. At least, if this was death, then it appeared he also had come to some sort of transformative end. He hadn't expected this outcome, though. Was there existence after death?

He was aware that he was floating in a white, and very dense cloud-like mist and he seemed to be non-corporeal. He was without a body, yet he could 'see'. Well, it wasn't really seeing so much as it was some kind of otherworldly awareness of something other than himself. It was as if his entire body were an eye, and Magus could occasionally 'see' other beings near him as they passed briefly within his 'sight' in the mist, like the vague shapes of people passing in a dense fog.

One of these passing shapes 'brushed' against him, and he immediately perceived that she was a young woman with long and striking black hair. She didn't seem to notice that she'd 'touched' him, but Magus 'felt' everything about her. It was as if a violent electric shock filled with her personal information passed through his ghost fingers and arched up his ghost arm to his ghost brain. As they touched, he had a jumbled flash of emotions, including love, fear, excitement, and sexual tension, all mashed together like debris from a flash flood. It faded quickly as she too disappeared into the fog, leaving him exhausted if that were even possible in this state.

Magus tried to fathom what had happened. His physical form no longer appeared to exist, yet he obviously wasn't dead, unless self-awareness was an aspect of death. These others, these fleeting entities in this fog, he was aware of them, but they seemed unaware of his presence. Had the device reduced him to pure consciousness? No, he didn't think so. If he was simply consciousness now, then why could he feel the distinct presence of his magnificent power? It had always been a tangible thing, a part of him, but also apart from him, like the white noise created by the flow of water in a river, present but not intrusive, an old friend that was always close by, hovering in the background of his ambitions, ready to assist him in accomplishing his goals.

Another being 'brushed' against his presence, and he felt anxiety and fear ripple uncomfortably through his essence. He didn't like that. Magus didn't acknowledge fear or recognize anxiety. He was the master of fear! He was the one who created anxiety. Angry and impatient with his altered state, he began to 'reach out' to other ghost-like figures around him, each encounter was accompanied by a flash of unwelcome emotions and foreign memories. He kept going, searching for what seemed like hours. Or was it merely seconds? The explosions of mental and emotional energy weakened him with each encounter until he sensed something familiar, like an old, much-worn, and beloved winter coat.

How strange, he thought. I'm not sentimental, yet this feels like it belongs to me.

The being was a young man, tall, muscular, and physically powerful. Magus reached out, 'touching' the man. The blast of this person's essence coursed across his non-corporeal self, like two charged wires suddenly touching and creating a complete circuit. This time, he 'felt' his old friends, hatred, jealousy, envy, and perhaps Magus's most favourite of all, a commitment to winning at any cost.

This was home to Magus. He knew this place. It was pleasant, and he wanted it for his own. Was that possible, he wondered?

He pushed his ghost-self to 'embrace' this being, to consume this entity who seemed so familiar to him, and suddenly the strange sensation of not having a body spun on its axis and turned into one of feeling like he was being pulled apart, cell by cell as if he was being dragged into the event horizon of a black hole. That had happened to him once, decades earlier in a confrontation with one of those League do-gooders, and despite the almost impenetrable bubble of energy that protected him at all times, he'd barely survived the experience. This was similar but far more painful. He felt his soul, his very mind, being stretched like the tail of a comet as it skirted past the intense solar winds of a star. Yet not just in one direction, but in every possible dimension of space and time. It was excruciatingly painful, and he loved it.

Magus screamed. At least it sounded like he was screaming, although he had no mouth to scream with. Then suddenly, he did.

A long cry of agony, both horrible and pleasurable, exploded from lips that weren't his but had now become his. Gravity suddenly gripped him, and he crumpled. His head smacked something hard, and then unfamiliar, yet somehow familiar hands were reaching out to help him. The others, these entities from the fog, were now solid beings and they were crowding around him, their hands touching him, grabbing him, pulling him to the feet of this body that he now possessed.

"Damn, Thomas, are you all right?" one of them asked.

Magus turned his head and saw faces he didn't know, yet somehow he felt that he did. They were young, in their twenties or thirties, a quarter his age, his real age, not this body's age. He felt something burning in this body's right hand and raised it awkwardly to his face to see. The disc. It had made the journey with him, to wherever this was. The hieroglyphics on it might mean something, he thought, but he didn't have time to bother with such wonderings. Magus was proud that patience wasn't one of his virtues. He slid the disc into a front pocket of the Armani slacks he knew he was wearing, and quickly scanned his immediate surroundings, feeling the repulsion of these hands on his new body.

There was no Mighty Titan and no immediate and obvious threat. Good.

He pried one hand from his left arm, pushing it away. The owner grumbled. He was in a large room with floor-to-ceiling windows that looked out onto a typical city landscape of more buildings and bits of colour from green spaces jammed between those buildings. It all looked familiar somehow. The sun, judging by the angle of light streaming into the room, suggested it was past mid-afternoon.

So, he thought to himself, I'm no longer on the dark side of Earth. But where? What continent? Or perhaps, if this was not Earth, what planet?

The room had an impressively large wooden table with coloured presentation folders, sheets of shiny white paper, and computer tablets carefully laid out in equally parsed spacing. The orderliness of it all irritated Magus even more since, after all, chaos was his friend. The table was flanked by standard office chairs, so it was a conference room of sorts, he supposed. He flicked another repugnant hand away from his right arm. The owner squeaked in pain and complained. Various coloured charts and graphs describing marketing goals and strategies were projected on a screen at the far end of the room. Glancing over his shoulder, he saw a table with what looked like liquid refreshments near a tall but closed door. The last to be touching Magus, one of the men, well dressed with coifed blond hair, whom he somehow sensed was known to the previous owner of this body, was holding onto one of his arms and a shoulder.

"Hands off me, worm," he demanded, twisting, and pushing the man away.

"Thomas, what the hell?" the man said, as he stumbled back into a woman.

Suddenly Magus heard a terrified voice in his head.

Hey! Hey! What the hell's going on?

"Hah," Magus hissed, with barely repressed annoyance. "You yet survive within this body."

The voice inside the body whimpered.

What? What do you mean by 'within this body?' What is this? What's happening to me?

Magus laughed, as a girl with intense blue eyes set in a face with skin like chocolate took hold of his hand. He gazed intently at her. She had magnificent black hair pulled high atop her head, and he knew who she was.

"Thomas," she said. "What's going on?"

She was stroking the hand of the man Magus knew she loved.

He could feel her emotions, or rather, he surmised, the consciousness still inside this body felt them. He sneered but was then surprised to feel a stir of memories he'd buried for many years. His heart suddenly ached with a feeling he hadn't felt since Gloria, although she was better known and feared by all as Medusa. That worm Titan had killed her in battle. She and Magus had been lovers and partners, and together he and the terrifyingly powerful Medusa had terrorized the universe.

Gloria.

Magus rarely felt emotional pain, but her death had hurt like nothing else. Not even the terrible pain of what had happened only moments ago over Scotland between he and Titan compared—if it was only moments ago. Gloria had been the only person worthy enough to appreciate his true genius, to understand his formidable greatness, and then, in a moment, she was gone, killed by Titan. He grunted with derision. Titan was dead, and the score was settled. The all-powerful Mighty Titan was no more and somehow Magus had undergone a complete transfer of consciousness into another human's body.

He knew it was possible. The clever assassin Gal'E'thuhl had done something similar to a Syndurian life form on Midex Prime, but the transfer had only lasted for a few cycles of the exoplanet's rotation. However, it had been long enough to kill the entire royal family, including their pets, and then for the patsy, once Gal'E'thuhl exited the body, to take the fall for the heinous crimes. How the disc had accomplished something similar was worth exploring, but first, there was the matter of these annoying creatures to attend to.

He lifted his gaze to the five people facing him.

"What planet is this?"

One of the people facing Magus smirked.

"What planet is this? Really, Thomas?"

The voice inside the body of Thomas screamed again.

Help! Somebody help me!

"Shut up," Magus hissed, pushing the black-haired girl's hand away. " No one can hear you, worm."

"Thomas?" she said, stumbling away from him, her face a contrast of confusion and concern.

"What planet, worm," he repeated, pointing a strong, young finger at the blond-haired man, as he suppressed an immediate desire to vaporize everyone in the room.

The man laughed, his face barely hiding the ridicule he obviously felt.

"Uranus, dude. Where else?"

Help! Somebody help me!

Magus scowled and clenched a fist. He'd kill this one first.

"Uranus doesn't have a breathable atmosphere, you worm."

What? Kill Brad?

"Silence, Thomas. Thomas, is it?" Magus said harshly to the voice within him, without waiting for a reply. "I know you've wished him dead. I know the many ways you've imagined it. Sitting in your sad apartment with your girlfriend, you pathetic worm, wondering how to strip the very essence of life from your enemy. Musing over how to get away with it, rather than just doing it. Ah, yes, he very cleverly siphoned the Imperial Works marketing contract into his own private side job. Is it not so? He's your partner and he's working against you, behind your back?"

H-how do you know that?

"I know all!" Magus exclaimed.

He laughed to a stunned and confused Brad, who quickly stepped up to Thomas and touched his coworker's arm.

"Hey, what's up, man?" he whispered, glancing around slightly. "You know I'd never do anything to hurt the company, right? We're business partners. I wouldn't stab you in the back like that."

What a little shit. He's lying. Mehjoong at Imperial Works let me know just before this meeting that they awarded the contract to this shithead. Unbelievable. You can't trust anyone.

"Hah! See?" said Magus, smiling.

He relished Thomas's secret hatred of Brad, drawing strength from the repressed anger that had first drawn him to this body.

I can use this, Magus thought. If he was stuck with this whiny voice in his head, he'd use its anger. He glared at the young man, Brad, who'd dared touch him.

"Where am I?" he demanded. "Andora? Alpha Prime? Where?"

"Jeez, man," Brad said, as he took a step back. "Chill. It was just a contract, a small one. We don't want small, right? You said we're heading for the big times, right?"

"Chill? Never heard of it," he snapped. "Where is that? What star system?"

Star system? The voice inside his head exclaimed.

"Shut up," Magus hissed, through clenched teeth.

This little cretin in his new body was quickly becoming an annoyance. Another of the young men frowned and crossed his arms.

"What the hell are you doing, Thomas? We're in the middle of a meeting, one that you and Gloria called."

This one gestured toward the table and lifted both arms in a shrug as he shook his head.

What an ass. I shouldn't have hired him. He's a waste of skin.

"Shall I kill him also?" Magus asked. "You've also thought of killing him have you not?"

"What?" said the young man, leaning back into the enormous table.

What? No!

Another of the room's occupants, a redheaded woman whom Magus suddenly knew Thomas had begun an affair with only a week earlier, pulled a device from a back pocket of her red slacks. Sex, yes, they'd had sex in one of the building's bathrooms. It had been quick, feverish sex, driven by the threat of discovery, and lust. Then they rented a room in an out-of-the-way hotel the very next day, for another lust-filled rendezvous.

"Ah," Magus smiled deliciously, pointing at the redheaded girl. "You're cheating on your girlfriend, with her."

What? How do you know that?

"What?" the black girl with intense blue eyes gasped.

Magus could see the shock of betrayal on her face.

"I'm calling 911," the redheaded girl said, stepping back as she pushed her thick hair aside and lifted the phone to an ear.

Oh, god. What's going on?

Magus began to laugh. He laughed loudly and the people around him repulsed in unified confusion and alarm, their tailored clothes holding up their groomed heads, their collective expressions an idiots' gallery of comic shock. He let the laughter fill his chest, as he pushed both his hands together to coalesce his power. He'd form a plasma blast and kill them all, every one of them, except the girl with the blue eyes called Gloria. How odd that her name was the same as Gloria from his universe. He might let her live a little longer.

No! I'm not going to let you do this!

Magus ignored the little fly buzzing around inside his head.

"Prepare to die, cretinous vermin!"

He let the words rise ominously and from deep within his being, like the violent geyser eruptions on one of Str'a'guun 5's volcanic moons where he'd sometimes go to find solace after being thwarted by Titan or one of his minions. The eruptions were spectacular, blasting through the moon's thin sulphuric atmosphere, molten metals, and caustic liquids spidering out into the vacuum of space, hissing as they kissed the subzero temperatures. He imagined that his attack voice was similar to this spectacle. It was melodramatic, but it struck great fear in the hearts of the already fearful. It was his trademark, and a very good one, he thought with a certain amount of manic glee. His fingers began to tingle, to spark, faint arcs of blue energy dancing around his fingertips, the familiar sensation creeping into his palms, and then—

Nothing.

Well, nothing except that the young adults around him looked at him with open mouths, and then began to laugh. No one had ever laughed at Magus and lived, and he felt his fury rising as he rubbed his hands together harder, faster, with greater ferocity. Still no plasma blast. Nothing, except he felt the skin of these hands heating up. He let them fall slowly to his sides, his mind racing for an explanation.

I won't let you kill them.

"How have you done this?" Magus growled through clenched teeth, lifting his hands again and flexing his fingers as he gazed at them.

He felt a moment of uncertainty, confusion even.

I won't let you kill them!

"You can't stop me, Thomas," Magus growled.

I'm not a murderer. I'm not.

"Yes, you are," Magus said slowly, aware of the anxious eyes upon him. "I can hear your every thought."

"What the hell, Thomas?" Brad said, pulling his own cellphone from a back pocket.

Who are you? How are you doing this?

Magus smiled slowly, reaching up to adjust the collar of the expensive silk shirt he was wearing. It was a pale purple, and the silk tie around his neck was a deep blood red, projecting the confidence of a young business owner destined for more than boardroom meetings and the next corporate ad campaign.

"I am a god. I am Magus, destroyer of worlds, the scourge of the universe, killer of all who dares oppose me."

"You need to go to the hospital, man," someone said.

"He must have hurt his head when he fell," another added.

"Hello? Yes, we have an emergency," the red-haired woman was saying into her device.

How is this happening?

"Sweetie?" Thomas's girlfriend pleaded as she stepped up to him again.

He suddenly knew that she was also his business partner. She rested her warm hands against the smooth silk covering his broad chest, as she looked with concern into his eyes. She slowly pushed two fingers through the gap between buttons and he could feel her playing seductively with the hair on his chest. His breathing suddenly felt constricted. She was beautiful and she excited him. But she too had laughed.

"You must have banged your head when you fell," she said, her words etched with concern.

Magus smiled maliciously down at her, lifting a hand to let his fingers caress her beautifully thick hair. So much like Gloria's, he thought

Don't you hurt her! I won't let you hurt her!

Magus cast his gaze around the anxious faces of the small group. Something was very wrong. This person, this Thomas in his head, had managed to stop him from utilizing the formidable power that he knew had been transferred into this new body along with his consciousness. He'd felt it, his power had been his lifelong companion, its powerful energy coursing through his being like an old friend. It was here, within this body now, and this snivelling being still holding on inside his new body was somehow keeping him from accessing it. That wouldn't do! His mind flashed back to a time, the time before The Event that had so wonderfully transformed him. He was a different person then, weak, pathetic, hawkish, and normal, and he hated that person. He hated these people. They were the weak ones, well, except maybe the body he'd entered. Magus could feel the familiar rage that simmered beneath the young man's facade of civilization. He could use that rage. He could also feel the immaturity and uncertainty of his host. He could use that, too.

Don't you hurt them!

"Give me a chair," Magus said as pleasantly as he could, as he carefully pulled the girl's hands from his shirt and pushed her aside.

No! Don't do this!

Magus laughed.

"You want this, Thomas. I know you want this."

I'm outta my mind. This can't be happening.

"Oh, this is happening," Magus said, calmly.

The universe's mightiest villain smiled gleefully at the people standing before him. They were corporate monkeys, clambering over each other to reach a summit that had no summit, to grasp at the nothing they all thought was something. Thomas was one of them, but not anymore. He chuckled softly, no, Thomas was about to become a whole new Thomas.

The one called Brad reached around and grabbed a chair, pushing it so it rolled forward across the tightly woven carpet to stop in front of Magus.

"Here, man. Sit down. Chill out."

"Thank you," Magus said calmly, as he leaned over to grip the back of the chair with these strong, young hands.

He could feel his power tickling his flesh, hesitant, but present, hovering somewhere just out of reach, but close. Oh, it was so close. His smile thinned, as his eyes narrowed and focused on the face of the young man Thomas had often fantasized about killing.

He would kill this one first.

TWO

"Who the hell are you and

how are you inside my head?"

HUNTER MACKENZIE CLEARED PUMP NUMBER SIX on the console while waving through the window at the frowning older man who was waiting impatiently for him, so he could fill his battered old Jeep Wrangler. Hunter sighed and slumped back down onto the only stool behind the counter. The top had compacted into a hardened and uncomfortable surface from too many years of use.

Working Fridays sucked.

"Sorry you're so grumpy," he said quietly, as he monitored the activity around the two fuel pump islands.

Most customers who came to Earl's Gas and Convenience Store simply inserted their cards at the pumps, filled their vehicles then drove away, but Stanley Gruber insisted on using the one pump that hadn't yet been upgraded to be fully automated. He didn't trust banks, he'd often told Hunter.

"Who's grumpy?" a voice suddenly asked behind him.

Hunter spun around on the stool, its worn bearings squealing as he did so. He jumped up.

"Mia!"

Mia Kim, her broad face wearing a smile that spilled from her dazzling brown eyes, wrapped her arms around Hunter as he slid his around her waist. They hugged quickly, he was at work after all, and then she stepped back, slipping her hand into his as they kissed, also quickly.

"Juwon let you in the back?" Hunter asked, casting a nervous glance at the door with *Staff Only* stencilled on it in important-looking tall black letters.

Mia nodded and laughed, her long black hair swaying to the movement.

"I parked in the alley. I brought his wallet, he forgot it this morning."

She frowned and looked past him and out the window.

"Who's grumpy?"

Hunter shrugged and pointed.

"Oh, just Mr. Gruber, the guy with that beat-up Jeep Wrangler out there. I've told you about him. He comes in every few weeks, pays cash, never smiles."

"Oh, him. Poor guy. Maybe he's all alone in the world."

Hunter squeezed Mia's hand and looked into her kind eyes. There was something humanizing about her view of people that always gave him hope, and it had been that way since the day he'd truly noticed her, two years earlier in Grade 11.

"Yeah, maybe he needs someone like you."

She smiled in response, her face continuing to shine.

"Aw, Hunter, you're such a nice guy," she said, tossing a glance at the *Staff Only* door. "I'd better go before Juwon catches me fraternizing with his employees."

Mia kissed him quickly, squeezing his hand before letting go. He watched her stride to the staff door, her long black hair swaying with the motion of her long legs, before turning briefly to blow a kiss at him.

"See you tonight," she mouthed, before disappearing behind the door.

He sighed and turned back to the plexiglass window that separated the public from the tills. Mia had always been able to cheer him up, even when he didn't know he needed it. Her 'magical talent,' as she called it, came from being the child of immigrants, where in order to fit into a mostly Eurocentric culture, one must always be cheerful, she'd once told him. He laughed at the thought, remembering how she'd tilted her head, then frowned deeply, when she'd first made the comment. It didn't seem fair somehow that being part of a minority population meant you had to appease the majority, but his experience since they'd first started dating had shown him that she was honestly an upbeat and happy person.

His attention was suddenly drawn to a teenage boy who'd just entered the store, his hands stuffed in his oversized jacket pockets. The temperature was in the low twenties Celsius outside and, suspicious of the big, heavy coat, Hunter immediately began keeping track of him.

Stanley Gruber came in immediately behind the teen and paid cash for his gas. He was wearing the same disapproving gaze he reserved for all suspicious-looking young punks, as he slid two twenties through the pass-through at the bottom of the plexiglass shield. Hunter suspected there were many he was suspicious of. What a sad way to live, he thought.

The teenager, someone Hunter vaguely remembered from a younger grade in his high school, was slowly perusing the chip aisle, his eyes occasionally flitting slyly to the concave mirror in the back corner of the store. The store had cameras, but cameras couldn't chase you.

Shoplifters always acted like they were extremely interested in things as if they had a pocket full of cash and their presence was doing the business a huge favour. He'd already stopped two shoplifters that month, and three the previous month, not to mention the kid with a can of spray paint who'd been considering adding to the mess of tags already on the store's delivery door. Hunter was good at catching the young and dumb, Mia had once told him.

"Oh, great, he's gonna do it," he muttered to himself.

He glanced quickly down at his running shoes to make sure the laces were tied. They were. The teen slowly slid a large bag of chips up and under his jacket and casually made his way toward the exit, looking at both sides of the aisle, as if he couldn't make up his mind and was just going to leave. Hunter pressed the buzzer under the countertop. He could hear its faint ring in the back of the building. The teen heard it too and for a tense second, their eyes locked in the frozen moment of 'what ifs' that separated them.

Hunter smiled at him.

He's thinking about it, wondering if he can do it. Just put the bag down and walk out. It's that easy, he thought as his eyes followed the teen.

It was the glassed-in counter that fooled would-be thieves into thinking they had a chance. It looked like the attendant was locked behind it until you got close enough to see it was just a hanging partition over the service counter. It took only seconds to get around.

The kid ran for the doors.

"Juwon!" Hunter yelled as he swung around the service counter, hitting the faded lino in a run. "We've got a shoplifter!"

The kid looked back with fear and surprise, but he was in motion, already pushing through the doors, his back hunched, and head tucked for a quick getaway.

He sprinted across the two islands of pumps, dodging a large black SUV that was just pulling in, the driver honking their displeasure. The teen cast a glance over his shoulder, spotted Hunter then swerved, flailing a sharp left to duck down the alley that ran along the back side of Earl's. Hunter was fast too. He corrected course, avoiding the SUV as well, and sprinted into the alley a little more than a metre behind. The kid had tossed the bag of chips and was running as if his life depended on it. As far as Hunter was concerned, it did.

"Stop, you little punk!" Hunter yelled, ignoring the bag of chips.

The bag had hit the building's wall and burst open, spilling its orange-coloured triangles out across the filth of the alley. A sharp pain suddenly stabbed Hunter in the forehead, but he shook it off, pushing his concentration to focus on the runner. The thief kicked some empty crates over in an attempt to trip Hunter up, but he cleared them easily and was just reaching out to snag the kid's floppy coat with his outstretched fingers when he heard the man's voice. It was as loud and as clear as his own.

Hello?

A second later, lights flashed before Hunter's eyes like strobes at a concert, and the pain in his head intensified, beginning to pulse back and forth between his ears. He wanted to stop running, to scream at the pain, but he was so close. His fingers touched the collar of the kid's coat.

"I said stop!"

The pain grew, and he stifled a scream. He was so close. The teen briefly looked back in alarm, his eyes wide.

Stop?

What was going on with his head? Hunter's fingers brushed the fabric of the coat, but the stabs between his ears began to feel like a sharp knife was being shoved into his skull, causing tears to stream from his eyes, blurring his vision.

"Stop!" he yelled at the youth, but also at the blinding pain that was stabbing into every part of his head.

Stop!

Hunter stopped.

He completely and instantly stopped running. His body was leaning forward, fully engaged in the run, his one arm extended, the fingers of its hand slightly curled, ready to snare the teen's coat. One foot was flat to the pavement, the other bent mid arc but stalled, the heel pointing downward to the concrete, anticipating what normally should have followed. However, contrary to the laws of physics, he was frozen, like a sprinter captured in a photograph. The energy from his abruptly halted momentum transferred painfully to the thigh and shin of the one leg touching the pavement. Then suddenly, he could move his arms and he fought for balance, almost falling over, but his body awkwardly adjusted of its own volition, the leg in mid arc pulling sharply down to the hot pavement. The youth cast a startled glance over his shoulder and dove through a poorly kept hedge along the end of the alley.

"What the hell?" Hunter gasped, as the pain in his head intensified, causing black specks to chase each other across his vision. He grabbed the sides of his head and pushed, willing the pain to leave. What was happening to him? He couldn't move his legs, and there was a horrible pain in his head.

"What the hell?" he barked again, keeping his hands pressed to his head as he struggled to move his legs.

His feet appeared to be glued to the grime beneath his shoes. Then, as if it hadn't happened, the pain was gone. Relieved, he dropped his arms and tried again to move his legs. He could move his torso and arms, but his feet refused to budge. He could feel them and sense the heat through his shoes that had built up over the long hours of the summer day, but he couldn't get them to obey the commands of his brain.

Where is this?

He heard the voice distinctly this time. It sounded familiar. He looked rapidly around, but he was alone in the alley.

"Hello. Who's there?"

Where am I?

"Where are you?"

He continued to cast quick glances around. Other than the drone of traffic on the other side of the hedge that sheltered the side alley from the busyness of 14th Avenue, he was definitely alone.

Is this Earth?

"What the hell?"

You use that phrase often.

It was a statement and it appeared to be coming from within his own head.

"Where are you? How did you do this to me?"

I am uncertain of where I am.

"What the hell?"

Hunter grabbed one of his legs with both hands and tried to pull it free from the pavement. His feet and the pavement had become one.

Remain calm.

The voice spoke firmly, but Hunter was anything but calm. He tried to move his other leg, but it too seemed impervious to the commands coursing unheeded from his cerebral cortex.

"What the hell!"

Again, with that phrase. I ask you to remain calm. There must be a perfectly rational explanation for what is happening.

"Rational? There's nothing rational about this," Hunter exploded. "I can't move my feet and there's a voice in my head."

I am in your head? Is that where I am? I am looking through your eyes at this horrible wasteland. Has there been a worldwide calamitous event?

"Oh, my god. I must be having a stroke," Hunter gasped.

A stroke made sense. The stabbing pain, the blurred vision. He'd read about this.

"Juwon!"

Juwon?

"Juwon!" Hunter cried again.

There is no need to call for additional help. The Mighty Titan is here. I will assist you.

"Juwon!"

Juwon appeared from the store's stockroom entrance, a few meters away from where Hunter was inexplicably anchored.

"What the hell, Hunter?"

He employs this phrase as well.

"Shut up," Hunter said, as he thumped the side of his head with a hand.

"Hunter?" said Juwon, frowning from the doorway. "What's up? Did you get him?"

Hunter?

Hunter gestured desperately at his feet.

"I can't move."

Juwon pushed through the heavy door, propping it open with an empty crate, as he gestured back into the building.

"There's nobody at the counter, man."

Hunter blinked.

"I know that. I can't move."

You are called Hunter?

"What do you mean, you can't move?"

Juwon stepped toward him, looking down with an annoyed expression at Hunter's feet.

Hunter Mackenzie?

"Shut up!"

Juwon stepped back.

"What's wrong with you?"

"Not you, Juwon. Don't you hear that voice?"

Juwon glanced up and down the alley, looking confused.

"What voice?"

You are Hunter Mackenzie?

"That voice!"

His supervisor, Mia's older brother, glowered at him with the look all young convenience store managers reserve for employees not much younger than themselves.

"Get inside. I need you out front. There's nobody at the counter."

"Juwon, there's something's wrong with me. I'm having a stroke or something. I can't move."

Juwon frowned again, shaking his head as he watched Hunter flailing his arms.

"You're moving."

"My feet aren't."

Be silent. I must think.

Suddenly Hunter couldn't move or talk. His body went rigid, and his eyes grew wide, unblinking.

"Hunter?" Juwon growled.

He marched in front of the one employee he regretted having to manage. It was never a good thing to manage your sister's boyfriend, he fumed.

"What's wrong with you? Get out front."

Hunter tried to speak, to move, to blink, but his body was somehow completely out of his control. He felt his weight pressing through his runners against the ground in the alley, felt the slight summer breeze ruffling the hair at the back of his head, but he couldn't move or make a sound. Wait, he wasn't breathing either. Panic began to rise in his chest.

Where am I? What did Magus do to me? Why am I in this body? There was a long pause then the voice asked, *Where is my body?*

Juwon pushed against Hunter's shoulder.

"Hey! Quit fooling around. Get up front."

I can't breathe, thought Hunter. *Hey, voice in my head. I'm not breathing.*

"Hey!" Juwon bellowed, poking Hunter in the shoulder again. "What the hell are you up to?"

I can't breathe! Hunter screamed in his head.

His vision began to fill with little tiny flying specks that seemed to be lulling him to sleep.

Oh, dear, I am depriving this body of oxygen.

Hunter suddenly gasped, sucking in long drafts of hot alley air, as the tiny specks in his vision flitted away.

"This is nuts!" he gasped.

Take me to a mirror.

Hunter's feet began to move, awkwardly, like someone else was controlling them.

"Hey, if it weren't for my sister, I'd fire your ass for this," Juwon grumbled, as Hunter stumbled past him into the back of the store. "There's nobody at the counter."

"I'm not doing this, Juwon."

"You're also not making any sense, either. Lay off the Red Bull, will you?"

Where is the restroom?

"I'm not doing this, Juwon. Can't you hear that voice?"

"What voice?"

Yes, restrooms are usually in the back of these establishments.

"That voice! Can't you hear that? He wants to go to the restroom."

"Yeah, right," Juwon said from behind him. "I'm gonna fire your ass for sure. I'd do it, too, except Mia would never forgive me."

Hunter stumbled into the crate that held the side door open, sending stabs of pain coursing through his shin. He hoped he wasn't having a stroke, as he thought of Mia's blown kiss, and the promise to meet later.

Where is the restroom? Ah, here it is.

Hunter suddenly jerked to his left and shouldered through the staff bathroom door. He couldn't help himself. The voice was in control of his legs.

"What the … Hunter," Juwon said, as Hunter's arm elbowed the door shut. "I need you out front."

Hunter stood in front of the bathroom's mirror and flexed his right arm, which seemed to be back under his control. He reached for the door handle, but then his arm stopped and pulled back to his side. It was no use fighting, the voice appeared to have complete control of his body if it wanted.

"Just give me a minute, okay?"

Look in the mirror.

Hunter lifted his head and saw what he always saw—himself. Unruly and thick dark brown hair, brown eyes, the pupils circled with a hint of cream, and that zit that had been annoying his left cheek for a week. That was it, just the same old Hunter MacKenzie.

Except the voice said, *What the hell?*

Hunter laughed.

"Oh, so now you're using *the* phrase?" he said, able to make air quotes.

I apologize. It seemed appropriate at the moment. I seem to be me, but not me.

"What does that mean?" he groaned, "Is that why you sound like me, only an older me?"

His shoulders shrugged of their own volition and the voice spoke again.

I am me, but me of more than a century ago.

"Right, like that makes a lot of sense. And," he grimaced at himself, surprised that he could point a finger at the reflection in the mirror, "I'm certified. I'm talking to myself."

Juwon banged on the door.

"Hey, man. I need you out front."

"Gimme a sec!"

"Hurry it up."

"Yeah, yeah."

I must have travelled back in time.

"Say what now?"

Something in Magus's Black Energy must have sent my consciousness back to this particular time in my life. However, I do not recall working in such an unkempt establishment. I suspect by your lack of a Scottish accent that we are not in Aberdeen.

"No, this is Canada. Who the hell are you and how are you inside my head?"

You use far too many expletives for such a young person.

"Expletives?"

Hunter peered into the mirror closely, scanning his eyes, half expecting to see a tiny face looking back at him in them.

"Who are you? How is this happening?"

Who am I? Why, I am the Mighty Titan. Indeed, we are the Mighty Titan! Earth's greatest defender, the champion of—

"Oh, my god. This can't be good!"

I assure you, I am as real as—

"I-I think I'm dying."

I assure you, you are not dying. The disc Magus used to attack me has somehow

—

Juwon banged on the bathroom door again.

"C'mon, man. We have customers."

"Shut up!"

"Screw you, man," Juwon shot back, as Hunter heard his footsteps retreating to the front of the store.

He sighed and called after him through the door.

"No. Not you, Juwon."

Go. You must attend to your required duties for this establishment. This is an unprecedented situation, and we must not arouse suspicion. Our identity must be protected at all costs.

There were five customers, all exhibiting various states of annoyance and impatience, waiting along with a miffed Juwon, who was helping the first couple on the second cash till. He made sure Hunter was aware of how unhappy he was with a pinch-faced glare as he stepped into the booth. The voice in his head fell mercifully silent as he took care of the remaining customers. A cherry slushy and ketchup chips for one, sixty bucks of gas plus a six-pack of pop for another, and a litre of oil and a lottery ticket for the last one.

"Hey, good luck with the lotto, man," he said as the final customer left.

He flopped down onto the stool next to Juwon.

"Sorry, man," he said, casting a quick glance at his supervisor. "I don't know what happened to me. I literally couldn't move my legs."

"Whatever," Juwon said, as he stepped out of the booth and headed back into the building. "You're weird, you know."

"Yep," Hunter sighed, as he ran his fingers through his hair.

He caught his reflection in the glare of the window that separated him from the outside world. Was there really a voice in his head, he wondered, turning slightly to see a stack of on-sale 12-pack pop cases that Juwon had asked him to organize into a proper pyramid. Customers had been grabbing them and the display was looking more like a half-made Transformer. He stood up and sighed again. He was just beginning to think that maybe he'd imagined the entire episode when the voice spoke again.

We must leave this place at once.

"Oh, god, it's still here?"

He dropped his head into his hands.

Unfortunately, yes. I do not seem to be able to leave your body. We are somehow fused into one being. Tell your supervisor we must leave. We must return to the Fortress.

"The what?"

Magus may have been pulled back to this time as well.

"Who?"

We must contact the League.

"The League?"

The safety of the world is at stake.

"The world?"

Yes, we may have a chance to stop Magus before he continues his reign of evil.

"Reign of evil?"

Yes, do you not understand me? Why do you keep repeating my words?

"Oh, god."

Hunter slumped back down onto the stool and threw his head back and looked up at the stained ceiling tiles above his head. He'd always found the blend of pop splatters, dehydrated insect cadavers, and the tile's pattern of dots interesting. At times he could almost make out the faces of celebrities or constellations.

What is wrong with you?

"What's wrong with me? I think something really frightening is wrong with me. There's a voice in my head. This is definitely not normal."

He pulled his cellphone out of his pants pocket, swiped it on then pulled up a browser. He typed 'delusions of superhero grandeur' into the search box.

Is this your communications device?

Hunter ignored the voice and pressed the search button on the browser. A list of options appeared:

Superheroes with mental illness

From Superman to super-villains: mental illness and delusions of grandeur

Is Deadpool psychotic?

People who actually think they're superheroes

This is not necessary. We are not delusional.

Hunter tapped the fourth link. A webpage popped open, and he skimmed through an article explaining the phenomenon of schizotypal personality disorder, in which those afflicted have difficulty distinguishing between reality and fantasy. The affliction was often characterized by magical thinking. The article suggested that a few signs of the disorder were social anxiety, being a loner, and belief in special powers. He abruptly stopped reading and swiped the page away, before slipping the phone back into his pocket.

"No, that's not what's happening."

Of course, it isn't. We are not delusional or suffering from this disorder your device suggests.

"Right," Hunter sighed. "Yet, there's a voice in my head."

That may be true, but for me, I am not in my body, and I do not understand how this came to be.

Hunter grimaced as he watched a vehicle pull up to the pumps.

"Why is this happening?"

I seek the same answer, young Hunter. However, we are Earth's greatest superhero, and we must ascertain whether Magus arrived here as well, wherever or whenever this is. Time is of the essence.

Hunter puffed his breath out between his lips and popped the tab on a can of Red Bull he'd left sitting on the counter. He took a long swig—it was warm and unpleasantly syrupy—then placed the can down and shook his head.

"Wow. This is really unexpected. What'll I tell Mia?"

You must tell no one.

"Something like this could end our relationship."

He took another swig from the can.

"Sure, she's probably the most caring and understanding person I know, but a voice in my head?"

You must not tell anyone, least of all someone you have a relationship with. Their life would be in danger.

"Wow, this is freaky."

He turned to look out the window and mindlessly watched a customer filling up an old Dodge Charger. The vehicle looked partially restored.

"And my dad, he already thinks I'm not living up to my potential. What'll he have to say about this?"

We do not have a dad.

"Oh yeah, we do," Hunter sighed, deeply. "And I'm not exactly his dream child."

We are the Earth's mightiest…

"Yeah, yeah, mightiest superhero. Whatever."

"We must leave at once!"

"Not a chance. I don't get off for another three hours."

"Time is of the essence."

"You've already said that."

For a moment the voice fell silent, but then spoke again.

Hunter?

Hunter groaned in exasperation then downed the final mouthful of the Red Bull, in one long draft.

The voice persisted.

Hunter?

Hunter looked at the empty can. He needed help, didn't he? A voice in your head wasn't a good sign. But, if he was having some kind of breakdown, how had the voice-controlled his body earlier, or was he just doing that himself?

Hunter?

"Oh, my god. What?"

Are you not working here in this menial but essential service job as a front to protect your true identity?

"You mean my identity as a gap-year gas jockey?"

No, your identity as the Mighty Titan.

"You know, every time you say that you sound," he said, tapping the side of his head, "I mean, in my head, this Mighty Titan thing, it's not helping."

That is our name. It strikes fear in the hearts of evildoers across the galaxy.

Hunter laughed, wearily.

"See? Hearts of evildoers! I can't believe this is really happening."

Are you not the Mighty Titan?

Hunter drew a long, slow breath and effortlessly crushed the empty can of Red Bull between his two hands, top to bottom, perfectly flat, as he let the air rush out through his lips. He lifted the flattened disc, looked at it closely, then grunted and shrugged.

Hunter?

"Sorry, I have no idea who this Mighty Titan is."

He casually flicked the flattened can toward the blue recycling bin that sat next to the *Staff Only* door. It was more than three metres away and he'd never once made it into the bin from that distance. The flattened can arced beautifully through the air, almost in slow motion, reflecting light from the LED pots in the ceiling, before curving silently down through the bottle-sized opening in the top of the bin. He heard a little tinkle, as it hit other cans in the bin.

"Huh," Hunter exclaimed. "I've never done that before."

Please, are you not the Mighty Titan?

Hunter groaned.

"Look, I'm just plain old Hunter MacKenzie, who apparently now has a voice in his head. Could this day get any worse?"

Oh.

Hunter chuckled.

"Does that disappoint you, voice in my head?"

The voice replied, without hesitation.

Yes, this is worse than I could imagine.

Hunter leaned back on the stool, as a woman with two children sporting superhero-themed bicycle helmets pushed through the doors.

"Oh, perfect."

THREE

"Oh, Thomas, you know you enjoyed it."

MAGUS WAS HUMMING JOYFULLY TO HIMSELF as he scrubbed the blood from beneath his nails, the soap lathering into a pink froth before it was swept away under the flow of water from the tap. The swift, brutal killing of this body's acquaintances had sent an explosion of adrenalin coursing through this body—his body. It was heady, and sensual, and he felt a compelling desire to do it again. It had been decades since he'd killed with his bare hands. The plasma bolts were so thorough, so clean, his victims were vaporized and reduced to a wisp of molecular dust, but killing with one's own strength, while messy, felt so natural, so fulfilling on a primal level. He loved how it made him feel and he especially loved this young body.

The voice inside him suddenly broke his revelry.

Why?

Dampening a handful of paper towels, he wiped splatters of blood from his face.

"Oh, shut up, you whiny little cretin."

Magus leaned in closer to the mirror over the glistening sinks in one of the building's bathrooms. The reflection revealed an angular young man's face, with strong features and intense, piercing, almost black eyes. The hair was thick and dark, the skin tanned, and the shoulders and upper body were toned from whatever physical activity this young man had been enjoying.

Wait.

He stepped back.

No, it couldn't be.

This was his body, from at least a century ago. And there were no scars. Titan had given him those scars, three that had dissected his face, from brow to chin, forever marked by his enemy's formidable power. The wounds had healed, like any wound he'd ever had, but he'd willed the scars to remain as a reminder of his hatred for Titan.

Yet, this was his face. How was this possible? Had he travelled back in time? No, he'd lived in the United States in the years before The Event, the incident that changed his life forever, and he'd never been a business owner, and never made it past his first year of college, much less earned a business degree. In fact, he'd never been anything noteworthy before his transformation into Magus. His early years, willfully not remembered, had been marked by numerous demeaning and insulting jobs. As an adolescent, he'd dreamed of attending a university, perhaps to study business, but his parents divorced, and any help from them to pay for tuition had dried up like their love for each other. He was angry, his life cast adrift in a sea of dead-end jobs, that is, until The Event. Magus shivered. He didn't like to remember that person. He wasn't that person, and, apparently, he wasn't that person in this, what, in this universe?

Had he travelled to a parallel universe? He'd heard of such things, fanciful and wishful, but dubious science at best, yet what other explanation was there? There was a Thomas Stewart and there was—he turned his head to study the cowering black woman who had pushed herself in between a toilet and the thin wall of a stall next to the sinks after he'd dragged her into the bathroom—there was also a Gloria Musa in this universe. However, she, or rather they, weren't the Thomas Stewart and Gloria Musa of his universe. Somehow, the Black Energy had brought him to this parallel universe and into the body of this Earth's Thomas.

He sneered at the woman, despising her fear. This wasn't his Gloria. No, his Gloria was long dead in that other universe. How unfortunate, she'd have found this situation intriguing. Perhaps in this universe, he and Gloria had been destined to find each other, but both of these versions, the Thomas in the mirror and this Gloria were weak. Her eyes stared at him, fearful, confused. She was not the Gloria he'd once known, and definitely not the powerful woman he'd moulded into the fearsome killing machine he'd named Medusa.

Why? Why did you do that?

Magus looked back into the mirror, seeking to see the unseen voice behind his eyes.

"Oh, Thomas, you know you enjoyed it."

No! They…they were my friends.

"Oh, come now, surely you're lying. They weren't your friends. Those fools were riding on the coattails of your genius. Besides, I spared your precious Gloria."

Spared her life? You want me to thank you for sparing her life? My friends, I, I needed them—

"Tut, tut, don't lie to me," Magus chided. "Tell me, where is this place? What city?"

You don't know where you are?

Magus leaned into the mirror to look at his eyes.

"Tell me, fool."

Nepean.

"Nepean?" he spat the word out, like a bitter drink. "Where the hell is that?"

Ontario. Where are you from?

"Certainly not this knee-peon, wherever that is."

It's in Canada.

"Canada? I'd never lived in Canada," he declared, frowning at himself. "How could you bear to live in such a boring place as this?"

The bathroom door suddenly swung open, banging into and bouncing off the doorstop embedded in the glistening floor. Magus could see in the mirror's reflection that a portly uniformed security officer had charged through the opening, stopping almost comically as the door slammed back into his elbow. The man yelped then shoved the door back, using his foot to keep it open as their eyes met. An unusual-looking weapon was gripped in his visibly trembling hands.

"F-Freeze!" the man barked.

Fear filled every nervous cell of his body. He reeked of it, and Magus smiled back at himself in the mirror.

Now you're in deep shit, the voice in his head sneered.

"I think not, my ill-informed parasite," Magus said quietly, as he eyed the odd weapon in the officer's shaking hands. "It's you he sees, not me."

Shit!

Magus turned around very slowly, raising his hands calmly to chest height. It was always best to placate one's enemy. It made them feel as if they were in charge, it set them off guard and primed them for the kill.

"Don't move, you sick bastard."

The weapon trembled almost as much as the man's voice.

"Why'd you do that?"

Magus let a smile slowly dissect his face.

"Do what, exactly?"

The security officer's eyes stared back, wide, and shocked.

"Why did you—did you—?"

"Why did I kill—those people?"

He said it slowly, the smile never leaving his face. He always liked this part, when a soon-to-be victim struggled to comprehend his magnificent maleficence.

"You're crazy, man," the officer said, gasping at the callousness in Magus's voice. "Get down on the floor."

I didn't kill anyone!

Magus laughed, softly.

"I'm afraid you did, my dear Thomas."

Why are you doing this to me?

"Au contraire, I'm doing this to us. You are me, you see."

What the hell are you talking about?

The officer disengaged one hand from the device and fumbled for a two-way radio comm hanging from his shoulder, then pressed a button on it.

"I have one suspect. He's on the fifth floor. Men's washroom. I need help. I need backup."

Do not engage, the radio squawked. *OPP will be there in three.*

What do you mean, I am you?

Magus ignored the voice in his head and angled a finger down at the security officer's weapon.

"What is that?"

"W-what?" the man stammered.

His eyes darted around the room, as he gripped the weapon again with both hands. The object continued to tremble, despite his fierce grip on it.

"That," Magus gestured calmly again, but with two fingers this time. "Is that some foul instrument of mass destruction?"

The man's eyes fell to his own hands.

"It's, it's a taser, asshole. Now get on the floor!"

Magus kept smiling and didn't move.

"Well, Thomas, what's it to be? Prison or domination?"

What?

The officer cast his eyes anxiously around the bathroom again, the taser jerking with his motions.

"Who the hell are you talking to, man?"

Magus chuckled and tilted his head slightly to the side while angling a finger at his own head.

"The little boy inside me. He can't decide if he wants us to turn ourselves over to your capable hands," he replied, chuckling happily, "or kill you."

"What?" the officer stammered, edging back slightly.

What? I don't want to kill anyone. I didn't kill anyone!

"Oh, Thomas, c'mon, I know you can feel the power within us. We can do anything, be anything, have anything. We're invincible. We are Magus."

This is bullshit!

"Is it? I know you can feel what we are. I know you hate your life, I know you hate the sucking up you've done every day of your pathetic existence to lesser talented people, and to achieve what? An insignificant paycheque? Your quaint sixth-floor apartment overlooking, what, a parking lot for a strip mall? Sex with your very pretty partner?"

Shut up!

"Get down on your knees! Now!" the officer squeaked, nervously.

The taser in his hands was shaking so uncontrollably that Magus wondered if the guard was able to fire it off, would whatever come out of it actually come close to striking him.

"Excuse me," Magus said to the officer, while slowly waving his hands.

He squinted at the man's name tag.

"Oliver, is it? I apologize, but my younger self and I are having a life-altering moment here."

"What the—"

"I know, I know. You woke up this morning, just another day in the sad life you live, not knowing that today you'd find yourself in this bathroom, which is quite pleasant and very clean I might add, facing the most fearsome and powerful being the galaxy has ever known. It's okay, Oliver. Just give me a moment here, and we'll soon end your sad, little existence."

"Shit," the guard gasped, jamming his finger hard against the trigger on the taser.

No!

Both electrified prongs and supporting wires snaked across the space between the two men like a python launching at its prey. One prong stopped about a half-dozen centimetres from Magus's left shoulder, while the other paused slightly closer over the centre of his chest. Electricity arched in the air across the front of his shirt, making sharp buzzing and snapping sounds, as the device sent an electrical current violently through the wires. The two quivering prongs hung suspended, floating weirdly, like they weren't sure what they were supposed to do next, but then they suddenly fell to the floor in a shower of muted sparks.

"Hah! You wish to rule!" Magus said, enthusiastically.

Thomas had relinquished control of a good measure of the power that had been lurking just out of Magus's reach. The malignant energy raged through the molecules of this frail human body, burning its way down into his atoms, into nuclei, and deep into the quantum fabric of his existence, changing the very nature of its relationship to the laws of physics of this universe.

Shit! I won't kill anyone. I'm not a killer.

"Of course, you aren't a killer," Magus chuckled, softly. "I'll do the killing for you."

He knew his younger self would release the energy that had been Magus's dark companion. Earlier, as he'd taken the lives of Thomas's friends, one by one in a blinding fury of speed and deep dedication to his one true love, his own magnificence, he'd felt the familiar tingling in his hands. He'd sensed his younger self's fascination with the violence, and could feel Thomas lingering just short of releasing the full potential of Magus's energy. There was no way a normal human being could have moved as fast as he had in the room where his essence had first appeared or could have ripped apart the chair that that fool had rolled toward him to use as a delightful and brutal weapon. No, Thomas had been a reluctant but willing participant. He'd wanted what Magus always wanted, which was to crush anyone opposing him, to take what had been denied him all of his young life, gaining absolute control of his own destiny.

Magus saw the conflict his younger self was wrestling with. He saw the memories, the emotions, and the carefully hidden rage behind the firm handshakes and thin smiles. Thomas was twenty-six and he'd started his own business with his partner, Gloria. Yes, this Gloria who was, but also wasn't Magus's Gloria, in an industry that chewed up people like them. He'd unexpectedly landed a large government contract, rented elegant floor space on the fourth floor of the Albright Business Building, and had the most beautiful and intelligent woman he'd ever known as his lover and partner. But always, deep inside, hidden between the relentless drive for more power, more control, and the constant annoyance of feeling compelled to calculate how much was too much, was the secret desire to just let go of caring about other's feelings or wants, giving in wholly to taking whatever he wanted. Take it all, do whatever needed to be done to get what he wanted, and damn the cost. Gloria had tempered that harsh desire within him, offering a voice of reason, of calm, but this power he was sensing in this being that had suddenly invaded his world, this raw unimaginable power was letting him see a path he couldn't have imagined. He could take whatever he wanted, be whatever he wanted. He didn't need partners and didn't need people who pretended to be his friends. He would be the most powerful being in the world.

Magus laughed softly. Thomas was like a toddler, taking his first steps towards embracing the promise that came with the power. He was letting go of the weak, pathetic excuses that kept lesser beings ensnared in the shackles of compassion. Indeed, Magus could smell the metallic odour of ozone, as the tendrils of destruction reached out, drawing energy from the lights and conduits in the bathroom, like a maestro searching for the perfect notes and time signature.

"On the floor! Now!"

The officer had pulled a small handgun from a side holster, his mind still reeling from the sight of the taser prongs stopping, with no effect, just short of the young man's body.

Magus shook his head slowly, his hands still at chest height.

"No," he said, calmly.

The pistol wavered, as beads of sweat careened down the sides of the officer's tight, terrified face.

"What? This isn't a taser, man."

I don't want to die!

"You won't," Magus said.

"Get down, or I'll shoot you!"

"Irrelevant," Magus said, while slowly and blissfully breathing in the officer's fear.

It tantalized his senses, like a lover's sensual touch, and he enjoyed it almost more than his own power. He could feel Thomas reaching out and touching the fear, drawn into the euphoria of the beginning of the smallest of understandings that he was more powerful than anything in this universe, and no one and nothing would ever be able to oppose him.

What is that? Is that what you've been talking about, your power? It—it feels—

"Yes, it feels wonderful, doesn't it? Only one other being is as powerful as we are, and he's dead."

Yes, yes, I feel it. It—it's—exhilarating.

"Yes, it is. Now give it all to me. Let me have full control of my old companion, let me show you what we've been and what we can become, my dear Thomas."

But I won't kill anyone. I'm not a killer.

"Of course, you're not," Magus said gently, not once believing the hollow words sputtering between his ears. "No one thinks you're a killer.

You just want what belongs to you, don't you? Why can't people just see that? There's no crime in being allowed to be who you are, is there?"

I—maybe—do I just let it go, just let you do whatever you want with this power, this feeling, this remarkable feeling?

Magus laughed.

"Yes, Thomas, I know how to use my power. I've wielded its strength for decades. Let me have it, let me show you who we are."

Magus gasped, sucking in a short, sharp thrill of a breath as Thomas Stewart fully relinquished the hold he had on his power. The air around his raised hands began to shimmer, like the waves of heat off the tarmac on a hot summer's day, and both he and the officer turned their attention to the phenomenon. Magus had never grown complacent with the beauty of the event. Fresh air after a torrential downpour, that's what the buildup always smelled like, in a breathable atmosphere, that is. The fragrance was an oddity, considering that what followed was a harsh and somewhat immediate death. Refreshing death, he liked to think of it.

The officer mumbled in disbelief.

"What the hell?"

Those would be his last coherent words, as his finger tightened on the pistol's trigger.

Magus slowly lowered his hands, pointing the fingers of both toward the officer. Blueish-green energy crackled and arched from his fingertips like spidery lightning bolts, sizzling across the space between the two men, finding its way to the head of the security officer. The little gun rocked in the guard's hands, as a bullet erupted from its short barrel. The tiny piece of lead fizzled and disintegrated, as it passed through the crackling stream of energy.

The spectacular energy continued to flow from Magus's hands, wrapping around the man's head, embracing him like a windblown scarf of silk. He jerked and froze, his mouth gaping open in surprise. It was a look Magus had seen on countless faces or reasonable assumptions of faces from a menagerie of species across the galaxy. He laughed with glee, embracing the sheer elation of the moment. Translucent blue flames danced across the man's white teeth, coursing up and out through his nostrils, filling his eye sockets and pouring from his ears, turning his skin and cartilage transparent. Shock and then horror filled the man's face, as he dropped the weapon. It hit the bathroom floor with a sharp clatter, as his flesh began to peel away in layers, vaporizing like morning mist to the rising sun.

Magus's eyebrows rose slowly at the spectacle. His power didn't seem to be at full strength, so the effect of molecular deconstruction was slower, and much more painful for its victim. The man screamed in terrible agony as his body contorted, as every cell, every molecule, was rent violently apart. However, his screams of terror were brief. His vocal cords quickly disintegrated, followed a moment later by skin, muscles, tendons, organs, then finally a naked structure of bones, the man's skeleton, dissolved into dust.

Oh, my god.

The bathroom door, no longer held open by the weight of the guard's body, slowly swung shut, pulling an empty shoe with it that jammed between the door's edge and the sill. For a few seconds, particles of what had once been a human being hung suspended like tiny dust specks caught in the sunlight. They then slowly glided down in a shimmering blanket that coated the officer's clothing as they crumpled to the bathroom floor. If the death hadn't been so horrific, one might say that it was beautiful to watch. Magus nodded in approval, appreciating the magnificent slowness of the kill.

Oh, my god.

"I know you were just doing your job, officer."

Magus mock saluted the pile of clothing and then held his fingers close to his face. The tips were hot as if he'd briefly touched an open flame, but otherwise, he was in exceptional health.

"I was just doing mine."

That was—that was—

"Beautiful?"

Yes … and amazing. I've never seen anything like that, but—you shouldn't have done that. That was wrong.

Magus laughed derisively and turned to the whimpering woman with the striking blue eyes in the cubicle, the one person he had not killed with his bare hands, the Gloria of this universe. She'd overheard the entire encounter and her mind was filled with visions of horror she couldn't have imagined and wouldn't soon forget. Magus stretched a hand out to her. He remembered this hand. It was young, muscular, with strong, long fingers. Perhaps he'd play the piano again, he thought. It had been years.

Too much time was wasted fighting that stupid League and the annoying Mighty Titan to enjoy the simple but powerful pleasure music brought. Well, his enemy was dead, and he wasn't. Whatever miracle the Black Energy had forged, it was time again to play. The world would be his piano and he'd fondle its ivories with intensity and rigour unseen and unheard of since the first musical notes rose from the primordial creativity of a thousand species in a thousand star systems.

"Come, Gloria," he entreated her, with a flick of his fingers.

Don't you hurt her!

"Oh, Thomas," Magus sighed. "Do you not yet understand? I'm you, and you're me?"

You're right, I don't understand. How do you know who we are?

Magus sighed then impatiently twitched his outstretched fingers towards Gloria. The girl's swollen eyes fell to the hand, and she repulsed back alongside the toilet. Mascara ran in muddy streaks from her eyes to her glistening chin, and her broad lips trembled with fear. Magus could detect the sound of her fearful heart pounding behind her breasts. It excited him.

How are you me? How is this possible?

Magus shrugged.

"Call it magic, if you will, but we must leave this place before more of these," he gestured dismissively at the ashes on the floor, "arrive."

We're just going to walk out of here? I hear sirens. The police are here.

Magus laughed.

"We don't walk out of anywhere. We fly."

Fly?

"Yes, my poor ignorant Thomas, we fly. Come, Gloria."

He smiled, flicking his fingers again while softening his eyes.

"I wouldn't harm the love of my life. You may not be the woman I once loved, but I may yet find you useful."

The girl, transfixed by the eyes she knew, and confused by the horrific change in the young man she loved, slowly reached out a hand. Magus gently took it and a subtle electrical charge passed between their bodies, a small reminder, he thought, of the powers that had made him and his Gloria, Medusa, feared threats to the League. Magus sucked his breath in with exhilaration and pulled her up and out of the stall. He hadn't felt that sensation since his Gloria. Magus was pleased.

"I don't understand," she said, her voice hoarse. "Why? Why did you kill them?"

Magus drew her to his chest, tilted her chin up with a hand and gazed coolly, but fiercely, into her pleading eyes.

"They're nothing, my darling. You may not yet understand, but you will. I am Magus, Lord of all the known galaxy, master of your fate, sworn enemy of the League, and dispatcher of that ridiculous Mighty Titan."

Then he kissed her hard, passionately letting a hand run down the side of her body, brushing against the side of her breast, coming to rest on the curve of her hip, remembering, longing for what had been, before pulling away to gaze intently into her bloodshot eyes.

"You may have no powers in this universe, you may be a mere sad shadow of who you were elsewhere, but you're still Gloria, my queen."

FOUR

"There are no real superheroes, they're fictional."

HUNTER GLANCED AT HIS CELLPHONE. 7:33 p.m. He was tired, confused and had lost an hour of just-above-minimum-wage pay by asking—no—by begging Juwon to let him leave early with the promise of coming in an hour earlier on his next shift, which happened to be the following morning. Leaving was at the insistence of the voice, of course. He had to save the world, he must find the League, it was imperative that they stop Magus, blah, blah, blah.

Do you live here? In your parent's basement?

The voice asked Hunter, as he dropped his backpack on the floor and flopped down onto his unmade bed.

"Seriously? I'm only nineteen. Where else should I be living?"

And you live in Calgary? In Canada?

"Um, yeah."

He responded with some hesitation. He was answering a voice in his head after all and was understandably struggling to comprehend that he was even having such a conversation. He'd taken to just simple engagement with the voice, otherwise, it wouldn't stop asking for a response to its many questions. He'd ridden his bicycle to work at noon, listening to The Beatles' White album through his phone, and he'd ridden his bicycle home at seven, listening to the manic ramblings of a perplexed superhero in his head. He was exhausted.

This situation is intolerable. I cannot believe you are me.

"Why do you keep saying that you are me?"

You are Hunter Angus MacKenzie, are you not?

"Yes, why?"

That is my name, and when we looked in the mirror earlier, I saw my face, but from more than a hundred years ago when I lived in Aberdeen, Scotland.

"We could just have the same name, that's possible," Hunter argued, feeling increasingly awkward debating with himself.

I wish it were so, but my memory is flawless, and I am you, and you are me.

"But I'm a Canadian and you say you're from Scotland, why don't you have an accent?"

I once did, but I left my homeland more than a hundred years ago.

"I guess it's possible," he admitted. "So, you're like another me?"

Oh, so now you believe in me?

"No, I believe I'm having some sort of episode where, for whatever reason, there's the imaginary voice of a character in my head who claims to be a superhero and who weirdly sounds a lot like me, only like an older me."

I am not an imaginary character. If it were such as you say, would I have been able to assume command of your body? Such as I am now?

Hunter suddenly sat up, twisted so his feet dropped to the carpeted floor, then stood up, completely without his willing it. He immediately put both hands on his hips and bowed, remaining bent over, facing the smattering of dirty socks and t-shirts at his feet. He tried to move but couldn't. The voice had control of his body again.

"Whoa, wait, what the hell? Let me go."

Suddenly, his body relaxed, and he was able to stand upright. He sat back down on the bed and stared at his hands.

"How is this possible?"

I apologize, that was inappropriate and unethical.

Hunter frowned.

"Inappropriate, yes, but how was whatever you just did to me unethical?"

This is your body. I may inhabit it at the moment, and I may seem to have complete control of it if I wish, but it is still your body. I apologize.

"I see," Hunter said. "So, if any of this is real and not just a delusion of my mind, if you get access to my body, what do I get out of this deal?"

Titan hummed.

My power, my abilities, my knowledge, I suppose. If that's what this transference is meant to accomplish.

Hunter lifted his hands again and looked at them closely.

"Well, that's convenient, isn't it? You can take over my body anytime you want, but I don't seem to have any of your powers."

Yes, I suppose it does support your case for what has happened as merely being a delusion of your mind.

Hunter nodded.

"Yeah. If you actually have powers other than controlling me, what might they be?"

I am unaffected by all forms of gravity.

"You mean you can fly?"

Yes, I can fly, but that's an inefficient term for what it is I am capable of.

"I don't understand. I think you're real, I think this is real, but how did this happen? How are you inside me?"

Magus, my arch enemy, had some sort of device that he assumed would destroy me, but it in effect seems to have transported my consciousness into you, my younger somewhat uncooperative self.

"Thanks. You can understand why I doubt this is real, right?"

I do not understand myself. I'm here, in your body. I can control it, but I do not seem to have access to that which has made me a superhero.

"There are no real superheroes, they're fictional."

Not where I come from. There are many brave and gallant beings that are superheroes.

"Why don't I have your powers then?"

I am unsure. I can sense it within your body. It is a presence I have known for much of my life.

"What? Your power is here, in my body?"

Yes, but I do not seem to be able to avail myself of it.

"You don't seem very powerless to me," Hunter complained. "Taking control of my body, making an ass out of me in front of Mia's brother."

Moving your limbs is not one of my powers. I have the power of a thousand suns resting in the very fibre of my body.

"This is crazy. Things like this don't happen in real life."

I assure you, I sincerely wish it were otherwise, but here we are. We must prepare to protect the Earth from Magus.

"Magus?"

Yes, my greatest foe, the Earth's greatest enemy …

Hunter nodded slowly, pushing the disembodied voice to the back of his mind as he found the TV remote in the folds of his sheets. He hit the power button, cranking up the sound as the flatscreen flared to life. Maybe he could drown out the voice until he could make sense of what was happening.

He let his gaze fall to the TV remote in his hands. Would his life as he'd known it be over? Would he spend the rest of it sharing his brain with a lunatic personality? Hunter recalled a classmate who had suddenly dropped out of school a few years earlier and that he'd later heard was living with schizophrenia. What was his name? Jarod or something like that? He was doing okay, he had heard, but he'd transferred to another school where people didn't know him. Is that what this was, schizophrenia? What about Mia?

We must contact the League.

The sudden demand startled Hunter.

"The what?"

The League, we must make contact with the League.

"Uh, there is no League and no superheroes, not real ones anyway."

He tapped the volume down on the flat screen and flicked through the sports channels.

No League? How is that possible? This is Earth, is it not?

Hunter blinked and looked away from the TV.

"This is Earth, but there's nothing called the League, at least I'm aware of."

No Momentum?

"Who?"

Only the fastest B'Tubian anywhere in the Milky Way! It has twelve legs and four arms and can exceed the speed of light merely by running.

Hunter sighed.

"Uh, sorry, no Momentum alien thing."

Impossible. How about a courageous hero called Voltage?

"Nope."

Madam Odds?

"That's a name for a superhero?"

Of course. Her mind is a cybernetic construct. She can calculate the odds of any situation within one-one-quadrillionth of a possibility.

Hunter nodded slowly and turned his focus back to the TV. This was happening.

"Right, of course, she can."

But this makes no sense. You are me. There must be a League. How is it possible that you do not know who you are? The energy that struck me from The Event transformed my body when I was fourteen, and you are much older.

"The Event?"

Yes, a massive surge of energy erupted from the giant black hole at the centre of the Milky Way. I was fourteen when this happened. The wave spread rapidly through the galaxy by a factor of 10 times the speed of light, clearly defying Einstein's special theory of relativity. It altered the genetic makeup of random individuals from twenty-seven-star systems and became known as The Event. Those affected were transformed in ways that the scientists of my universe have not yet been able to explain fully.

"Wait, you're saying there are alien civilizations out there, among the stars?"

Yes, of course. There are many, and twenty-seven of these civilizations, including Earth's, were affected by The Event and the Second Event.

"A second Event?"

"Yes, there was a second energy pulse 70 years after the first.

"Well," said Hunter, laughing lightly, "there's your problem since this Earth hasn't experienced either of these events."

Titan groaned, a genuinely odd sound coming from inside Hunter's head.

This is bad, very bad. We may be the only hope your universe has of stopping Magus.

"We? Stop the super villain guy? How do you know he's even here?"

His name is Magus, and I cannot know for sure that he came to this universe when I did. It is highly probable, though, as our final struggle involved the disc he had used to injure me. We may be the Earth's only hope.

"We're Earth's only hope?" Hunter mumbled as he muted the TV.

He slipped his cellphone from his pocket and quick-dialled Mia's cell. He could have texted her, but he needed to hear her voice. It rang several times before she answered.

"Hunter? Hey, I was just talking to Juwon," she said. "He said you were acting weird at work.

Who is this person?

"He told you that? I need help, Mia. Something crazy's happening to me. There's a voice in my head, some sort of super being. He says he's from another universe."

Who is Mia?

"What's in your head?" she asked.

Mia? Do not talk to her. She must not know our secret.

Hunter switched the phone to his other ear.

"I was chasing this shoplifter at work, and like, bam, I suddenly start hearing this guy talking in my head, and he doesn't use contractions, ever."

Terminate this call.

Mia laughed.

"Contractions? I'm sorry, Hunter, I know we're supposed to hang out tonight, but I'm heading over to my halmi's. Her back's out again. You know how my grandmother is, she still thinks she's a young woman. I'm going to stay the night and run some errands for her tomorrow. Can I call you back?"

Terminate.

"No," said Hunter.

"No?" Mia repeated. "What's wrong?"

"There's a voice in my head."

Mia laughed again.

"That's nice, Hunter. I'll call you back."

"No, I meant what I said, a guy is talking in my head."

"Hunter, I'm staying the night at my grandmother's. You know, you sound a little like a tto-rai."

"What was that again?"

"A nut job. Crazy."

There was a sudden burst of laughter in the background over the phone, and Hunter could hear Mia's mother saying something rapid fire in Korean.

Mia laughed.

"Mom likes your nickname, tto-rai. Lay off the Red Bull. I'll call you later, K?"

You must terminate this call.

"Shut up. No, not you. I mean, the voice in my head."

Terminate now!

Suddenly his hand pulled the cell away from his ear, and his thumb pressed END.

"What the hell? Don't do that. This is my body. That was my girlfriend."

He tried to redial, but his hand wouldn't cooperate, jerking and weaving with every attempt he made to stab REDIAL

I apologize for interfering with your free will, but we must always protect our identity. Who is this Mia?

"Mia Kim, she's my girlfriend, and she's my best friend!"

"Hunter? Is everything okay, honey?"

Hunter flinched and glanced around the room as if the Mighty Titan were visible. His mother was standing at his bedroom door.

"Hey, mom. I'm good. I was just talking with Mia."

This is your mother? We do not have a mother.

Hunter grimaced and smiled painfully at her. He knew his mother loved her only child, but he sensed she was worried he was becoming even more inscrutable to her than he already was. When he was twelve and curious why he was an only child, she'd told him that she'd struggled through her pregnancy with Hunter, and another childbirth hadn't seemed like something she could manage. Not that she and his father had wanted more children. She had a successful career in real estate, but Hunter wondered if they shouldn't have tried for one more child, a spare, he'd often thought. Then the entire MacKenzie family legacy wouldn't rest solely on his shoulders. She frowned and then smiled in return.

"Well, your dad's made his famous lasagna," she said with raised eyebrows as she made air quotes. "I saved a plate for you in the fridge if you want something to eat."

She smiled again and walked away, her footsteps brushing against the carpet of the basement stairs as Hunter listened.

"We have, I mean, I have a mother," Hunter whispered to the entity in his head.

We do not. We are orphaned.

"Orphaned? Why are superheroes always orphaned?"

I am, others are not. I fail to understand your point.

"It's a classic superhero origin story," Hunter replied.

Do you also have a girlfriend? That is very dangerous. Our enemies could take advantage of this. You have put her life in grave danger.

Hunter grimaced.

"Look, I don't have any enemies, and Mia and I are planning a future together."

Together? Do you have a sexual relationship with this female person?

Hunter choked.

"Uh, what? Sexual? No, not quite. Well, I mean, we make out sometimes, but, like, no, uh, no sex—not yet."

I apologize. I have made you uncomfortable.

Hunter shrugged.

"Yeah, well, Mia, we're serious, we have plans, but we're not going down the sex road yet. Shit, I can't believe I'm talking about sex with a voice in my head."

I was merely asking the obvious. Your body temperature rose 1.75 degrees celsius, and your heart rate increased significantly while you were talking to this Mia.

"You can tell all that from what's happening in my body?"

It was quite pronounced. What are you and this Mia person serious about?

"Uh, you know, we're serious about each other. I like her, she likes me. Don't you understand that phrase? What kind of world are you from?"

Again, I apologize. I have lived for a very long time as the Mighty Titan. I am Hunter MacKenzie, but I rarely assume that identity anymore, as I have outlived anyone who knew me at a young age. The universe is a vast place and requires much of my attention.

Hunter frowned.

"You take care of the universe all by yourself?"

No, not at all. After several years, many of the beings changed by the effects of The Event formed a coalition as a way to use our powers responsibly. It is known as the League. Together we protect the galaxy against such threats as Magus.

"I'm sorry, but there's nothing like this League here."

The voice sighed.

This is all wrong. There is no League, no superheroes, and you have a mother and a girlfriend? This cannot be Earth, yet you are me, but not me.

Hunter groaned, still doubting his sanity but feeling a twisted intrigue.

"This is Earth," he insisted as he unmuted the TV.

Yes, it may be, but it is not my Earth. This is another Earth, and indeed not the same time stream. You are considerably younger than I. And you are powerless, yet my power seems to be here within your physical frame, and I cannot access it. I am afraid that all is lost if Magus has come here as well.

"Magus? That's such a corny name. Sounds like maggots," Hunter interrupted.

He is evil.

"So, he's like a super villain?"

Yes, if he is also here, your planet will experience an apocalypse unlike any other.

Hunter laughed.

"There have been other apocalypses?"

Yes, many. He is evil.

"C'mon, no one's all evil."

Magus is all evil.

"So, are you all good?"

I cannot imagine doing evil, as you say. It is not something I would contemplate.

"So, he's all evil, and you're all good? That's not how life works. Nothing's as black and white as that."

I do not understand. Are you suggesting that I may be both evil and good?

"Not in the literal sense, but have you never done anything wrong, like, I don't know, creep through a stop sign when you're driving?"

I do not creep through stop signs.

"Okay, so like, you've never lied, not even about something as simple as telling someone they look nice today when they actually don't."

I do not lie.

Hunter grunted.

"So, let me get this, you say you never do anything wrong?"

That is a relative question. What is wrong on this planet may not be wrong on M'd'prione Prime.

"Now you're being evasive."

I speak only the truth to your question.

Hunter frowned.

"Okay, so here on Earth, or your Earth, I guess, you'd never fudge things to get what you want? If you bought an ice cream cone and the vendor accidentally gave back too much change, would you keep it?"

I would seek to rectify the situation. To do otherwise would be an affront to all that I am.

"And Maggot Man would do the exact opposite?"

He is called Magus, and yes, without question, he would not rectify the error. He is evil and seeks only to exploit and destroy all that is good.

"What kind of Earth do you live on?"

Titan hesitated before answering.

Not yours, I surmise.

"I was joking."

This is nothing to joke about. I fear for the safety of this Earth and this galaxy.

"Relax. What if he's like you, just sitting in some poor punk's head, powerless?"

That would not stop him. He is pure evil. He has no conscience. He will bring down a reign of terror, unlike anything your planet has...

Hunter laughed.

"Whoa, we have laws here. They'll bust his ass."

If he is like you, then yes, but if not, then I fear the worst.

"Like me?"

Powerless. Weak.

"Thanks."

He will rape your world for its wealth, and I will be unable to stop him.

"Wow," Hunter said slowly.

Are you amazed at the extent of the evil of my nemesis?

"No," he said, then chuckled. "It feels like I'm trapped in a comic book with a dumb storyline. I just didn't think being delusional would be so interesting."

You are not delusional.

"Oh, yeah, I'm pretty sure I am."

"Are you okay, son?"

Hunter's father was standing at his bedroom door, his eyes narrow and scrutinizing the son he was increasingly feeling confused by.

"Jeez, dad," Hunter exclaimed as he jumped. "Can't I have any privacy around here?"

His father shrugged.

"My house," he replied as he stabbed a thumb over his shoulder. "My basement workshop. Shut your door."

"Yeah, all right. Got it. Could you…"

"Everything fine with that job?" his father interrupted.

It was always 'that job.' His father had high expectations for his son, and Hunter could feel the disappointment. It oozed from every look and gesture. You could be anything, he'd said many times to Hunter, especially as he entered the senior grades and seemed to hold a 3.9 GPA effortlessly. For whatever reason, for whatever the motivation was that propelled him, Hunter purposely chose to only get excited about one particular career path.

He loved designing computer programs and loved playing computer games. It was that simple. He ate, slept, rode his bicycle as much as possible, hung out with Mia and a few other friends from his high school days, and worked at the gas station to save money for university. That was his life so far, and he liked it.

"It's all good, Dad."

His father frowned.

"Uh-huh. You were just talking to yourself."

We must leave at once.

"Shut up," Hunter muttered softly through his teeth.

"Excuse me?" his father said, leaning further into the room.

Hunter sighed and turned his head back to the flat screen.

"Nothing. I chased a shoplifter down today, I'm just a little tired."

Say nothing of us.

"You catch him?"

"No."

"Uh-huh," his father said dryly as he pulled the door shut. "I made lasagna. There's some in the fridge if you're hungry after your exhausting shift."

That is your father?

"Yup. My dad. Our dad, I guess, if what you claim is true."

This cannot be.

"Of course," Hunter said, as he flopped back onto the bed, "now that I have this voice in my head, I'm sure he'll be even more disappointed in me. Uh, in us. Whatever."

How can this be?

"Mighty Titan, you're seriously throwing a wrench into my life."

I am you. We are both throwing wrenches, as you say.

Hunter flipped to a news channel and paused. There had been what the reporter was calling a killing rampage that afternoon at a marketing firm in Nepean, Ontario. Four dead. They were bludgeoned to death in 'horrible ways.' A security officer was also presumed dead. Authorities found his clothing in a washroom, along with a pile of ashes, but no sign of a fire. As well, a young female and male, a couple who were also owners of the firm, were unaccounted for, and the police were seeking them for questioning. Two side-by-side photos of the woman and her boyfriend flashed on the screen. The young man had nice wavy hair and dark moody eyes, Hunter thought. The girl was African-Canadian, with a head of neat cornrows decorated with coloured beads. Her eyes were unusual, blue, which contrasted the dark tone of her face. *They're too cute to be killers,* he thought.

"That sucks," Hunter said as he switched the channel.

Wait. Return to that channel.

"Oh, god. I thought you'd left."

I cannot leave, I am you. Return to that channel, please.

Hunter flicked back to the channel.

A harried, unblinking reporter with her hair pulled tight to her head was talking.

"… and as far as building security and officers on the scene are willing to say, Tricia, the two may or may not be involved in this horrific crime. A colleague of the victims, who was first on the crime scene and called authorities, has told Channel Five News that a cryptic message, written in blood on the walls of this terrible crime scene, warns of a so-called coming apocalypse from a…."

She tilted her head down to read from a notebook.

"… an all-powerful … maggots?"

She lifted her gaze back to the camera.

"Maggots? A truly bizarre tragedy unfolding here. Chelsea Billingsworth, Channel Five News, Nepean."

The scene switched back to a brightly lit news anchor room, and Hunter muted the TV.

"Satisfied?"

His mind was quiet, and for a brief moment, he wondered if the voice had somehow managed to leave him.

"Hello?"

He is here.

Mighty Titan spoke quietly and with such gravity that Hunter felt the hair at the back of his neck prickle with electricity. Hunter frowned.

"How can you tell? He looks like anybody."

That was Thomas Stewart and he is Magus. That was his name before The Event. The Thomas I know is much older, but that is Thomas when he was a young man. He is here.

"What? Here? On Earth? How?"

He must have entered his younger self as I have joined with you.

"That's nuts."

That was him, Thomas Stewart, who became Magus in my universe. He is here, in his counterpart in this universe, and I do not seem to have control of my powers.

FIVE

"Your girlfriend is a blubbering idiot."

THE BLACK ENERGY HAD SOMEHOW transferred his being, mind, consciousness, and power to this universe and into this pathetic version of his younger and decidedly stupider self. Had he travelled back in time?

He was also unsure of the status of this universe's super-powered beings. He'd not seen any yet, but indeed the carnage he'd created in this city of Nepean would draw out at least one of them. Maybe that annoying Dazzler with her plasma pulses. Or perhaps that odd-looking High Top. Magus had never been able to tell if it was a human male, a Bopsium female, or some other non-gender specific being from god knew what planet. Whatever it was, it had once been able to deliver a fierce blast of subatomic sound that had left Magus deaf for several hours until his power repaired the damage. Of course, it didn't matter who showed up now. The members of the League together were still far weaker than Titan, and the aforementioned do-gooder was dead.

He smiled at the thought, looked at the half moon, and then searched for Mars, quickly spotting its inviting red glow. A half a minute later, he was hovering a metre over the dusty, wind-blown southern ridge of the Red Planet's Hellas Basin.

Gloria screamed, her grip tightening even more around Magus's waist.

"W-what's going on," she whispered, her eyes wide with confusion and terror as she looked fearfully at the gleaming bubble that surrounded them, keeping them from the harsh environment of Mars. "H-how are you doing this, Thomas?"

"Damn," Magus bellowed in anger, turning quickly to look about, his mouth agape and his head shaking in disbelief.

Nothing but a rock-strewn wasteland. No New Denver, no spaceport, nothing. The planet hadn't been terraformed yet.

"This … this is inexplicable."

Holy shit! We're, we're on Mars? The voice in his head shouted. *I, I don't understand.*

"Shut it!" Magus growled.

"Thomas?" Gloria whimpered. "I want to go home."

Magus lifted his hand and smacked it to his forehead in frustration.

"Will you both shut up?"

Hey, you can't talk to me like that. I can take your powers away, remember that.

Magus smirked.

"Go ahead, you idiot, we'd die in seconds. This is an inhospitable planet, is it not?"

Thomas muttered and swore.

Fine. We've been crisscrossing the Earth while you grumble about what's missing and what should be here or there, and now you suddenly bring us to Mars? And, how the hell are you doing this anyway?

Magus grunted dismissively as he stared out at the vast landscape before him. The sky was the wrong colour, the lifeless ground a dry, blistered mat of weathered stones and boulders, and there wasn't a single piece of vegetation. There should have been a thriving city of several million inhabitants waiting to be exploited and terrorized.

"The how doesn't need explaining. I am Magus, I am a god, and I do as I please when I please. As for the why, I need answers."

Wow, that's a pretty stupid answer. I could help. Let me help.

"I doubt it. Be quiet and let me think."

I can't believe we're on Mars. Holy shit. What's Gloria doing? Is she seeing this?

Magus groaned loudly.

"Your girlfriend is a blubbering idiot. Now shut up."

Fine, fine. Go ahead and do your thinking.

After he'd dissolved a section of the wall in the bathroom in Nepean, he'd flown through it with this universe's Gloria held tightly by the arm. It took only a few minutes to realize there was something quite wrong with this Earth. Everything was familiar but slightly off, old even, as if he were in a different century. Even Paris wasn't the same. There was the Eiffel Tower, for instance. The damn Eiffel Tower! He'd destroyed it more than half a century earlier in a fierce globe-spanning battle he and Medusa had fought against Titan and the League. He'd periodically return to tear it apart, molecule by molecule, whenever the French government foolishly attempted to rebuild it, and, he grudgingly admitted, only if Titan was off-planet. It was petty to keep thwarting French efforts to rebuild it, but he knew it pissed off the mighty do-gooder.

So, this universe still had its Eiffel Tower, but worse yet, there was no 'secret' fortress where Titan's useless band of super-powered goons hid out in the far North. Oh, he knew where the fortress was, in the frozen wasteland of northern Greenland, where Titan's band of idiots plotted against him and Medusa back in the day. It was probably the most heavily fortified facility in the entire galaxy. He'd imagined destroying it with its detestable occupants many times, but for whatever reason, it simply wasn't there. Where were they hiding in this universe?

Even worse, it occurred to him, was this universe's Gloria. She was the doppelgänger of perhaps the only person he'd ever considered loving, or rather, felt something emotional for. Here she was, the spitting image of his ferocious partner in villainy, prematurely taken from him by the murderous Mighty Titan. All this version of his lover could manage to do was endless crying and pathetic bouts of begging for him to let her go. Even now, she was sobbing in his ear as the relentless winds of Mars whipped around the energy bubble that kept them safe. Where was her awe, her admiration for the impressive power he'd just displayed in spiriting them to this barren, lifeless rock, the fourth planet from Sol? Why, before The Event, Earth astronauts would while away for months in chemical-propelled tin cans to get to the Red Planet, and here he'd done it in less than a minute. If he'd been at full power, he could have made the journey in the blink of an eye. But, no, he wasn't precisely his former self yet.

Hey, hello? You done your thinking yet? I can help. I'm not useless.

Magus sighed loudly. There was a feeling of weariness in his chest.

"This body isn't yet up to managing the tremendous power I've brought to it. We need to rest."

What? Here? On Mars?

Magus ground his teeth together.

"No, you idiot. Back on Earth. Somewhere out of the way to spend the night while I plot my next steps."

I don't like being called an idiot.

Gloria sobbed, and Magus grasped her chin with his hand, turning her face to his.

"Preferably somewhere where her confounded crying won't arouse suspicion."

She's frightened.

"And you're not?" he demanded as he released Gloria's face from his grip.

Her head lolled to the side as it shook from her sobs.

Why should I be frightened? This power you have brought to me opens up possibilities I've never imagined. We're on Mars!

"It's my power, but smart answer. Yet, she's afraid."

You killed our friends.

"They weren't your friends. They were using you to build their petty kingdoms."

You murdered them.

Magus laughed, the sound hollow in the bubble of his protective energy.

"No, my dear Thomas, you murdered them," he replied, holding up his free hand, "These delightfully young hands dispatched their useless lives."

Shit. I didn't want that.

"Of course, you didn't."

I didn't!

"Enough! Where on Earth can we stay the night?"

The voice was quiet for a moment, then spoke again.

Go back to Nepean. I know a hotel. It's not four-star accommodations, but it's where I, uh, I …

Magus smiled and looked down at the anguish-filled face of the woman he was holding onto.

"Oh, I see. She doesn't know."

She doesn't have to! Now take us back to Earth, to Nepean.

Magus's smile grew as he quickly rose off the surface of Mars, leaving its dusty surface behind as his thoughts turned to Earth, to Nepean.

SIX

"I don't want to meet him in battle.

He sounds dangerous."

HUNTER DREW A LONG, LUXURIOUS BREATH before stretching his legs and opening his eyes.

"Wow, what a crazy dream."

Ah, you are finally awake.

Hunter jerked and quickly sat up, feeling his skin crawl as if a disembodied voice had suddenly spoken aloud in his bedroom's morning gloom and aloneness. He flopped back onto his pillow and groaned loudly. The night had been long and troubling, fitful at best, a nightmare at worst. He kept having flashes of otherworldly events, costumed beings, some human, some extraterrestrial, and of planets and alien cultures he couldn't have imagined. When the insistent prodding in his head from Titan finally pushed him out of this wild dreamland, the superhero in his head was jubilant.

Arise, young Hunter. We must begin preparations for our attack.

Hunter flung an arm over his eyes.

"Oh, my god. I was hoping none of what happened yesterday had been real."

I apologize and regret that I cannot undo what has happened to us.

Hunter could hear the pelting of rain on his window, along with the occasional peel of thunder pounding through the concrete of his basement bedroom. How was any of this possible? And why didn't this guy use any contractions when he talked? It made the voice in his head sound like a robot.

He propped his head up on one hand.

"So, you're still here, and you still sound weird."

Weird? Explain.

"Yes, you use very few contractions when you speak. What's up with that?"

Oh, well, I suppose it is because I have taught myself to talk in this manner. I communicate with many different species, and the subtleties of contractions can be lost on those with only a rudimentary grasp of Earth languages.

"Wait, what? So these other alien species speak our languages?"

Of course, since the two Events, humans have travelled between the stars and now many alien species, as you say, speak English, French, Spanish, Hindi, and many other Earth languages. Earth's people have also learned many non-Earth languages as much as we are physically capable of doing so.

"So, all these alien species hang out together in your parallel universe because of these events?"

Yes, it was the impetus for what is now called the Great Galactic Connection. The two Events changed many beings from different planets, and like those of us from Earth, we felt a connection to one another, even across the vast distances of space. As those who were transformed could now traverse great distances very quickly, we travelled out into the depths of space to seek each other out. This led to remarkable advances in interstellar travel and the most significant exchange of culture, ideas, and technology in the history of our galaxy.

"Wow." Hunter rolled back onto his back and laced his fingers together under his head. "So, these Event things only affected intelligent beings?"

Ah, an excellent question. No, there are a handful of creatures of lesser intelligence that were changed by the two Events. The transformation has led to increased intelligence in these beings, and the League often works with them on projects where their abilities are needed.

"Cool, so like superhero pets."

No, not pets. They are partners in our work throughout the galaxy, as all those in the League are.

"Huh," Hunter remarked.

"So, if we live in parallel universes, why are you older than me, and how come this hasn't happened here? Shouldn't parallel universes be the same? Isn't that why they're called parallel?"

Hunter could hear Titan start, stop, and then finally reply.

I am afraid I do not have a complete answer for you. One could assume that a self-contained plane of existence that coexisted with my own would be identical, but obviously, it is not. Perhaps the variants of each universe's reality allow for some overlap of events, but not all.

Hunter's eyebrows shot up.

"Wow, Mia would love to chat with you about that idea."

She must never know. It would significantly endanger her life.

Hunter nodded, but he knew he'd tell Mia. He simply had to. He rolled out of bed and pulled open the bottom drawer of his dresser, where he had several comic books and graphic novels in plastic sheathes that he'd collected in his early teens. He searched through the pile, pulling out a bunch of titles. He flopped down on the bed and splayed his choices on the quilt.

"Can you see these?"

Yes, I see whatever you are looking at. What is it you wish to do with these funny books?

Hunter chuckled.

"Funny books? I don't think people call them that anymore. These are comic books and graphic novels."

I see. How do these help our mission to stop Magus?

"Well, you say you come from a universe filled with superheroes—"

I apologize, my universe is not 'filled' with superheroes. There are currently two hundred and twenty-seven beings from many different star systems that have abilities beyond what is normal for them.

Hunter nodded.

"Ah, so of those two hundred and twenty-seven, do you recognize any of these?"

He flipped the first comic around and pointed to the stylized name. "Superman?"

No.

He pushed that comic aside and pointed to the next one. "Iron Man?"

No.

He flipped another one over. "The Flash?"

No.

"Monkey D. Luffy?"

Most certainly not.

"Any god-type superheroes, like Thor, Zeus?"

No, well, yes, but they are Norse and Greek myths.

"Ah," Hunter said excitedly, "so, in your universe, there are all the usual historical myths but no fictional superheroes, just the real heroes and villains you've told me about?"

Titan sighed.

This is pointless. I fail to see the importance of discussing fictional heroes and villains. Magus is here, he is very real, and you must begin training to meet him in battle.

Hunter sighed.

"I don't want to meet him in battle. He sounds dangerous."

He is dangerous, and many have died by his hands.

"Yeah, thanks, that's reassuring."

I only tell you the truth. It does not benefit either of us to lie to you.

As they'd bantered back and forth, Hunter realized he was beginning to believe and accept that another being was inside his body, somehow sharing the same space with him. Also, he was starting to feel that he was somehow different. It wasn't huge, yet, just a sense and a feeling that he wasn't entirely himself. Not in a bad way, but perhaps in a leap over tall buildings kind of way, like he might be able to do that sometime in the future. He dropped his feet to the floor and stood up, stretching. The idea that there was a universe with actual superheroes and supervillains, along with aliens of every imaginable description and some that he'd never have imagined, and interstellar travel between star systems was as common as continental air travel was in this universe, was incredible. However, he still had questions.

"So, voice in my head, why can I hear you, but you can't hear my thoughts? I can hear you talking to me, but I have to talk out loud for you to hear me."

Titan made what sounded like a grunt.

I do not know. I have not experienced this phenomenon before. Whatever Magus caused to happen with the disc he called the Black Energy is unknown to me.

"Well, explain this then. You say you're more powerful than Magus, why haven't you just killed him? Why keep fighting him for, uh, how long did you say?"

Our battle has lasted for more than a century in my universe.

"More than a century? A whole century? Why not just kill him?"

I do not wish to kill anyone, even a being as terrible as Magus.

"But wouldn't killing him put an end to his reign of terror?"

Yes, killing him would end the terror he inflicts on the innocent, but that is the most challenging part of a life guided by justice, Hunter. Justice has to be for all, even those like Magus. These gifts bestowed upon me and many others do not make us judge, jury, and executioner. Our powers and abilities may far exceed those who were not so affected, but we are not gods. What each society deems as a just and fair punishment for crimes against members of their societies is not ours to execute or contravene. There are places in the galaxy where Magus would have been executed for his crimes, but carrying out such judgments is not the prerogative of superbeings.

Hunter interrupted Titan.

"Wait, couldn't you just bring Magus to one of those civilizations where he committed crimes so they could put him to death? That would solve your Maggots problem."

Yes, that would, as you say, solve the problem of Magus, but those fortunate enough to have been altered by the first and second Events and who have chosen lives of service rather than violence must live outside of the corporal laws of each civilization. Otherwise, we could quickly become pawns between warring civilizations and ideologies. We see ourselves as caretakers of the galaxy. Our motto is to protect, assist, and bring comfort.

Hunter slowly nodded.

"Wow, this seems very complicated. I think I understand, but that must suck for you, knowing you could put an end to Magus, but you're bound to this moral code of honour."

Yes, it does suck, as you say, but this code of honour is what separates those who have chosen to use this power for good and those who have chosen a destructive path. Justice cannot be extended to only those you like or agree with, it must extend to those you do not like and those who do not hold the same values.

Thunder crashed outside, and Hunter tapped his cellphone, the screen flaring to life, revealing the time. He had less than an hour to get to work. He'd promised Juwan he'd come in early to make up for the missing hour the day before, the hour that the superhero inside his head had cost him.

We must leave this place.

"Yes," Hunter agreed, "I have to get to work."

Work?

"Yes, at Earl's. You know, my job at the gas station."

We do not work. We must prepare to battle Magus.

Hunter slipped on the pair of jeans he'd stepped out of the night before, hopping briefly on one foot.

"Sorry, as you heard yesterday, since you're living inside my head and can see and hear everything, I promised Juwan I'd be in early today."

Work is irrelevant. Magus must be stopped.

Hunter grabbed a clean t-shirt from his dresser and slipped it over his head as he fumbled for a pair of socks from the dresser's second drawer.

"Yeah, no, not in my universe."

Hunter's body froze. He was bent, standing precariously on one foot while slipping a sock onto the other.

"Aw, come on. You said it was wrong to do this to me. I have to get to work," he complained, trying not to panic.

He should have fallen over, but his body was resisting the push of gravity. He could feel the strain in his calf.

We must prepare for battle. Your world depends on us.

"Look," Hunter sputtered as he stared at his half-socked foot. "My world depends on me getting to work on time and making a good impression on Mia's brother so I don't get sacked."

What you wish to do is relevant. Magus must be stopped.

"Unfreeze me. I can't fight your battle for you."

You must. I am you and you are me.

"I don't have your powers. You can't make me do this."

Irrelevant.

However, Hunter was suddenly free and stumbled, grabbing the dresser to steady himself.

"Thank you."

I apologize. I indeed cannot force you to fight our greatest opponent. It would be wrong.

Hunter sighed, snagged his backpack from the floor, and opened his bedroom door, looking out into the hallway.

"Well, thank god for your code of honour. Okay, let's compromise. Let me go to work, and then we can figure something out about this Magus character."

His head fell silent as he ran up the stairs into the kitchen,

"Well?"

"Well, what?" his mother said unexpectedly from the small kitchen table that sat against one wall.

"Oh, hey, Mom," Hunter said, laughing nervously.

"Off to Mia's? Isn't it a little early?" she asked, a mug of coffee halfway to her mouth, her other hand holding a tablet.

Hunter grabbed two bananas from the counter's fruit basket and a muffin from the fridge's freezer.

"No, I promised Juwan I'd come in early today. I might see Mia later tonight, but she's over at her halmi's. She's not feeling well."

His mother frowned, putting her mug down with a small click on the table.

"Oh, I hope she's okay. I enjoyed meeting her."

Hunter smiled. The only time his parents had met Mia's grandmother had been a few weeks earlier when they'd been invited to a BBQ in the Kim's large backyard. She was an immigrant to Canada, but she'd lived in Alberta since she was young and was very proud of her English. However, his mother had assumed she didn't speak English well and had spoken to her in a slow and loud voice. Mia's grandmother had been very gracious and touched his mother's arm to interrupt her.

"Oh, very nice. Your English is excellent," she'd said with only a hint of a Korean accent.

It had caught Hunter's mother off guard, knowing she'd made an assumption, but the older woman just laughed, and it was soon forgotten.

"It's her back again. Mia spent the night with her and will help with some chores and shopping today."

His mother nodded, turning her attention back to her tablet.

"She's such a nice girl, isn't she?"

Hunter grinned, slipping the food into the backpack.

"Gotta go, Mom."

"Take your coat, it's raining," his mother called.

"Love you," he said.

Her response was lost in the groan of the back door closing and the sound of Titan's voice in his head.

Yes, excellent plan, go to your work. Perhaps this will allow me sufficient time to determine how to awaken my powers within you.

Hunter groaned as he ran to the side of the garage to his chained-up bicycle. It was going to be a long shift.

SEVEN

"I didn't want to compromise the crime scene with my puke."

"DETECTIVE, OVER HERE."

A sombre-faced constable gestured to an open door, one of a handful along a picture-lined hallway on the fourth floor of the Albright Business Building.

Detective Kathy Shimooka tapped her cellphone off and slid it into the back pocket of her slacks, which was a little too shallow for her liking. She should have worn her black pants, she thought. The pair she'd grabbed from the closet after the call from her partner had interrupted her day off had faux pockets in front and a single half pocket in the back. Grumbling, she quickly pulled on a pair of latex gloves as she nodded at the officer and examined the large photographs on the hallway walls. Lion, tiger, leopard. All cats, all aggressive, and all poised for attack. The leopard picture had been ripped from the wall and thrown to the ground, its thin glass covering shattered into a thousand shards on the carpet, the print crumpled with the impact.

The words 'The apocalypse is coming' were scrawled in copious amounts of blood in the space left on the wall by the destroyed picture frame. It had been written with a finger and was signed. The signature was impossible to make out clearly. Margaret? Maggot? She wasn't sure. The author had used blood to write the body of the message and appeared to have run out for the signature. She slipped her cellphone from her pocket and took several images of the message and the damaged picture on the floor.

Stepping back, she walked to one side of the hallway, avoiding two sets of bloody footprints that made a disturbing trail exiting the room where the officer was standing guard. His face was deathly pale, and he seemed to be trying to keep his breathing under control, sucking air between clenched teeth underneath trembling nostrils. Shimooka understood from the initial reports of those first on the scene that the crime scene was ugly, and she silently prepared herself. The initial 911 call had turned frantic and graphically descriptive before suddenly ending.

The officer stepped aside. Shimooka could hear the rattle of his rapid breathing.

"You okay?" she asked, letting a hand rest briefly on the man's arm.

The officer grimaced and shrugged, keeping his eyes on Shimooka.

"Where's the crime scene people?" she asked.

"Next floor up," he said almost too quickly, "the other crime scene."

Shimooka nodded, turned her eyes to the room, and immediately sucked in her breath. The odour of human blood slapped her nostrils. Sharp, acrid, and overwhelmingly heavy, like the abattoir her grandfather had owned in Southern Alberta. She'd spent summers visiting Jiji and Baba as a child, just south of Calgary, and the smell of the slaughterhouse had never left her memory.

"Chikushō," she swore loudly, using her mother's favourite curse word.

The Nepean City police officers who were first on the scene had called in four deaths, all young adults, ranging in age from twenty-three to thirty-one. What they hadn't called in was that they lay in various grotesque repose in, on, and under a large wooden table in this spacious conference room. A young blonde-haired male, his eyes wide and glazed over with death, lay on the floor nearest the door, grotesquely impaled by one of the table's large wooden legs. Someone had lifted the heavy, four-metre-long table and had driven one of its legs through his abdomen with an incomprehensible display of strength and force. She thought he must have bled out in agonizing pain. His spine was probably severed. The second of the male victims was spread-eagled face up on the table, one of his legs hanging limply over an edge, the plastic arm from one of the many chairs in the room sticking straight out from his chest, his blue tie twisted around the metal support of the arm that stuck out at a right angle from his impaled chest. One of the two women in the room sat almost casually in a chair, except her head was twisted at a bizarre angle, almost facing backward from her torso, her lifeless eyes gazing unseeing toward the room's floor-to-ceiling windows as if she was thoughtfully pondering the Nepean skyline. The other female, her long reddish hair shrouding her face, lay on the floor at the opposite end of the room, a laptop plunged crosswise into her chest. Shimooka was sure it was most likely sticking out the other side of her.

"How is that even possible?" she asked, trying not to breathe in too deeply.

The splatter in the room was horrific, as if a blood bomb had exploded.

"That explains the disturbingly graphic footprints in the hallway," Shimooka muttered. This was a vicious, violent crime, a bloodlust rampage that lacked even a hint of humanity. What kind of person was physically able to kill four people without a lethal weapon and with such extreme violence? This would take days, if not a couple of weeks, to process, she fumed as she swallowed hard.

Shimooka suddenly retched, turned and lurched into the hallway. She had the presence of mind to peel off one of her latex gloves and empty her convulsing stomach into it. There wasn't much. She hadn't eaten since the previous evening. Finished, she took several deep breaths through her nostrils and pinched the hot, bulbous glove shut.

"Damn."

"You okay, detective?" the officer asked.

He stared in alarm at the bulging glove, his voice quivering.

"Chikushō," Shimooka growled again.

She was angrier at herself for losing it than at the question.

"Yeah, I'm good."

Shimooka felt a bead of sweat traverse across her brow, down into one eye, stinging it. The young constable was looking at the vomit-filled glove in her hand. He wasn't smiling.

She caught his glance.

"I didn't want to compromise the crime scene with my puke."

He smiled weakly and nodded his head toward the room.

"Have you ever seen anything like this, ma'am?"

Shimooka could tell he almost turned his head to look into the room behind him, but she saw his neck muscles tense, and she felt a tinge of admiration for his resolve. She shook her head in reply, running a hand quickly across her eyes, wiping the sweat.

"No."

She smiled thinly at the constable.

"So," she began, "what's this place, and who were these people?"

The constable seemed happy about the distraction. He sucked in a deep breath, then pulled a small coil notebook from a breast pocket on his uniform.

"First call came in at 3:36 p.m., from, uh, one of the victims as the incident was happening. The second was a few minutes later, by building security personnel. Six rooms, including this one, along this hallway, belong to a startup design company called MajiGrafx."

He spelled it out for Shimooka.

"The deceased are all employees, with the exception of the one with the, uh, arm from a chair sticking out of his chest. That's Bradley Ashton Manual. He and the two missing persons are listed as the company's owners."

"Two missing persons? How do we know they're missing?"

"We have a witness who puts all six in the room at the time of the, uh, the, uh, incident."

"You have names of the missing?" Shimooka asked.

"Uh," the constable said, as he flipped a page, "ah, yes, Thomas Alexander Stewart and Gloria Adaego Musa."

"I guess that makes them suspects," Shimooka said.

Bonnie and Clyde. Damn. She pulled her tablet from her shoulder bag, swiped it open and called up a blank incident form. Pecking with a finger, she began filling in the required fields. She preferred paper and pen, but, well, the new commander was hot to make the small Nepean police force leap forward dramatically into the twenty-first century. At 53, Shimooka wasn't too interested in digital workplace devices or jumping forward into anything except maybe retirement someday. Nepean was supposed to have been her way of coming down after decades of front-line police work out west. She sighed as a popup window blocked her view of the incident page.

There are 19 wifi networks available. Do you wish to connect to Studmuffin_7659?

Frustrated, she tapped exit on the popup and silently cursed modern police technology.

She looked at the constable, who was staring off down the corridor. She cast a glance toward where he was looking, at the writing on the hall's wall—scrawled in the blood of the victims.

She sniffed loudly.

"So, there's a secondary crime scene?"

He nodded briskly as their eyes locked.

"Yeah. Next floor up, in the men's bathroom. It's a building security guard. Uh, I mean, we think it's him."

Shimooka let her eyes fall to the horrific scene outlined by the doorway behind the officer.

"Think? It's worse than this?"

"No, ma'am. Just a pile of clothes and what looks like about a kilo or so of ash."

"Say what?" she asked, swiping the tablet off and slipping it back into her bag.

The officer shrugged.

"Yeah. His uniform and a pile of ash, bits of bone we think like he was cremated on the spot, but not his clothes."

She scanned the face of the young officer.

"The building security officer's clothes are there but not him?"

The officer scratched his arm nervously.

"His clothes, unburned, and a pile of ash, some bone. Couple of kilos, maybe, of ash. A few shards of bone, like when my dad was cremated. And then there's the hole."

"A hole?"

"Uh, yes, there's a hole in the exterior wall of the bathroom."

"A bullet hole?"

"No, ma'am, like someone blew a hole in the wall with explosives, only, uh —"

Shimooka raised a hand.

"Only what, constable?"

The man grimaced.

"It's perfectly round like the wall was melted through, with something really hot and big. There's, uh, no debris, inside or out, and it's big enough to walk through."

Shimooka frowned in disbelief.

"Our suspects escaped through a hole in the wall on the fifth floor? They fly or rappel?"

The officer shrugged.

"What the hell?" Shimooka said, then grabbed the constable's hand, placing the vomit-filled glove into his palm. "Here. Get rid'a this."

EIGHT

"How do I make this stop?"

THE MIGHTY TITAN REMAINED SURPRISINGLY quiet for almost half of Hunter's shift. Oh, there was the occasional sudden interjection that startled Hunter and left him struggling to answer discreetly, especially if there was a customer at the counter or Juwon was lurking. It might have been easier had it been a running conversation, but Titan would suddenly voice a thought or a question.

Why do you drink that syrupy liquid?

"Because I like it."

It is not healthy for your pancreas.

. . .

The people that come into this establishment buy many lottery tickets.

"Yes, they do."

They rely on a near statistical impossibility to better their lives?

"Uh, I guess so."

. . .

Do you feel any different yet?

"Uh, I think so. I'm not sure."

Are you experiencing anything unusual, like super hearing? Supervision? Super smell?

"Super smell? Seriously?" Hunter balked. "That's a thing?"

Of course. All our senses are enhanced far beyond the standard human capability. They help find individuals trapped in a landslide or collapsed building. Our senses also assist in solving cases of criminal activity against the beings we protect.

A customer had just left, and Hunter found himself feeling oddly comfortable with a being existing inside his body. It was weird as hell, for sure, but if it had to be, he reasoned, it was far better to have someone as interesting as the Mighty Titan than, say, a cartographer or an accountant. Of course, he wasn't entirely sure that Titan wasn't just some lunatic from another universe who believed he was a superhero.

"So, other than flying, what exactly are these powers of yours? Can you see through walls, leap over tall buildings?" he asked.

Yes, I can do all those things and infinitely more, although I fail to grasp why I would need to leap over a tall building.

"Ah, it's what that fictional Superman guy I told about can do."

I see.

Hunter shrugged as he punched the button for Pump 4, clearing it for the next customer.

"Here, in my universe, superheroes, I mean, fictional superheroes, usually have a dominant power. It makes them unique and usually decides what name they choose. They communicate with insects or animals and can assume their strengths and abilities, or they can make their skin super dense, or they run or fly fast. What's your specialty?"

Interesting. It is fascinating that the peoples of this Earth have no such powers as you describe, yet they imagine beings with these powers. It is amusing.

"It's hard to imagine a universe like yours, with many super-powered people. So, what's your power?"

We, you and I, have many abilities. I can feel it within this body. You must simply believe in them and concentrate on using them. However, we do not have a dominant power to answer your question. There is nothing we cannot do.

"So, as far as superheroes go in your universe, you're good at everything. Like, you can see through solid objects? That would be cool, you wouldn't have to answer the doorbell to see who's ringing it. You could just look right through the door—"

Suddenly a painfully bright light exploded across his vision like someone had shone a powerful flashlight into his eyes. He gasped and blinked rapidly, but then the counter he'd been sitting behind began to fade, becoming translucent. Hunter could now see into it, see through the grimy sliding wooden doors that concealed what was under the counter. He could see the various cleaning spray bottles, extra pop and drink bottles, and the box of chips staff kept there to replenish shelves out in the store. He jumped off his stool and stepped back, bumping into the counter behind him. He grabbed its edge with the palms of both hands to steady himself as a wave of nausea swept over him.

"What the hell?" he said, as he blinked profusely, trying to see normally as he looked around the store.

He saw through shelves laden with bags of chips and confectionary, through the slushy machine and straight into Juwon's office. His supervisor was leaning back in his swivel chair with his feet up on his always-organized desk and was reading a romance novel, *The Lonely Buccaneer*. The phenomenon didn't stop there. Hunter saw into and through Juwon's eyeball and brain matter and then out through the back of his head and into the bathroom behind the office. Yet, at the same time, he could still see what was directly in front of him. The effect was unnerving.

Ah, yes, our supervision is returning! My powers are manifesting in you.

"Supervision?" Hunter gasped. "How do I make this stop?"

Oh, yes, we can do many amazing things with our eyes. Peer through the perceived veil of physical substance. We have telescopic vision, microscopic vision, infrared, heat vision—

"Yes, awesome, totally sick, but how do I make it stop?"

Hunter winced as he looked away from the bathroom and Juwon and up through the ceiling above his head. He threw his hands over his eyes, but he saw through them and up through the rumbling old air conditioning unit that leaked during hot summer days, sending droplets of water down over the counter area and onto whoever happened to be working at the time, and still further up, and up, his vision racing away from where his eyes were set in his head. He saw the sunshine-coated outline of a passenger jet angling overhead, descending towards the Calgary International Airport. His vision zoomed in, involuntarily locking on the plane, then carved a visual hole through its skin, through the cargo, each layer of the aircraft peeling before his eyes, revealing the craft's contents like the layers of an onion. Boxes, plastic crates stuffed with smaller containers, suitcases, three dogs in cages, then up through the wiring and ducting in the floor of the flight deck, through a section of seating, through part of one person and part of another, bones, muscles, his vision flashing, flashing red, black, green, strobing—

"Oh, god, how do I make it stop?" Hunter begged, fearful that the rising panic in his voice would attract the attention of Juwon.

Titan laughed.

You have control of our power. Use your mind to control it. Think it so.

"How?"

Hunter slammed his eyes shut, but he saw through his eyelids. His eyes were still tracking the plane. A woman was pushing up the seat tray in front of her. He could see up through her nostrils. He could see the texture of her dark skin, see the bones in her forearm, the sinew flowing along a thin bone, connecting to her wrist, veins, muscle—

Calm yourself. Tell your power what you want it to do.

Hunter squeezed his eyes even tighter, pressing the palms of his hands into them while tucking his head down. His vision pulled away from the plane in a crazy, jarring menagerie of images—women on the plane, the cargo hold of the aircraft, then sky, ceiling, and then they were prying into the cement floor at his feet. He imagined the act of 'seeing' as it had always been for him, imagined that when he opened his eyes, he would 'see' the counter before him and not see through it.

Then suddenly, his vision jumped back to normal, and he opened his eyes. He saw what was like a brief lag in a streaming video. His visual world stuttered, paused, and then returned to normal. He had to grab the counter's edge before him to keep from keeling over.

"That was insane."

"Hey," he heard Juwon call from the Staff Only door he was holding open. "What's up?"

Hunter turned to see half of Juwon's face peering around the half-open door. For a second, his vision peeled Juwon's face, looking into his brain, but Hunter flinched, trying to regain control.

His manager's face became instantly solid, normal.

"Oh, uh, nothing. Was listening to a soccer game."

He smiled sheepishly, quickly pulling his cellphone from his back pocket and holding it up so Juwon could see it.

"Not during your shift, Hunter, you know the rules. Stock the shelves, eh," Juwon barked as he pulled the door shut.

Titan spoke excitedly.

Practice. Do it again, we must practice.

A wave of nausea tumbled through his stomach again, and he flopped down on the stool, feeling sweat pushing across his forehead.

"Are you nuts? How is this even possible?"

The voice shouted with glee.

You are the Mighty Titan. Everything is possible!

"This is seriously happening?"

You must practice. The whole point of coming to your workplace for these precious hours was to give us time to awaken my powers within you. They are awakening!

Hunter blew his breath out loudly.

"Look, I thought I was losing my mind and might still be, but I didn't think any of this was real. You have to give me some time. I'm not you. Superheroes aren't real."

I am sorry, Hunter, but Magus has already killed and will do so again. We have very little time.

Hunter stood up and pulled the box of chips out from under the counter.

"I don't even know how I made that happen, it just did. I have to stock shelves."

I know how you did it. You were talking about seeing through objects, that's when it happened.

Hunter shrugged as he pried the box open.

"Okay, maybe that's how it happened, but I need to stock shelves now."

Did you not find it thrilling? Why I remember the first time it—

"Okay, okay, fine, I'll practice while I do this."

Switching the ability on and off became easier as Hunter practiced looking through everything and everybody who came into the station or pulled up at the pumps. His eyes could zoom in on birds sitting on power poles several blocks away. The sparrows were as clear and sharp as if he'd been using a high-powered telephoto lens. He could also look deep into his skin, revealing cracks and crevasses that looked like river-carved canyons. There was nothing that he couldn't see into or look through to see what was behind it or inside it.

The voice in his head cheered him on.

Yes, the power infusing your body extends your existing abilities. Your vision is enhanced far beyond normal capabilities. Your hearing will become—

"Wait, my hearing? Is that going to go all crazy, too?" he interrupted.

Titan sniffed.

I'd hardly call any of your remarkable abilities crazy…

At that very moment, Hunter felt a sharp pain in his ears.

"Ow," he reacted, pushing his hands against the sides of his head.

Then, as if someone had turned up every music station and TV channel within a kilometre to full volume all at once, his head was filled with the sounds of everything. The hum of the cash register, the pump management panel, the pop machines, and the coolers along the back wall that held ice and drinks, Juwon talking to his mother in Korean on the phone in his office while he tapped a pencil's point on his desk, thump, thump, thump! He heard the gasps from the air conditioning unit metres above his head on the roof, the electrical buzz in the pumps out in the bays, the grating symphony of noise coming from vehicles close and far away, and people, so many people, talking, yelling, arguing, hating, whispering, laughing, crying, all at once. Hunter slid off his stool and sank to the floor, his knees hitting the hard floor while his hands pressed into his ears.

"Make it stop," he begged as tears broke from his clenched eyes.

Super hearing!

The voice celebrated, adding to the cacophony that was assaulting Hunter's mind.

So, the manifestation of our abilities appears to be directly related to your belief in their possibility. This may be the answer we are looking for. We must explore this avenue to be ready to confront Magus.

But Hunter was no longer listening to the voice in his head, it had become one of the many sounds pummelling his mind. The noise was too much, too loud, too everywhere, and too everything. Hunter opened his eyes and saw a million black flies swarming across his vision. He felt as if his brain was about to explode, about to push through his skull and splatter the inside of Earl's, and he'd be the one told to clean up the mess.

Then he felt himself falling over into the welcome silence of darkness.

NINE

"If you weren't me, I'd kill you this instant!"

"MAGGOTS?"

Magus bellowed in rage as he leapt up from the edge of the hotel room's only bed and directed a kick at the screen of the TV. The old, heavy cathode tube television tipped precariously back but quickly settled on its stand. He'd rented the room using strangely coloured currency from Thomas's wallet. The room wasn't a palace by any measure and certainly nothing like his fortress on Vagus Prime, but it would have to do until he could increase his fortunes.

It irked him that they'd been hiding out the entire day in this hovel of a hotel, watching television and ordering food and refreshment from something called McDonald's and something else called Bob's Ribs and Pizza, which was delivered by another something called Dash-It, all requiring a free giveaway of the funny looking currency with each delivery, plus what Thomas had called a tip for services rendered.

Magus the Magnificent did not 'hide out.' The Scourge of the Galaxy did not hide his face. It was a despicable way to spend his first full day in this new universe, but he wasn't fully back to his powerful self. Still, every cell of his being wanted to, or rather screamed to, be released to go out and pillage and crush any opposition, should he find any on this pathetic imitation of his home planet. The night before, after Thomas had led them to this out-of-the-way hotel, Magus had locked Gloria in the bathroom, concerned that she might try to escape and lead authorities or super-powered beings to him. It wasn't that he was afraid, no, far from it. He could feel that his great power was slowly infusing every cell of this body, but it was taking time. Thomas had given him complete control of his power—the worm—but this younger body was still adjusting to its new reality. It reminded him of the days after The Event, when he was first struck by the mysterious field of energy that rapidly coursed across the Milky Way. Even then, it had taken days for him to understand what was happening to his body. Two days from now, he thought, he would be at full power. Then, the Earth will know who Magus is.

Magus, he'd chosen that name. It was a mashup of the words magnificent, stupendous, and glorious, something he'd gleefully pulled together a year or so after The Event, when he was beginning to realize that there was very little he was incapable of doing. He could defy any number of the laws of physics. He could fly at astounding speeds, ignoring the laws of gravity and inertia. He could look through any solid object, his body could resist any physical or elemental assault, and best of all, the electrifying and very destructive blue energy that leapt from his hands merely by thinking it made any and all kneel before him.

Well, that might have been an exaggeration, but for those who didn't kneel, he learned he could simply dispatch them with a more concentrated blast of the energy. Oh, how exhilarating those early days had been, exploring his powers, gradually realizing that Thomas Alexander Stewart, the once pathetic college drop-out and all-time loser, who had failed at just about anything and everything, had become the most powerful being on Earth. Yes, there were others who had been transformed as he had been and were also learning what they were capable of, but they were nothing compared to Magus. No, he knew what he wanted to do with this unexpected gift. He tried to make the world bow to his will and have every living thing fulfill his every desire, and he wanted revenge on every snivelling, cowardly piss-ant who had ever insulted him, ignored him, or looked down upon him. Those first months had truly been the most violent and breathlessly ruthless of his long life. He ended his parents' lives in a slow and wonderfully glorious manner, for, of course, divorcing each other and ruining his future. He tore his coworkers apart with his power-hardened bare hands, for not recognizing his greatness and treating him with less respect and reverence than even the lowly janitors of the factory he'd worked at. Then, he killed one of the new supers, who had assumed the ridiculous role of protector of the innocent. It was that particular incident that had drawn the ire of the Mighty Titan.

The super had a name, Vashti Behman. She was a single mother of three from Ornans, France, though she'd taken to calling herself Azar, a Persian name reflective of the spectacular fiery nature of her powers. She'd have made a splendid partner in villainy, Magus had thought back then, but she'd done what many of the supers had begun to do: acts of kindness and heroism, saving people in distress or danger. It was revolting. They were giving themselves names and donning costumes and face masks to protect their identities, to allow themselves the freedom to explore how they could help the world. Help the world? Bah! The world didn't need their help. The world had ridiculed and cheated Thomas all his life. Yet, some, like Azar, had taken it upon themselves to fight against crime and injustice and even against the, unfortunately, few supers who'd decided to take a different path, a simple life of merely taking whatever they wanted, by force if necessary. They were gods, Magus had realized then. Why should they help those unfortunate souls far less worthy than themselves? It had made no sense to him then, and it still didn't. This was the path that Magus had taken, and it was what brought Azar and him into conflict.

He was beginning to amass gold, antiques, artwork, whatever he felt he might need, which was much, and which later would end up in his magnificent fortress nestled in the rugged spiral equatorial mountains of the fifth planet of the Vagus system, Vagus Prime. He hadn't yet ventured far into space, not yet realizing that his powers could carry him safely anywhere in the galaxy, just by the very thought of it.

While at the BNP Paribas headquarters in Paris, as he was quickly robbing its subterranean vaults, the do-gooder Azar unexpectedly attacked him from behind with her consuming fire. The blinding pain caused by the near nuclear fusion temperatures of the flames that poured from her hands so enraged him that he returned the attack with such ferocity and relentless rage that he barely remembered the epic fight between them, which reduced the global financial institution's hulking edifice along the Boulevard des Italiens into a heap of smouldering rubble. However, he recalled the blue, crackling flames of his magnificent plasma energy coursing gleefully around her head, her terrified eyes bursting like squashed grapes, as his power choked the scream and life from her convulsing body. It was the first time he'd killed someone with the full force of the energy that filled every cell of his body, ultimately rendering her whole being into particles that would have barely filled a dessert dish. The act had filled him with, well, elation and clarity of purpose, and he'd do it again and again with whoever annoyed him. Killing her had been the beginning of his journey to utter ruthlessness.

The Mighty Titan, that self-appointed leader of the newly formed so-called League, had not taken kindly to her death. Oh, no, he was furious in fact, and their seesaw battle raged for most of the following century, back and forth, battle after battle, decade after decade, but, well, Titan was dead now, at last, at long last. Finished by the hands of the man once known as Thomas Stewart, who was now and would forever be known as the Magnificent Magus. That Thomas had been long gone from his mind, yet here he was, in this weasel of a universe, unexpectedly returned to this young body, which still harboured his pathetic former self. He sighed. Maybe this was a sort of redo, a chance to improve his already glorious feats of villainy.

Magus laughed as he tossed the remains of a greasy pork rib toward the small plastic-lined bin near the relic of a television. This sustenance wasn't terrible, he had to admit, especially if one was holed up in such a place, waiting for his power to grow to full strength. Plus, the Canadian beer was pleasing to his senses. The television also provided some entertainment for passing the time. Still, police procedurals, game shows, reality TV, and movies of fictional superheroes and villains were all eating away at his already wafer-thin patience, almost persuading him to abandon any real reason not to destroy this entire universe simply for its stupidity.

"These so-called heroes aren't even real?"

What are you talking about? Of course, they're not real.

"How utterly useless and such a waste of time, creating fictional beings to emulate what's real in my universe."

The hourly newscast again grabbed his attention, the same one that had been playing all day across several news stations. Every time the piece ran, sometimes with additional information on the unfolding investigation, his blood boiled.

"—Maggots? A truly bizarre tragedy unfolding here. Chelsea Billingsworth, Channel Five News, Nepean," the reporter said.

"Maggots? How stupid a place this Nepean must be not to recognize the Magnificent Magus!"

Magus is a stupid name. You must have had better options.

"Shut up! It's a greatly feared name and the name of a god."

Magus launched his foot at the television again, and this time the old device flew backward and embedded into the stained drywall behind its stand. Sparks exploded from it and the screen blacked out in a burst of momentary brilliance.

A god? You call yourself a god, and you give yourself the name Maggots? Who would fear that name?

"Magus!" he growled. "Magus, you imbecile! It's a brilliant mashup of magnificent, stupendous, and glorious, all of which I am and more! So much better than Thomas."

He raised his hands toward the ceiling.

"Who could be afraid of a name like the Terrible Thomas or the Magnificent Thomas."

Magus is a stupid name. It means nothing to anyone here.

Magus shoved his hands into his pockets.

"If you weren't me, I'd kill you this instant!"

Some god you are.

"I am a god. I'm the most powerful being in this and any other universe. You'd do well to understand this since you're me."

Why do you keep saying that, that you're me?

"Because, unfortunately, we're the same being," Magus muttered, scrunching up his face in disgust at his predicament.

He'd never shared the glories of his power with any being except with his beloved Gloria. The situation was intolerable, and as soon as he could figure it out, he'd rid himself of the snivelling other Thomas inside his head.

"You're me, and I'm you. I was once known as Thomas Alexander Stewart, although I'm better than you in every way."

I'm not you.

Magus sighed.

"Our father beat us mercilessly when we wet the bed."

What? How—

"He left us when we were eleven, walking out the door without so much as a goodbye. He left us alone with that wretched, despicable, abusive alcoholic, our mother, although I dare say she was anything but motherly."

How—

"You vowed that night to always put your life first, to always be in charge, to never, ever let anyone control your destiny."

I—yes, but how?

Magus sneered.

"You spent the first twenty years of your miserable adult life living in poverty in Philadelphia, unable to hold onto even menial jobs."

What? No. I'm almost twenty-seven, but—

"Bah," said Magus, waving the conversation away. "I am you, and you are me, a situation I find most unfortunate."

I don't understand.

"Oh, shut it! I must think."

Somehow Thomas could control the flow of Magus's power, but Magus held Thomas's body. It wasn't the most desirable arrangement, Magus admitted, but at least the whiny voice inside his head didn't seem to be able to hear his thoughts. If he could have, Thomas would have trembled at the many and varied ways that Magus was planning to kill him, should it become possible. Still, Thomas hadn't stopped him from killing his friends. He'd let enough of Magus's energy flow into the young Thomas's body to carry out the horrifically magnificent killings in that office. And from the moment Thomas had chosen preservation over-incarceration and allowed Magus to disintegrate that security guard, he'd not taken back control of his powers. After all, they'd flown to Mars and back to this pathetic hovel of a hotel. Thomas had dreams of greatness, of supremacy over any who might be a competitor. Magus could sense it like a shark smells blood in the water. Thomas's growing awareness of the potential of Magus's power to attain whatever he wanted was something Magus could use to his advantage. As long as Thomas saw how easily he could rule the world through Magus's genius and power, then all would be well. He'd make this inferior version of himself into something powerful.

He gazed at his image in the cracked full-length mirror that hung on the wall near the bathroom of this shabby room, placing his hands on the wall on either side, peering in at the youthful face that was now his again. The waning light of the day flowing through the grimy window formed a slight glow around Magus's reflection. The clothes he'd stolen from bins behind a Goodwill Thrift Store on the flight over the city were sad and ill-fitting, hardly worthy of his greatness. The clothes the annoying inner Thomas had put on the morning before were soaked with the blood of his victims, Thomas's acquaintances. As he'd rifled through the bins of donated clothing while forcing Gloria to do the same, Magus had reflected on his glorious former days of hands-on villainy, of the days of blood and carnage before he'd begun dispensing his enemies with the spectacular but clean plasma blasts.

His eyes drifted across the mismatched well-worn Armani shirt and faded green cargo pants with worn knees he'd removed from the bins. At least he still had Thomas's costly leather Versace loafers. The blood washed easily off their finely tooled leather. He'd forced this whiny version of his Gloria to remove the blood stains from them. One day, one day soon, he'd return to his former glory. This world would know and fear his name, as so many other worlds had.

He reached into his pocket and slid the Black Energy disc out. It was hot to the touch, and he assumed that if he were to focus his power on it, it might become a challenge to hold onto. This device had brought him here. How did it do that, he wondered? It might not be the ultimate destroyer of all things he'd hoped it would be.

What is that thing?

"Power," Magus said, with apparent awe, "something very powerful."

Where'd it come from? That wasn't in my pocket before you took over my body.

Magus shrugged.

"It travelled with me to this god-awful place."

What's it do?

"Unimaginable things, things that we shall explore in due time."

Gloria whimpered.

Magus turned to look at the woman who so painfully looked like his long-dead Gloria. She was curled against the black velvet headboard of a queen-sized bed that had seen far too many bodies to be still comfortable. Sobbing, she pressed a lumpy pillow to her chest, watching in horror as her partner in business and in life talked to himself. Magus had demanded she repair her makeup when he'd let her out of the windowless bathroom that morning, and she'd done so as best she could. Her entire body hadn't stopped trembling since he'd pulled the office chair apart with his bare hands and then proceeded to beat Brad and their employees to death. She was nothing like his Gloria, nothing like his Medusa.

"Maggots?" Magus roared again, his rage at his name's mispronunciation rising again. "What's wrong with this Nepean? Have they not heard of me?"

He swung his attention to Gloria, levelling a slim finger at her, but she shrunk away from him.

"Tell me, Gloria," he demanded, "have you not heard of the all-powerful Magus?"

No one's heard of you, dipshit.

"Shut up! Shut up!" Magus screamed, smacking the sides of his head with his palms. "You weak, pathetic worm!"

Weak? I have control of your power, asshole.

"Yes, well, that may be."

Angered, he turned his attention back to Gloria.

"Well?"

Gloria smiled weakly and shook her head.

"Yes or no, answer me," said Magus as he stepped to the foot of the bed.

"You're, you're Thomas," she stammered, unsure if that was the correct answer.

"Thomas? Thomas? Thomas is weak!" Magus screamed as he drove both fists into the mattress at his knees. "I am Magus! Have you not heard of me?"

But Gloria continued to sob and pulled the pillow tighter as Thomas pleaded.

She doesn't know who you are. We've never heard of you!

"Never heard of Magus the Conqueror?"

He stood up, then slapped a hand to his chest, his mouth agape with incredulity.

"You've never heard of Magus the Magnificent?"

No!

"No," Gloria said, shaking uncontrollably, her mind a jumble of confusion. "Thomas?"

"Not Thomas! I am not Thomas! Thomas is pathetic, Thomas is weak. Perhaps you know me by my other grand names? Magus the Terrible? Scourge of the Universe? Pillager of Planets?" he shouted, accenting each word with a stab of a finger that sliced the air with spurts of blueish energy.

"No," she answered weakly.

Leave her alone, or you'll never use your powers again.

Magus stared at her, disbelief displacing the anger in his mind. He slowly turned around and slumped down to the edge of the bed.

"What the hell kind of Earth is this?"

"I-I don't understand, Thomas," Gloria said, trembling.

He waved a dismissive hand.

"You're not you, and I'm not me."

Where are you from?

"Not from this universe, obviously," Magus muttered.

He crossed one leg over the other and leaned forward, cradling his chin in hand.

"Mars is uninhabitable, Earth has no planetary defence system, and no super beings, well, other than me."

Us, other than us, you mean.

"Yes, yes, whatever. This isn't the Earth I know. Somehow I've been transported to a parallel universe where your heroes and villains are fictional, solely for entertainment."

He smacked his forehead with his palm.

"And I don't exist here, other than as this pathetic version of myself?"

Hey, that's unfair. I'm not pathetic.

Magus sighed.

"Yes, in this universe, you are pathetic."

Universe? Are you from another universe?

Magus ignored Thomas and focused on Gloria.

"Does the Mighty Titan exist here?"

Gloria stared at him.

"Well?"

"Tommy?"

Magus sighed and then tapped his temple with a finger.

"You in there. Tell me, have you ever heard of this worthless waste of power, the Mighty Titan?"

The Mighty Titan? No, unless he's one of those pro wrestlers.

"You don't know a so-called super being called the Mighty Titan?"

No. It's a stupid name, too.

"No, there's no Mighty Titan," Gloria whimpered, her eyes red and swollen, as she blinked back more tears.

Magus turned back around and slapped his knee.

"Excellent. No Titan to impinge my future quests."

He turned to Gloria, tapping two fingers on his lower lip in thought.

"Have you heard of the League?"

Gloria continued to blink, her mind racing to find an answer that might calm her boyfriend.

"Do you mean like a soccer league?"

We don't know what you're talking about.

"Most excellent," Magus bellowed with glee.

He turned back around and plopped his chin back into the palm of his hand. The foot of his crossed leg was tapping in rhythm to the pulse of pleasure he felt parading through his veins. What did all this mean, he wondered? Was he free to roam this version of Earth unimpeded by these silly costumed do-gooders?

A hand touched his shoulder.

"Tommy, honey, what's wrong? Why did you kill—"

Magus's free hand flew into the air, a finger pointed toward the ceiling, as he twisted around to see her.

"One more word, and I'll kill you, even if you are my queen."

You will not!

Gloria cowered, pulled back and closed her eyes, wishing she'd awake from her nightmare.

"Fine, fine, fine!" Magus grumbled.

He was growing ever more impatient with the duelling conversations.

"This isn't my Earth," he mused aloud. "These people have never heard of me nor felt the power of my wrath. They've never heard of nor experienced the supreme annoyance of the League or the Mighty Titan, either."

He smiled at that thought and quickly stood up, turning back to Gloria with a gaze of self-affection upon his face.

"I can't believe my good fortune. Somehow the Black Energy has transferred not just my consciousness but also my power into this useless younger self, in a dimension that's like a ripened peach waiting for the picking. Isn't that just the most amazing stroke of luck?"

Gloria stared at him, not comprehending if he was asking her a question or simply making a statement. Magus brushed her off with a wave.

"Hah. Weak-minded child, you may look like my Gloria, but you're not her. I'm the great Magus. I'm the great, magnificent, stupendous, conquering Magus in this and every universe. And," he paused, pointing a finger at Gloria, "my Gloria, my Medusa, was by far the most powerful being ever to walk upon a thousand planets! She was twice the destroyer I am. You will never equal her."

He strode purposefully to the room's only window and threw open the curtains with a flourish. Dust cascaded down from its rod, and Magus coughed and swore. The room was on the ground floor at the back of the hotel, with its sole window facing out onto a garbage-strewn alley through a rusted bank of security bars. A dishevelled older man was digging through a bin, picking out bottles and other money-making recyclables and placing them in a cart he'd stolen from another dishevelled older man. Magus placed a hand against the glass. It dissolved into its molecular components, a sheath of glittering particles that drifted away in the stench of the breeze that blew through the alley.

That was cool.

"Yes, cool, as you say," said Magus, laughing. "We can do many amazing things. Are you not glad you've decided to join me on this journey? We'll rule the world, you and I."

I won't kill anyone.

"Of course not," Magus responded slowly.

He then raised his voice, beckoning to the man.

"You there," he called.

The man, pushing his grimy baseball cap back to see better who'd spoken, saw the young man with black hair standing behind the security bars in the open window, pointing at him.

"Yeah, what the hell d'ya want?"

Magus raised a hand dismissively as a feudal king would do to a serf.

"Tell your government I'm prepared to accept its terms of surrender. Quickly now."

What are you doing?

"The obvious, fool."

The man was used to suffering abuse at the hands of young, well-off punks. It was a hard life, and he knew it came with a price. Yet he'd long since quit caring. Scrounging enough coin to buy a cheap bottle of wine was his only goal now. Get the wine, a mickey if he was lucky enough, then crawl back into the ravine under the Rosedale Bridge and get roundly smashed. He hated these little shits who teased him, however. He used to be one of them many years ago, but life had been unfair, and well, here he was. It was what it was, he'd always told himself.

"Go to hell," he growled, raising his middle finger as he turned back to the cart filled with the remnants of his tattered life.

Magus disintegrated him, laughed exuberantly, and then vaporized his cart for its own sense of retributive pleasure.

Shit. Was that necessary?

Magus chuckled.

"Was that sad wretch of a human being necessary?"

Magus turned back to the cowering Gloria, throwing his hands in frustration.

"Can you believe this, my dear, sweet Gloria? This Earth is plagued with unbelievers. I need to make a statement, so the entire world will know that I, Magus, am here."

He placed both hands against his chest and sighed in exasperation. He then strode to the door and fused the lock and strike plate including the three hinges along the doorframe, making it impossible to open or for Gloria to escape should he fall asleep that night. The security bars on the window would serve as bars in her prison. He then turned to her.

"My queen, we shall find me a warrior's suit befitting the world's greatest super villain in the morning."

He paused, placing a finger to his lips.

"I wonder if Atreasium is on this pathetic version of Earth?"

Atreasium? What's that?

"Oh, you poor bereft souls," Magus sighed, clutching a hand to his forehead. "Only the greatest tailor and armourer in the universe, who happens to live on the Midwestern portion of the North American continent. He's superior to any other so-called clothing designers."

Magus spun on his heels and pointed to Gloria.

"Atreasium, have you heard of this magnificent craftsman? He's clad the most fearsome of villains, though—"

He paused, tilting his head slightly up.

"I prefer to call us the true heroes of the people."

"Who?" Gloria stammered.

We don't know who that is.

"Ah," Magus fumed, his fingers beginning to tingle with the energy of his anger. "Of course, you don't. There are apparently no worthy beings here, save me. I have half a mind just to incinerate this entire planet."

He reached out and snatched one of Gloria's hands, cupping it between his hands as he leaned into her tear-streaked face.

"Tell me, my queen, where can one such as I acquire a suit, a royal costume, if you will, of such magnificent malevolence as to strike terror in the heart of my greatest foe? Who, by the way," he said, as a chuckle escaped his lips, "is no longer among the living. Sad, I should have enjoyed killing him once more."

Gloria cringed at the touch of her boyfriend's hand, which no longer belonged to the man she knew. Something had happened to the young and ambitious Thomas she'd fallen in love with. Was he having a psychotic episode, she wondered? He'd always seemed strong and confident, ruthlessly ambitious even, but to suddenly kill their coworkers, some of them close friends, wasn't her Thomas. She searched his face, looking for anything that might help her understand. Yet the man she thought she loved no longer seemed to be there. This was a different Thomas.

"My dear, my sweet, sweet queen," said Magus.

He softened his face, the closest thing to a comforting smile creeping across the features of his younger self, as he let one hand caress the face of the woman who looked like his beloved.

"Where can I acquire a costume?"

Gloria took a deep breath and looked Magus in the face.

"Um, you, you want a costume?"

Magus rolled his eyes, shocked that she'd even have to ask.

"Yes, yes, of course, I do. I can't present myself to this world's leaders dressed in such average attire. Would you have me be laughed at?"

He narrowed his eyes.

"I cannot bear the laughter of fools."

Gloria smiled timidly, then swallowed.

"Um, maybe Party Costume?"

Magus pulled his hand away, chewing the words over in his mouth.

"Sounds as pathetic as this planet, but it'll have to do."

He turned his attention back to Gloria.

"I suppose, knowing the uselessness of this Earth, they wouldn't be open at the moment?"

She looked apprehensively at Magus, then glanced at the clock radio on the bedside table.

"Uh, probably not."

Magus huffed his frustration, letting his power swirl slowly around his hand as he watched it. How pretty, he thought, how exciting, how very, very sensual. He let the energy fade to nothing and turned his eyes back to Gloria, allowing them to sweep salaciously over her body as she held herself in fear on the bed. He slowly reached out to touch her face, but she pulled away. Smiling, he leaned into her, forcing her to push back and press against the headboard. He slid his fingers gently along her strong cheekbone, along the side of her head, and up into her hair, gripping the blossom of her dreads as he pulled her face close to his. Oh, his Gloria had known how to set his inner desires aflame.

Seriously? She's my girlfriend, you know.

Magus laughed, and Gloria flinched.

"Yes, she is our girlfriend."

TEN

"It's just a carrot."

HUNTER.

A vehicle's horn was honking.

Hunter, get up.

More honking.

"Hunter!"

It was Juwon, calling him from a million miles away and painfully right next to his head. Hunter rolled over onto his side and sat up, reaching blindly above his head on the counter with his hand for the refresh button on pump number Six. He found it and gave it a push. The honking stopped, but the roar of noise in his head didn't

"Hunter, where are you?"

Hunter stood up, waving at him. Juwon was leaning out from behind the *Staff Only* door.

"Sorry, I was just restocking the shelf down here."

Juwon frowned and disappeared.

Hunter squinted out at the person using the pump. He could hear every little click and tick and snap and flick of the man's use of the machine.

"How do I make it stop?" he begged, hoping he was whispering and not actually screaming.

Titan laughed.

The same as your vision. You have control. Simply will it to stop.

"Will it to stop," Hunter mouthed over the roar, jamming his eyes shut to focus.

It stopped. Blissful auditory normalcy returned, and he opened his eyes to see a bemused man looking at him through the plexiglass shield.

"Uh, lottery?" Hunter asked.

The man frowned, set two cans of pop on the counter, and asked for a lottery ticket.

"Superhearing?" Hunter mused after the customer had left. "How do I keep it from being like standing next to a speaker stack at a rock concert?"

A rock concert?

"You know, a music concert."

Ah, I see. Yes, that was unexpected, but I recall a similar event occurring when I was first infused with these powers. Unlike you, I had no one to coach me through this process. However, it was not difficult to gain control, as it is no different from controlling your supervision. Focus and tell your power what you want it to do. You control it, it does not control you.

This day has been crazy, Hunter thought as he rode his bicycle through back alleys and parks on his way home after his shift ended. He'd been practicing listening for the last hour. He'd had no idea that the world was such a noisy place. He could even hear the staccato taps of an ant's six legs as it crossed the concrete pad by the pumps. Titan had encouraged him to use his enhanced vision to see the ant and his pumped-up hearing to listen for the insect's rapid transit.

"Wait until I tell Mia."

You must not. You cannot. It will put her in danger.

"You don't know Mia. She's not afraid of anything."

That may be, but my experience has been that loved ones must never know your true identity. The villains you face would find great pleasure in destroying those you care for.

"Right," Hunter said as he pulled up to the back fence of his parents' house.

He opened the gate and pushed his bike through. He locked it to the metal bike post his father had installed on the side of the garage, then made his way up the back steps, pushing his way into the kitchen.

His parents were there, making a pasta dish together. They'd always enjoyed cooking as a couple, especially on weekends. It was a family tradition. A soccer match was streaming on the laptop sitting on the kitchen island. Hunter glanced at it as he slipped off his running shoes.

"Ah," his father said. "Just in time."

"Hey, Hunter," his mother added.

She smiled while tossing a raw carrot at him. Hunter watched it flip toward him, moving in slow motion.

Your enhanced vision can make fast-moving objects appear as if they are moving in slow motion, so you may decide how to engage with them. It allows you the opportunity to avoid being struck.

"Funny," Hunter said quietly while snagging the carrot from the air before crunching it loudly between his teeth.

Amazing.

Hunter frowned.

"It's just a carrot," he whispered.

No, it is incredible that you have parents.

Supper with his parents was weird and uncomfortable, not because eating with them was weird or uncomfortable, but because the voice in his head was incredulous that Hunter had living parents. He peppered him with questions throughout the meal, creating a difficult-to-follow three-way conversation between Hunter whispering answers to the being in his head and answering questions from his parents about his day. It was complicated, and the only thing that made it bearable was that Hunter could look into his parents' heads, literally.

"So," his mother began, employing her standard method of initiating a conversation at the dinner table, "how was your day?"

We have a mother. This is incredible. Do we have siblings?

Hunter cleared his throat.

"Uh, no."

"What?" his mother said, a fork of chicken Alfredo halfway to her mouth.

He caught his father frowning at him out of the corner of his eye.

"Uh, sorry, yes, uh, the day was good."

"Oh," she said, slipping the pasta into her mouth.

The 'oh' was meant as an invitation to continue with an explanation of the day's events, whether they may have been interesting or not. That's how this nightly conversation routine was supposed to go. It lasted for about half the meal, filled with awkward silences until it mercifully ended when one of his parents would push their chair back and say 'well' or something similar.

So, in between trying to manage three conversations, Hunter looked into his father's skull, letting his vision push slowly into his brain, then out the other side to where the dining room window looked out onto the backyard. It was exhilarating to see the inside of someone's head. It should have been dark since there was obviously no light inside his father's head. Still, somehow his enhanced vision was able to compensate for that, and every bit of veined white and grey matter was as visible as if it'd been splayed out on a mortician's table under a bright light. He also listened to his parents' heartbeats, the slow hiss of their breathing, and the tiny clicks and squeaks of insects in the walls. He wouldn't have minded doing this the entire meal, zipping in and out of his parent's bodies, listening to the gurgling sounds coming from their stomachs as they ate. However, there was a voice in his head, unheard by his parents, but a voice that wouldn't stop talking.

You should not invade their bodily privacy in such a way.

Titan reprimanded him after Hunter had been looking through the table at the bones and veins of his mother's feet and ankles. Hunter grunted quietly in turn.

How fortunate you are to have parents. As I said yesterday, I am an orphan. My parents were killed in an automobile accident shortly after I was born. The nuns of Holy Christos Orphanage raised me.

"Right, you're an orphan? Nuns?" Hunter said out loud. "A classic origin story."

"Excuse me?" his father asked, frowning.

His mother also frowned.

"Who's an orphan?" she said. "What about nuns?"

Hunter shook his head.

"No, sorry, I was just thinking out loud."

"About nuns?" his father asked, frowning even more deeply than usual.

Hunter smiled.

"Uh, no, uh, it's a new graphic novel I bought."

You lie so quickly.

Hunter grunted.

"Yeah, sorry, my day was pretty ordinary."

I think not. This day has been anything but ordinary. I have never experienced anything like this, ever.

His father cleared his throat.

"Chasing and not catching a shoplifter was an ordinary day for you?"

"A shoplifter?" his mother repeated excitedly.

She leaned toward her son, her fork, wrapped in thin strips of linguine, was in mid-twirl in the spoon she was holding over her plate.

"That sounds exciting."

"That was yesterday," Hunter corrected. "No one tried to rip off Earl's today."

"Ah," his father nodded, wiping his mouth with a brightly coloured napkin.

Yes, yesterday. That was when I entered his body. He was chasing a young man who was embarking on a criminal career.

Hunter grimaced.

"No, he wasn't a criminal. He was just a kid making a terrible decision."

"I never said he was a criminal," his father said as he artfully spun pasta on his fork while using a spoon as a base.

"Oh, a criminal?" his mother echoed.

Indeed, your parents must be very proud of you.

"No, I don't think so," Hunter muttered, trying to speak into his shoulder.

"What?" said his mother, as she leaned in closer. "You don't think what?"

I can see I have missed much by not having a family. Although, in all honesty, the League has been more of a family to me than the nuns ever were.

"Oh, I wouldn't say that," Hunter whispered.

"Say what?" his mother asked.

His father sighed and stabbed a piece of chicken.

"He didn't catch him, the non-criminal shoplifter, that is."

Your parents are very nice.

Hunter sighed.

"I caught three last month, Dad. Sometimes one gets away."

An uncomfortable silence suddenly hung like a cloud over the table. It wasn't the first time and probably wouldn't be the last. Being an only child was difficult at times. There was no sibling to bounce the conversation to. The entire dialogue always rested on the three of them being able to pull it off without the nightly event becoming too dull. Hunter had often thought that not much happens from one day to the next. How much can three people talk about, day after day?

"Well," his father said, pushing back his chair.

"I'm gonna call Mia," Hunter said after a moment, standing. "But, I'll clean up the dishes first."

ELEVEN

lol I'm your Super Mia

MIA KIM SLID AN ARM AROUND her halmi, helping her grandmother rise out of her favourite chair, the one that sat squarely in front of the large flat-screen TV in the apartment condo she'd lived in since shortly after her husband had passed away, more than a decade earlier. It was a comfortable two-bedroom apartment with a view of Calgary's Bow River. Well, a view in the fall, after all the leaves had fallen off the dense bank of poplars that lined the building's east side. Mia had heard her halmi brag to friends about the view but would only invite them over in the autumn, after the leaves had fallen, to show off the barely visible strip of glistening water that could be seen from the small balcony.

"Thank you, little Mia," her halmi said as she made her way to the condo's tiny kitchen. "Tea?"

"Of course, halmi," Mia said, following her. "Let me help you."

They'd spent the entire day sorting through boxes of clothing and dishes her halmi wanted to give to Goodwill. Her grandmother had been deep into the task when she'd hurt her back lifting one of the boxes the day before. Mia had always felt close to her halmi, especially after the death of her hahl'bee, her grandfather, when she was seven. That was when she'd begun spending nights with her grieving halmi, inviting her to tell stories of their early days in Calgary and what it was like to be one of the few Korean families in the city. It had made little Mia feel important, bringing comfort to her halmi. Family was important to her grandmother, and it was to Mia. The Kims had lived in Alberta since the 1960s. Unlike many Korean families back then, who had chosen to immigrate to Toronto, her halmi and hahl'bee had travelled by air to Calgary, landing in the city in mid-February during a chinook, a spell of warm, humid weather. Halmi had told the story many times about how the weather had tricked them, jumping from 50 Fahrenheit on the day they'd arrived to 15 Fahrenheit the next day. Her grandfather had been a chartered business accountant, and the province's growing oil and gas industry had provided a comfortable living for them as their family grew.

However, there wasn't a large community of Koreans in Alberta, which meant that Mia often only had her family to share the traditions they'd grown up with, which held them together. Her grandparents had two sons, one of them being Mia's father. His brother had three children, but they'd moved to Vancouver shortly after hahl'bee's death. Uncle Steven couldn't bear to live in the same place where his father had died, she'd heard him tell her father one night during an unusually heated discussion. She texted and video-chatted with her cousins often, but it wasn't the same as when they were kids and went to the same school.

As her halmi was pouring the hot water over the loose tea, and Mia was laying out flowered teacups and saucers on the counter, her phone chirped. She pulled it from her back pocket and glanced at the screen. It was Hunter.

"Your young man?" halmi smiled, a twinkle of mischief in her eyes.

Unlike her mother, she didn't seem to mind that Mia was dating a white boy. Of course, Hunter was such a nice guy, was very comfortable around her family, and was especially sweet to her grandmother. He was a fan of her traditional winter dish, kimchi, which was pretty good, and he was always interested in hearing stories of the early years when everything was new and exciting for the Kims in the land with enormous skies and flat, flat ground.

Mia chuckled.

"Yes, halmi, but he can wait, I'm here with you."

"Oh, no," she beamed, waving her away with a hand. "I'll make us some soup. You go tell him how much you miss him."

"Oh, you," Mia chided as she slid into one of the chairs around the kitchen's small table.

Her mother, who adhered to a few cherry-picked Buddhist teachings, was sure Hunter would bring suffering to her daughter, but Mia wasn't convinced of that. He wasn't like the other boys in their high school. Hunter was kind, and she sincerely felt he wanted her for who she was as a person. She was intelligent and loved the sciences, and he made her feel like her mind mattered, that she was a human being first and not just a pretty Asian girl that he could brag about hooking up with to his friends. He just wasn't like that. Maybe it's because he's an only child, she thought. Perhaps that made him less competitive and more interested in other people's lives.

She swiped her screen open. The message from Hunter was a text.

Hunter: Mia???

She texted back.

Mia: Hey hunter. I'm still @ halmis staying another night but b home in the a.m. come over after breakfast

Hunter: sure hug your halmi for me hope she's ok

Mia: nothing help from super mia can't fix how was work

Hunter: lmfo super mia. I like that speaking of super I need to tell you something

Mia: lol I'm your super mia ;)

Hunter: lol there's a super being from another universe in my head

Mia: ?

Hunter: not jking there's a voice in my head says he's a superhero from parallel universe

Mia frowned and looked at her halmi, who was loudly chopping some cabbage on a cutting board. Another message came in from Hunter.

Hunter: not jking serious there's a voice in my head and he has powers and it's doing something to my body :(

Mia looked at her phone, puzzled, and typed a new message.

Mia: I don't understand you talking about a new graphic novel :)

Hunter: no there's a voice in my head says he's from another universe is a superhero wants me to fight a villain from that universe

Mia: i don't get jk

Humter: no jk

Mia: call me, k i don't get jk.

Hunter: k no jk

"How is your young man?" her halmi asked, grinning widely, as Mia stood up and slipped over to the stove, where a pot of broth and vegetables was beginning to boil. Mia shrugged.

"I'm not sure. He's going to call me."

Halmi smiled and patted Mia on the arm.

"Ah, your Hunter is a very nice boy."

"Yes, he is," Mia said, reaching for soup bowls from the corner cupboard near the fridge.

Hunter never called.

TWELVE

"Look, I can't do this."

IT WAS EARLY SUNDAY MORNING, just past seven, and the Mighty Titan had cajoled Hunter out of his sleep long before he would usually have bothered to roll out of bed.

Good news! My powers continue to grow. They are greatly diminished but appear to be infusing your body the longer we are joined in this manner.

Hunter sat on the edge of his bed and grabbed his cell from the nightstand. He swiped through his text messages. There was a lone response from Mia the night before.

Mia: Hunter?

He quickly typed a reply.

Hunter: Sorry, I'll explain. c u soon.

"Uh, yes, you said diminished?"

Yes, but I believe they are returning to their full power the more you become aware of them and utilize them.

"Utilize?"

Yes, we are one being, but separate. You are you, and I am me, but we are stuck, if you will, in the same space in this universe. Magus's Black Energy disc must not have been a weapon, per se, but perhaps a trans-dimensional transporter.

"Trans di-what?"

Yes, a trans-dimensional transporter that requires massive amounts of energy to activate. That would explain the damage he inflicted on me in our last battle. My contact with the disc was draining my power, weakening me, and allowing him to injure me quite seriously. Clasping the device between our hands must have given it enough power to initiate the transporter, bringing us both here.

Hunter stood up, stretched, and reached for his jeans from the chair near his bed.

"Wow, I don't think I understood any of that. How old are you?"

Is that relevant?

"Well, I think it is."

I am one hundred and thirty-seven-Sol years.

"Woah, a hundred and thirty-seven? You don't sound that old."

My power slows the aging process.

"Do we still have our hair?"

How is that relevant?

"My mom's dad is bald. It's relevant to me."

Yes, we have hair.

"Cool. So, why are you so much older than me if you're me? If you came from a parallel universe, shouldn't things be the same, like shouldn't we be the same age?"

You are assuming that our universes share a similar time dynamic. I suspect not, judging by your age and that of the young Thomas Stewart we saw on your visual device. Assuming there are multiple universes, each may be populated with the same beings but not all share the same flow of time or even some of the same significant events.

"Like this Event thing you talked about that gave you superpowers?"

Yes, neither of the two Events has happened in this universe.

"Oh, right, you mentioned two Events yesterday. So, this is like a reoccurring thing in your universe?"

No, it has only happened twice.

"But it could happen again?"

I cannot say.

"So, what's this power or energy that changed you and others in your universe?"

There has been much research into it, by some to understand the two happenings, and by others in an attempt to replicate it and create more super-powered beings. The consensus is that the energy that erupted from the Galactic Centre may have caused a HIGGS Field inversion on a temporal micro level, which permanently altered the laws of physics for the living beings the field passed through, such as myself.

"Uh, right."

This is the reasoning behind my use of the phrase that those of us affected by The Event exist outside of the laws of this universe. We can manipulate the laws of physics in this universe while existing within our micro-universe. I can travel at speeds exceeding the speed of light, which is an impossibility in this universe, but not in the one my actual being resides in. My physical being exists within a universe where its physical laws allow me to do what appear to be impossible actions simply by thinking so. Because I am also physically present in this universe, and both universes occupy the same overlapped space and time, I am able to manipulate this universe's laws by using the ones I exist in. Do you understand?

"Uh, no. That made absolutely no sense to me."

No matter, the HIGGS Field inversion explanation is theoretical at best. No scientist has yet been able to replicate the effect. Others have theorized that the energy field may have created a type of quantum entanglement, but we do not have time for this discussion. We must prepare for battle.

"Uh, yeah, let's not do that. Mia's back home, and I need to talk to her after I eat."

We do not need to eat.

Hunter frowned and laughed.

"Uh, yeah, we eat breakfast, lunch, and dinner. You don't eat? How do you get the energy to, you know, to keep on living?"

The transformation that occurred in my body during the first Event allows it to feed on the background radiation of the cosmos, I need nothing else.

"How is that even possible? So, you don't get hungry?"

I do not eat for the sake of eating. If necessary, I will join in a culturally based feast, but I do not eat. There is no point in this conversation. We must leave.

"I need to eat breakfast."

The voice was still for a moment.

We will leave after you eat.

"Where are we going?"

I must teach you how to use our other abilities. The awakening of our enhanced vision and hearing will not be enough to defeat Magus.

Hunter laughed.

"Well, I could beat him in a staring contest."

That would not suffice. I did, however, experiment on you last night.

"What?" Hunter said as he pulled on clean socks. "You experimented on my body while I was sleeping?"

It is our body.

"Did you like, um, anal probe me?"

There was no probing.

Hunter looked both ways out his bedroom door. No dad in his basement shop and no mother lurking.

"What did you do to me?"

I made us fly.

"What? Fly? Where to?" he whispered as he crossed the hall to the bathroom.

We did not leave your bedroom. I made your body float over the bed. My power is growing within us, though it appears to be weakened from the effects of the transfer from one universe to another.

"I don't understand, I thought I was in charge of your powers?"

Yes, you are, but in your unconscious sleep state, I appear to have some influence over it.

"Huh, so you made me float above my bed?"

Yes, and I made you spit.

"What? Spit?"

Yes, it appears to be the limit of what I was able to achieve beyond levitating.

"Why spitting?"

Look at the wall behind your bed.

Hunter turned around at the bedroom entrance. He focused his vision and found two dime-sized holes in the wall facing his pillow, where his head would have been lying. The holes were nearly perfectly round, a few centimetres apart. He peered closer, pushing his vision into the holes.

The two punctures extended quite deep, punching through the drywall, the wooden framing behind, the depth of the house's concrete foundation, and the dirt behind that.

You may try if you wish.

He frowned, pulling his vision back to normal.

"Try spitting? At my bedroom wall?"

Yes, it is something of force, at least.

"What, just spit at the wall?"

Yes.

Hunter grimaced but searched his mouth for saliva then spit halfheartedly in the direction of the two holes. The spittle exploded between his lips and hit the wall, the impact sounding like a gunshot. Hunter jerked back and then leapt forward to the wall to inspect the third hole. It was slightly larger than the other two and was irregular in shape.

"That's nuts. I have super spit power! Is that such a thing?"

Yes, it is something offensive, at least. I would hesitate to boast about it.

"Oh, my god, this is so crazy," he said, running his fingers over the holes. "Uh, I really need to do something."

Yes, I concur. I can feel it within you.

"You can feel my need to, uh, you know?"

Yes, it is strange for me, too.

"What, you don't poop?"

I do not.

"How is that even possible? Every living thing defecates."

That is true, but the power within me has made my physical body extremely efficient.

"Well," Hunter said, as he crossed the hallway to the basement bathroom, "I'm not that efficient, plus my dad's lasagna has superpowers of its own."

The basement bathroom was mainly for his use, although his dad occasionally used it when working in his shop. Hunter caught his reflection in the vanity mirror. He looked normal, well, as normal as he'd ever been, he thought. There was a voice of a being from another universe in his head that had somehow given him superpowers to fight another super-powered being. Oh, and he didn't poop. He sighed.

"Look, can you go somewhere in the back of my head or something while I, uh —"

I cannot.

"Oh."

Moments later, after a quick shave to remove the stubble from his face, Hunter ran up the basement stairs, entering the kitchen. He was surprised to see his parents were up so early. He could see them through the window over the sink, sitting at the glass-topped table on the backyard patio and reading from their tablets while drinking coffee. It struck him how normal they looked, not something he'd thought before. His mother noticed him and smiled. He waved. His father saw the movement and cast a glance at Hunter. He nodded once. The prairie sky was blue and vast above the row of houses he could see from his backyard. It was looking like it might be a lovely morning. Hunter made two slices of toast smothered with jam and peanut butter and downed a glass of milk before heading for the front door.

Where are you going?

"I told you, I have to tell Mia."

No, we must not. She must not know about us.

"I have to talk to someone, and she's someone I can talk to."

Out of the question. We must protect our identity. It would not be safe for her if she knew.

"Wait," Hunter implored, but Titan took control of his legs. "We can't just run off and save the day."

Why not?

"Because you'll get me killed."

I've been dead before.

"What? Really? You actually just said that? Did you steal that line?"

I do not understand.

"It's from a Star Trek movie. Never mind, where are we going?"

Somewhere secluded. You must practice if we are to stop Magus.

"You promised you wouldn't take control of my body."

I am sorry. This is not ideal, but there is little time, and we must prepare.

"You have no idea where you're going, do you?" Hunter said as his body turned left on the sidewalk in front of his house.

We need privacy.

His body kept walking briskly, leaving his neighbourhood and turning onto a cross Street. It was extremely unsettling, having his legs head in one direction while his mind wanted to run in the other, covering the three blocks to Mia's house. He walked past a bus stop and tried to reach out and snag the edge of the bench, but his body jerked away.

"C'mon. Just stop. You obviously don't know anything about Calgary. We need to think this through."

His body stopped. The Mighty Titan had decided to save the world, but this wasn't his Earth, and he didn't know where he was. Hunter smiled.

You may be correct. So, think this through.

"Can we sit down at least?"

His legs turned him around, and approached the bench Hunter had just tried to grab. They sat.

Think.

"Look, I'll do this, whatever it is you want me to do, but only if we go straight to Mia's right after."

Impossible.

Hunter shrugged.

"Then I'm not cooperating."

Silence.

"I'm serious. We go to Mia's after, or I don't help you."

Silence.

"I mean it. Please, I have to talk to her. I need to know—I need to know I'm not just talking to myself, and I'm not just imagining the super spit and that I can see through things."

Titan sighed.

If it advances our cause.

Hunter nodded.

"It will. Mia has a brilliant mind."

Then, yes.

Hunter scratched his arm, glancing around to see if anyone was watching him talking to himself. The situation was already intolerable, to quote the voice in his head, and he didn't need any further complications.

Talk, or we commence our training.

"Okay. Relax. Do we even know where this Maggot guy is?"

Magus.

"Whatever. Where is he?"

Your visual device said Nepean.

"It's called a television. You don't have TVs?"

Nepean, Hunter. Focus.

"Nepean? Right, that's across the country."

We must leave now.

Hunter chuckled.

"It's a lot further than you can make my legs run. We need transportation."

We must fly.

"I don't have that kind of cash just laying around. I have money in the bank, but I'm going to university this fall."

We do not need money. We will fly.

"What? How does levitating over my bed equate to flying?"

Levitating was simply a test to determine the level of my powers in you. You are the Mighty Titan. We will fly.

"No, I'm not the Mighty Titan. I'm this universe's much more useless version of you."

Not so, Hunter. My power is within you. You are me. You just don't fully realize it yet.

Hunter shook his head slowly.

"Right. I'm me. Oh, god."

Trust me.

"Right, trust the voice in my head?"

You are very stubborn.

"And so are you."

Yes, we are very stubborn. Please stand.

Hunter rose from the bench.

"Now what?"

Listen.

"I have no choice, in case you hadn't noticed."

Titan laughed, which was a little troubling to Hunter as he hadn't yet heard the voice in his head laugh. It was definitely creepy.

When I defy gravity, whether in a planetary atmosphere or the depths of interstellar space...

"What the hell?"

Yes?

"Listen to yourself. You sound like a comic book."

I do not understand.

Hunter groaned.

"You know, cartoons, illustrations, sometimes funny, sometimes serious? Superman, Thor, Pooch Cafe. They're not real. They're stories written by someone with imagination and drawn by an artist."

Ah, yes, the funny books you showed me yesterday. I understand humorous illustrations intended to make one feel hilarity, but I do not know how I sound like one of these fictional characters.

Hunter sighed.

"Never mind. Go on. You defy gravity and stuff."

The voice sighed, which was equally as odd as the earlier laugh from within his head.

Very well. As I was saying, I defy gravity with the power of thought. I make it so by thinking it so. My thoughts reorganize the very fabric of space and gravity around my body. I control both, they do not control me. I traverse through the fabric of this universe thus. I am a part of it, yet not a part of it, within it, yet outside of it.

Hunter grimaced.

"Right," he said. "Do it then."

As we have already discussed, I do not seem to be able to do so. My being is somehow interconnected with yours. We have exchanged abilities, it would seem, I can control your body, so conversely, you should be able to control the energy that has made the journey with me. We share the same space in this universe but seem constrained to accessing only each other's abilities. You must make it so.

"That doesn't make sense. You made me fly or levitate while I was sleeping."

Titan sighed again.

I managed to make you levitate, but you were in a paralytic state brought on by your sleep cycle. Perhaps if you were unconscious, I could assume complete control of my powers.

Hunter laughed.

"Ah, and how would you suggest I make myself unconscious?"

Without injuring you or drugging you, I do not know, and I am sure that doing so would be highly unethical.

Hunter laughed again.

"That is a conundrum," he said as he glanced about.

Indeed. Therefore, we have no recourse but to instruct you in the manner of using my power and thus learning to fly.

"Ah, yes, Obi-Wan, teach me how to use the Force so we can achieve lift-off."

I know not of this Obi-Wan or this Force, but if by lift-off you mean fly, then yes.

"I can't do that. I'm not you."

Yes, you can. Yes, you are me. Think it so.

"Seriously?"

Yes, seriously. Think it so.

Hunter looked up and down the street. Too many vehicles with too many sets of eyes might notice a shaggy-haired young adult blasting off from Mother Earth.

"We must get out of sight if this is going to happen."

Yes, that is very wise. Forgive me, we must protect our secret identity at all times.

"Uh-huh, protecting the secret identity."

Hunter nodded slowly as he walked to an alley that dissected the street. He found a spot behind a row of refuse carts.

"Wouldn't want anyone to assume that we are crazy. Now what?"

Think it so.

"What? Scrunch up my eyes? Concentrate hard? What do I do?"

It is no different from using your enhanced vision. It should require no more effort than breathing. Just think—

"Yeah, yeah."

Hunter made air quotes, something, he suddenly realized, feeling more nerdish than usual, he'd been making a lot of lately.

"Right, okay, just think it so."

Hunter sighed. He'd also been doing that a lot in the hours since the 'possession' had started.

"Right. Think it so. Think it so."

There is no need to make a mantra of it.

"It helps."

He jammed his eyes shut, slightly afraid that he might start 'seeing' through things again. There was a momentary translucent flash, but he concentrated. Think about flying, think about not seeing through your eyelids—

Open your eyes. I wish to see your progress.

"There is no progress," he muttered, keeping his eyes shut while clasping his hands to his head. "Look, I can't do this."

Open your eyes. I must see.

Hunter opened his eyes. A black cat with a white streak down its chest, its head tilted to one side, was sitting on a blue cart, watching him.

"See?" he said, gesturing at the cat. "I can't do this."

This is most unfortunate.

"I'm afraid I'll start seeing through stuff again."

You are overthinking this. Let your power do the work by thinking about what you want it to do. Close your eyes again and concentrate.

"I told you, I can't do this."

Do it.

"Fine."

Hunter leaned against the cart. The cat, startled by his sudden move, leapt indignantly to the grimy pavement of the alley and toddled away, its tail flicking in time with its perceived annoyance. Hunter crossed his arms and jammed his eyes shut.

Just like we practiced yesterday with your vision. The objects may be solid, but you can peer through the perceived solidness. Your visual acuity acknowledges that you are in this alley, but your mind must gain control of your senses. Envision space.

"Outer space?"

Indeed. Outer space, but not in space, as you call it, but outside of space. You may or may not choose to interact with it. Outer space is cold and inhospitable to the human body, but you will not feel it unless you wish to. In either case, your body remains contained with its minor universe while manipulating the energies of this vast universe. Thus, we fly.

"Hey, inner me, that makes no sense."

I apologize. Perhaps if I may, I can explain it in another way. We are like an orange—

"Enough!" Hunter declared as he opened his eyes. "I'm going to Mia's. You may or may not come with me."

We must not.

"Oh, really? And why not?"

Magus must be stopped.

"Let the police deal with it," Hunter growled as he struggled to move his feet.

They will be no match for Magus.

"Let me go."

You are the most powerful being in the universe. You are the galaxy's greatest hero.

"Really? Powerful? I can't even fly. All I can do is look through things and into people's bodies, and look—"

He slapped himself hard across the face.

"Uh, hey, that didn't hurt."

He slapped himself again, even harder.

"Wow. That should have hurt."

Invincibility! You are growing more powerful by the moment.

Hunter looked at his hands, flipping them back and forth, frowning at the latest development.

Go ahead. Strike one of your fists against that pole over there.

Hunter looked over at a tall wooden utility pole. It was standing up against a fence, behind a few bins, and held an array of electrical equipment high above his head.

"Punch that?"

Yes, but gently. Your super strength is no doubt awakening as well.

Hunter's eyebrows rose.

"Super strength? Right."

Hit the pole, but not too hard. You will not feel the pain generally associated with such a foolish act.

"Foolish act, right."

He stepped over to the bins and pushed them out of the way, relatively easily, he thought. He sensed their weight but didn't feel the weight in his arms. Standing in front of the pole, he slowly placed his fist against it, feeling the coarse, weathered wood against his knuckles.

"So just hit it?"

Yes, but gently. We do not wish to annoy anyone who may be inconvenienced if you knock it over.

Hunter grimaced.

"Right."

He gave the pole a little tap with his fist, just a gentle punt. It shook with a slight tremor as if a car had backed into it. He looked up and saw the wires bouncing lightly.

"That shouldn't happen, right?"

Did you feel any pain?

Hunter looked at his knuckles.

"No. I didn't feel a thing. I didn't hit it very hard, though."

He drew his fist back.

No, do not do that!

Hunter hit the pole, tempering the movement, so it was about as gentle as if he'd tapped Mia on the shoulder. The sound of the impact was shockingly loud but not nearly as surprising as seeing his fist push effortlessly into the aged and hardened wood, creating a split in the pole that traversed upwards for two metres.

"Oh, shit—"

Oh, dear.

"That's crazy!" Hunter yelped as he grabbed the shaking pole to steady it.

Despite being damaged where he'd tapped it, the pole looked like it might not break apart.

There is nothing crazy about it. You are me. You have many abilities that make you unique. You slapped yourself and felt no pain. You damaged this pole and felt no pain. I am virtually indestructible. I have flown into the hearts of supernovas and harnessed the power of black holes to save entire civilizations. I have withstood the ferocious onslaught of countless foes, mechanical or organic, human or alien, real or imagined. Until two days ago, I led a band of like-minded heroes, the League, who together have defeated every diabolical force that has arisen to assume superiority and dominance over the everyday freedoms of sentient beings from across the known galaxy. I am the Mighty Titan, I bend space and time, I have the strength of a thousand suns, and I control within my hands the power to protect an entire star system from attack or natural disaster. That is who we are. This is who you are. Do you finally believe Hunter MacKenzie?

"Oh, man," Hunter said, shaking his head. "That was a really crazy speech."

Do you believe it?

"Yes, I think you've proven I'm not going crazy. I'll need more than being able to punch out utility poles and seeing through stuff to fight Maggot boy."

Agreed. However, I feel the longer we share the same space, the more you can access my power. By this time tomorrow, based on the rapid progression we are witnessing here today, you should be able to avail yourself of all that my power is.

"And then what?" Hunter asked, knowing the answer.

Then we hunt down Magus and defeat him.

Hunter let go of the pole, feeling sure it wouldn't fall over. Besides, he was positive he'd heard a back door slam in the yard behind the fence. Someone had noticed the sound of his punch and was coming to investigate. He turned and began walking briskly toward Mia's neighbourhood.

"Oh, and let's not forget the almighty super spit power. That'll come in handy in a fight," he added, glancing over his shoulder to see if anyone was inspecting his handiwork.

Defeating Magus will require far more than what we have accomplished here this morning.

The voice spoke with a deep sense of gloom.

Hunter, if you cannot avail yourself of the fullness of my powers, then we are doomed.

Hunter ignored Titan's grim comment and launched into a jog toward Mia's house. He had so much to tell her.

THIRTEEN

"You sound like you need help."

MIA, HER LENGTHY HAIR PULLED BACK into a ponytail and held in place by a purple scrunchy, leaned forward as if to hear better what Hunter had been struggling to explain. Voice in his head? Super being from another universe controlling his body? He sounded more than a little unhinged at the moment. His texts the night before had been cryptic, but then Hunter had always been a little different.

"He will bring you trouble," her mother had reiterated when she'd called her from her halmi's and mentioned the strange texts.

"Oh, Mom, he's not like other guys. He doesn't just think of me as his Korean girlfriend who can cook him dakjuk," she'd replied, laughing.

Mia didn't cook dakjuk or kimchi, but her mother had often said that in Asian culture, food is love, and Hunter loved both her mother's and her halmi's cooking.

He was different, though, certainly nothing like any of the other guys she'd been interested in. Hunter gave his full attention to her, talked with her, and didn't need to impress her or prove how macho he could be, and he hadn't insisted they have sex. They loved each other, she was sure of that, as far as either of them understood what love was. She wasn't naive, she knew that when they were alone and kissing, their hands playing seductively over each other's bodies, she was very aware of what was happening to Hunter physiologically. Their foreplay was fun, full of teasing and innuendo, and maybe one day they'd go further, but not yet, and he was comfortable with that. It was this very thing, this sense that she had autonomy over her body and what she did with it and when she chose to engage sexually, that made her feel safe with him. It seemed very mature of Hunter, she'd often thought, but she knew he liked her for who she was as a person first. They could talk about anything, and that's what couples did. But, did couples do this? Have conversations about universe-hopping super-powered beings?

Mia glanced at her bedroom door again. This was getting too weird, and if her parents overheard his strange ramblings and confirmed that this Caucasian boy would be nothing but trouble, their relationship would be over. She remembered her mother's warning when they started to date early in eleventh grade, telling her that if she wanted a white boy, it would be her fault if it didn't work. Now, here was Hunter, rambling on about voices and super beings. She'd never live the shame down.

"It, he, this voice in your head, calls himself the Mighty Titan?" she ventured, hoping this was just some elaborate but incredibly lame joke.

Hunter was sitting on the edge of her bed, nervous, fidgeting, his thick hair looking even wilder than usual. Mia had been sitting next to him on the bed, but as his weird tale progressed and her concern had grown, she'd positioned herself on her desk chair, so she faced him. Surely his declaration of possession by an alternate universe superhero was a joke. Hunter wasn't always the most serious of persons, but he repeatedly promised her it was all true.

"Yeah, and he won't shut up."

"He's talking? Now? To you?" she asked.

She peered at his face, hoping to see a hint of deception, but he was as serious as she'd ever seen him.

Hunter shrugged.

"Listen, I'm not that nut job you called me in Korean earlier. There's a real voice in my head."

Mia laughed.

"And he's talking to you right now, tto-rai?"

"Too-ray?" Hunter struggled to imitate her.

Mia laughed as she curled her hands forming claws, and lowered her eyebrows.

"No, tto-rai. To yok or insult someone with any authenticity in Korean, you have to get your entire face and hands into it."

Hunter sighed and chuckled.

"Well, yes, he's talking, but he's mad at me and I think a little discouraged. It sounds like he's pouting."

"It's pouting?"

"What?"

Hunter suddenly thumped the side of his head, and Mia sat upright.

"You're not discouraged? Oh, right."

He held up both hands and made air quotes.

"We're all doomed if I don't figure out how to use his power. I'd call that pouting."

Mia sat back and crossed her legs, exasperated.

"Hunter, why are you here?"

He flopped back on her bed, looking up at her stippled ceiling.

"He didn't want me to come. He threatened to stop me, but I trust you, Mia."

Hunter pulled himself back up and slapped his legs with his hands.

"At least his almightiness let me come over here."

Mia frowned.

"Let you? Like, in gave you permission? Or, like when he did that controlling thing you said happened at Earl's?"

He grimaced.

"Yeah, he can control my body, but I control his power. He says he's my older self from another universe. He says he's over a hundred and thirty years old. It sort of makes sense if you believe in parallel universes."

Mia nodded.

"Look, I want to believe you, but—"

Hunter sighed and turned to look out her window.

"Yeah, I know. I'm sorry. Maybe he's right, I shouldn't have told you."

"Aw, Hunter, I'm sorry," Mia said.

She was suddenly conscious of how plastic the smile on her face must look. *He so desperately wants me to believe him*, she thought.

He caught the look.

"You don't believe me, do you?" he said quickly.

Mia shrugged.

"Well, no. I mean, I don't know, Hunter. It sounds farfetched, doesn't it?"

"That massacre in Nepean two days ago, on Friday," he pressed on, raising a finger in the air. "I told you about that Maggots—what?—oh, right—this evil super villain called Magus, he did that."

"Magus? Supervillain? Listen to yourself, Hunter. This sounds—"

She raised her hands and grimaced. Hunter sighed and looked at his feet.

"Crazy?"

Mia shrugged.

"Does it really?" said Hunter.

Mia nodded slowly.

"Yeah. If you're a hundred percent serious right now, and you believe completely that there's a man with superpowers talking to you inside your head, then you sound like you need help."

He suddenly stood up, the springs of her bed creaking noisily.

"Look, I can prove it. The Mighty Titan says I have his powers, but I haven't figured out how to use them. Not yet, anyway. There are things I can do that I definitely couldn't do before."

"Oh, really?" Mia smiled uneasily as she looked up at his face. "Like what?"

Hunter grimaced.

"Well, I can see through stuff."

Mia leaned forward slightly.

"You know this is really weird, right?"

Hunter sighed and sat back down on the bed.

"I know, but it's true."

"Prove it."

"You're wearing blue underwear!" Hunter blurted.

Mia laughed and grabbed the bottom of her top, pulling it up.

"I have a short top on, so you could have seen them sticking out over the top of my pants."

"Uh, yeah, okay, right."

He pointed to the bottom drawer of her dresser.

"There's a stash of three Mars bars in a little pink bag, with a picture of that K-Pop band you like. It's at the back of the drawer."

Mia blinked.

"How could you know that?"

"I can see it, well—what? He says it's not seeing through things so much as I see the thing's energy—uh, yeah, molecules, yeah whatever — and my brain interprets it to look like I'm looking through—what? Really? He says I'm explaining too much."

He shrugged.

"My panties have energy?"

"Uh, well, no, yes, I mean—"

She did have blue underwear on, and yes, she'd hidden the chocolate bars in her bottom drawer to keep Juwon from teasing her about liking cheap confection, but Hunter could have quickly snooped while she was in the washroom earlier. She sighed quietly. He was so confident that something was happening to him. But why this? Why something so bizarre?

"Mia?"

Mia turned her face to Hunter, sensing his discomfort.

"Fine. What other superpowers do you have besides panty X-ray?"

He grimaced.

"Well, I'm sort of invincible?"

Mia frowned.

"What? Like bullets bouncing off of you kind of invincible?"

Hunter laughed and shrugged.

"Well, we didn't try that. I mean, my dad doesn't have any guns—"

"Seriously, Hunter?"

"No, really, look—"

He reached into his pants pocket and pulled out a Swiss Army knife, one with two blades and a pair of scissors.

"It's my dad's. He leaves it in the glass bowl on our dining room bureau. I borrowed it."

"Hunter, this is going too far."

"No, really, just watch. It's cool," he said as he pulled the longest open.

He then drove the point of the blade as hard as he could at his hand. Mia stifled a scream and gasped as the blade bent slightly from the force of the blow, then bounced and skittered off the back of his hand. The blade then collapsed against the pinky finger of the hand holding the knife. There should have been blood everywhere, but there wasn't.

"See? Cool, eh?"

Mia jumped up.

"Hunter MacKenzie, you jerk. Why are you doing this?"

"What?"

"That's a fake knife."

Hunter tried to pass it to her, but Mia shook her head and brushed him away.

"Enough, Hunter. What's going on with you?"

Hunter grimaced and looked away toward her bedroom window.

"I get it, this seems so weird, but Mia, this is freaking me out. This isn't a fake blade."

He held it up, then tried to collapse the blade back into the body, but it was bent. Puffing with frustration, he easily straightened the blade using his thumb and forefinger, closed it and slid the unit back into his pocket.

"Titan believes other more, er, substantial manifestations will follow. What? Shut up. Let me talk."

"Excuse me?" Mia said, placing her hands on her hips.

"No, not you," Hunter groaned. "Him. He's being all dad-like, saying you think I'm mentally unstable and that you want me to leave."

Mia shrugged and smiled tensely.

"Well, this is way past being weird, Hunter. Pretending you're invincible, and panty x-ray powers?"

She smirked and slowly shrugged.

"I'm starting to—"

"I know, I know. You're starting to think I'm a two-ray," he said, shrugging.

Mia laughed.

"It's tto-rai, you ass."

Hunter smiled meekly.

"There is something else I can do."

Mia slumped in resignation and crossed her arms over her chest.

"What is it?"

"It's weird."

"You're weird."

"Honestly, it's weird but kinda cool."

Mia sighed. He wasn't going to let this go.

"What is it, super farts?"

"Don't laugh. Promise?"

"For god's sake, Hunter, what's this amazing superpower? It can't be more bizarre than looking at my underwear."

"I can spit really fast."

The room filled with an awkward silence as Mia's eyes widened, then she laughed. Hunter raised his hands and sat back down on the bed, frustrated.

"I know that sounds stupid, but it's not what you think. I can spit through walls, concrete walls. I have three holes the size of dimes in my bedroom wall, and it's made of concrete!"

Mia laughed even louder, doubling over in the chair, the relief of knowing he was joking sinking in. What a stupid joke, she thought. Why would he do this to her? Super spit?

"No, really," Hunter pleaded. "I'll show you."

"Oh, please do," Mia chuckled. "Do I need goggles, or should I get my raincoat?"

Hunter sighed and turned his head toward her dresser.

"Keep your eye on the mirror."

"Okay," she said slowly.

Hunter took a deep breath and spat.

The spittle exploded with an unexpected deafening crack from his lips. Mia's hands flew to her ears. The projectile was very fast, but she still managed to catch a glimpse of something small piercing her mirror from the corner of her eye. The force of the impact rocked the dresser on its stubby legs. Cracks from the impact on the glass spidered out in a dozen directions as the high-velocity saliva punched through the layers of the wall behind the mirror. A second later, a car alarm went off outside and a voice, faint but angry, bellowed in the complaint.

Mia jumped to her feet, putting her hand against the cracked mirror.

"What the hell, Hunter?"

"See! See!" he said, punching a fist in the air.

Mia looked between the back of the mirror and the wall, her hand feeling for the exit hole, before turning her face to Hunter. How had he done that? Super spit? He was telling the truth, or at least what he thought was true. But, a being from another universe with superpowers living inside him? That was impossible. That was comic book stuff.

"Do it again," she said, her eyes narrowing. "Only this time, open the window first. Dad's gonna kill me when he sees that hole."

Hunter, laughing, walked to the bedroom window, cranked it open as far as it would go then removed the screen. Mia slid beside him, pointing out the window to the backyard below.

"See that compost barrel against the fence? Shoot that with your super spit."

Hunter smiled and shrugged, feeling some vindication for proving himself right and a twinge of guilt for damaging Mia's mirror and wall.

"Sure."

Mia plugged her ears with her fingers as Hunter took a breath, wiggled his lips around, searching for more saliva, smiled comically at her, then took careful aim at the faded green barrel next to the backyard fence. He squinted his eyes and drew in a slow breath, aiming, concentrating.

He spat.

Half the back fence exploded thunderously in a shower of splintered pieces of wood and timbers.

"Oh," Hunter exclaimed slowly. "Wow."

Mia became aware that her mouth was open and her heart was pounding madly in her chest. She turned to look at the face of someone she thought she'd known. They'd been going out officially for almost two years. He'd asked her one day after school.

"Do you want to, like, you know, hang out, like, you know, officially?" he'd said.

"You mean, like a couple?" she'd replied.

"Sure!" he'd said, smiling excitedly.

That moment had turned them into a couple, and their friends seemed okay with that. Her parents seemed happy with Hunter, although she suspected they thought it was just an infatuation that would pass, and she'd settle down and marry a nice Korean boy someday, maybe after university. They'd known each other since Grade Six, and easing into each other's lives as a couple had been fun and comfortable. He wasn't her first boyfriend, but maybe her first real one, or at least the first one she'd felt serious about.

Mia took a deep breath as she turned back to the fence, which now looked like someone had driven a truck through it. Whatever this was, whatever was happening to Hunter, she wanted to be a part of it. She reached out and slid her hand into his.

"You missed."

FOURTEEN

"This universe knows nothing of my kind."

PARTY COSTUME WASN'T WHAT MAGUS had imagined, not that he imagined much about such mundane things. However, it could have been more authentic to its promise of costumes suitable for all occasions and seasons.

"This is a travesty," Magus grumbled.

He looked up at the stuffed piñatas in the shapes of giraffes and gorillas and other mostly unrecognizable creatures hanging from the store's high warehouse-style ceiling.

The rows of costumes, obviously ill-fitting and poorly made, inspired him to wish for the flaming end of all humanity. Nah, the screaming, flaming end of all living things. The costumes were thin, poorly fitted (one size fits all, my ass), and represented what his inner companion, Thomas, said were the outer trappings fictional super beings wore in this super being-less universe during annual festivals and parties. Superman, Batman, Green Lantern, Thor, Shang-Chi, and countless others that Thomas tried to explain represented the Earth's mightiest fictional heroes, hung like cheap imitations of the universe Magus had known most of his illustrious life.

Now, Atreasium, he was a true genius. That was the gender pronoun Magus gave the creature for no reason other than he deemed it inappropriate to call him an 'it' given his formidable size and exquisite skills. Atreasium wasn't human, of course, nor was his name actually Atreasium, it was given to him by some long-forgotten first-contact super, who couldn't wrangle the species' remarkably complex language into anything manageable by beings such as humans that used lips and vocal cords to articulate language.

Atreasium was from the planet of Isthmastrium, another mangled translation, fourth in a solar system unlike any other. Twenty-seven planets charted twenty-seven precarious courses around a binary star system. One sun larger, the other half the size, they danced nervously around each other, taking less than an Earth Sol day, their energies swapping back and forth between them like interstellar boxers, the lesser destined to one day be reduced to a white dwarf or a black hole. The eighth planet, comparable in size to Sol's Jupiter, was the only one with life and what life it was. Due to the planet's extreme gravity, all living things were squat and dense, the vegetation emitting gases toxic to all alien creatures that dared venture upon its surface. The dominant species was a broad armoured multi-pedal creature with wide eye stalks that could see a staggering range of the light spectrum and multiple dexterous appendages that could manipulate a half-dozen tools at once. Their large brains, composed of nineteen lobes scattered throughout their magnificent bodies, had long mastered the science that governed such a harsh environment. No other costume maker anywhere in the galaxy was as qualified and exacting as Atreasium, and he took no sides. Heroes and villains alike availed themselves of his services. When the hulking three-ton alien had immigrated to Earth and established his business in a pressurized dome in the Sonoran Desert, along the Arizona border with what had once been California, he quickly became the darling of supers far and wide, seeking impermeable but functional, armoured costumes. Magus was his most ardent fan.

When Magus had taken his Gloria to Atreasium for the first time, and they'd stood side by side in the glowing holographic display area affixed to a portion of the costume designer's pressurized dome, she'd squealed like a child, her excitement was that real. It had only been a few weeks since he'd plucked her from the silly ramshackle fortress she'd built on the side of some desolate snow-covered mountain in British Colombia. It now was her time to be attired with a costume befitting her emerging and formidable powers.

Her armour was dark, like her skin, with slashes of rich blue, the colour of her eyes. No cape, just jagged shoulder and torso armour that made her look fierce while also designed to deflect anything those useless Leaguers might throw at her in battle. Those were the best days, the early days with Gloria. They had so much fun. Their combined power was fearsome, and together they committed countless brilliant acts of violence. Gloria, Medusa, was such a beautiful and sensual woman.

Damn you, Titan, he thought, wishing all kinds of evil on anyone who had known Titan.

"Are there no costumes here worthy enough to symbolize my true greatness?" he bellowed in seething anger, startling a nearby customer.

This isn't your Earth. I told you, people like you don't exist here.

Magus dropped his head and sighed again.

"Thomas?" Gloria whispered, trying to smile and reassure him. "This is the best place to buy a costume."

"Unbelievable," Magus muttered, resisting the desire to simply incinerate the building and find a costume elsewhere. "How will I present my true greatness to these worms if I can't find something that reflects how truly magnificent I am?"

It was a rhetorical question, of course, and Gloria started to stammer and explain her choice of shopping venues. Her fear swelled in his senses like an ocean tide, but Magus held a finger to her lips.

"Tut, tut, my dear. This universe knows nothing of my kind. Need I expect anything different from this," he said, waving a hand broadly, "this sad costume establishment?"

Moments earlier, Magus, with Gloria holding onto his torso with all the strength she could muster, had shot straight up from the grimy alley behind the hotel into the morning's gloomy skies. She'd been surprisingly unafraid, Magus thought. She might not be his Gloria from his reality, but there was a part of her that was as fearless and as adventurous as his Gloria had been. Once she was able to determine the general direction of the costume store from their high vantage point, they quickly soared above the residential areas of Nepean, angling west to a small Kanata strip mall anchored by an overly large Party Costume store in what had once been the space occupied by a Woolco department store. Colour variations in the stained beige side of the building revealed the spaces where the original letters had been.

Gloria had been unwilling to speak with him in the morning, the anger and betrayal of the assault from the previous evening raging in her eyes. Still, after threatening her with unimaginable violence, Gloria told him that she'd been to this particular mall only a few days earlier to buy streamers and cheap party plates for his, Thomas's, upcoming twenty-seventh birthday party. Once she started talking, her words became a rush of mashed sentences, telling him that she'd considered getting herself one of the Halloween costumes that had just been displayed. It had been a little early in the season to peddle the spooky holiday she'd gone on, but they were on sale, and Thomas was a big fan of things being on sale.

She's rambling. She's worried when she does that. I know, we've been together for three years.

Magus grunted.

"How interesting, and yet you cheated on her."

Gloria's hair clipped Magus's face as she suddenly turned her head at his comment. He matched the heat of her gaze and smirked.

"I believe she's angry with you."

It was nothing. She needs me. Besides, she wouldn't have gotten this far in the business without me.

"Yes, we have that effect on women. They're nothing without our greatness. She's nothing."

His gaze turned to the gathering crowd beneath them as they floated over the parking lot.

"And last night? You wanted her to be forcibly taken by me."

I, I, uh, she's not one of us. She's not prepared to do what we must to be at the top.

"Ah," said Magus, nodding. "Now you see what I see, my dear Thomas. She isn't our Gloria, so she'll only hinder who we're to become in this universe."

"Thomas?" Gloria asked, her eyes searching his face. "I don't—"

"Should I drop her, Thomas?"

What? No!

"Ah, but you just said she's not like us, not one of us, not ready to do what's necessary to be one of us."

Gloria tightened her grip around Thomas's waist.

"Thomas? What are you saying?"

No! Don't you dare let her go. I'll take back your power, and we'll all fall to our death!

Magus smiled and then laughed.

"There it is. Yes, you do have what it takes, my dear Thomas."

"Thomas? What—"

"Shush," Magus hissed, touching her lips with a finger. "These worthless nothings deserve an entrance they shall not forget."

A handful of people in the mall's parking lot and a few more coming out of various stores had seen the two slowly descend out of the overcast sky. No parachute, no futuristic jet pack, just a young, attractive couple rapidly dropping to the cracked and worn pavement that hugged the equally cracked and worn sidewalk in front of Party Costume's dirt-streaked display windows. The method of their arrival caused quite a stir. Cellphones whipped out of pockets and purses, lifted high as morning shoppers photographed or live-streamed the strange spectacle. When Magus and Gloria's feet settled on the pavement, a crowd swarmed around them, peppering them with questions.

"Who are you?"

"Is this a stunt for a new movie?"

"Have we seen you in anything recent?"

Magus ignored them, brushing curious people aside with a slight pulse of his power as he pulled Gloria toward the store's entrance. It was only at the store's sliding doors that he suddenly stopped and turned around with a flourish, dragging a stumbling Gloria with him. He slowly scanned the crowd, barely concealing the disdain he felt. More than fifty people had gathered, spilling out onto the parking lot from the sidewalk, blocking a few vehicles whose drivers had stopped to catch the sudden commotion.

How pathetic, he thought, *how utterly repulsive and like children, they are, clambering for a glimpse of royalty. Wishing to touch what they can't ever have or attain, insects hoping to fly with eagles.*

"People of Earth," he roared, deepening the timbre of the young voice of his young body while tilting his head to one side and smiling thinly. "I have come to save you from yourselves. I, the Magnificent Magus, will rule over you with a fair and just hand."

He lifted a hand slowly, palm up.

"And you will serve me, as others have throughout the known galaxy."

He bowed his head slightly. A young man, holding a penguin-shaped piñata under one arm, reached out and touched Magus's arm.

"Who are you, dude?"

Magus smiled even more thinly as he touched the impertinent human with a finger.

"I am your death, imbecile," he hissed

The man's face froze with anguished surprise. A second later, his body was engulfed in a flash of dazzling blue arches of plasma that spiralled around his entire body before it was pulled apart to form a cloud of sparkling sunlit dust that slowly caught the rising wafts of hot morning air rising from the warming pavement of the parking lot. The piñata dropped with a crunching sound to the pavement as the shimmering, glittering remnants of his deconstructed body trailed away over the heads of the awestruck crowd.

There was a moment's pause as people looked at each other and at the strange couple who had turned and were walking through the sliding doors of Party Costume. Some were already uploading their cell videos to social media platforms, thinking of the instant fame and clicks the spectacle would bring them. Someone began clapping, and others followed hesitantly, followed by a cheer that grew and expanded like the supposed special effect they thought they'd just witnessed. Magus sneered with pleasure at the cheering as he entered the store. As the doors slid behind him, he stopped, looking up aghast at the rows of piñatas.

"This is a travesty."

FIFTEEN

"People do terrible things to each other."

DETECTIVE KATHY SHIMOOKA'S HANDS were trembling. That didn't happen very often, but this was the worst human-engineered carnage she'd had the miserable misfortune to see in almost twenty-five years of chasing bad guys. Yes, bad guys, primarily men behaving badly.

It was Sunday morning, her second day on the scene, and even though the bodies had been removed, the area still reeked of death and the horror that had led to their deaths. She stuffed her hands into the pockets of her dark slacks. It didn't pay to show weakness in a vocation dominated by men. She'd worked her ass off to get to where she was, and there was no way in hell she would allow anyone to think she was a gender equality promotion or, god forbid, a race promotion. She was damn proud to be a fourth-generation Japanese Canadian. Although her grandparents, along with two uncles, had been sent from Alberta to a BC internment camp during World War II, her family had a long and proud history as Canadians. However, that had nothing to do with how good she was at her job. She had a nose for sniffing out the truth from the tangle of lies and subterfuge spun by those looking to twist the law to their ends or by those who just simply ignored it.

She heard the huffing, gasping breath and shuffling steps of her partner behind her. She thought he must have climbed the stairs, another attempt, no doubt, to stay within Ontario Provincial Police health guidelines. Detective Martin Friedman, Marty to his friends, coworkers, and enemies for that matter, offered Shimooka a paper cup filled with what she assumed was coffee. He was sweating, and his breathing was raspy as he tucked a loose end of his shirt into the expanse of the waist of his pants with one hand while balancing the two coffees in the large palm of his other hand.

"Thanks," Shimooka said, extracting the hand she felt was quivering the least to grasp the cup.

She passed a cursory glance over Marty. His jacket was wrinkled, probably slept in, and he reeked of stale cigarette smoke and old cologne. Nothing new, Shimooka grunted quietly. Marty was a good cop, a bit unkempt but oddly quick on his feet despite the girth around his waist. He also was pretty good at thinking outside the box of normal or what was considered normal, and this situation wasn't looking normal.

"Had to wade through the damn media out there. You ever see anything like this, Shim?" Friedman asked.

"No," she said flatly in response.

Shimooka took a tentative sip of coffee and immediately regretted letting Friedman bring the java. It was almost unpalatable and might require three or four antacids later on if she drank the whole cup. Too strong, plus he'd probably picked it up from one of those food trucks over on Elgin, where some vendors, she'd heard, never washed their cauldrons and reused the grinds. Rumours, of course, but still, the worst and the best coffee in Ottawa came from the streets. This cup was close to being the worst.

She placed the undrinkable cup of sludge on a window sill that overlooked a small strip of grass nestled peacefully between buildings. A group of teens were kicking a soccer ball around in a small wedge of grass tucked between copses of trees, unaware of the aura of death above their carefree heads.

"You don't like it?" Friedman grunted with a smirk, lifting his cup.

"It's crap, Marty, like your fashion sense."

He laughed, took a gulp and grimaced, making a half-hearted attempt to look like he was enjoying the dark sludge.

The CSIs had cordoned off the fourth and fifth floors where the murders had been committed. She and Friedman were standing alone in a small meeting room populated with plastic chairs, a whiteboard, and a large flat screen television perched on one of three long tables. She was waiting for eyewitnesses to be brought in by uniforms to give statements. It was going to be a very long day.

Friedman grunted and continued to sip his coffee.

"Worst shit I saw. Worse than the Horkowski murder a couple of years back. R'member that?"

"God," Shimooka groaned.

She recalled the Horkowski woman's face, her eyes wide-open but lifeless. She hadn't been able to look in the mirror for days, well, maybe it was for weeks, without seeing those eyes masked over her own. She pushed both hands deep into her pockets.

"That was bad. This is a thousand times worse."

"Hmmm," Friedman grunted. "Damn, what a way to start the summer, eh?"

Shimooka's cellphone chimed. She pulled it from her back pocket and swiped it on. It was her mother. She turned to Friedman.

"Sorry, I should take this. She's probably seen the news coverage and has tips on how to solve the case."

Friedman chuckled and walked over to the large windows lining the wall, lifting his coffee to his lips while laughing.

"Make sure you tell Okaa-san I'm still single."

"As if, Friedman," Shimooka said as she tapped the screen and placed the phone to her ear. "Okaa-san, I'm very busy."

Her mother's commanding voice was diminished now with age, she was eighty-nine, after all, but she was still able to make Shimooka feel like a little girl.

"Have you seen the news, Kat?"

Shimooka knew that her mother would call as soon as a serious crime made it to local news channels. It was inevitable, like the sunrise after the night. When she'd been promoted to a detective with the OPP more than fifteen years earlier, Okaa-san had called several times a day, almost earning her a verbal reprimand from her CO. Luckily, her commander was of South Asian heritage, so he fully understood the culture of strong mothers and had asked her to keep the calls to one or two a day, if possible. She managed to convince her mother that once a day would keep her in good standing with her CO, and so, every day, especially if the crime were serious and on multiple television channels, her mother would call with an interrogator's list of questions. Had she solved the crime yet? Had she shot anyone? Had she found a suitable man to marry? Shimooka couldn't fault her mother. She was traditional in many ways, and having an unmarried daughter, the eldest child no less, who'd wanted to be a police officer since she was a teenager, was definitely untraditional. When her father had died several years earlier and her mother had moved into a senior condo facility several kilometres from her apartment, the worrying only increased. Of course, being unmarried didn't help, Shimooka grumbled. If she had a husband, her mother would call him to see how her daughter was faring. She smiled at that thought.

"Yes, Mom, I've been assigned to the case."

"Terrible, such terrible things," said her mother. "Why do people do these things?

It was a rhetorical question, one her mother would ask depending on the severity of the crime, especially if it was exceptionally gruesome. Thankfully, it wasn't that often in the Ottawa area, just lots of shootings and domestic violence crime.

"I can't say, Mom. People do terrible things to each other."

She heard her mother sniff with derision.

"Very bad, karuma. Very bad."

"I'm sorry, Mom, but we're interviewing suspects. I need to go."

"Yes, yes, make sure you make them understand you are in charge."

"Yes, Mom. I really need to go."

"Promise you'll be safe," said her mother.

Friedman turned to look at something behind Shimooka. She glanced over her shoulder and saw a uniformed officer standing in the doorway with an apprehensive-looking young man.

"I promise, Mom."

"Daisuki desu."

"I love you, too, Okaa-san," Shimooka said as she ended the call.

A uniformed officer nodded at her and led a young, blond-haired male wearing rumpled slacks and a shirt nearly as out of sorts as Friedman's. Shimooka nodded to the officer as he left, then gestured to the nervous witness. She smiled at him, trying to appear reassuring. Cops made people nervous.

"How's Okaa-san?" Friedman asked, a knowing smile sliding across his face.

Shimooka shrugged.

"You know my mother. I think she'd be here helping us if she could, making sure we're catching the warumono."

Friedman chuckled as he pulled out a small coil notebook with a chewed-up pen stuffed into the coil.

"Yeah, if your mom caught all the warumono, I could retire then."

"Have a chair," Shimooka said to the young man.

She indicated the three chairs they'd set up facing the two that she and Friedman planned on using. The man, nervously wiping his brow with the back of a hand, sank into one of the chairs as Friedman flipped his around and straddled it. Shimooka slowly slid into hers while pulling her tablet out of her shoulder bag. She swiped it on and searched for the case file folder. She also drew a small digital recorder from her bag, tapped it on then placed it in the middle of the table near the young man.

"We're recording this. You okay with that?"

"Uh, sure," he stammered, looking down at the device like it might jump up and attack him.

Shimooka smiled warmly.

"It's okay, this is what we do," she said as she gestured to the recorder. "It helps us old people remember everything that gets said here."

She found the case file on her tablet.

"You have the right to have a lawyer present," she offered as she looked up at the kid.

He shrugged and shook his head.

"Okay, witness declines a lawyer."

"What's yer name?" Friedman asked while slipping a cellphone from his shirt pocket. "Mind if I take a picture? For our records?"

The young man shrugged again, looking back and forth between the detectives.

"Sure. I guess."

Friedman took a couple of shots as the young man smiled uncomfortably. He blinked every time the phone's fake shutter sound pierced the awkwardness of the moment.

"What's your name?" Shimooka repeated.

"Ryan. Are you going to catch them? I, I think I'm out of a job."

"We're trying. Last name?" Shimooka answered as she pecked out the kid's first name on her tablet with a finger and then waited for him to reply.

He looked at her, then Friedman, then back at Shimooka.

"Oh, sorry, Ryan Philips," he replied, then spelled it out. "Philips, like the appliances."

He snorted. It was meant to be a laugh, but his lips were trembling.

"Thanks," Shimooka said as she typed his last name. "The officer outside explained why you're here?"

Philips nodded vigorously.

"You work here?" she asked.

He nodded again. The nods were short, little pumps of his head. He's terrified, Shimooka thought.

"I understand that you saw something that might be helpful to this investigation?"

"Sure did."

Philips breathed the words out heavily, glancing down at the recorder. Then he stared at the detectives, his mouth agape.

Shimooka waited.

Friedman waited.

"Well?" Friedman finally said, tapping the chewed end of his pen in his notebook. "What the hell did you see?"

The young man grimaced. He was more than frightened, he was terrified, Shimooka surmised. It was reasonable, given what had happened.

"It's okay, Ryan," she said. "Just tell us what you saw. It'll help us catch whoever did this."

Philips blinked several times, then drew in a long, shuddering breath.

"It was Thomas. Thomas Stewart. I saw him, saw them. He's my boss, one of the owners. I saw them go into the ancillary meeting room. I was in the hall, I was going to go in there, but, but, I have this information course I've been streaming, you know, workplace self-improvement. Normally I'd have been in the, in the room with them, but, you know, the course. I was waiting for the umbrella, er, I mean the elevator. Well, I mean, that's when it started, the screaming. I heard the screaming. I thought it was like, you know, one of those office massacre things you see in the States, but, like, there weren't any gunshots. There was just screaming."

He lifted his hands to his head and pressed his palms hard into his eyes. Shimooka reached across the space between them and touched his elbow. He flinched.

"It's okay, Ryan. Deep breaths. You're doing great."

He trembled and brushed tears from his face with the backs of his hands. Shimooka sat back and tapped a few lines into her tablet.

"How do you know it was Thomas Stewart?"

"I hid," he stammered. "I'm alive because I hid."

"Yeah, yeah, great you're alive," Friedman interrupted.

Shimooka glared reproof at him, but the detective leaned toward the shaken man.

"How do you know it was Stewart?" said Friedman.

"I, I, like I said, I hid. I didn't get on the elevator, I, I didn't want to get trapped, you know, like in the movies, so I hid in this room."

He nervously flicked a hand to indicate the room they were presently in.

"When the screaming stopped, I looked out, out of this room, I was in this room, and saw Thomas and his girlfriend in the hall. He was, he had blood all over his clothes—like he'd painted himself with it. Oh, god."

"His girlfriend, his business partner, was with him? That's the 'they' you mentioned?" Shimooka asked.

"Yeah," the kid nodded. "Gloria. Uh, Gloria, something…"

"Gloria Musa," Shimooka interjected.

"Yeah, Gloria Musa. She has amazing eyes, uh, she's also one of the owners of, of MajiGrafx. She's the one who interviewed me back in, back before—she was terrified. She was terrified and crying, and he was pulling her by her arm, and she was crying—"

"So," Shimooka said, nodding at Friedman, "He's added kidnapping to the count."

She turned to her partner.

"We need to contact her family again. If this is also a kidnap situation, Stewart may call with demands once he's cooled off from yesterday's rampage."

Friedman's phone began to klaxon loudly, followed almost immediately by Shimooka's device, with the same alarming klaxon sound. Ryan's phone began sounding off with the same intensity in his shirt pocket.

"What the hell?" Friedman muttered as he looked at his screen. "It's the public alert system."

A uniformed officer suddenly pushed his way into the room. Shimooka looked up, annoyed, but held her tongue as she caught the anxious look on the man's face.

"Uh, sir, ma'am. I'm sorry for the interruption, but, um, Channel Five news, you gotta see this."

Something was playing on the cellphone in his hand, but he looked down at it and then at a large flatscreen television perched on a table in the corner of the room. He strode over to it, hunted for it and eventually stabbed the power button, then stepped back, grabbing a remote sitting next to it on the table.

"Does this have cable? Can I stream to it?" he asked, turning to the wide-eyed Philips.

"I, I, uh, yes, there's cable. Go to the TV icon," he replied as the flatscreen flared to life and the sound of a car chase slammed the tension in the room.

The officer swore, keying down the volume as Shimooka and Friedman both stood and approached the screen. Philips leaned over in his chair to see around them. Shimooka read the alert on her cellphone as the officer fumbled with the TV controller.

"Friedman, you see this?" she asked, tilting her phone toward him.

He nodded and shrugged, turning his attention to the flatscreen.

The officer used the remote to flip through channels. He stopped at a local news station. The screen framed a long camera shot of a white male floating in the air. One of his arms was wrapped around the waist of a black woman. Both were floating, hovering, suspended maybe by some wires or something they couldn't yet see, Shimooka thought. The two were several metres above the large grassy field, the quadrangle, in front of the Centre Block on Parliament Hill. Something off-camera erupted, showering debris across the camera's field of view. The camera shuddered, tilting, so images were blurred, and then panned back as a blueish flame, or maybe it was electricity, Shimooka couldn't quite tell which, seemed to be arching from the capped individual's free hand. It danced and expanded through the air toward the iconic East Block, striking it near the south end with such force that about ten metres of the end of the building appeared to shimmer, or tremble, and then immediately erupted outward into a massive ball of flame and flying chunks and pieces of the building. If it hadn't obviously been a news channel, Shimooka could easily have assumed the officer had turned to a strange Canadian movie.

The camera suddenly zoomed in on the flying couple as a steady stream of gunfire off-camera was aimed at them. The bullets and what looked like artillery shells hurtling at them appeared to stop dead, hitting some invisible bubble-shaped field. The shape was only detectable by the impact debris of the armament hitting against whatever the forcefield was made of. Then the armament seemed to disappear or be absorbed by the invisible bubble. The effect looked fake, Shimooka thought. Then, as the camera pulled back, she could see that the costumed male was using the blue energy he shot from his hand to vaporize the squad directing the fire at him. Several soldiers and a handful of OPP officers simply disappeared, dissolving into nothing. That also appeared fake.

A woman reporter, off-camera but clearly near the scene, was excitedly detailing the event.

"Yes, Rob, roughly thirty minutes ago, Parliament Hill was attacked by these unknown assailants. This remarkable, no, this, uh, unbelievable spectacle happening on Parliament Hill, which was first believed to be a publicity stunt, has since been confirmed to be some sort of terrorist attack from these unidentified flying individuals, one dressed in a mishmash of superhero costumes and the other, a woman, with, uh, no apparent costume, uh, just regular clothing."

The camera panned across the settling cloud of dust and debris that had been a good portion of the East Block. Off to one side, Shimooka could see running military personnel. The camera then zoomed in again on the instigators of the destruction, the flying, caped man and the woman. Another stream of bluish flame leapt from the man's hand. This time, several military assault vehicles, which had been angling along Wellington toward the flying man, blossomed into balls of orange flame and flying shards of metal. One of these crashed through the Queen's Gate, flipping over and landing upside down against the Centennial Flame, causing a sudden geyser of fire to erupt upward, stabbing the sky like a yellowish finger.

"This can't be real," Shimooka muttered.

Friedman grunted in agreement.

"Say, doesn't that blue stuff look like the electricity coming out of, you know, the hands of that emperor guy on Star Wars?"

The disembodied voice of the reporter interrupted him.

"Oh my god, Rob. He just, he just took out that entire armoured group. Oh, my god. How is this possible and why is it always men who do these things?"

The television picture suddenly separated into a split screen. One side was a tight shot of the man and the woman, while the other half showed a young, well-dressed and intense-looking male news anchor.

"This a Channel Five exclusive. If you're just joining us, minutes ago, two flying individuals, one male, the other a woman, used some sort of energy beams, yes, that's right, energy beams coming from the male's hands to level the south end of the East Block on the Hill. Our reporter, Carol Black, is live on Parliament Hill, where this man, dressed in a green costume, who is apparently flying without any apparent visible means of propulsion, and this woman, whom the man seems to be holding onto, attacked the Hill, yes, attacked the Hill, just a few minutes ago. They've done significant damage to the East Block and some damage to the Peace Tower, and while still unconfirmed, they're alleged to have also killed and or wounded several military personnel who arrived on the scene from Canadian Forces Station Leitrim. We haven't received a comment as yet from the Prime Minister or the Minister of Defence."

The news anchor looked into the camera.

"Carol?"

The right side of the screen continued to show the images from a camera panning across the carnage.

"Carol? Have these individuals made any demands?"

Carol, the voice, cleared her throat.

"These terrorists, Rob," she said, "these flying terrorists came from out of this, uh, beautiful early morning sky approximately thirty minutes ago and demanded the surrender of the Canadian government and its armed forces."

The caped individual engulfed another armoured vehicle with the same blue flames, followed by percussive explosions that caused feedback in the camera's microphones.

"Other than these demands, Carol, has either of these individuals given a reason for this unprecedented and shocking attack? Do either have a name?"

"No, Rob," the woman responded, her voice shaky as if she'd just run up a set of stairs. "No other demands other than the initial call for surrender. The male perpetrator did give a name."

There was a pause before she continued.

"Um, uh, the Magnificent Margaret? Or maggots? We're not sure at this point."

"Excuse me, Carol, did you say—"

The news anchor touched his earpiece.

"What? I've just been told our Ottawa affiliate has a live feed from one of the terrorists being fed to us from a drone. Uh, the military on scene seems to be halting their assault on the perpetrators. Uh, the caped man's hand is up, he's waving. He appears to be signalling he wants to surrender, or, or perhaps to communicate."

The news anchor was replaced with a scene that a banner scrolling across the bottom of the screen indicated was breaking news and exclusive drone coverage for Channel Five. The drone's camera focused on a young man. He was in his early twenties, Shimooka guessed, Caucasian, full head of black hair, deep eyes, and clothed in a rather snug fitting Green Lantern costume, with a large blocky M emblazoned in red across the chest where the familiar comic book hero's iconic lantern symbol should have been. Shimooka regretted that she knew this about the fictional hero. She'd dated a guy long ago who'd been into cosplay and Manga. They had fun together, a nice break from her early days of routine police work on the beat. The sex had been great, but the relationship got a little weird when he began insisting on dressing up as a fictional character called Berserk, especially in the bedroom. The drone's camera focused on the M. The letter appeared to be strips of red masking tape stuck to the thin material of the costume. The drone pulled back, revealing a Batman cape of flimsy black material hanging from the man's shoulders, its serrated bottom fluttering soundlessly in the wind. He was also wearing a pair of plastic Iron Man boot fronts, the kind that straps around a cosplayer's calves, leaving their shoes exposed. And, Shimooka noticed, whoever this was, they were wearing a very nice pair of Oxfords.

The woman was black, wearing a loose-fitting pair of dark slacks and a blouse that shimmered in hues of deep purple. Her hair was arranged in a large number of dreads, pulled back and tied up in a massive knot on the top of her head that bounced with each blast of energy from the male's hand. Her eyes were an unusual blue, and they were unblinking, swollen from crying, and filled with terror.

"She's a hostage," Shimooka said quietly.

Friedman grunted in agreement.

"She has blue eyes. I didn't know, uh, you know, I didn't know—"

"Know what?" Shimooka interrupted, lowering her eyes at her partner. "That black people can have blue eyes?"

Friedman shrugged.

"Uh, yeah."

"It's rare. I had a partner back when I worked for the city police in Edmonton. He was of Nigerian heritage. He had pale blue eyes. It's some sort of pigment disorder."

"Oh."

Of course, unusual eye colouring aside, what made any of this anything more mundane than a video clip of an insane cosplayer and his hostage, was the fact they appeared to be floating, or hovering, apparently unaided, several metres above the scorched grass and the debris from the damaged East Block. Shimooka peered closer at the TV, looking for wires. The man suddenly extended an arm and finger and pointed at the drone. Obviously fearing its destruction, the operator pulled rapidly back and down, keeping the vehicle and the lens pointed at the two. The costumed man let his gaze and pointed finger follow the movement, a somewhat maniacal grin distorting his handsome face. His expression seemed a trifle overacted, Shimooka thought.

"Hear me! I am the mighty Mag—" he began as a blast of wind muffled the drone's microphone. "The destroyer of the Mighty Titan, eternal enemy of the League. I am the mighty Magu—"

Another puff of wind briefly obscured the word again.

"Did he just say maggots?" said Friedman, turning to Shimooka.

She shrugged and glanced at her cellphone and the emergency alert that had appeared only a moment earlier. The message was for the Ottawa Gatineau region and was telling people to stay indoors until further notice because of a serious police incident.

"Is this alert for that?" she asked the officer, pointing to the flat screen.

"Ma'am," the officer replied shakily, quickly raising both hands. "Yes. The call came in from OPP minutes after the, uh, attack. Thirty-seven dead thus far, various military and police vehicles burned to the ground, and as you just saw, the West Block, I mean, the East Block! Half the friggin, pardon me, ma'am, the military's heading out there. The country's on orange alert are the air force, army, the whole friggin, pardon me, ma'am."

"Why attack Parliament Hill?" Shimooka mused.

It wasn't a significant military target nor a logical place to make a statement from if you had whatever kind of crazy military hardware this person appeared to have. The perpetrator obviously possessed the power to reduce half the East Block to rubble with a wave of his hand, so why not go after the White House? That would get the world's attention, she thought.

"That's Thomas!" a voice exploded from behind her.

Philips pushed between them and stabbed a frantic finger at the screen.

"That's Thomas Stewart, and that's Gloria!"

"What the hell?" Shimooka muttered. "These two incidents are connected?"

SIXTEEN

"Why can I breathe? I'm in space."

"I GUESS I STILL DON'T QUITE UNDERSTAND," Mia said. "He's inside you right now, inside your head?"

Hunter shrugged.

"He says our molecular identities are fused, uh, right, he says like atom to atom, down to a quantum level. I guess that means he's inside my entire body."

Mia smiled.

"Ah," she said. "I get it, the two of you exist simultaneously in the same space? The older Hunter MacKenzie from another universe has joined to his younger version, meaning you, in this universe. I wonder if it's a quantum entanglement where the two of you share a common, unified quantum state?"

She is very astute.

Hunter laughed.

"He knows what I know."

"What's that?" Mia asked.

"That you're the most intelligent person I know."

They'd left through the front door, evading Mia's mother's enquiries from somewhere in the house over the sudden and deafening explosion in the backyard. Sirens could be heard approaching from somewhere not far away, and neighbourhood dogs were barking their disapproval. Hunter felt it best to get as far away as possible.

"Sorry about the fence," he gasped as they cut through a connecting alley and made a quick pace for McKinley Park.

The park was an older playground installation that needed upgraded materials that would be less bone-crushing than the solid steel from which they'd originally been made. Hunter had snapped a collarbone in fifth grade after bouncing like a tossed rag doll through a lattice of metal pipes disguised as a child-friendly climbing dome.

"You spat and blew up my fence," Mia said, bemused, as she slid her hand into his.

He squeezed her hand, and she his. It was their thing, their silent sign of affection, something they'd been doing for almost a year after her halmi had told them that she and her late husband had done the same. It was a way to stay connected without using words.

Titan then spoke, although without much conviction.

You should not have told her.

"I had to."

"You had to blow up my fence?" Mia choked.

Hunter laughed.

"No," he said. "His Mightiness is telling me I shouldn't have told you about him."

"Ah," Mia said, nodding as they quickly ran together to cross a street and enter the park through an open gate. "He's talking to you? Right now?"

"Yeah," Hunter replied as he pulled Mia along, heading for the climbing dome.

We do not have time for this. We must fly to Nepean. We must intercept Magus.

"Now he's telling me we need to fly away," Hunter added as he pulled himself up onto one of the climbing dome's cross pieces.

It and the rest of the playground seemed far worse for wear than he remembered. The metal slide he'd attacked not that many years ago, pretending to be an alien with suction cup feet and hands, was wrapped in yellow tape with an official-looking sign that warned of potentially serious injury if used.

Mia followed, sliding in beside him on the metal dome.

"So, like up, up, and away, fly?"

"That's what he says. I tried doing it earlier, but it didn't work."

"You tried flying?" she asked. "To where?"

"Nepean, Ontario. That's where this super villain is or was yesterday."

Mia frowned.

"Ontario? That's about a six-hour flight from here," she said. "And then Nepean? We'd have to change flights since neither of us is old enough to rent a car."

Hah! Mere seconds for us!

Hunter chuckled.

"What? He's talking again?" Mia asked, leaning back to look Hunter in the face.

She wondered if she'd see a tiny superhero face somewhere in his eyes.

"Yeah, he says," Hunter replied, as he made air quotes, "it's mere seconds away for us."

Mia nodded, then dropped to the packed sand outside the dome.

"So, fly then."

"What?"

"If the Mighty Titan says you can fly, then you can fly."

Hunter laughed.

"And then what? So, I fly to Nepean and, what, super spit the Marvellous Maggot to death?"

Mia laughed.

"You blew up my fence, and you can see through things!"

You are far more powerful than your ability to destroy fences with your spittle.

"Like what?" Hunter demanded, then pointed to his head and addressed Mia. "He's telling me I'm powerful."

You may not be as fully powerful as I was before I was transported to your universe, but I can feel the pure cosmic energy flowing through your body. My powerful energy is within you, it flows through your entire being, down to the smallest particle you are made of.

"You'll have to prove that," Hunter answered.

"Prove what?" Mia asked, leaning closer.

"Prove that I'm as powerful as the Maggot."

Even in this state, you are more powerful than my enemy.

"I highly doubt that."

Lift your right hand toward that cordoned-off child's play apparatus.

Hunter smirked.

"He wants me to do something to the old slide," he said to Mia.

Mia twisted around to see the slide thousands of children had played on over the years and laughed with glee.

"Do it."

Hunter grimaced.

"Blow up the slide?"

Not blow up. Disassemble it. Imagine removing the powerful electrical bonds between molecules, between quarks, matter and anti-matter. Take it apart in your mind and make it happen through your hand.

"How?"

Think it so.

"Think it so? Just imagine it being pulled apart, uh, molecule by molecule?"

Yes.

"He wants you to pull the slide's molecules apart?" Mia asked, her mouth agape with wonder. "That'd be cool to see."

Hunter nodded.

"Yeah, like take it apart with my mind."

"Cool," she exclaimed as she pulled her cellphone from a back pocket. "Don't do it yet. I want to record this."

Hunter lifted his hand and spoke to Titan.

"If I just have to think it so, why do I have to lift my hand?"

Your hand is a point of exit for your power. You could as easily use your nose, but your hand will suffice. Now, quickly, disassemble that apparatus.

"Fine. Fine," Hunter said, lifting his hand and directing it toward the slide. "Okay, imagining, tearing it apart bit by bit."

"Wait," Mia said, stepping back so she could get both Hunter and the old slide on her cellphone screen. "Okay. Do it!"

Hunter groaned.

"I'm trying, I'm thinking, I'm gonna blow up the slide."

Be quiet. Focus. Take it apart in your mind.

"Fine," Hunter hissed.

He narrowed his eyes, wishing the damn thing would fall apart or disintegrate into nothing and disappear. Suddenly, a blast of blueish energy surged from his outstretched fingers. The bolt, about the diameter of his arm, arced through the air and enveloped the slide, which immediately and soundlessly exploded into nothingness. Its age-weary structure vanished in a cloud of sparkling dust particles that settled on the trampled sand, where it had stood unmoving for decades. It happened so fast that it looked like the slide was there one second and then not there the next.

Hunter yelped, and Mia smacked her knee as she stared at the playback on her phone.

"Wow, Hunter, that's way more awesome than super panty X-ray vision. Here, take a look."

She held the phone up so Hunter could see the playback.

"Oh my, god," Hunter exclaimed as he looked at the screen.

The blast of energy from his hand looked like spider webs shooting from his fingers. The strands of energy wrapped themselves around the old slide, almost like they were squeezing it until it suddenly disappeared in a cloud of particles. He stared at his hands. He'd felt very little sensation when the energy erupted from his fingers, maybe a tingling sensation, like a feather had briefly touched his skin, but that was it. At his command, the energy had simply shot from his hand. He quickly looked around to ensure no one had noticed the strange sight.

"I can't believe that worked."

Obviously, you did, or it wouldn't have happened. Now fly.

"He wants me to fly now."

"Yeah," Mia declared as she pointed to the ground. "Get down from there and get up there."

She then pointed to the sky.

"This is amazing, Hunter. You're doing things that no one has ever done before, not in this universe anyway."

Hunter groaned.

"I hadn't asked to be the first."

Your girlfriend is more of a believer than you are.

"I can't fly."

Yes, you can.

"Hunter, if he says you can, then you can," said Mia, laughing as she pointed to the large sandy area where the slide had stood since before either of them had taken their first breaths. "There's science behind what you just did, just not science this universe has known before. He's not asking you to believe in magical thinking. He's asking you to believe in the abilities he brought with him from the other universe."

She pointed to where the slide had been.

"He said you could make the slide disappear, and, well, look!"

Oh, I like her.

"Shut up."

"What?"

"No, not you, the Mighty Titan."

Mia reached up and grabbed Hunter's pant leg.

"He agrees with me, doesn't he? C'mon."

Hunter sighed and slipped through the worn bars, landing easily on the sand.

"I can't fly. That's ridiculous."

It is not ridiculous. As Mia said, what we do is within the laws of science within the universe we exist in. We exist outside the science that defines this universe's theory of gravity! I have flown through the rings of Saturn, though the Chrimeria Cloud of the Greater Antiqu—

"Oh, please, stop talking," Hunter moaned, placing a hand on the side of his head. "I can't fly."

Mia reached out and took Hunter's hands into her own.

"Look, I thought you were crazy when you first told me about this Mighty Titan, but you made that old slide disappear just by thinking it. At the very least, you're less crazy than I imagined, and there might be some weird being living in your head."

"Oh, great, thanks."

I am not weird. I am the Mighty Titan.

"I think you've offended him," Hunter whispered.

She laughed and squeezed his hands in hers before squinting and looking closely into Hunter's eyes.

"I'm sorry, Mr. Titan, I meant no offence."

She drew her head back and smiled intently at Hunter.

"I don't know what's going on. What you just did was impossible from everything I know and understand about physics, but I saw that news piece on the Nepean massacre yesterday. If this super being inside you thinks you two can stop whomever it is that did those horrible things to those people, you have to try at least. Right?"

Hunter sighed, looking around. The playground was empty.

"Right here? Right now?"

Yes.

"Yes," Mia echoed Titan, without knowing she had.

"It didn't work in the alley," Hunter reminded her. "Why would it work here?"

Because you are me, and I am you. I am a hero, and it is within you to be one.

"He's giving me another hero speech," Hunter said as Mia let go of his hands and stepped back, pointing her cellphone at him.

"You can do this, Hunter," she said, smiling brightly.

She laughed and took another step back, adjusting her phone, so Hunter filled the screen.

"What? You don't want to fly with me?" he chided.

"Seriously? You'd have me fly with you on your maiden voyage?"

"Well, I—" said Hunter, as he grimaced and shrugged.

Mia laughed.

"You go first. If you die, I can tell your dad about it when they find your frozen body in orbit."

"Gee, thanks."

She is not helping.

"He says you're not helping."

Mia laughed again.

Close your eyes. Focus.

"He wants me to close my eyes and focus. I can't do this," Hunter pleaded. "People don't fly."

We are not normal people.

"Trust him, Hunter," Mia said. "You blew up my fence with your spit, and you disappeared that old slide, just by thinking it. That was impossible. Why shouldn't you be able to fly?"

Hunter smirked.

"That's a bit of false equivalency, isn't it? My spit flew, not me."

Mia chuckled.

"C'mon, Hunter. Something amazing is happening to you. If the voice says you can fly, then you can fly."

She is a sweet child.

Hunter groaned and looked around. A small boy had just walked onto the park grounds and headed for the low swings.

"There's a kid over there," he said, pointing.

Never mind that. Close your eyes. Focus. We just need to levitate a few feet off the ground. You need to practice to prepare before we take the next step.

"The next step?"

Mia looked over at the kid, who was maybe eight or nine years old. She stepped over to Hunter and squeezed his hand before letting go to focus her phone's camera on him again.

"Hunter, concentrate," she said. "Just do what he's telling you to do."

Hunter could feel his heart beating in his chest as he closed his eyes.

We fly, Hunter, we defy gravity. We are untouched by the laws of this universe. We exist in and outside of all that you know and see. Fly.

"Fly?" Hunter whispered, his eyes jammed shut so tight he was beginning to see stars behind his lids.

Yes, just rise slowly from the Earth, just a short distance. The gravitational fields of Earth have no control over you. Rise up!

"Fly, Hunter," he could hear Mia say softly.

Her voice calmed his beating heart. If she believed, maybe—

He heard a squeal, like air escaping from a pinched balloon. Hunter opened his eyes. He was staring into a black void. No, wait, his eye quickly adjusted. There were stars, millions of stars. He looked down. The Earth was a shiny, cloud-painted, giant blue, green and brown ball beneath his feet.

"Oh, god!"

Excellent. A little further than I believe we intended, however, my power has grown mightily within you.

"Oh, god!"

He was an unknown number of kilometres above the Earth, on the outer edge of the planet's stratosphere, and he was breathing. He was alive and in space, and he was breathing, and he was flying, and he was breathing, in and out, and he wasn't cold, he wasn't dead, he wasn't frozen. He was breathing in space, in and out, breathing—

Hunter threw up.

Bits of chewed toast, peanut butter, jam, and curdled milk spewed out into space, immediately freezing into a long, oblong blob as it entered the frigid temperatures of space a hand's breadth from his face. Driven by momentum, it slowly twisted and spun away into the starry void.

That was unfortunate.

"How did I get way up here?" Hunter gasped as he wiped stomach acid and spittle from his mouth.

Yes, well, you were not thinking very clearly. It is most fortunate that we did not end up many light years away. You must think clearly and exactly where you wish to travel to.

"Why can I breathe? I'm in space."

His voice sounded hollow and muffled in the space around his body.

You are in space, but you are also not physically within the space you see.

"What? What the hell does that mean?"

Your visual acuity acknowledges that you are indeed in space, as you call it, but you are, in fact outside of space. You may or may not choose to interact with it. In either case, your body remains contained with its universe while the immense power fused to our very being manipulates the energies of the universe you see. Thus, you breathe, as you say, in space.

"That makes absolutely no sense. Where's the air I'm breathing coming from?"

I apologize. Perhaps if I may, I can explain it in another way. We are like an orange—

"I'm really flying!"

Of course. You are the most powerful being in the universe. You are the galaxy's greatest hero.

"What else can we do?"

What else can we do?

"Yes, I mean, could we go to the moon or Mars?"

Anywhere you wish. You just have to think about it. Turn slowly and take note of your orientation to astrological bodies, as viewed from your position in this solar system.

"How is this even possible?" Hunter said.

He imagined turning slowly, and suddenly he was facing the curvature of the Earth as it disappeared into the darkness of the planet's far side. He could see a sliver of the moon poking over the edge of the planet. I should be afraid, he thought. I could fall at any moment and burn up in the atmosphere. They'd never find anything, nothing at all, not one little charred piece of his body. That would be horrible.

"Where's Mia?"

Beneath us, of course.

"I want to go back. How do I go back?"

We must pursue Magus.

"No, not yet. I want to see Mia."

And suddenly, the Earth rushed up to swallow Hunter. He screamed, throwing his arms over his head, anticipating the bone-crushing pain of his body slamming into the ground at a frightening speed.

"Oh, my god! You're back," he suddenly heard Mia say.

Hunter opened his eyes. He was in the park, in the same spot he'd left moments earlier. He crouched before Mia, his two feet solidly planted in the sand next to the climbing dome. His heart was pounding in protest beneath his heaving ribs, and he was having difficulty catching his breath.

Mia stepped up to him, helping him stand upright.

"I'm so glad you're not dead."

"Uh, thanks, me too."

She grabbed his arm.

"Just after you disappeared, my phone started chiming like crazy. Something's happening, you have to see this."

She was holding her cellphone in one hand, tapping the volume up.

"It's all over social media."

Hunter, his head swimming, his eyes blinking rapidly of their own volition, looked down at the phone. He saw Green Lantern, wearing a Batman cape, apparently floating several metres off the grassy field where he'd seen Canada Day celebrations on TV in front of the Parliament Buildings in Ottawa. The comic book character had an arm around a woman's waist. She had a lot of hair. Green Lantern was pointing directly at whoever had been videoing.

"Hear me! I am the Mighty Mag —" he said but then windswept Green Lantern's words away.

He has revealed himself! This is far worse than I imagined.

"—the destroyer of the Mighty Titan, eternal enemy of the League. I am the mighty Mag...."

Another blast of wind briefly obscured the remaining words.

He believes I am dead, and thus he has begun his quest to dominate this universe.

"Already? From Ottawa?" Hunter muttered in disbelief.

Magus must be stopped!

"Green Lantern?" Hunter mumbled, his vision slipping in and out of focus. "Why is he dressed like Green Lantern?"

"Is that the bad guy?" Mia asked, pausing the video and expanding the image with her fingers to focus on the man and woman.

Yes.

"Yes," Hunter echoed, as dark spots began to do battle before his eyes, like tiny little super-powered heroes and villains duking it out.

"Who's the girl?" Mia asked.

I am unsure. Magus does not take hostages.

"He doesn't know who the girl is."

"That Magus guy is attacking Ottawa?" Mia said.

Yes.

"Yes."

The spots were exploding into bursts of light and flashes of vibrant colours as Hunter continued to wonder why Green Lantern was the bad guy.

"Why Ottawa?" Mia said, shaking her head.

This is the seat of your government.

"This is really happening, isn't it?" Mia said quietly.

Yes.

"Yes."

"Should we be afraid?" Mia asked, slowly lowering the phone.

Yes!

"Uh, why is Green Lantern—" Hunter began to say, but then he felt as if his mind was leaving his body.

"Hunter," he vaguely heard Mia exclaim.

She sounded alarmed. Why would she be alarmed? Is Green Lantern real, too? He felt his head hit the packed turf of the playground, and the world exploded in a kaleidoscope of spinning fractal colours. This is the second time in two days that I'm passing out, Hunter thought. That can't be a good sign for a hero.

Then the darkness mercifully enveloped him.

SEVENTEEN

"That's not the look of someone
who's pulling the trigger."

"WHY WOULD ANYONE WANT TO ATTACK OTTAWA?" Shimooka asked out loud.

The question was taking on the form of a mantra as they drove toward Parliament Hill.

"Why attack Ottawa?" the detective mused again. "What's the significance of Ottawa?"

Detective Friedman glanced over at his partner as she piloted her unmarked squad car through noon-hour traffic along Elgin Street, lights flashing, yelp siren blasting at uncooperative vehicles and pedestrians. The streets were vicious at this time of day. He shrugged.

"Hell if I know, Shim," he said.

"I mean," Shimooka continued, "this is Canada, right? Why would anyone with that kind of ability or whatever it is, want to attack us, right? Why not the bloody Americans?"

Friedman shrugged again. This day was quickly becoming one of the most bizarre of his life.

"How is any of this possible?" Shimooka said. "How could any human do what he's doing? And, what about the girl? She doesn't seem to be an active participant."

Friedman grimaced and shook his head.

"Can't say. Helluva thing, though. I mean, when have you ever seen something like that? Fire coming out of his—"

"Electricity," Shimooka interrupted. "Military liaison says it's a type of electrical plasma. Like the sun."

"Yeah, electricity, and flying, what the hell?" Friedman said as he shrugged again.

Shimooka suddenly stepped heavily on the vehicle's brakes, throwing both of them forward so violently that their seatbelts locked. Military, Ottawa Police Services, OPP, and RCMP vehicles were parked haphazardly in the block approaching Confederation Square like a kid had spilled a bucket of Matchbox cars. Just beyond the National War Memorial, the monumental seven-storey arch epitaph marking Canada's involvement in various military conflicts, they could see the damaged East Block, large sections of its masonry walls and twisted sections of its copper roof laying in a jumble. Plumes of black smoke spiralled upward from the mess, like the fingers of a dying man reaching for the sky. Several helicopters, some from Canadian Forces and some from news media, faced some unseen objective. Thomas Stewart, Shimooka surmised. A flying human being with lightning erupting from his hands, like Hachiman, an ancient Shinto god of war deity, for god's sake.

One of the CF helicopters, its tail rotor almost up against the Wellington Building opposite the Parliament buildings, its nose angled down, was directing a steady stream of heavy gunfire at something Shimooka couldn't yet see. She gasped when the chopper was suddenly enveloped by tendrils of vibrant blue lightening that twirled and skittered across its rotors and down the sleek line of its tail boom. The craft appeared to shimmer, tip alarmingly up, and then explode, becoming a bright fiery ball of orange flame and black smoke as it spiralled out of sight. She saw a soldier jump from the tumbling aircraft.

Shortly after the morning's dramatic televised event, Shimooka had called into her chief and asked to be allowed to transit to Parliament Hill. He agreed and forwarded the proper digital credentials to join the local

OPS on the scene, along with RCMP and Canadian Forces personnel. This was her case, as grim as it was. It was hers, and Thomas Stewart was her prime suspect, as weird as that was becoming. That Green Lantern/Batman/Iron Man cosplay mashup? What the hell?

As they took the 417 Queensway from Nepean moments earlier, another video was posted by Channel 5. People were lapping this up, Shimooka thought, as Friedman watched on his cell. They probably thought it was a highly organized stunt for an upcoming superhero flick. But no, people were dying, shit was blowing up, and the prime suspect, Thomas Stewart, was the one making it happen.

The video was shaky, handheld, taken by someone lurching and dodging for cover as ribbons of electrical plasma, audibly crackling and popping like a downed power line, tore through buildings and vehicles and bodies, as if cutting through a brick of butter that had been sitting on a sunny window ledge. Heavily armed military vehicles melted where they stood, and OPP SWAT members exploded like balloons filled with confetti, their screams cut off like a cancelled soundbite. It was horrific, and Shimooka asked Friedman to turn the volume down on his phone. It was too disturbing because it was all too impossibly real.

All the while, as these destructive bolts of energy poured from Stewart's hand, he held onto Gloria Musa. Something wasn't right about her, Shimooka thought. She was his business partner and life partner. Had she known about his impossible superhuman abilities? What was her role in all of this?

"You ready?" Shimooka asked as she glanced at her partner, who she thought appeared apprehensive.

"Nope," Friedman mumbled as they opened their doors.

Both detectives were blasted by the chaotic sounds of rapid gunfire and the whoosh of RPGs somewhere close by as they exited the cruiser. With weapons drawn, dozens of military personnel and SWAT teams ran past the massive war memorial, angling up Wellington Street towards The Hill. Shimooka and Friedman passed through a barricade armed by anxious-looking OPP officers before pushing their way past Queens Street and onto the Square, where dozens of soldiers were positioned parallel to Sparks Street. None of them saw the detectives coming toward them, their attention on the staccato commands coming from their radios, along with the riotous explosions from the area up the street.

"Hey!" Shimooka bellowed.

One of the soldiers snapped his head in their direction, his weapon rising as he scanned the credentials both detectives held up. His face was haunted like he'd seen things he couldn't quite understand.

"You can't be here, ma'am, sir," he stammered, looking back and forth at both of them.

Shimooka quickly explained the connection to the murders in Nepean.

"I'm the lead OPP detective on the crime scene, Detective Friedman here is my second," she said. "Is what we've heard really happening here? Thomas Stewart is perpetrating this—"

"Whatever the hell that is," Friedman interrupted, a hand gesturing in the direction of the battle.

The soldier glanced over his shoulder as another explosion shook the ground and a flash of flame and debris rose into the sky. They all ducked as the soldier lifted his weapon to his chest, a finger playing nervously with the safety. He turned his ashen face back to them.

"Sorry, what, ma'am?"

"Listen," Shimooka began as she leaned in to read the soldier's name tag stitched to his chest, which read Chief Warrant Officer Tyler Gunther. "Gunther, is there a man and a woman over there, both floating in the air, with the man shooting electricity out of one of his hands?"

The young man stared at her and nodded.

"Yes, ma'am. Crazy shit, Sorry, ma'am. I was called up this morning when it, uh, he began to, uh—"

Shimooka held up her cellphone, turning it horizontal, open to the document that gave her and Friedman the authority to join the engagement. The soldier squinted at it, nodding as he anxiously read the order.

"Right, right, yes ma'am, I see," he said, nodding.

Suddenly his radio, hanging from a strap on his shoulder, screeched. Gunther reached up and toggled the volume down.

Friedman turned to Shimooka.

"Look, Shim, I'm as up for a fight as the next cop, but if the whole damn military isn't taking this guy down, this isn't just a simple cuff and stuff anymore. What the hell do you think we can do?"

"Excuse me, ma'am," the soldier interrupted. "I don't know any Thomas Stewart, ma'am, but they've thrown all sorts of shit, pardon my language, at those two, and it isn't doing a thing. I've never seen anything like it."

"We know," Shimooka barked. "They're our suspects. The male and female are suspects in killing five people at the Albright Business Building on Friday afternoon in Nepean."

The soldier's eyes widened.

"Shit, pardon my language, ma'am, I heard about that, but that," he said, as he jerked a thumb over a shoulder, "that, they're your suspects?"

Shimooka nodded vigorously.

"Yes, and we need to apprehend them before they kill more people."

"Damn it, Shimooka," Friedman growled, turning slightly toward the mess of vehicles. "We're outta our league here. I'm not into getting killed today."

Shimooka grabbed his arm.

"Look, I think that woman, Gloria, is a hostage. There's something wrong with how she fits in all of this."

Friedman shook his head.

"She's there with him. That makes her an accomplice or an accessory at the least."

"I don't think so," Shimooka said. "You saw her face on that newscast. That's not the look of someone who's pulling the trigger. We can at least physically see if she's a hostage or an active participant."

Suddenly the chatter from the soldier's radio dramatically increased. He reached for it and toggled the volume wheel, and they all listened as a man's voice shouted.

"We're pulling back. Repeat. We're pulling back to the Wellington line. A civilian female is in the line of fire. Civilian is in the line of fire. Pull back."

The soldier turned his attention back to Shimooka.

"Something's happening. They're pulling back to Wellington Street. I hear a pair of CAF F-18 Hornets or CAF F-22 Raptors from Joint Base Langley-Eustis are in flight, ma'am, sir."

"Jeez!" Shimooka rumbled. "C'mon, detective."

She turned to the soldier.

"We're going in before they get here."

The soldier laughed weakly, then waved to his fellow soldiers to let them pass.

"Good luck, ma'am, sir. They sent my squad back behind the line to guard the Square because, like, you know, we've never been in combat before, and he's killing us, ma'am. Nothing's stopping him. Shit, sorry ma'am, is just bouncing off'a him. I mean, how is that possible? He's laughing at us."

Shimooka patted the man on his arm and stepped around him.

"It's okay, soldier, nobody expects the Spanish Inquisition."

"What? Ma'am?"

But Shimooka and Friedman were already running toward the melee.

EIGHTEEN

"I just threw up in space!"

HUNTER, YOU MUST AWAKEN.

Hunter lay unconscious on his side on the hot sand of the playground. Mia was kneeling beside him, holding one of his hands while gently rocking his shoulder.

"Hunter. Hunter."

When he'd begun to collapse backward, Mia had leapt forward to try and catch him, but he was too heavy, and his head had hit the sand with a dull thud.

"If you can hear me, Titan, I think he's uninjured," she said, hoping the person inside her boyfriend wasn't also unconscious.

She'd rolled Hunter onto his side because that's what you do if someone faints, she remembered from her St. John's Early Childcare first aid course. Otherwise, they could choke on their tongue.

You must awaken.

Hunter moaned.

You are Earth's only hope.

Hunter groaned.

For the sake of all humanity and every living creature, wake up!

Hunter's eye fluttered, and somewhere deep within his brain, a giddy voice pushed through his consciousness. He'd gone to space. He, Hunter Mackenzie, had been in outer space. He'd defied gravity, blasted through the atmosphere, and stood, with the Earth beneath his feet, looking down at the planet he'd called home for nineteen years. That was insane. Oh, he'd also thrown up. That was gross but so cool. The puke had exploded out into—

"You threw up?" he heard Mia laughing through the fog that shrouded his brain.

Hunter opened his eyes and flopped over onto his back. Mia was looking down at him.

"Was I using my outside voice?"

Mia smiled.

"Yes, spaceman, you were babbling like a madman."

Hunter rolled over onto his hands and knees, then slowly stood up with Mia's help. His legs were shaking, his heart was pounding, and his mouth tasted bitter from vomit, but he, Hunter Mackenzie, had been to the edge of space.

Yes, yes, yes. You've been to space. Now we must defeat Magus before more people die!

"Are you all right?" Mia asked, not letting go of Hunter's arm.

He blinked rapidly and patted his chest and arms.

"I think so. You'd think I'd be cold or something."

We must leave here at once!

Mia stepped back, letting Hunter stand on his own.

"That was insane, you know. You shot up so fast I barely saw it happen. It was completely silent. You just took off!"

She slapped her hands together.

"That was nuts!"

Hunter, we must go!

"How long was I gone?" Hunter asked, reaching out to touch her arm.

Hunter—

Mia shrugged.

"Two minutes maybe, and then, snap, you were right back."

Hunter, there is no time for this conversation.

"He says I have to go," Hunter said.

Mia frowned.

"Go where?"

She held up her cellphone, the image of Magus on pause as he was electrocuting or blasting or whatever it was he was doing to the people on Parliament Hill on the screen.

"To Ottawa?"

Yes!

"Yes," Hunter sighed, peering closer at Mia's phone. "He thinks I can stop this Maggot guy."

Mia slowly lowered her phone.

"Then, you have to go. We have to go."

"What?" Hunter stammered. "Shouldn't I go to superhero school or something? I don't know what I'm doing."

Mia slipped her cell into a back pocket and grabbed Hunter by both hands.

"This is really happening, people are really dying, and that guy, the Mighty Titan in your head, thinks you can stop whatever's happening in Ottawa!"

Hunter cringed.

"But I can't do this. I just threw up in space!"

I am you, you are me. My formidable power is emerging within you. You will not be harmed. We will do this together. Magus must be stopped.

Hunter pulled away from Mia and began walking toward where the boy was swinging back and forth, pumping his way toward outer space, each arc of his transit causing the old swing to squeal in protest.

"I can't do this."

Mia quickly matched his step.

"Yes, you can."

She pointed to the space where the slide had been.

"You made that old thing disappear, and I just saw you fly up into space. You have whatever abilities this guy inside you has, and," she said, as she grabbed his arm and pulled him to a stop, "you won't be alone. I'm coming with you."

She must not. It is too dangerous.

"What?" Hunter choked. "Didn't you hear me? I just threw up in space, I just passed out, I'm nineteen. I sell gas at Earl's to make money so I can go to university."

You are the Mighty Titan!

"Oh, shut up, will you?" Hunter moaned, then addressed Mia. "Not you, him. In my head."

Mia reached a hand up to touch the side of her boyfriend's face.

"Look, I can't explain any of this, but you've been doing the impossible all morning, and I just saw you fly, Hunter. Maybe this Titan can help you do whatever is needed to stop—"

She reached back and grabbed her phone, flipping it around so Hunter could see the paused image of Magus and the girl.

"—whomever the hell this guy is."

Hunter stared at the impossible but real image of a man dressed as Green Lantern, sporting a Batman cape. Blue spidery arcs of electricity, frozen on the video like a still from a sci-fi movie, were reaching out from his free hand to choke the life of a group of green-clad and armed to the teeth Canadian soldiers, on the ground several metres below Magus. Their bodies were twisted, and distorted, some rising in the air, others collapsing like unstrung marionettes. Their contorted faces were almost comical, their mouths trapped in silent, gaping screams. Their bodies seemed to be out of focus, pixelated like photo editing software was pulling the image apart. It was horrifying and all too real. Mia restarted the video and the audio exploded, with the last terrifying cries these people had made, along with the rising shrill laughter coming from Magus, so maniacal and so unnerving that Hunter realized every horror movie he'd ever seen would no longer frighten him.

His shoulders slumped, as he looked away to see the boy letting go and launching from the cradle of the swing he'd commandeered as it reached the apex of its arc. His tiny body soared through the air, a gyrating tangle of arms and legs, the joy of imagination escaping his lips in a squeal of glee. The sound was cut off, as he tumbled onto the grass just beyond the border of the swing set's sandy oasis. The kid rolled over onto his back, arms splayed out, as he laughed the laugh of innocence.

"I—I chased a shoplifter this week," Hunter said, quietly. "A kid, really, but he was fast."

Mia smiled softly and squeezed his arm.

"Did you catch him?"

Hunter slowly shook his head.

"No."

NINETEEN

"No one laughs at us."

THE SUIT WAS TIGHT IN PLACES that pinched and hurt, and loose in others that made it awkward to bend over, but at least it was something. Party Costume had been an unimaginable disappointment to Magus. Not one villain costume was—wait—more accurately, not one fictional villain costume was magnificent enough or splendid enough for a truly superior being such as himself. They were all fashioned from hard-edged shapes of coloured plastic and thin pathetic pieces of cloth that had little form or function, other than to satisfy the empty-headed adoration of non-existent beings from these stupid humans. They barely fit, these wretched imitations of what should have been true, authentic greatness. Who were these faux heroes? Green Lantern? Batman? How horrid their names, how despicable these meaningless costumes. He even had to tape an M to the chest of this costume, covering over that pathetic and decidedly non-frightening lantern symbol. How could he possibly present himself to the people of Earth as a saviour dressed in such poorly fashioned attire? Magus was this close to simply incinerating the entire horrible excuse of a planet.

No, you can't do that!

"Ah, shut up," Magus growled. "There are many more planets out there waiting for us to rule over."

He and the almost totally useless Gloria of this universe were heading for Canada's Parliament Hill where the leader of this country was supposedly ensconced. They were flying low, tracking a few hundred metres above treetops, following the general direction of the twists and turns of what Thomas called the Ottawa River, and the endless clutter of cottages and houses that clambered for space along its banks. Thomas had assured him that the seat of this country's government was in a place called Parliament Hill and that the elected officials within its walls would heed his calls for the surrender of Earth. Magus was sure he'd never spent much time in this sparsely populated country called Canada. The United States had been his birthplace. He'd lived there until The Event had opened up the universe to him, but visit the huge landmass above his home country? He didn't think he had. As it existed in his own universe, it was a place of little consequence, certainly with no heroes or villains.

Heroes?

Magus cringed at the word. He was the only hero in the known universe, or for that matter, in any universe. The Mighty Titan and his ilk were the self-appointed defenders of the weak-minded rabble, the useless, and the powerless. Here, Magus vowed, he'd decree that he'd be called a hero, the only hero. He'd rule this Earth, this solar system, this galaxy, and every creature would bow before his glorious, magnificent hero-ness.

That's it. That's Parliament Hill.

Gloria mumbled something. Magus didn't catch it, but she was pointing to a jumble of beige-coloured stone buildings on the edge of a hill that overlooked the river, their copper roofs discoloured with the effects of oxidation.

"Finally," Magus shouted, as they swooped down and over the central building, the one with a single tower pointing like a finger to the heavens.

Magus came to a stop high over a large field that was flanked by the East and West Block buildings of The Hill. The droning voice in his head was explaining the layout. This was the quadrangle, that was the Peace Tower, blah, blah, blah. Magus didn't really care. He'd destroy all of this in due time. Below, several dozen people were wandering across the grass, while others seemed to be lining up to one side of the central building, as Thomas spoke to him.

There, over there to our right. That's a group of people waiting for a tour of the Parliament buildings. Those people in dark uniforms are security personnel. They'll know who we should speak to.

Magus zoomed in with his vision, scanning the people and area for any who might oppose him. He still wasn't totally convinced that there were no super-powered beings in this universe. The idea was unthinkable to him, although, he reflected, there had been a time in his universe when such greatness as his hadn't existed. Still, it didn't pay to let down one's guard.

My parents brought me here once.

"That's of little consequence," Magus responded. "This will soon be my throne and all the peoples of the Earth will make pilgrimages to see the splendour I shall create, once I remove these dull, sad monuments to an insignificant country."

"Uh, Thomas, honey? Would it be okay if I ask a question?" Gloria asked, her voice low and wavering.

He was surprised to hear her speak. She'd said so little in the previous two days, other than to whimper and occasionally ask him, the Thomas she physically saw, if he was feeling well.

Magus smiled as he surveyed what was soon to become his fortress, where all would come bow and offer him homage, as the heroic ruler of all the universe. He turned his gaze to her.

"Magus. I am Magus. Of course, my queen, ask me anything."

Gloria's face was only a few inches from her boyfriend's, so she tilted her head slightly back to see his eyes.

"I'm sorry, Thomas, uh, I mean, Magus, but you keep talking to somebody. Who are you talking to?"

She won't believe you.

"Oh, but she will. She must if she is to live."

I wouldn't be very happy if you killed her.

"Oh," Magus said, feigning surprise. "Would the all-powerful Thomas truly miss his weak, powerless Gloria?"

"Thomas?" Gloria pleaded, quietly.

I love her.

Magus groaned.

"Love, such a useless emotion. You don't love her, not in this universe or in any other. She's merely a small piece in the machine of your greatness. She can easily be replaced by a thousand others just like her."

I, I guess.

"Of course, my young fool. Do you think for one second that you've ever needed this pathetic woman to get you where you are today? Will she take you where you need to go tomorrow? Will you carry her powerless body everywhere you go, like a trophy you're holding onto, from some forgettable episode in your life before I arrived and revealed your true greatness, all because you feel what you consider to be love?"

"Thomas?"

Magus sighed, and pushed Gloria away slightly, in order to see her beautiful face. He paused, again amazed by her beauty.

"You're as beautiful as my Gloria was."

He could feel her grip on his hand tighten, as that single connection became the only point of contact keeping her from falling to her death.

"Do you not yet understand who I am, my queen?"

Gloria frowned and looked down at the odd shapes of the people walking beneath them before replying.

"I don't understand, Thomas. Who are you?"

"Magus, my name is Magus."

He smiled softly and gently moved a strand of Gloria's unruly hair that had worked itself loose from one of her dreads and had curled down over one eye. His Gloria's hair had done the same.

"I was Thomas Stewart, well, in another universe, but I'm not your Thomas Stewart. Oh, he's here inside my head, we share this magnificent young body. However, he's annoying, babbling on about this stupid Parliament Hill of yours and how much he thinks he loves you, although I suspect he's beginning to understand that you may no longer be all he needs or wants."

He leaned in slightly.

"He has potential, your Thomas, but his imagination is, um, shall we say, immature and limited in scope, a result, I should guess, of living a rather pathetic life."

That's unfair, I'm almost twenty-seven and I've accomplished many great things. I've imagined the most horrific things, too. You said so yourself.

Magus pulled Gloria back to him, her arm circling around his back underneath the Batman cape.

"Yes, I know you have, Thomas," he said.

Shouts below drew Magus's attention. Visitors to The Hill, their cellphones and cameras raised, had noticed the two hovering individuals. Magus smiled gleefully as he slowly, and with magnificent flair, stiffened his back and neck then descended to the foot of a broad concrete staircase that ascended a slight rise to the building with the tower. He felt the awe emanating from the gathering crowd. These people, with their recording devices, were following them up the stairs, asking questions.

"Who are you?"

"Is there a movie being filmed here?"

"Why are you dressed as Green Lantern?"

He could feel the excitement and the worship coming from these fools, and for the first time since his arrival in this pathetic universe, Magus knew he was destined to rule with utter impunity. This universe had no Mighty Titan, no League of extraordinarily useless and irritating heroes, just Magus, Magus the Magnificent, Magus the Conqueror. The adoration would be almost overwhelming, he thought, smiling.

"You feel it, Thomas? Do you feel the adoration?"

They don't understand. People don't fly like you do on this Earth. They think this is a movie stunt.

"Pathetic fools," Magus muttered, as he and Gloria took the last step. "They'll see soon enough."

Holding onto Gloria's arm, he guided them toward the line of people Thomas had pointed out earlier, and where several uniformed personnel were checking the contents of visitors' bags. Magus approached the one uniformed person who appeared to be in charge. He was a tall man, strong, his chin firm, his eyes bright with the power he was exercising over those wishing to enter the halls of the Government of Canada.

"You," Magus ordered.

The man turned his alert eyes to the commanding voice. They immediately narrowed, as he focused on the costumed man before him, the apparently frightened woman he was holding onto, and the crowd of people whom all seemed to be recording whatever was happening here.

You realize you're dressed as Green Lantern, right? No one will take you seriously. I told you, Darth Vader is much scarier.

"Shut up," Magus hissed quietly then pointed to the security officer. "You, take me to your leaders."

The man frowned and tilted his head slightly to one side.

"I'm sorry. What was that?"

Magus smiled thinly. He knew his magnificence spawned awe in lesser beings, one that often left them speechless. He took a deep breath.

"I wish to speak with the leaders of this country, to arrange the surrender of your government. Bring me to them."

We should just walk in. That will draw their attention.

Magus sniffed with annoyance.

"Thomas said you'd take me to the leaders of this country."

"What?" the uniformed officer said, slowly.

He's just a security officer. He won't understand who you are, how powerful we are. Just go into the building.

The security officer's frown was slowly replaced by a thin smile of his own.

"I'm sorry sir, are you part of this tour? What's your name?"

He lifted a clipboard and a pen from a table next to him, and, smiling at Magus, waited for an answer. Magus allowed a wispy stream of plasma to tickle the fingers of his free hand. It would be so easy to reduce this one to ash, he thought.

"My name is Magus the Magnificent, and I am part of no tour, cretin. I wish to speak with your leaders. Go and fetch them before I become angry."

The man's smile grew slightly.

"You're not the Green Lantern, then?"

See?

Someone in the crowd laughed. The officer frowned again, curiosity spreading across his face, as he looked at the group behind Magus.

"Um, I'm sorry, Mr. Lantern, if you want a tour, you'll have to cross over to the Wellington Building and reserve a spot at the ticket booth. I believe all the tours are full for today, but Mondays are usually slower, and there should be slots available for the morning or afternoon."

Magus reached out and pulled the clipboard from the man's hand. He flipped it over his shoulder with disdain.

"I'm not here for a tour, you foul, mindless toad. I'm here to demand the surrender of your government to the mighty Magus."

The security officer seemed shocked at first by this sudden action, but then a smile slowly spread across his face.

You should have gone with Vader or Freddy Kruger. Yeah, Kruger would've been awesome.

"This is a gag, right?" the man asked, looking around. "Am I on that show, *Just for Laughs?* Where's the camera?"

I told you.

"Shut up," Magus said, as he reached out and grabbed the man by his shirt. "I'm Magus the Magnificent. I am the conqueror of countless worlds across the known galaxy, well, the known galaxy in my universe."

The officer pulled back against Magus's unexpected move, but then a nervous laugh escaped his lips, followed by another less nervous one, and then he smiled, as he laughed even more. Some of the people standing to the side of Magus laughed as well, hesitantly at first, but then full-hearted. Others behind them began to chuckle and laugh, their cellphones and cameras trained unwaveringly on the strange spectacle. Then people in the security lineup, who'd gradually been drawn to the odd exchange, began to laugh, and Magus's eyes narrowed and filled with seething hatred, the hatred that had been his lifelong friend and had spawned decades of unimaginable carnage.

They're laughing at you.

"They're laughing—at—us," Magus whispered, harshly.

Yes, they are. I don't like it when people laugh at me.

"What then, Thomas? What shall we do about this situation?" Magus hissed, between clenched teeth.

"Tommy?" Gloria said as Magus felt her hand caressing his chest, her fingers pressing against the large M. "Let's just go. Please?"

Magus looked down at her pleading eyes, filled with such silly innocence, such foolish compassion for such insignificant beings.

"You are weak. We don't need you."

We don't need her, right? Right? I mean, she's always trying to get me to dial my ambition down.

"Come, come, Thomas. You've already cheated on her with that lovely young redhead we killed, twice in fact. You've already decided she's not going to go where you're going."

I—I guess. Yes, but, you shouldn't have killed Megan.

Magus laughed, "There's no debate here, worm, we have never needed anyone to prove our superiority. What's it to be? They're laughing at us, Thomas, what are we going to do about this intolerable situation?"

Use our power. Make them stop laughing. I don't like it.

A rush of excitement coursed through Magus, like a sensual fire, aching for release. Gloria's eyes were lined with the mascara of fear, brimmed with the tears of knowing, knowing full well what was about to come, for she'd seen it when he'd arrived on Friday when he'd first inhabited this body and slaughtered their friends and employees, and she'd seen it at the hotel, and at that infuriatingly useless costume store. His Gloria would have already torn this pathetic security officer molecule from molecule. Magus smiled and turned his head, letting his eyes drift down the length of his young, muscled arm to his strong, veined hand, the one gripping the officer's clenched neck muscles through his starch-stiff shirt. That hand began to bristle with energy, its blue tendrils snaking out like living things, hungry for flesh, encircling a spidery web of translucent energy around the man's chest, strands of it climbing up over his chin and into the gaping hole of his mouth, which had spread wide with the sudden horrifying realization that what was happening to him wasn't a gag.

"No one—"

Laughs—

"At us!"

No one!

TWENTY

"You've been alone a long time,

haven't you?"

MIA WAS SQUEALING LIKE SHE WAS on a speeding rollercoaster ride. She was holding onto Hunter's right arm with both her hands, as they rose up, standing in the air, with the grass of the park rapidly receding beneath their feet. Looking down at the shrinking park, Hunter could see the kid who had only moments earlier shot out of the swing, landing in a tangle of arms and legs and innocence on the grass. He'd seen them and had jumped to his feet, open-mouthed with amazement as he watched the two of them rise straight up into the sunny Alberta sky and then suddenly veer away, sailing over the houses that lined one side of the park. They were heading for Hunter's home, as the Mighty Titan spoke.

You must disguise yourself. You must always protect your hero identity or those you love will suffer.

There was a slight sadness in the way he said it, which caused Hunter to take him seriously.

"How?" Hunter had asked.

"How what?" Mia had asked, before realizing that Hunter was probably talking to the voice.

"He says I have to protect my identity. How do I do that?"

"Seriously?" Mia had said. "You're the comic book junkie. You need a mask or something, right?"

I am liking her more and more.

This time, Hunter didn't shoot off into outer space. This time he imagined moving from one point in the universe to another, imagined moving from the park to his house. Mia's grip relaxed a little, as she realized she wasn't going to plummet to her death. They arrived in seconds, dropping out of the sky into Hunter's backyard between the garden shed and the old cotton poplar tree that his father had been threatening to have cut down. It was ancient, in prairie terms, some branches not leafing out after a cold winter, but today, the tree Hunter had known all his life offered some cover for them.

"I only have a few old masks from my Halloween days," he said, as Mia let go of his hand, steadying herself after the short journey.

"That was so cool," she exclaimed. "I wonder how long it will take to fly to Ottawa?"

Seconds.

"He says seconds," Hunter offered.

"Unbelievable," Mia breathed as they entered the back entrance of the house. "Who knew I'd wake up today and you'd be infected with some other-universe superhero?"

"Infected?" Hunter's mother said, unexpectedly.

She was standing at the kitchen sink, a bag of potting soil and garden implements arranged around a sad-looking begonia plant that was sitting in a pot in the sink.

"Oh, hi, Mom," Hunter said, as he and Mia turned to go down the stairs that led to the basement. "We were just talking about Mia's brother. You know, Juwon. He's got an eye infection."

"Sorry to hear that. Hi, Mia," Hunter's mom said, as they disappeared through the basement door.

You lie with so little effort.

Hunter shrugged.

"I can't tell her what we're about to do," he whispered. "She'd freak."

You are most fortunate to have a mother.

"Hi, Mrs. MacKenzie. Bye, Mrs. MacKenzie," Mia called over her shoulder, as she followed Hunter down the stairs.

"Wow, you lie easy," Mia said, as they entered Hunter's bedroom.

"You, too?" Hunter choked. "His highness just accused me of the same thing."

Mia laughed.

"Well, this is a side of you I don't think I've really seen, yet."

"Oh, c'mon," he complained. "I couldn't tell her the truth."

Yes, that was very easy for you, but necessary to protect your identity.

"Titan thinks so, too," said Hunter, laughing. "He says I have to protect our identity."

Mia shrugged.

"You're right. In my family, we only lie to protect someone from hurt. When my mother had to have eye surgery last year, we told my halmi that she was visiting some friends that day, so she wouldn't worry."

Yes, this is what I mean. It is lying, but it is not meant for harm, but to protect.

"Titan agrees," Hunter said. "So, wearing a mask is for the same reason. You hide your face not because you have something to hide, but to protect those you love."

Exactly.

The Halloween masks were from Hunter's junior high school days and had been stashed in the back of his closet in an old school backpack. He quickly pulled four masks from the pack—Iron Man, the Wasp, the Ninja Turtles Michelangelo, and Ant-Man—laying them out in a row on his unmade bed.

"Will these do?" he asked his inner voice.

I do not know whom these represent. Are they villains or heroes?

"Does it matter?" Hunter asked.

"What's he asking?" Mia said.

"He wants to know if they're good guys or bad guys."

It matters because you are the good guy and if you disguise yourself with these plastic replicas of your fictional heroes, you will be associated with their deeds, whether they are imaginary deeds or not.

Hunter sighed.

"Wow. This is complicated."

He pointed to the Iron Man mask.

"Okay, he's a good guy, stops lots of crime and stuff. The Wasp is Ant-Man's partner and girlfriend. That one's a mutant human-sized turtle and also a ninja who fights bad guys, and this one is Ant-Man, my favourite, and he's definitely a good guy."

Mia laughed.

"Why do you have The Wasp?"

Hunter looked at her and grinned.

"I bought it for you, remember, two years ago for the school costume party, but you had a cold and couldn't come."

"Oh, right," she said, laughing again and smiling broadly at him.

"I know. I'm such a nerd."

Mia reached for his hand and squeezed it, before kissing him on the cheek.

"Yes, you are, and I like your nerdy self, but it's not only that. It's just that, well, you're having a conversation with someone I can't see or hear. It's strange."

Hunter nodded.

"Tell me about it."

Mia picked up the silver-coloured mask of the Wasp character, turning it over in her hands, feeling the elongated nose and large yellow eyes. It was designed to completely cover the head, with a broad dark mesh in the back to hold it in place.

"I want this one. I can tuck my hair up into it."

She twisted her hair up into a knot and slid the mask over her head. Hunter could just see her eyes through the mask's large, bulbous eyes.

She cannot come with us. You will be impervious to Magus's attack because we are one being, but she will not.

Hunter ignored the voice and grabbed the Ant-Man mask. It and the Wasp mask had cost him almost eighty dollars from the comic shop over on 16th Avenue. They were cosplay pieces and were designed to be used, so the plastic used for the eyes on both had good visibility, while carefully hidden slots in the earpieces on the sides allowed the wearer to hear well.

He turned it over, and slowly pushed it onto his face, closing the back of it so the front fit snugly against his cheeks and forehead.

Our mission is too dangerous.

He glanced around his bedroom. His field of vision was reasonable, and the plastic lenses, though adding a tinge of red to everything he looked at, were clear with only a slight distortion around the edges. He turned to look at Mia, who was looking back at him through the large eyes of her mask. They laughed.

Her death may be at hand if she comes.

"I need her," Hunter said, quietly. "There are soldiers and police there. We can leave Mia with them once we arrive, but I need her to be there."

Why? I see only a selfish reason to do so.

Hunter sighed, catching Mia watching him out of the corner of his eye.

"It may look selfish, but we're a couple. We're a team. I need that."

There is no need to endanger her life. You are invincible, she is not.

Hunter lifted the mask up over his head and turned his back to Mia.

"She believes in me. I can't do this without that belief."

That makes no sense. You are me, I am you. We do not need another person to help fulfill our mission, especially someone who isn't—

"Isn't what? Invincible like us?"

She could die. You would not like her blood on your hands. That is very difficult to live with, I know.

Hunter sniffed.

"You've been alone a long time, haven't you?"

It is necessary when you are who I am.

"What?" Mia asked, touching his shoulder. "Who's alone?"

Hunter turned around and sighed.

"He doesn't want you to come. He thinks you could get killed and that I wouldn't want your blood on my hands."

Mia pulled the mask from her face, dropped it on the bed, grabbed Hunter by his shoulders and looked him in the eyes.

"I agree."

"You do?"

She does?

"Yes, I know this isn't a game. I know this will be very dangerous, and yes, I could get hurt and maybe even die. But you won't let that happen to me, will you?"

"Uh, I—"

Mia's eyebrows lowered as she frowned, shaking her head slowly before tapping a finger to Hunter's forehead.

"No, not you Hunter, the other you inside you, the almighty, all-powerful being inside you. You won't let that happen, will you?"

I am beginning to understand why you have such affection for her. She is formidable.

Hunter chuckled.

"Uh-huh."

"I think I should go pee, first," Mia said, grabbing her mask as she headed out of the bedroom.

TWENTY-ONE

"Take me to your leader? Seriously?"

AS SHIMOOKA AND FRIEDMAN SIDESTEPPED slabs of limestone and twisted metal of what remained of the South end of the East Block that faced Wellington Street, they could see Stewart floating about twenty metres above the quadrangle and about half that distance out from the steps that led up to the Centre Block's arched entrance. Stewart was standing upright, his Batman cape flapping in the afternoon breeze, both his hands bristling with that strange blue energy. He seemed to be waiting, slowly turning his head back and forth, scanning the battlefield of his own making. He also appeared to be having a conversation with someone, his mouth occasionally moving, sneering, and laughing, but he was alone. Beneath him, the charred grass of the quadrangle was littered with burning military and police vehicles, the mangled fuselage of a wrecked helicopter, and the bodies of at least a dozen military and law enforcement personnel. Shimooka knew from reports there had been many more casualties, but their bodies wouldn't be found. They'd been vaporized. Vaporized? How was that possible?

"Damn," Friedman said as they snaked past the rubble and around a damaged statue of Nelly McClung, taking up a position behind what had once been a massive carved oak door. "I think that statue used to be way over on the North end of the East Block."

Someone sensible had ordered a retreat and a ceasefire, Shimooka thought, as all personnel had pulled back to the far side of Wellington Street, hiding in government buildings, behind wreckage, planters, or any available cover. Whatever Thomas Stewart was, he was far more powerful than anything that had been thrown at him thus far. Shimooka looked over the top of the damaged oak door. Much of the South end of the East Block had been smashed, windows blown in, and sections of rustic Nepean limestone wall slumping like an old man. To her left, the Confederation Building, the Justice Building, and the Wellington Building, and on the far side of the quadrangle, the West Block, all had signs of being struck either with the electrical plasma Stewart generated or, as in the case of the Wellington, pieces of an Air Force helicopter that had crashed into the office space at its base just as she and Friedman had arrived.

Friedman bumped her elbow.

"Why are we here again?"

"The girl," Shimooka hissed, turning her gaze back to Stewart.

He was simply floating there, looking like a man waiting for a bus, only floating in midair. What the hell was going on? She let her eyes scan the quadrangle, searching among the wreckage-strewn pathway that led to the broad steps that climbed up to the Centre Block, looking for Gloria Adaego Musa. She spotted her almost immediately and slapped Friedman's arm.

"There," she said, pointing, "the girl's right there."

Musa seemed very small, sitting on the top step to the entrance of the Centre Block, her arms cradling her legs to her chest. Her eyes appeared to be on Stewart, but Shimooka couldn't tell if she was a victim or an accomplice from her distance. One thing was clear, though, there was no indication that she had the unnatural abilities of her boyfriend. All the violence thus far had been perpetrated by Stewart.

"Hey!" a voice suddenly barked from behind them.

Shimooka turned and saw a soldier crouched low in a defensive posture. She was in full combat gear, wearing a helmet and flak jacket, and her hands gripped an automatic rifle, with a thumb lightly touching the safety. A C7A2 5.56-mm, Shimooka noted. If fired at this close range, they'd be cut in half.

"What the hell are you two doing here?" the soldier demanded.

Shimooka held up the OPP badge hanging around her neck and jabbed a thumb toward the carnage on the quadrangle.

"Stewart's the suspect in Friday's Nepean killings at the Albright Building. I'm the lead detective, this is my partner, Marty Friedman."

Friedman flashed his badge at the soldier without taking his eyes off the assault rifle in her hands.

"We shouldn't be here," he mumbled.

Dupuis lowered her weapon.

"Shimooka, Friedman, I'm Lieutenant-Colonel Rachel Dupuis. My commanding officer, Colonel Art Johansen, mentioned you two might be showing up."

She chuckled and gestured in Stewart's direction with the barrel of her weapon.

"Not exactly the reinforcements we need, are you?"

Shimooka smiled thinly, ignoring the jab.

"What's the status of your operation."

Dupuis shrugged.

"City police and Hill security cleared the buildings of personnel and visitors once it was determined Stewart was a threat. We arrived shortly after he took out," she said, waving a hand at the rubble they were standing in, "the damn end of the East Block. Thank god Parliament's on summer recess."

"What about Gloria Musa, the woman?"

Dupuis looked past Shimooka's shoulder and shook her head.

"When your suspect, Stewart, arrived at 0937 hours, the female was with him."

She glanced at the watch on her wrist.

"Shit, about two and a half hours ago. Eyewitnesses say they just dropped out of the sky, flying, like friggin' Superman. We have security footage to collaborate that claim. Dropped out of the sky—"

"Was Musa flying, too?" Shimooka pressed.

Dupuis shook her head and shrugged.

"Well, she arrived with him, which was by flying, however, the hell they're doing that. However, as far as we can tell, the male was holding onto her, possibly carrying her. She's made no effort to communicate, as he has, and though she was physically at the male's side during the attacks, he alone has fired those bolts of whatever from his hand. I suspect she's a hostage, although Stewart hasn't indicated as such."

"What happened when they arrived," Friedman asked. "You know, besides all the blowing up shit and stuff? What did Stewart want?"

Dupuis shifted the weight of her weapon.

"Near as we can tell from CTV footage and Hill security cameras, they landed on the quadrangle, just there by the main steps," she replied, pointing generally, "and walked up the steps. There was a tour lining up at the side security entrance, and there was Hill security present. Parliament's on summer break, eh, so security's not heavy. They then approached the security personnel and said something like take me to your leader."

She turned her eyes back to Shimooka.

"Yeah, Stewart said, take me to your leader."

"Take me to your leader?" Shimooka repeated. "Seriously?"

Dupuis nodded.

"Yeah, it's on CCTV. Take me to your leader."

"Then what?" Friedman asked, sweeping a hand toward the destruction. "How the hell did this happen?"

The soldier took a deep breath and blew the air out through her nose, her eyes widening.

"The Hill security laughed at him. They laughed. I saw it on CCTV. He did that thing with his hands, and they just disappeared."

"Disappeared?" Shimooka said.

"Yeah," Dupuis nodded slowly. "I saw the video. I thought it was a special effect, you know, like in a movie, but no, he made them disappear. Turned them into dust, some of the Hill visitors, too. He was mad as hell that they laughed at him. Turned them all to dust. Shit."

"Like the pile of ash in the bathroom back in Nepean," Friedman said slowly. "We shouldn't be here, Shim. We can't apprehend someone with this kind of weaponry."

Shimooka ignored her partner.

"What about Musa? You're convinced she's a hostage?"

Dupuis turned her eyes to the small figure crouching on the top of the steps of the Centre Block.

"Most likely. I viewed the CCTV footage of the first thirty-five minutes after they arrived. She's done nothing but appear fearful of Stewart. He seems to have some sort of fascination with her."

"They're lovers and business partners," Shimooka offered. "They've been living together in Nepean for about three years. Met at the U of T."

Dupuis nodded.

"Yeah, when we showed up, and the shit show really started, he held onto her and assumed a position over the North end of the quadrangle. During the fight, he was protecting her somehow, like a, you know, like a force field or something, like in a sci-fi movie. When we were throwing all sorts of shit at him, it was absorbed by whatever was protecting them. But he put her down on the steps just before you showed, and we called a ceasefire because the Colonel wasn't prepared to assume she wouldn't be a casualty if we kept up the attack."

"Any communication since that Channel 5 piece?" Friedman asked.

Dupuis shook her head and laughed.

"Yeah, they high-tailed it outta here when he took out one of their camera crews. But no, we sent a white flag out to establish a line of communication, but he bloody disappeared the entire unit. Then we sent out a robotics unit with a comm strapped to it. We got a sentence outta him before he disappeared that too."

"What's he want?"

Dupuis grunted.

"The surrender of the planet."

"Damn," Shimooka muttered. "And the woman, since he put her down?"

Dupuis shook her head, the straps of her helmet slapping the sides of her face.

"She's just been sitting over there, not moving. She doesn't appear to be injured, but we didn't want to endanger a civilian if that's what she is."

Shimooka's cellphone chimed. She slipped it from her back pocket. Her mother. Not now, she thought, as she declined the call.

"Sorry, it's my mother. She calls every day, sometimes two or three times a day."

Dupuis nodded and smirked.

"I have one of those."

"Uh—" Friedman began, but Dupuis didn't hear and cut him off.

"As I said, this situation is way outside of anything we're prepared to handle. It's bloody crazy."

Shimooka shook her head as she touched the soldier's arm.

"Yeah, it's like something out of a comic book."

Dupuis shook her head briefly like she was trying to rid her mind of the madness she'd witnessed for the past few hours.

"And how do you explain that?" she asked Shimooka, jerking her clutched weapon towards the floating Stewart, a tiny, almost insignificant figure hovering over the quadrangle.

The detective's cellphone chimed again. She looked down at it. Her mother. She sighed and swiped it open.

"One second," she said to Dupuis.

She placed the phone to her head, plugging her other ear with a finger.

"Okaa-san, I'm so sorry, but I can't talk. I'm—"

"You're there, aren't you, Kat? I saw you on TV with all those soldier men."

"What? Yes, I'm here, and I'm sorry, but I can't talk."

"Please, be very careful. This is very bad."

Shimooka sighed.

"Yes, Mom. I'm sorry, but I have to go."

"Al-suru."

"I love you, too, Mom."

"Um—" Friedman said.

Shimooka slipped her phone into her pocket and eyed Dupuis.

"Sorry about that. You should have seen what he did to those kids in Nepean. None of this has a simple explanation. Stewart was an average nobody a few days ago, and now," she said, as she turned her eyes to the distant Stewart, "now we have whatever that is."

Gunshots, and close by. Shimooka looked at Dupuis, who was peering in the direction of the War Memorial. Friedman suddenly stood up, an arm rising, a trembling finger pointing back the way they'd just come.

"What the hell is that?"

Shimooka turned and saw her partner standing up, his head and shoulders in the line of fire, should Stewart choose to vaporize him from this distance. She grabbed his belt to pull him down but caught a glimpse of his face. His mouth was agape like he'd lost the ability to close it. She followed his gaze and felt her mouth drop. Two people were floating, an impossibility until that morning, or flying, or standing up and doing both, hand in hand like they were on a date, gliding casually over the arch of the National War Memorial. As they drew closer, she saw that they were wearing colourful masks. The two suddenly veered and dropped down towards their position. Shimooka could hear the shouts of the soldiers they'd seen stationed around the memorial when they arrived and wondered if that's where the gunfire had come from. A second later, Dupuis's radio crackled.

"Uh, ma'am, bogeys heading your way. Uh, they look like civilians, teens maybe. We fired warning shots, but they had no effect. Uh, they're flying like that other guy—"

"Shit."

Dupuis had twisted on the ground, keeping low, to follow Shimooka and Friedman's gaze. She grabbed the two-way radio handheld strapped to her shoulder, jabbing the send button with her thumb several times before growling.

"Yes, Lieutenant, I see the subjects. Hold your position, and stop that damn shooting."

Shimooka's knees popped in protest as she stood up.

"What now?"

TWENTY-TWO

"Don't let go of my hand."

THE JOURNEY HAD TAKEN 'mere seconds' across the country to Ottawa.

Titan had said the rapid journey would be less disturbing if Hunter and Mia ascended a few kilometres before streaking across the sky towards Ontario. It was only slightly less disturbing. It felt to Hunter that the Earth had become a giant ball that was suddenly spun in one direction beneath their feet. No inertia, no wind-in-your-face, nothing in the way of resistance to physically mark their transit, other than the unnerving appearance of the movement of the 5.9 trillion-trillion kilograms of their home planet beneath their feet. Mia squealed in his ear as they sped high above the patchwork quilt of Saskatchewan farm fields, the grain fields and lakes of Manitoba, the glistening, vessel-dotted surface of Lake Superior off to the right, Thunder Bay, shrouded in cloud, hugging its western end. If it hadn't been for the massive Great Lakes, Hunter wouldn't have known where they were.

Okay, he thought, get over Superior and follow the shoreline of Lake Huron. They were a little unnoticeable dot skimming high above clouds, forests, rivers, towns, and cities. Over there, the polluted haze of Toronto is off to the right. Then, boom, dropping down through thin cloud cover to Ottawa. No, wait, that's not Ottawa. I believe that's Orillia, Mia says. Back up above the clouds, looking—looking—

You are overthinking this. My power is fully integrated into your cellular structure. Just imagine where you want to be, and it will take you there.

"You talk as if it's alive like it has a mind of its own," Hunter said.

Yes, you are beginning to understand. It is like a living thing, and we are in a symbiotic relationship with it.

"My phone doesn't work up here," Mia said while moving it around, holding it close to the bulbous eyes of her Wasp mask, looking to see if she was getting a signal. "I thought maybe I could do a search and get directions."

We are not within your universe. Her device will not function properly.

"Oh, he says it won't work when we're flying," Hunter responded.

"That's okay," Mia replied, pointing ahead and downwards. "I think it's over there. That's Lake Ontario so that Ottawa will be just north of that."

It was. Hunter took them down to just below the thin cloud cover. Off to their left was the Ottawa River, wriggling through the landscape. They followed it until they came to where it separated the city of Ottawa from the town of Gatineau, Quebec. Mere seconds, Titan had said. The journey had been a little more than a minute, but Hunter almost threw up again. Mia, on the other hand, laughed and laughed.

It took another few seconds to spot the seat of the Canadian government, keeping watch over a bend in the roiling waters of the Ottawa River. Multiple columns of dense black smoke rose above the sprawling government complex before being pulled eastward by an afternoon summer breeze. The view from above was stunning, a grid-work of streets, buildings and parks, almost peaceful if not for the pulsing lights from dozens of emergency vehicles and sirens rising to meet them as Hunter slowly approached from the West, keeping just above the office buildings and hotels that lined Sparks Street.

"Hey," Hunter said, "if we're flying in a separate universe, how come we can hear the sirens, but Mia's cell doesn't work, and we couldn't feel or hear the wind as we flew here?"

Ah, a brilliant question. Yes, our power exists in a small universe of its own, and when we move within our bubble universe, we can interact with the space we pass through. In this instance, your mind is focused on the activity below us, and our power knows this and allows for the sound from the activity to enter our universe, completing the image of what you see and logically should expect to hear. Thus, we hear or see, or if we wish, we may touch the universe outside of our own bubble. Devices, such as Mia's phone, cannot interact beyond our bubble.

"Ah, okay," said Hunter, nodding, although it still didn't make sense.

"What'd he say," Mia asked.

"Uh, he says we're in a bubble universe, but the bubble is, uh, in the larger universe too, and we can touch this universe and manipulate it using the, uh, powers that come from the bubble one. Our phones can't do that, though, I guess?"

Clearly, you do not fully understand.

"He doesn't think I get it."

Mia laughed and nodded.

"Yeah, the concept is complex. I think I get it, though. If, when we're flying, we're in a bubble inside our larger universe, then that means we look like we're defying the laws of our universe, but we're just traversing through it. You can observe and interact with this universe because the bubble Titan's power creates is hyper-local, existing within our massive universe."

She is grasping the basic concept.

"Am I right?" Mia queried.

We must focus on the specifics of our attack.

"He says you are," Hunter said, then turned his gaze toward the small dot floating above the quadrangle.

He zoomed in with his vision. It was Stewart. His arm was around his girlfriend like Hunter's was Mia.

"That Stewart guy and his girlfriend are just floating there," said Hunter.

Then suddenly, Stewart flickered over to the entrance of the Centre Block and placed the woman on the steps. Flickered was the best way to describe what Hunter saw. The movement was so fast that it appeared like a flicker or glitch in a streamed film. The woman stumbled backwards and slumped down to the steps.

"He just put his girlfriend down by the front of the Centre Block," said Hunter before Stewart was suddenly back over the quadrangle. "Oh, man, he's fast. He's already back over the field."

Mia pulled Hunter closer.

"Wow, I wish I could do what you do. He's just a speck from here."

"I think we should get out of the sky, he might see us," Hunter said.

He quickly dropped down, hoping Stewart hadn't already seen them. Staying about fifty metres above the ground, he swung south to Laurier Avenue and then north along Nicholas Street so they could approach the Hill from the East. Hunter became aware that their journey above the streets was attracting attention from people below. Ignoring the occasional shout and horn honk, he took them over the ByWard Market area, turning south, so they flew along the black and brutalist architecture of the American Embassy. He then went up behind the high peaked pinnacled roof of the picturesque Chateau Laurier Hotel, swooping down over the Rideau Canal before realizing the area below them was crawling with armed soldiers. Hunter quickly rose to hover as high above the arch of the War Memorial as he could without coming into Stewart's line of sight.

"We need to find somewhere else to hide, those soldiers are going to see us," Hunter said quietly.

He was too late. Shouts suddenly erupted beneath them, announcing that they'd drawn the attention of the multitude of soldiers around the memorial.

We must speak with this city's military forces, and assure them of their safety and our imminent victory over Magus.

Hunter looked down at the armed soldiers pointing not just fingers but some serious-looking weaponry at them.

"I don't think that's a good idea."

"He wants us to go down there?" Mia exclaimed. "They don't seem thrilled to see us."

"Yeah, that's all they need, another flying menace."

Nonsense, we are Earth's mightiest hero. No sane military force would see us as an enemy. We defend justice. We uphold the weak.

"Wow," Hunter gasped, "you really are from another universe."

Yes, I am, but that does not change the fact that it is to our advantage to assure the forces of this city that we are not the enemy.

Suddenly, a weapon beneath them fired, then another, then a series of sharp pops rose above the din of sirens.

Plunk. Plunk. Plunk. Plunk.

Bullets were smashing into some kind of invisible force about half a metre away from them. Hunter could see their crushed shapes collapsing like plastic water bottles crushed against a wall, then they simply disappeared, apparently absorbed into the field around them.

"Cool," Mia said as she peered at the disappearing bullets.

"They're shooting at us," Hunter yelled, wondering if maybe it had been a terrible mistake to come to the city. "We need to leave."

No! They cannot hurt us. Remember, you are not in their physical universe. Their weaponry will not harm us. We must talk to them to assure them of our benevolent intentions.

Mia gripped Hunter's hand harder and pulled herself closer to him.

"Oh my god, if this weren't so dangerous, it'd be cool."

Hunter, we must stop Magus, and we will do that by assuring this city's military that we are not a threat.

"What's Titan saying? What are we supposed to do now?" Mia said, pointing to the soldiers below as more bullets were stopped by whatever was protecting them.

"We shouldn't have come. This is stupid. I'm not a superhero," Hunter exclaimed.

"What's he saying to you, Hunter?"

Hunter groaned.

"He says we have to talk to them to let them know we're not the bad guys."

"Hey," Mia said, pointing to the jumbled mess of the East Block. "There are three people over there. I see only one gun. We could talk to them."

Hunter focused his attention on the three individuals and zoomed in. As they jumped into sudden clarity, he could see there was only one huge gun and two smaller ones. Although, Hunter mused, they couldn't hurt him or Mia as long as she held onto his hand. He squeezed her hand just for good luck.

Good thinking. Two of them look like law enforcement, and the other is most likely military. Proceed.

"Okay," Hunter agreed with both Mia and Titan.

He began to angle along Wellington Street, dropping down toward what was left of the southern end of the East Block. He could see the three people crouching behind a massive wooden door turned up on its side, held in place by rubble.

"Don't let go of my hand," he said to Mia, "not for a second."

TWENTY-THREE

"But that's an Ant-Man mask."

"UH, HI, WE COME IN PEACE."

The masked male spoke as he and the female, Shimooka was pretty sure it was a young Asian woman, landed a couple of metres away from their position, stepping down onto the rubble-littered ground as if they'd just hit the bottom landing of a staircase. Both were dressed in jeans, running shoes, and lightly coloured t-shirts, the female's tee had stylized, multi-coloured flower art that began at her waist and swirled up over a shoulder. The male's mask was definitely from the Ant-Man movie, Shimooka noted, and the females might be as well.

"Are you the people in charge?" the female asked, looking back and forth between Shimooka and Dupuis.

Shimooka opened her mouth to demand who they were, but Dupuis suddenly pushed her to the ground, forcing her words into a choked scream. Almost simultaneously, the soldier whirled around and kicked Friedman's legs out from under him, so he flopped down on his backside, his breath flapping out through his lips like a tire rupture. She then rolled to one side to assume a kneeling combat posture, as she gave a guttural roar while flipping off the safety on her C7A2. She levelled the lethal weapon at the two people who'd just flown out of the sky and squeezed the trigger. Round after round chuffed out of the barrel, accented by the sharp staccato cracks of each bullet and the continued warrior cry from Dupuis. The magazine emptied, and the soldier ejected it while reaching behind her to secure a fresh one. It was only as she snapped it into place and fed a round into the chamber that she paused, the barrel of her smoking weapon lowering slightly as she stared at her target.

The two youths were still standing and hadn't been struck by any of the lethal bullets. A dozen or more spinning projectiles were floating in midair, a circular pin cushion grouped about thirty centimetres in front of the chest of the male, who'd pulled the female behind him when Dupuis began firing. By this time, Shimooka had rolled over onto her knees, her hands pressed hard to her ears to ward off the assault of noise from the close-quarters gunfire.

"Well, what the—" Dupuis mumbled.

She flipped the safety on, sighed in frustration, and stood up, still keeping the barrel trained on the two teens.

"Unbelievable," Shimooka said under her breath as she stood up, her knees protesting royally.

The spinning bullets, looking very much like a swarm of large bees, were trembling as if the kinetic energy of their explosive escape from the soldier's C7A2 was trapped and looking for a release. But something else was happening. They were also disappearing, dissolving like an antacid tablet in water. Bubbling, dissolving, fading away into nothing. It was unlike anything she'd ever seen. Of course, her list of Things I've Never Seen was growing exponentially.

The female was peeking from behind the male, who was peering down at the dissolving bullets that Dupuis had skillfully aimed at his chest, the kill zone. The bullets should have torn them to pieces, Shimooka noted.

"Cool," the female said.

The male grunted.

"No, not cool."

These two were like Stewart. They could fly, and the soldiers at the Memorial had been shooting at them, and the bullets must have just disappeared like the ones from Dupuis's weapon had done and like the munitions fired at Stewart had also done. If they were associates of Stewart, why hadn't they attacked when they arrived? Coming from behind was an excellent flanking maneuver when all eyes were on Stewart. Why the masks? Were they protecting their identities, unlike Stewart, who seemed so self-assured in his prowess that he didn't bother to hide his face? And, why say something so absurd and cliche?

A thought occurred to Shimooka. She placed a hand on her forehead and chuckled, nodding to herself.

"Of course."

Lieutenant-Colonel Dupuis raised her weapon and stepped in front of Shimooka and Friedman, who'd managed to compose himself, along with his gun.

"Not a step closer," she barked. "Who the hell are you?"

Shimooka sighed and shook her head before pushing past Dupuis, her finger resting lightly on the trigger of her unholstered weapon, although she failed to see how it would make the slightest bit of difference if she decided to use it. This situation was rapidly moving beyond anything anyone on Earth had ever dealt with.

"Listen," she said, "please excuse my friend here. I apologize for that little display of Canadian military might, but you're the good guys, right?"

"Uh, yeah," the male squeaked.

It was a squeak, Shimooka thought. He'd just been fired at, point blank, with a very powerful weapon. I'd squeak, too.

"What?" Dupuis growled.

Shimooka could feel the heat of the soldier's glare on the back of her neck. She turned around to face Dupuis.

"Look, as preposterous as this may be, it just makes sense. So far, this day has been filled with the most impossible, the most unimaginable, out-of-this-world shit."

She pointed toward Stewart.

"Flying human being, bombs and bullets have no effect on him, laser beams coming out of his—"

"Plasma bolts," Friedman corrected.

He coughed nervously as he peered at the two young people, one hand gripping his gun, the other holding his cellphone. He was recording.

Shimooka nodded impatiently.

"Right, plasma bolts. Thank you, Detective Friedman. This day has been right out of a freaking superhero movie, soldier. Can't you see? It just makes sense that there would be flying good guys if there's a flying bad guy, right?"

She'd learned that much from her two years living with the cosplayer. Certainly, superheroes and supervillains were fictional, but hey, when faced with the impossible, the impossible suddenly becomes possible—flying bad guy, flying good guy. It was the Yin and Yang of good and evil.

"Detective," Dupuis began, "I'm in charge of this operation. Step aside."

"And do what? Shoot them to pieces again?" said Shimooka, as she jabbed a finger into her right ear. "I don't think so, officer. Besides, I can't possibly handle another barrage of gunfire from your weapon. I already have difficulty hearing out of this ear as it is."

Shimooka turned and took another step toward the two masked individuals, who, she noted, hadn't stopped holding hands, even when Dupuis was unloading 5.56-mm bullets at them.

"You're the heroes, right? You're the ones who've come here to stop that," she asked, as she stabbed a finger back toward where Stewart was out of sight behind the rubble, "that asshole, right?"

The female moved from behind the male to stand next to him, still holding tightly onto his hand like they were new lovers, and she was loath to let him go. She looked at the male and then pointed a finger at him with her free hand.

"He is. He's the one with the superhero from another universe inside him. I'm just here for moral support."

The male adjusted his mask.

"Uh, yeah, I guess."

The plastic mask muffled his voice, but Shimooka heard the hint of hesitation.

"You guess? What the hell does that mean? Are you a match for Stewart or not?"

"What he means," the female said quickly, lifting their clasped hands to pat the back of the male's hand, "is that, yes, we're the good guys, and yes, we're here to stop that guy over there."

"Bullshit," said Dupuis, her weapon unwavering. "I've lost good people today because of that piece of shit over there, and you two show up out of nowhere."

She jerked the barrel of her weapon toward the afternoon sky.

"You drop down out of the sky, same as Stewart. What the hell do you think I'm supposed to think, detective?"

"Lieutenant Colonel, please," Shimooka said. "Let's get some answers first. They could have disappeared us by now, right?"

The Ant-Man, Shimooka wasn't sure what to call him, lifted his free hand.

"Look, I'm sorry we didn't text or something first, but we just came from—what? No—okay, all right."

He sighed again and pointed.

"Like, uh, she said, we're here to stop Magus."

"Who are you?" Friedman said, his voice sounding oddly small for a man his size.

Shimooka turned to look at him and saw that his face was ashen. His cellphone was still directed at the two youth, but his right hand's grip on the Smith and Wesson was so tight that the tendons on his knuckles were bulging white strips under his pale, liver-spotted skin. She slowly reached out a hand and rested it on the top of his weapon, gently pushing it down.

"Put it away, Marty. It's useless, and you're gripping it so hard, you're liable to shoot one of us mere mortals."

Friedman smiled weakly, lowering the weapon, so it only partly pointed at the pair's feet. Shimooka turned back to the masked couple, motioning for Dupuis to drop her gun.

"So, who are you?"

"Oh, uh, I'm Hunt—what? —Oh, yeah."

Ant-Man turned his head slightly to the side.

"I can't say that. They'll laugh—No. No—That's stupid—"

Shimooka could feel her face hurting from the frown pasted on it. As if this day couldn't get any weirder. Was he talking to himself, or did the costume helmet have a radio setup inside it? In which case, who was he talking to?

Ant-Man groaned.

"My name is, uh, the, uh, I can't—Really?"

He sighed audibly loud through the plastic mask.

"Fine—I'm the Mighty Titan."

"The Mighty Titan?" Shimooka said slowly, letting the words roll off her tongue, scarcely able to believe she was saying them. "But that's an Ant-Man mask."

The male shrugged.

"It's all I had. I have to protect my identity. You know how that works."

Friedman, who was now standing next to Shimooka, still holding his pistol and cellphone while awkwardly lighting a cigarette he'd retrieved from somewhere within his jacket, nodded slowly.

"Yeah, like Spider-Man, or Batman. Right?"

"Exactly," the female said enthusiastically, her voice muffled by the mask.

The two of them couldn't be more than eighteen or nineteen, Shimooka thought, and there was a peculiar innocence to how they were treating this utterly bizarre moment. They'd floated down from somewhere up in the sky, flying from god knows where, as if that was a completely normal thing to do. Dozens of people were dead or disappeared by the plasma thing Stewart did with his hands, and a large section of the one hundred and fifty or so years old East Block of the Parliament buildings was lying in ruins around them. These two just show up dressed in jeans and cosplay headgear, and they were worried about their identities? What the hell was going on, on planet Earth?

"And who are you supposed to be?" Shimooka directed the question toward the female, who seemed to balk at the question.

"The Wasp, of course. Ant-Man's partner, you know, from the movie," she replied enthusiastically.

"Ah, right, the Wasp," Shimooka replied, putting a hand to her chin. "I haven't seen that movie yet. The sequel, right?"

Her voice began to rise.

"Maybe when we're done putting Mr. Stewart behind bars, you can all just come over to my place and we can watch it together on the couch. I'll dress up as the Scarlet Witch!"

She looked down at her handgun and laughed, flipped the safety to on and then jammed it into her shoulder holster, way harder than she needed to.

"You do realize you're interfering in an official police and military operation, right?" she said as she gestured toward Dupuis. "We could arrest you, right here on the spot."

Friedman coughed nervously behind Shimooka.

"I doubt they'd let us do that."

Shimooka nodded vigorously.

"Probably not, detective, based on the futility of the recent actions taken here by our grand military. How about the two of you quit playing your cosplay routine with us and tell us who the hell you really are and what you're doing here?"

Dupuis suddenly lunged forward. Shimooka had sensed her inching slowly up beside her, but the sudden burst of motion from the soldier was unexpected. She exploded across the few metres that separated them from the pair with such force and speed that Shimooka's mind took a few seconds to acknowledge the new reality. By the time she comprehended what Dupuis had done, the military officer had hit some sort of invisible barrier, the same one that had stopped her earlier firepower. Dupuis grunted explosively and was immediately thrown back, like she'd been pushed, her legs and arms grabbing at the air and ground in an effort to regain a defensive position. She failed and flopped hard onto her butt at Shimooka's feet, her helmet flying in one direction, her automatic rifle clattering to the ground a metre away against a slab of stone. The police officer looked down at the hulking soldier and then at Ant-Man and The Wasp. The two hadn't moved, flinched maybe, but they seemed unfazed by the unexpected attack.

"That was really cool," she heard the female say.

Shimooka snickered and crossed her arms, her right hand feeling the familiar bulge of her now not-so-lethal firearm. Kudos to the Lieutenant for trying, but these two hadn't been harmed by the barrage of bullets just a moment earlier, not even a nick or a scratch. It seemed they might have the same tech or whatever Stewart used to nullify the weaponry the CAF and local police had been lobbing at him since his arrival on The Hill. It's been that kind of day, she thought. It is what it is. She reached down to help the cursing Dupuis up.

"Lieutenant-Colonel, this day is seriously weird enough without either of us adding to the craziness."

She stepped around the complaining soldier and approached Hunter and Mia.

"Now, two questions. Can you do what he does with his hands, that plasma zappy stuff," she asked, as she jabbed a thumb over her shoulder in Stewart's direction, "and will that take him out?"

TWENTY-FOUR

"My god, you could have warned me."

"SO, THOMAS STEWART IS THIS MAGUS?" Detective Shimooka asked again. "From another universe, a parallel universe?"

Hunter nodded.

"And so is Titan, the super being inside me, uh, from the same parallel universe."

Shimooka frowned and shook her head. Hunter shrugged.

"Look, don't ask me how it works. Titan showed up Friday afternoon, and I guess based on what happened in Nepean, so did Magus."

"You know," Shimooka said as they peered around the wooden door, observing Stewart hovering over the quadrangle, "if this were anything other than what it impossibly is, you'd be in a psych ward by now."

Hunter turned and looked at the detective's face through the red tinge of his mask's eyepieces.

"If this weren't what it was, I'd put myself there. I thought I was losing my mind."

Mia laughed under her mask.

"I thought for sure he was joking," she said, shrugging. "Or having a breakdown when he said he could see my underwear through my pants."

The detective frowned.

"See your underwear?"

Mia chuckled and smiled, squeezing Hunter's hand.

"Uh, another time maybe, if there's another time," Hunter redirected. "What's he waiting for?"

Stewart hadn't moved from his spot above the quadrangle nor made any attempt to communicate since he'd put Gloria down at the arch.

Titan spoke ominously.

You, he's waiting for you.

Shimooka shrugged.

"After the white flag debacle, the military sent out a DSU. Uh, that's an armed robotics unit. They attached a two-way comm to it. Stewart didn't destroy it immediately, so we managed to get his one demand."

"One demand? What's he want?" Mia asked.

Shimooka slowly shook her head and shrugged.

"Oh, just the surrender of the entire planet's governments."

As I suspected. Magus has always been a megalomaniac.

Mia laughed.

"From Ottawa?"

Shimooka chuckled.

"My thoughts exactly. Why here?"

"Maybe he's an idiot and is unintentionally buying the rest of the world some time to figure out how to stop him," Dupuis growled.

"Yeah, time to do what, though? Nothing seems to be able to stop Stewart, except maybe these two," Shimooka said, then pointed at a pile of rubble. "What else can this thing inside you do besides reconstruct rocks?"

"Uh," Hunter said, nodding to something Titan was saying. "He prefers to be called the Mighty Titan. He's a human being like us."

Shimooka nodded slowly.

"Right, like us."

Moments earlier, the two OPP detectives and the CAF colonel had required multiple displays of Titan's powers to convince them of Hunter's claims of a superhero from an alternate universe living inside him, who claimed to have the ability to defeat Magus. One of those displays had been several examples of 'disappearing' and 'reappearing' various pieces of sandstone from the damaged building. Hunter dutifully disassembled the molecules of three massive blocks of broken wall and then willed them back together, the latter being something Titan had only just informed him he could do. It might have been fun if it hadn't been for the purpose of proving Titan's power. That morning, he'd merely destroyed the old metal slide in the park, which was spectacular, but this was even more so. The violence of disassembling the blocks had surprised everyone, including him. Still, Dupuis sniffed and told Hunter she wasn't entirely convinced and was counting on the arrival of a squadron of F-22s flying in from Joint Base Langley-Eustis.

He may be waiting for someone worthy to challenge him. Someone like us.

"I thought you said he doesn't know you're here, in this universe?" Hunter replied to Titan.

I am not convinced of this. Attacking your parliament buildings makes no strategic sense. Canada, in my universe, is a peaceful and well-respected country, but to demand the surrender of Earth's collective governments from the legislative buildings of your country is illogical. The United Nations would be a more appropriate venue.

"I didn't think the mighty Maggot would be considered logical," said Hunter, laughing.

Detective Friedman, who was on his fifth cigarette since it became apparent the two young individuals were like Stewart, waved a hand in front of Mia's mask to get her attention.

"He's talking to your super friend, that Titan guy?"

Mia nodded, her Wasp mask bobbing slightly on her head.

"Yeah. It's a little weird when the two of them get going like that."

"Huh," Friedman grunted. "Yeah, weird."

He waved his hand again.

"So, uh, why are you two holding hands like that? You haven't let go since you showed up."

Mia looked at the detective, seeing the fear in his eyes.

"I'm sorry, I can't tell you that," she said.

"Oh," Friedman nodded, taking a step back as if the girl in The Wasp mask might 'disappear' him at any moment.

The first ten minutes after Dupuis's two spectacular and failed attempts to hurt or capture them had been tense, with rapid-fire questioning from Detective Shimooka and the Lieutenant-Colonel, who obviously was struggling to believe or comprehend what was happening. Hunter and Mia had explained as much as they knew, two super beings from another universe, using the advanced technology of a small black disc, transferred into the bodies of their doppelgängers in this universe, along with their formidable otherworldly powers. Thomas Stewart seemed far more powerful or maybe more adept at using Magus's power than Hunter was at using Titan's at the moment, a situation that Hunter relayed was concerning to the superhero.

"Do you have one of these discs?" Dupuis asked, her eyes scanning Mia and Hunter.

"No," he answered. "Titan isn't entirely sure how the disc works or even how it brought them to our universe. When it happened, he told me they were duking it out in space over Scotland."

"Duking it out? They have a lot of these battles?" Dupuis asked, appearing to be taking the conversation seriously.

Hunter nodded.

"Yeah, for over a hundred years, good versus evil stuff, just like in superhero movies. Titan is the hero, and Magus is the villain."

"So, nobody ever wins?" Dupuis said.

"Not really," Hunter shrugged. "I've asked Titan why he doesn't just kill him, and he says it would be unethical to end Magus's life, even if he deserved it."

"A hundred years? That's a long time to be waging war," Shimooka noted.

"Well," Mia interrupted, "didn't he say Magus was angry because he accuses Titan of killing his super-powered girlfriend?"

"Yeah, he did. What? He says he didn't kill her, and her name was Medusa. Oh, I see, that was her villain name. Her real name was Gloria Musa."

"Gloria Musa?" Shimooka winced. "Gloria Adaego Musa?"

Yes, that was her name. How does she know her name?

"Uh, he says yes, and he wants to know how you know that name," Hunter responded.

Shimooka pointed in the direction of Stewart.

"Thomas Stewart was with a woman when he killed those people in Nepean two days ago. He arrived on The Hill, flying while holding onto a woman. He's killed dozens of people here and did all this destruction while holding onto a woman named Gloria Adaego Musa. They're a couple."

In my universe, Gloria Adaego Musa was Magus's protege and lover. She is dead. I watched her die. Magus believes I killed her, but I watched Gloria turn her power upon herself, and she died.

"Uh, he says there was a Gloria Adaego Musa in his universe. Her superhero, er, I guess her super villain's name was Medusa. She was Magus's girlfriend, but she died, uh, a long time ago, in that universe."

It is possible that when he entered the Thomas Stewart of this universe, he saw Gloria was alive here and has taken her. The Gloria of my universe was extremely powerful, likely more powerful than I am, but I always felt she was conflicted about her alliance with Magus. Like you, however, since The Event has not happened here, this universe's Gloria will have no powers of her own.

Hunter relayed this to the detective.

"So," Shimooka mused, "this, uh, this universe's Gloria, sitting over there on the steps leading into the Tower, is a hostage?"

Most likely, but take a closer look with your vision.

"Uh, yes, he says she probably is," Hunter told Shimooka. "He's asked me to take a look with, uh, my supervision."

Yes, engage your telescopic vision.

"You have super vision, kid?" Dupuis balked, shaking her head. "What the hell does that mean?"

Mia laughed.

"Yeah, he really does. He can see through solid objects, too."

The soldier grunted and cast an exasperated look at the detective.

"Shit, you're right, this is like a comic book."

Hunter ignored the soldier.

"Right, okay, I need to see Stewart so I can zoom in."

"Zoom in?" Shimooka asked.

Hunter nodded.

"Yeah, I can see faraway things up close, like a pair of binoculars, but better. We were practicing yesterday."

We merely scratched the surface of what our vision is capable of. You could see a coin on the moon if it was necessary.

"Really?" Hunter replied.

Mia slugged him in the arm.

"You and your one-sided conversations. What's he saying?"

Hunter laughed.

"He says I could see a coin on the moon if I needed to."

Dupuis groaned.

"Unbelievable. The most serious terrorist incident this country has ever seen, and we're working with a child with supervision. Does this mean you can see the woman from here, and how the hell is that possible?"

Hunter faced the soldier, exasperated.

"I'm sorry, I'm not a superhero, this just happened to me on Friday, and I don't know how any of this works, it just does."

We don't have time for this discussion. Go look.

"Yes, yes, I'll go look," Hunter fumed, letting go of Mia's hand for the first time since their arrival.

He climbed over a large slab of masonry and shattered windows to get a clear visual line on the Centre Block.

You did not need to do that, you can merely look through the rubble to see the woman with your telescopic vision.

"Yeah, right," Hunter fumed as he looked towards the Parliament building for the woman. "I'm not sure I can do both things at the same time yet."

You are quite capable of doing both.

"I'm already up here," he replied, then called over his shoulder, "Where is she?"

Shimooka had followed him close behind.

"He put her down, right there," she replied, pointing over Hunter's shoulder. "Beneath the Peace Tower, in the Porte-cochère."

"The what?"

She means the archway.

"The archway there," said Shimooka, as she pointed again.

Hunter groaned but squinted, letting his eyes track along the grass and various bushes at the Centre Block's base until he saw a small figure sitting, her arms holding her knees to her chest.

"I see her."

Hunter focused, leaning into his vision, staring at the woman, bringing her closer to him, and suddenly her face filled his entire vision.

"Wow," Hunter exclaimed. "I'm still getting used to this. Yesterday, when I was practicing, it was just cars and houses around the neighbourhood, but this is like she's right here."

"What do you see? Is she hurt?" Shimooka whispered.

Hunter turned his head back and forth.

"Crazy, and I can still see everything else between here and there. It's like a picture-in-picture effect."

"Hey," Shimooka hissed. "Practice later. What do you see?"

"Right, sorry. Uh, she looks upset. I don't see any blood," he said as he pulled back a little to see her fully. "She's looking at Stewart, I think, but— it's like she's not there. I mean, it's like she's zoned out or something."

He guessed the woman was in her mid-twenties. Her hair was arranged in dozens of dreads, which were pulled up and held together at the crown of her head, creating a bouquet of strands that hung like a cloak down her neck, lightly brushing against her shoulders. He zoomed in until her face was all he could see. Her eyes were a deep blue, but they were distressing to look into. She was staring at where Stewart was floating, but those eyes were eerily unblinking. He pulled back a little, noting that her face was drawn. Her eyeliner, which should have accented the intense blue of her eyes with thick lines of blue eye shadow, was smudged and streaked from the tears she'd been crying. Her lips were moving as if she was talking to herself.

Hunter tilted his head a little and focused his hearing on her. He'd done this the day before at the gas station, but this was far more intense, the weight of the moment resting on him. He heard clicks from insects in the quadrangle between them, creaks from the archway she was leaning against, and voices somewhere inside the Parliament building. Police, or somebody else in the building, whispering, watching—

He was reaching too far. He pulled back.

Good work, now focus on whom you want to hear.

Then suddenly, he heard a whisper, a woman's voice, hoarse, broken, Gloria talking to herself.

"I didn't do this. I didn't do this. This isn't me. I know. I know. We'll be fine."

"What do you see that I can't see through my binoculars?" Dupuis barked.

She'd clambered up behind them and peered with her binoculars in the same direction as Hunter was looking.

"She's been crying, still crying, I think," Hunter offered. "And she's talking to herself. She's saying she didn't do this. She's telling herself she's not a part of what's happening. It's the same words. She's repeating them over and over. She didn't do this."

"Damn, you can see way more than these," the soldier huffed.

"She's a hostage then," Shimooka said quietly. "We have to get to her."

Dupuis was suddenly hissing behind them and pulling on the detective's coat sleeve. Shimooka turned to see her waving the arm that held the binoculars.

"What?"

She was holding her radio's handheld in her other hand.

"The F-22s. Three minutes out. We need to clear out."

"Shit," Shimooka muttered, reaching out to grab Hunter's shoulder. "We gotta go, kid. Fighter jets are gonna drop ordinance on the quadrangle."

Hunter imagined pushing his vision away from Gloria. She zoomed out, returning to her small, sorrowful self far away under the Peace Tower.

"Fighter jets?"

They will be destroyed.

"Yes, c'mon," Shimooka replied.

She grabbed his arm and pulled him back behind the wooden door.

"They're going to bomb the Parliament Buildings? Is that legal?" Hunter asked, steadying himself as he stumbled over masonry in their haste to get away.

The military must not engage with Magus again. They are no match for his power.

"I think we're past legal in this situation, super kid," Dupuis growled.

"Uh," Hunter said as he tripped around a block of stone to approach her. "Titan says Magus will blow up the jets. They have to turn back."

"Bullshit," Dupuis spat. "They're armed to the teeth."

She lifted her weapon and pointed it at Mia, who stepped back, alarmed.

"Try anything, and I'll take her down. I know she's not like you, kid. Holding onto her hand was protecting her somehow."

Magus will destroy those fighter planes. Tell them.

"Lieutenant, step down," Shimooka barked as she stepped between Mia and the soldier.

Dupuis shook her head.

"It's Lieutenant-Colonel, detective, and not a chance. Those F-22s will incinerate that bastard."

They will not.

"They won't," Hunter yelled.

His super hearing detected the rising scream of the approaching jet engines.

Those pilots will die. We must stop Magus from doing this.

Hunter shifted the universe, so he stood beside Mia. He moved so rapidly that Detective Shimooka was still looking where he'd been, and the Lieutenant-Colonel was in mid-sentence, continuing her threat against Mia. He took Mia's hand and ascended several hundred metres instantly, causing Mia to shriek as she and Hunter were suddenly high above the battle-scarred Parliament Hill.

Excellent move.

"Hunter!" Mia squeaked. "My god, you could have warned me."

He pulled Mia close, putting his arms around her waist and holding her tightly.

"I'm so sorry. I shouldn't have let go of your hand. I thought we were safe. I thought we all were on the same side."

Mia held him, placed her head against his shoulder, and spoke softly into his ear.

"It's all right, Hunter."

He pushed Mia away to see her eyes through the mask's bulbous eyes.

"If that asshole had shot you—"

She shook her head.

"She didn't. You kept me safe. Now, what do we do about him?"

She pointed in the general direction of Parliament Hill, far below.

"Titan's saying we must stop those jets, or Magus will destroy them."

Yes, it is time to reveal ourselves to Magus. It is time to engage him and put an end to his evil plans.

"I'm not ready to do that. I barely know how to do anything with your powers," Hunter argued.

"He wants you to attack him?" Mia asked.

Hunter nodded.

"Yeah. I'm just not sure I can do this."

Hunter, you have my powers. I will assist you in what you must do, and together we will defeat Magus.

"And Titan's more powerful than Magus, right?" Mia asked.

I am. He has never defeated me.

"He says he's never been defeated by Magus," Hunter said as he grimaced.

"Really," Mia said, "then if Magus has never defeated Titan, and Titan is more powerful than Magus, why is this happening? Why hasn't Titan ever locked this guy up? If he had, he might never have come to our universe."

I have. Many times, but he and his cohorts are resourceful.

"We had this conversation yesterday. It's a moral thing, he could kill him easily, but he doesn't want to kill—"

A glint caught Hunter's attention. He zoomed in with his vision. The jets were streaking just above the city, coming in low from the Southeast. They'd be over The Hill in less than a minute.

We are out of time. Hunter, we must act now.

Hunter turned his attention on Stewart and zoomed in. The young man, dressed as Green Lantern, his Batman cape tangled between his legs, had spotted the planes. He was smiling, and Hunter could see sparkling tendrils of energy forming around his hands, the same blue arcing he'd seen in the video on Mia's phone earlier.

"He sees them," Hunter said. "He seems happy about it."

We must do this now, or more lives will be lost.

"Okay," Hunter said, as fear threatened to collapse his chest. "What do we do?"

"You're asking me?" Mia gasped.

Hunter shook his head.

"No, sorry, Titan."

We must preserve the lives of those here as much as possible. Take Mia to this universe's Gloria. She can get her away from the building, out behind where we saw those paths leading down to the river. Then put ourselves between Magus and the fighter planes.

"Really?"

"Really, what?" Mia asked, leaning back to look into Hunter's face.

He grimaced and explained the plan to her.

"That should work. I think. What? He says it'll work."

Mia nodded.

"Well, it's nice to be able to do something helpful."

"Okay," Hunter said slowly, focusing his thoughts on the tiny figure of the broken woman far below by the Porte-cochère. "Hold on."

And then the Earth moved, and the two of them were hovering a metre away to the side of Gloria. Mia dropped lightly to her feet, her face taut with the tension of the moment. She grabbed Hunter by his shirt, pulling him down to her.

"Be careful," she said, as she hugged him.

Hunter smiled slightly as she pulled away. He was desperately hoping she wouldn't sense the fear oozing from every pore of his body. It wouldn't do for Earth's first and only mightiest superhero to look like he was about to wet his pants. He waved a little awkward wave and shot up, moving so fast it seemed he blinked out of existence.

TWENTY-FIVE

"Puh-lease, have you learned nothing yet?"

WHAT ARE WE WAITING FOR?

"Patience, Thomas, once this country's pathetic military realizes they can't resist my power, they'll surrender to me. I could easily destroy everything and every enemy here, but what would be the purpose? I want these idiots to adore me, to bow down before me. Patience does have its merits, at times. This shall be the first of many glorious conquests in this universe. Besides, I've been quite enjoying myself. You can't imagine how refreshing it is not to be interrupted by Titan or that silly League."

After Magus had abandoned Gloria on the steps of the Centre Block, he rose above the quadrangle, waiting for what he knew would be the next attack from these impudent, weak cretins. He'd decided that protecting this universe's Gloria no longer held any purpose for him, and Thomas Stewart had reluctantly agreed. She was dead weight, and if she died in the crossfire, then she died, it wouldn't be a loss. Magus's Gloria, the formidable Medusa, had been a true partner, although, he admitted smugly to himself, she'd still have been nothing without him. She'd never have reached her full potential if he hadn't rescued her from her pathetic mountain hideaway. It saddened him a little to think the Gloria of this universe would never compare to his Gloria. Oh, this woman was as beautiful, but this cowering, whimpering person was no Medusa. His Gloria, his Medusa, outfitted in her magnificent uniform, with her crown of lustrous black hair commanding attention high on her head like a Medusa's crown of snakes, was a fearsome sight. And oh, so sensuous.

If the truth were told, there had been a time, in the beginning, after he'd given her a home, that he'd become wary of what she could do, even to him. The immense power that flowed through her being was undisciplined, without direction, and she could have easily destroyed him. But, he mused as he observed a group of soldiers sneaking around a barricade, he was far more clever than Medusa. She might have been more powerful, but he was far more ruthless, a manipulator on a grand scale. He wasted no time in grooming the young, impressionable Gloria into a weapon that had fealty for only Magus. They became lovers, she became dependent on that love, and he'd won the battle of dominance over her. She'd never attack him, no matter how punitive and manipulative he could be. Medusa was his.

Had been his, he reminded himself.

Magus sighed deeply, how he hated the Mighty Titan for taking her from him. How glad he was that he'd been the one to dispatch his foe from existence, from all existence. Perhaps, he pondered, when he was done taking over this Earth he'd find this world's Hunter MacKenzie and, well, incinerate him just because he could.

There was movement again. The soldiers had found a sheltered spot just past the barricade, behind a blackened hulk of a truck. He raised his arm, pointing his hand towards them. All four saw the motion and ducked and rolled, fleeing and diving behind the concrete barricade. Magus laughed. Fools.

Wow, like everyone's afraid of us.

"Ah, you're still here. I was wondering if you'd faded into oblivion," Magus said, not bothering to hide the disappointment in his voice.

No, I've been thinking.

"Don't hurt yourself."

You're such an ass, you know.

Magus grunted derisively.

I was just thinking maybe we should go to the United Nations. That might be a better place to demand the surrender of Earth's nations.

Magus sniffed.

"United Nations? Are you referring to that pathetic United Planetary Alliance? I'll crush them mercilessly."

No, uh, I've never heard of that body. I was referring to the United Nations, a body of——

But Magus tuned him out. Mindless prattle from a foolish child. He saw movement again and zoomed in with his vision. The same four soldiers were making their way to a few scattered planters in front of what a scorched sign claimed was the Wellington Building. The wreckage of one of the helicopters that had attacked him earlier blocked much of the front of that building. Magus could see through the wreckage to a small group of soldiers and police who'd gathered behind it but now appeared to be pushing further away from the battlefield. Cowards. They're in retreat, he grumbled.

Magus shook his head.

"Have you finished talking, Thomas? I grow weary of your babbling."

Movement caught his eyes again, this time off to his left, among the rubble of the building he'd damaged shortly after the first military and local police had arrived. He zoomed in with his vision. There was a dishevelled man, a serious-looking woman holding a small weapon, a heavily armed soldier, and two young people wearing odd-looking face masks. The soldier had a large weapon pointed at one of them and they appeared to be arguing with each other. Magus smiled as he took notice of the high-pitched sounds of the approaching aircraft. His vision quickly found the planes skimming low above the city. They seemed to be carrying lots of pointy weapons. Magus laughed.

That doesn't look good.

Magus rolled his eyes.

"Puh-lease, have you learned nothing yet?"

His hands began to bristle with the excitement of further battle.

TWENTY-SIX

"I don't want to disintegrate him."

"NOW WHAT?" HUNTER DEMANDED.

He'd taken them high above the thin cloud cover drifting lazily across the Ottawa Valley. The capital city was a tangled mess of civilization far below. Sunlight flashing off the two approaching aircraft below drew Hunter's attention again.

We must confront Magus. Drop down between him and the military aircraft.

Hunter puffed air out of his mouth.

"This is getting serious, you know?"

Yes, this is serious, but we are and have always been far more powerful than Magus. Together, we can stop him from doing further harm to the people of Earth.

"I don't know what to do."

I will tell you. The power infused into every cell of your body will protect us, and I will tell you how to defend ourselves against his plasma energy.

Hunter grimaced.

"How? This is real-time. I can't just run off and Google anti-plasma bolt deflection or something. How will I be able to do this?"

I know not of this Google you speak of, but Hunter, you are the Mighty Titan. See the Earth below us? You are defying the physics of gravity, the bullets from those misguided soldiers when we arrived did not impede our mission, nor did the weapon from the woman soldier harm us. You have learned to control my energy to create a fearsome weapon of attack and defence. Magus cannot resist us. I have defeated him every time.

"Not every time," Hunter corrected.

Yes, that is true.

"Yeah, about that," Hunter said. "That Black Energy thing, does he still have it?"

I am unsure. It was a painful experience, unlike anything I have ever felt. However, as we discussed earlier, I believe it somehow brought us to your universe.

"Could it take him or you back to your universe?"

I am sorry, I do not know this. However, I can only surmise that if he still had it in his possession, it is unlikely he would still be here. Of course, this depends on whether he understands the disc's true purpose.

"Right," Hunter said quietly as he used his vision to bring Magus into focus.

He looked strange from this high vantage point. He appeared squashed, the Batman cap flapping like a thin line, no feet, no arms, just head and shoulders. He was looking slightly upward and smiling.

"Uh," Hunter stammered. "I think he sees those jets."

Then we must descend immediately! Take us down, Hunter. Place ourselves between our nemesis and the warplanes. The world awaits!

"Uh—"

You must do it now, or those pilots will die.

"Okay, older self, let's do this."

Hunter moved the universe in a blur of motion, stopping about ten meters in front of Magus, and placing the incoming aircraft to his back, which was tingling and itchy with fear. Magus seemed unfazed by their sudden appearance, except that the look on his face became filled with glee.

"At last," Hunter heard Magus declare as he laughed.

It was more like a cackle. The sound of it surprised Hunter. He was expecting something more profound, more menacing. This laugh was like the laugh of a cartoon character. Still, seeing Magus up close like this was terrifying. He was a killer, and Hunter had never known anyone like this. He swallowed hard, his heart thumping loudly in his chest. He'd role-played both heroes and villains in computer games, but an otherworldly and powerful being was floating not far from him. This was about to get real, and the adrenaline thrill of excitement that had brought him to this point over the last two days suddenly fizzled.

He might die.

Magus, his hands bristling and crackling audibly with his blue energy, drifted slowly up towards Hunter. Hunter drifted back and up, his hands weren't bristling.

"He's coming closer," Hunter whispered.

Do not retreat. You are Earth's mightiest hero. We do not withdraw.

"His hands are shimmering and blue."

It is a show meant to intimidate.

"I'm intimidated."

Stop retreating. Demand his surrender.

Hunter stopped moving away from Magus. Magus stopped as well. Hunter realized his mouth was open. He closed it, feeling his teeth clack together.

You must demand his surrender.

"Um," Hunter began, trying to project his voice before he whispered to Titan. "Just say surrender or else?"

Yes, he must surrender, or we will incapacitate him.

"Right. Incapacitate."

Magus suddenly moved to within two metres of Hunter.

"Who are you? Why do you wear this strange covering you have on your face? You know I can see through it, don't you?"

"Uh," Hunter stammered.

"You're just a child."

Ah, he does not recognize me from when I was your age. He does not know who we are.

"Are you the defender of this pathetic planet?"

Hunter grimaced behind the mask.

"Uh, what do I say?" he whispered.

This is to our advantage. We must reveal ourselves. It will frighten him, catch him off guard.

Hunter swallowed hard again. The blue energy crackling around Magus's hands was distracting and disturbing.

"I," he stammered. "I am—"

"Yes, well, Mr. I am," said Magus, glaring. "You're obviously a super-being."

He gestured toward the ground beneath them.

"You obviously can defy gravity. Who the hell are you?"

Titan laughed inside Hunter's head.

Now hit him with a blast of our energy. He will know I am here then.

"What?" Hunter said.

Quickly, like before, when you revealed our power to that detective. Point your hands at Magus and think about disintegrating him.

"I don't want to disintegrate him."

Magus narrowed his eyes.

"Are you mentally deficient? Is this all you can do, fly and babble like a fool?"

You will not actually disintegrate him. His power will keep that from happening, but you will stun him. Now, Hunter!

Hunter raised his hands, his palms facing Magus, who frowned as if confused by the move. However, that lasted only a second as Magus raised his crackling hands.

Do it!

When Hunter had blown up a chunk of limestone from the East Block for the detectives and that trigger-happy soldier, the resulting sound had been minor, like a firecracker going off. There was no blue energy like that which was glowing around Magus's hands, just the quiet tearing apart of the stone's molecules. To be honest, Hunter had thought at the time that the process looked like a cheap CGI effect. Zap! Poof! The limestone block was gone.

Focus, Hunter.

"I'm trying," he muttered.

He kept his palms pointed toward Magus and imagined energy flowing from them in the direction of this young man dressed as Green

Lantern. He thought of the vast, powerful explosions of energy coming from the hands and eyes of fictional super beings he'd seen in movies and comic books. He recalled blasts of energy that crushed villains or stopped asteroids from destroying the Earth when he suddenly felt the shockwave from a massive thunderclap, as a flash of dazzling, bright light erupted from his own hands. Pure white energy exploded from his palms, flashing instantly across the space between him and Magus. He caught a brief glimpse of a surprised Magus before the energy hit the target so hard and decisively that it pummelled him over a dozen metres directly back into the Peace Tower's south-facing clock dial. The circular dial exploded, sending glass, stone, and metal shards outward as Magus crumpled into it. The Peace Towers 53-bell clarion hanging beneath the clock clanged in a cacophony of protest.

"Oh, my god," Hunter gasped. "I just wrecked the Peace Tower."

Yes! That was brilliant!

Magus appeared entangled in the twisted remnants of the clock mechanism, but then he slowly slumped forward and fell the eighty or so metres to the steps below. The thud of the impact of his body hitting the concrete steps was alarming.

"Did I kill him?" Hunter gasped as he looked down at Magus and then over at the severely damaged Tower. "I can't believe I just wrecked the Peace Tower."

Focus, Hunter. Quick! Follow him.

Hunter obeyed, letting his feet slam into the steps a short distance from Magus, who was lying on his side, gasping for breath. He felt the concrete crush beneath the impact of his landing, but his body felt no pain, not even pressure from the impact.

Magus was groaning and muttering angrily as he struggled to rise. Hunter turned to look for Mia and Gloria, standing about twenty metres from where he and Magus were. Mia was pulling on the black woman's arm, but Gloria looked back at them, her face filled with distress. Hunter looked down at his hands. They felt like they usually did, like his hands. The energy had been so powerful that he thought he should have felt something. Yet there was no tingle, no weird vibrations, nothing at all. Magus struggled to get to his feet, obviously stunned by the blast. He was also furious. His eyes, shrouded by his dark eyebrows, were focused like lasers on Hunter, who took a step back.

Something is wrong. That blast should have incapacitated Magus. I am not as powerful as I should be.

Hunter swallowed hard and whispered.

"What does that mean?"

You must hit him again. Concentrate.

Magus bellowed as the features of the youthful Thomas twisted in rage.

Hit him again! You must do it now!

Hunter lifted his hands again. Magus saw and rose quickly to his feet, raising his own hands, the spidery web of energy around them reaching out toward Hunter.

"How did you do that?" Magus growled as he lifted off from the steps. "Who are you?"

Hunter rose with Magus, backing hastily away, putting some distance between them. The success of his attack had given him confidence, but Magus, like the energy swirling around his hands, was bristling with rage, and Titan's words were quickly casting a shadow over that newfound confidence. Still, Hunter thought, maybe he could do this. Maybe the Mighty Titan wasn't exaggerating when he said he was more powerful than Magus. Maybe. He began to imagine the same energy pounding into Magus, tearing through his odd choice of costume, slamming him back into the ground.

We must stall for time. It seems my energy needs to rebuild.

Hunter winced.

"Rebuild?" he whispered. "What does that mean?"

I cannot say. Perhaps my power is somehow weakened by your uncertainty. We need more time. You need to believe in yourself and what you can do with this power.

"More time? I don't think I can call a timeout," Hunter gasped.

There is nothing you cannot do, Hunter, nothing that you cannot do. You must believe.

"I'm sorry. I'm trying, but this isn't like a movie."

"Are you done babbling?" Magus bellowed as his hands flared.

Let me talk to him.

"Go for it," Hunter said quietly.

He was aware that every part of his body was tingling, crawling with a thousand itches he couldn't possibly scratch at once. He was somehow pulling in energy from around him, like a sponge drawing in water. The power the Mighty Titan had brought with him from the other universe was preparing for another assault.

Hunter hoped this wasn't going to hurt.

TWENTY-SEVEN

"We needed those two!"

SHIMOOKA STARTED AS THE KID in the Ant-Man mask blurred past her, grabbed his masked friend, and disappeared upward.

"Damit, Dupuis," she shouted, gesturing over her head in the direction the two young people had fled. "We needed those two."

Dupuis flipped the safety on her weapon off and turned to the two detectives.

"We don't even know what they are."

She jerked a thumb in the general direction of the sound of the approaching aircraft.

"We need to clear the area."

Friedman holstered his weapon and walked past the soldier.

"No argument here," he said. "This is bullshit. I'm not dying today."

"Friedman," Shimooka called. "We have to get Musa."

Friedman stopped and glanced back at his partner.

"She's dead, Shim. We can't get to her in time before those planes drop their load. She's dead, and this," he said, as he swept his hands across the front of his coat, "won't look great in a body bag."

Shimooka shook her head as Friedman turned and began trotting toward the War Memorial. Dupuis was cradling her weapon across an arm, her body half-turned to leave.

"We can't save her, detective. She's an acceptable casualty considering what we're up against. The Air Force is going to end this now. C'mon."

Shimooka turned to look at the young woman in the distance, who'd moved to sit on the steps under the Porte-cochère, the southern arch of the entrance to the Centre Block. She seemed small and lost, a cowering figure sitting, leaning against the side of the cold stonework. She's a victim, Shimooka thought. I can't leave her. Suddenly, the two masked teens appeared beside the woman, hugged each other, and then suddenly, the male literally vanished. Shimooka shook her head in disbelief. The masked female held her hand out to Gloria.

"Look," Shimooka hissed, pointing. "Those kids are intervening."

Dupuis lurched up beside her, binoculars pinned to her face.

"Shit," the soldier growled again, reaching for her comms.

"You have to call off the air strike," the detective demanded. "Musa and whomever those kids are, they're not soldiers or suspects, they're civilians. How many casualties will be acceptable?"

TWENTY-EIGHT

"You have beautiful eyes."

THE WOMAN WAS PRETTY, MIA THOUGHT, and not much older than her, maybe in her mid-twenties. Her long hair, arranged in dozens and dozens of long, tight dreads, was gathered in a nut at the top of her head. It shivered and trembled with every movement from the woman as she sobbed.

Mia reached out to steady herself on the wall of the arch of the Centre Block's entrance and touched Gloria lightly on her shoulder. The woman gasped and looked up, her haunted eyes widening with surprise. Those eyes were a remarkable blue in contrast to the rich dark tone of her skin, but they were framed with the horror she'd witnessed. Blue mascara ran in long streaks down her cheeks. Mia ached for her. What a horrible thing for any person to endure, she thought.

"You have beautiful eyes," Mia said quickly, immediately regretting it.

That was all you could come up with, Mia chided herself. I don't have any superpowers. All I can do is try and get her away from here while Hunter and Titan attack that gaesaekki in the Green Lantern costume.

The woman blinked rapidly, the fear in her eyes seeming to lessen as they focused on Mia. There was also a kernel of something else as if an understanding was pushing through the cloud over her face. She unwrapped her arms around her legs and placed her hands flat on the concrete.

"Who?"

"Oh, wait," Mia added.

She pulled off her mask, setting it on the ground as she smiled reassuringly.

"Gloria, right? My name's Mia Kim. Are you injured? Can you walk?"

Gloria stared at her for a moment, then looked at the mask that lay at Mia's feet.

"That, that's the Wasp, isn't it?"

"Yes, we needed to protect our identity," Mia replied, nodding slowly, as she squatted down and gently placed one of her hands over one of the woman's. "I know this will sound weird, but my boyfriend and I are here with a super-powered being called the Mighty Titan. He's from an alternate universe."

Mia grimaced.

"Well, you can't see him, but his mind and special powers are inside my boyfriend's body. I'm here to rescue you."

Gloria's eyes began to glisten with tears again as Mia helped her stand.

"Magus?"

"Yes, I know this sounds crazy, Gloria, but there's another super-powered being inside your boyfriend, and he's a really bad guy. His name is, um, yes, Magus. How did you know?"

"Magus? Inside Thomas?"

Mia nodded, frowning.

"Yes. Inside your boyfriend, and we're going to stop him from killing anyone else. Okay?"

"It's true then, it's all true. I remember—Medusa—Magus," Gloria said haltingly.

She pushed her hands up against the sides of her head, her long fingers clawing at the rows of her dreads as she stared off in the direction of the man in the Green Lantern costume. Then she began to moan, her hands pressing the sides of her head.

"You must remember," she said forcefully. "You must remember!"

Then she dropped her hands and appeared to respond to herself.

"No, no, no, I left all this behind. I don't want us to remember."

Mia stared at her, confused. She reached out to touch the woman lightly on her shoulder.

"What are you saying? I don't understand. We have to get out of here," Mia pleaded as she grabbed Gloria's arm and helped her to stand. The woman continued to moan as if she were in pain as Mia led her along the sidewalk toward the West Block.

"I know this all seems out there, but there's a being from a parallel universe inside your boyfriend. I don't know how that's possible, but it is, and it also explains the terrible things that have happened in the last few days. He's inside Thomas, and he's making him do these terrible things."

"No," Gloria wailed, her voice choked with anguish as Mia continued to lead her away, "You said we wouldn't remember, you said your power would make us forget."

The taller woman stumbled, and Mia slid an arm around her waist, supporting her. The plan was to make their way west along the Centre Block and then around to the backside of the Library of Parliament, where paths led away from The Hill, some down toward the river. Mia would take one of those paths, and when Hunter and Titan had finished doing whatever they were going to do to Magus, Hunter would come and find them. That was Plan A, anyway.

Gloria suddenly cried out, pulling away from Mia, then fell to her hands and knees on the sidewalk. Mia jumped to her side, trying to help her up.

"We have to go," she begged, grabbing her by a shoulder.

"Why now?" the woman yelled, pulling away from Mia's grasp as her fingers tore into the hard concrete like it was made of butter, "I don't want to remember, remembering hurts!"

Mia looked down at the gouges in the sidewalk and Gloria's undamaged hands and stepped back. What was going on, she wondered, as Gloria grew quiet and slowly stood up, brushing her hands against her slacks.

"It'll be okay," she said calmly, "we'll be all right."

Mia reached out and touched the woman's arm.

"I'm sorry, Gloria, but we have to go. Magus has taken over Thomas's body. He's not your boyfriend anymore. The Canadian Air Force has sent fighter planes, and they're almost here, and Titan will attack Magus any second. We need to get clear."

"No," Gloria said, her voice barely audible, as she turned her face towards the sky over the quadrangle.

"Gloria, it's too dangerous."

The woman turned to Mia, her eyes steady and her voice remarkably calm and unwavering.

"I'm sorry, you don't understand. He'll kill them, he'll kill them all, including your boyfriend."

The statement was spoken calmly like she knew what she was talking about, and Mia realized that somehow she did know. This poor woman had seen a level of horror in the previous two days that no person should ever witness. She was clearly in shock.

"We can't stay, Gloria. We could die."

Gloria shook her head slowly and looked away.

"No, you don't understand what's happening. How long has he been here?"

"Who?"

Her eyes locked with Mia's.

"Titan. How long has he been in this universe?"

Mia frowned at Gloria, then caught a flash of movement over the woman's shoulder. Hunter had just appeared as a tiny figure opposite Magus, high above the quadrangle.

"Oh, no," she gasped. "Hunter and Titan are starting the attack."

Gloria swung around, letting her eyes follow Mia's gaze, then turned back and grabbed her by the arms.

"Mia, when did Titan enter your boyfriend?"

"What?" Mia stammered.

"How long ago did Titan enter your boyfriend?" Gloria repeated urgently.

"Uh, Friday afternoon, I think. Why?" Mia answered, trying to understand what was happening.

"Who controls the power, Hunter or Titan?" Gloria demanded, her voice firm.

Mia blinked.

"Uh, Hunter does. Titan can control his body, but Hunter's still trying to figure out the superpowers. But I don't understand. How do you know this?"

Gloria let her go and turned to look up at the two figures.

"It's the same as for us then, but we had years to find a balance between the two of us."

She held a hand to her mouth, and Mia could see her eyes widening.

"Yes, it's true then. Thomas is letting Magus do this. He let him kill our friends, our employees, and all those soldiers. He's letting Magus do what Magus does best, hurt people," Gloria said, her hand falling away from her mouth.

"Oh, Thomas."

"How do you know about any of this?" Mia asked again.

Gloria sighed heavily.

"Your boyfriend will not be ready for this battle. Titan isn't ruthless, and Magus will not stop until he gets what he wants."

The sky was suddenly filled with a flash of light so bright that Mia and Gloria suddenly had two shadows, one from the light of the sun and the other from a flash of energy that had come from Hunter's hands. His attack caused Magus to be thrown backward, smashing violently into the Peace Tower, and sending out a violent shower of glass, metal, and stone. The impact was loud from where they were standing. Hunter moved quickly, stopping a few metres from where Magus was embedded in the clock face. Mia swallowed hard. Magus slumped forward and slowly tumbled outward from the clock face, falling, twisting down to the concrete steps near where Gloria had been sitting earlier. The sound of the impact of his body hitting the steps was sickening. Hunter followed him down.

"Oh, no," Gloria said quietly as she watched Hunter descend rapidly, stopping near Magus. "I can't—no—I don't know how. You were that person, not me."

Mia looked at Gloria in confusion.

"What are you saying?"

Gloria looked down at the sidewalk at their feet, her eyes staring blankly as if in thought.

"You have to do this. It was just a story you told me."

She turned her gaze to the drama playing out at the foot of the Centre Block.

"Yes," she said. "Yes, you can have control."

Gloria turned to Mia. She reached out, touching Mia's face with the palm of her hand, smiling reassuringly. The anguish that had masked her face a moment ago seemed to have slipped away.

"Hunter MacKenzie is your lover?"

Mia nodded.

"Yes, I mean, he's my boyfriend, but how—"

Gloria interrupted her.

"I can see in your eyes that you love him."

Mia blinked and frowned, a thousand questions tumbling over her head. What was happening?

"I, yes, yes I do," she stammered. "He's the nicest guy I know, but we need to get away from here. I can't stop bullets like he can."

Gloria reached out, taking one of Mia's hands, and intertwining her fingers with hers. She turned her head to watch as Thomas and Hunter rose above The Hill, two people from this universe inhabited by two powerful beings from another universe, confronting each other, squaring off once more, launching attacks of white energy, then blue energy. Back and forth, circling, before firing, dodging and then shooting off a return blast. It was the same battle that had gone on for over a hundred years in another universe and was now carrying on in this one.

"Male ego," Gloria sighed, shaking her head while letting go of Mia's hand. "It always comes down to the fragile male ego, doesn't it?"

"I don't understand," Mia said, her eyes watching Gloria's face.

Suddenly a flash of Magus's blue energy shot out and enveloped Hunter, wrapping itself around his chest. A scream of anguish rippled through the air, rising in intensity as he began to fall. It was frightening to watch.

"Oh, my god," Mia gasped, grabbing Gloria's arm and pulling her away from the battle. "We have to get out of here."

Gloria resisted and pulled free.

"No," she said forcefully.

Mia turned to see Gloria reach up and pull her hair free from the broad band of multi-coloured fabric holding her dreads. They unfurled dramatically, cascading down her back, swooping out along her shoulders and around her face as if they were flexing their newfound freedom. Mia stumbled back as she saw what she thought had been a crushed woman, watched her stand straight, her neck stiff, shoulders pulled back, her eyes focused on the laughing Magus who was dropping toward the fallen Hunter.

"Thank you," Gloria said as she turned and lightly touched Mia's arm. "I came here to forget, but you've helped me to remember who we are, and right now, I must remember."

Mia continued to frown, shaking her head.

"I don't understand."

Gloria nodded and smiled in sympathy as she slowly lifted off the sidewalk, pausing to look down at Mia from above her head.

"Do your best to stay alive until I return."

And then she shot up into the sky, a barely noticeable blur streaking away from the carnage on Parliament Hill.

TWENTY-NINE

"I made you!"

THAT HURT LIKE HELL, MAGUS. Who is this?

This strangely masked youth was somehow the Mighty Titan, Magus was sure of this. It irked him to admit it, but no one else in the universe could have hit him with such force as Titan was capable of doing. Somehow, his arch-enemy had survived the assault over Scotland and, like himself, had entered the body of his parallel counterpart in this universe. But something was wrong. The initial blast of Titan's pure cosmic energy should have physically incapacitated him, as it had so many times before, a memory he despised. But this time, it hadn't. Oh, it had hurt, being knocked into the clock tower of the Parliament buildings and then falling to smash into the concrete of the steps far below. Yes, the blast from Titan had stung, and it had momentarily knocked the wind out of him. Still, as he and his oldest enemy began sparring, facing off above the seat of this country's government, Magus felt the same sense of finality, of the imminent victory he'd felt over Scotland only a few days earlier. Titan was weak, and Magus was going to kill him again.

There are no real superheroes in this universe. That kid's mask is from the Ant-Man movie, and it's just that, a movie. He's not real.

"Be quiet," Magus sneered. "My old enemy has somehow followed me to this universe."

What? That Titan guy? I thought you killed him?

"I did," Magus spat through clenched teeth.

"Who are you?" he demanded of the kid in the silly mask, playing for time as he directed energy to his hands, to the focal point of its egress. "Only one being has that kind of power, and I dispatched him without mercy!"

The two circled each other, around and around, their hands bristling with the energy of their powers. Magus noticed the boy was having a conversation with himself, or more accurately, with the super-powered being within his young body.

"Done babbling with yourself?" he asked.

He pushed a deliberately weak blast of energy at the masked figure, who lifted his hands and rebuffed the attack with a counter blast. Magus deflected it into the field below them.

"Titan?" Magus hissed as he made to circle his enemy.

"Maggots," the boy replied, matching his moves while occasionally looking over his shoulder. "Uh, was one universe not, uh, enough for you?"

Look, behind him, he's positioning himself to protect those fighter planes.

"Indeed," Magus whispered.

The Mighty Titan's greatest weakness was his foolish compulsion to protect lesser beings. He laughed. It would be the do-gooder's undoing, yet again.

"Hah, my old foe, there aren't enough universes to satisfy me. I see you've also inhabited the younger version of yourself."

He let a blast go, which was easily deflected upwards by Titan, where it dissipated like mist. It was another small release of energy, a test. Titan, in his younger self, seemed unsure, perhaps even weak. Magus gloated as energy continued to pour into his body, filling every cell, demanding release.

Kill him, Magus.

"These are not our bodies to take," Titan replied through Hunter, as the latter drove a blast of white energy towards Magus.

He deflected it with one hand. It veered into the West Block, blowing out a row of windows with a thunderous crash.

What are we waiting for? Even I can see he's weak. Finish him!

"Shut it," Magus growled under his breath, then laughed loudly. "That's rich, coming from the one who's now using his younger self to attack me."

He feigned a yawn as Titan spoke.

"You've left me no choice," his enemy muttered, pushing white energy towards Magus.

He blocked the pulse with a return blast, the two streams fizzling, crackling loudly, sparking, then vanishing.

Magus laughed.

"This one wants me. This one loves what I am and wishes to see what we can become together."

He then touched the letter on his Green Lantern costume.

"No costume, other than that silly mask? Does your younger self not want you, my dear Titan? Does he see what I've known all along, and have known in every battle with you, that you're not needed or wanted? You constantly interfere in the natural order of things, in the one fundamental law of nature, that the weak are dominated by the strong!"

God, this is why people like you always get defeated in the movies. You just won't shut up and kill your enemy!

Magus tapped the side of his head and spoke through clenched teeth.

"Patience, my dear Thomas. The mouse comes to the snake who waits."

What? What the hell does that mean?

Titan swooped around again, positioning the growing silhouettes of the approaching planes behind his body.

"Magus, this doesn't have to escalate any further. Uh, let's return to our universe and finish this there."

Titan glanced away again, no doubt looking for the military planes, which now appeared to be veering away. Magus laughed softly and seized the opportunity to consolidate the energy in his hands. He stretched out his fingers, reached for every molecule of cosmic energy, and focused it into one lethal blow. He released the gyrating, fomenting blue tendrils of power as Titan turned his attention back. It was a marvel to watch. His destructive old friend snatched his pathetic old enemy from the air, coursing around his youthful chest. Magus shivered with ecstasy as screams of anguish poured from inside the mask, filling the air around them with the cry of his defeat. Oh, how sweet it was, how marvellous to see his enemy, even in this younger form, twist in agony as he flitted down towards the field beneath them, like a leaf torn from its perch by the mighty wind that is Magus the Terrible.

Yes! Now that's what I'm talking about!

Magus laughed, circling the falling hero, shouting insults as his enemy smashed into the hard-packed grass.

"You're nothing, Titan. You've failed yet again!"

Finish him off!

"Oh, I will, I most definitely will. And this time, his death will be complete!"

The mask tore from Hunter's face on impact. Magus could see how weak this universe's Titan looked, how utterly unprepared this version of his old enemy was to stand against his power. Laughing riotously, he drew his hands together, spinning another web of molecular disrupting energy and directing it at the crumpled youth, watching the deathly blue tendrils dance across his face, crawl down under his t-shirt, slither out from his sleeves, wrap their fiery clutch around his chest for a second time. The boy screamed, his eyes bulging in horror, his back arching, his arms and legs flailing, heels and fingers digging and grabbing for release from the onslaught.

And Magus laughed. And Thomas laughed.

"I kill you yet again, my old foe," Magus bellowed as he swooped around the fallen Titan. "Can you imagine how marvellous this is for me? How appropriate that we should meet again, in another universe, and there you are, dying yet again by my hand."

He rose a metre over Titan's youthful form. He drove another mighty blast of plasma into the chest of the thrashing body, the air crackling violently, the smell of ozone rising like a tribute to the destruction he was exacting on his enemy. Titan screamed again, his body convulsing with the agony of the attack. And Magus drove another blast into his foe, the air shimmering and pulsing, electrical static playing across the grass, rivulets of energy violently stroking the green blades around Titan's writhing body.

And Titan screamed.

And Magus laughed.

And Hunter screamed.

And Thomas laughed.

But then…

"NO!"

A voice roared from behind them, so powerful and encompassing that it muted the cries of Titan. Magus spun around in the air, his hands trailing tendrils of blue energy as his power flared in anticipation, ready for an attack.

He froze.

"Glo-ri-a?"

The three syllables rolled from his lips, slow, foreign, laced with long-ago memories and reawakened fears. Thomas sputtered in his head.

That, that's Gloria? Magus, why does she look like that?

Gloria, the Gloria from the universe of Magus and the Mighty Titan, the formidable Medusa, was floating a few meters from him, the pale palms of her hands angled in attack position toward him, her body, emanating strength, crouching in the air, coiled and ready to attack. Her magnificent hair, black as the most starless night, was poised around her young and beautiful face like a living creature. But his Gloria would have been much older, like himself, if Titan hadn't killed her. No, this was this universe's Gloria. But how? No one from this universe had powers of their own.

Fear crept like a shadow into Magus's chest, squeezing it with confusion and uncertainty, as energy continued to issue from Medusa's body, like a fog, rolling in from the sea, clawing feverishly for the unsuspecting shoreline. Her power, a living, dark, twisting entity, was lashing angrily in and out and around her body, caressing her arms, then her abdomen, up and across the fabric of the blouse covering her breasts, then moving down her legs, whipping out to every point of the compass and then back, like a nest of angry snakes. Clouds slowly formed a few metres above and behind her, faint at first, like mist, then roiling and rolling, heavy with energy, angry, fierce, and threatening. Flashes of translucent golden lightning began coursing through the rapidly expanding cloud, lashing out, emitting thunderous peels as air, suddenly assaulted by the surge in energy, violently compressed and exploded. Excited oxygen molecules began to hurl themselves around, crashing into each other, creating fierce winds as the cloud grew, as jagged streams of lightening struck the damaged Peace Tower and pounded into the debris-strewn quadrangle around them, flowing and rippling across the ground, clawing up the sides of the buildings on Parliament Hill.

And Magus felt a terror like he'd never felt before.

I don't understand. She doesn't have powers like us. She's nobody.

"Yes," Magus muttered, almost inaudibly. "Gloria is nobody."

This universe's Gloria was a whimpering, cowardly nobody, worthy only of being cast aside like an unwanted thing. She was nothing. She had no power and no usefulness to Magus's universe-conquering designs. He'd dragged her powerless body around since he'd first arrived in this pitiless universe. She'd been so distraught, so overcome with emotion after he'd forced himself upon her. His Gloria wouldn't have done that. He'd had to force this Gloria to do something with the mess of her makeup from her insufferable crying and whimpering, forcing her to at least show him some respect as he allowed her to remain in his mighty presence. Even the inner voice of Thomas was done with her. This Gloria was nothing.

She was not Medusa.

"Hello, Magus," Gloria said thinly.

Her voice pierced the savagery her powers were causing to the elements as tendrils of her energy swirled vociferously around her body, like streamers of silk flapping and snapping in a summer gale.

"I'd hoped never to see your face again."

"What?" he managed to stammer, the sudden dryness of his lips entangling with the terror crushing his breath. "You've been here all along?"

This was his Gloria, his Medusa, yet she wasn't the same. She was different, confident and menacing, and Magus was uncertain of what this change meant.

"Know your place, Gloria," he said, as forceful as the fear in his mind would allow, while directing energy to his hands. "I shall slap you down like I have many times before. You were never a match for me."

How is this possible, Magus? Sure she's smart and all, but this—

"Shut it, fool."

Gloria slowly smiled, her white teeth growing as her lips spread in a way that made Magus pull away from the injured Titan. Something was off here. Something was very off.

"I don't need to hear the voice of this universe's Thomas to know he's confused, my old mentor," Gloria said, still smiling. "As are you."

What's she talking about?

"I saved you."

This isn't my Gloria. Who is this?

The smile remained large and confident, but her dazzling eyes disappeared as they narrowed. Her energy, slithering and writhing, swarmed like a million bees, filling the air around her with spears of lightning, crackling and snapping with impatience, longing for release. And Magus moved back further. He'd seen that power before, and fear, palpable and disgusting, began sucking at his bravado. He'd never really been afraid, even Titan wasn't to be feared, not really. Titan could hurt him, had hurt him, had imprisoned him many times, but he'd never worried that the do-gooder hero might destroy him. It was against the hero's code of ethics or some such nonsense. Their fight had always been a war between two beings of near equal power. They'd battled each other for almost eleven decades across countless planets and moons, from one end of the galaxy to the other, but he'd never once been afraid of death by Titan's hands. However, Medusa was another thing entirely.

"So, this is what became of you? You ran away, fled to this universe, and led me to believe Titan had killed you?"

Gloria leaned towards him, her eyes flashing flames of blueish fire.

"I got away from you!"

Magus recoiled, his mouth curling into a snarl.

"Got away from me? I made you, made you my queen. You were nothing without me."

Her power flashed, sending a volley of lightning strikes into the quadrangle beneath them as the two began to circle one another, their hands flaring with energy.

"I was young. You took advantage of my innocence and my ignorance. You gave me a life I didn't want. You made me into someone I didn't want to be!"

"Hah, make your excuses, Medusa," he shot back as the air around them continued to crackle with the building energies. "You made your choices. I never forced you to come with me that day."

"Yes, I made my choices, ones I've lived with my entire life, but no more," she hissed as the cloud of her power snapped and flashed.

"I saved you, Medusa. You'd have lived a meaningless life without me, but I saved you!"

Who is she? Can she hurt us?

"Shut up," Magus growled.

Gloria flickered and was suddenly within a hair's breadth of his face. Her hot, anger-fuelled breath burned like an out-of-control fire over his mouth, physically searing the flesh of his lips. Her blue eyes, cold and barely seen between the slits of her dark eyelids, were like flashing quasars, flooding his vision with everything he'd ever secretly feared about her.

"You didn't save me, you destroyed any chance I could have had to be someone better, someone that didn't become like you."

Her hands reached out and grabbed the thin fabric of the Green Lantern costume she'd helped him choose that very morning. Those hands were aflame with her power, burning against his skin, as she pulled him closer to her. Magus turned his face away from her wrath, tried to pull away, tried to summon every particle of energy into his hands, but a small part of his being realized it would be useless. In his peripheral vision, Magus could see the cloud of dark energy and the lightning strikes moving, twisting around them, above and below them, dancing madly across the quadrangle, a dance of revenge, something he'd hoped never to see.

"I, I command you! Release me, or I shall bring destruction upon you like nothing you've ever seen!" he screamed into her face.

Gloria's menacing smile disappeared from his view as she pushed her head alongside his.

"Not this time, Thomas," she hissed in his ear.

THIRTY

"I'm not 'posed to talk to strangers."

GLORIA ADAEGO MUSA WAS FIVE when the voice first spoke to her.

She was in kindergarten, a quiet, studious child, a wisp of a girl compared to others her age. Gloria was sitting cross-legged on the brightly coloured oval storytime carpet, her hands crossed carefully on her lap as Mrs. M'bituu read to her children. Gloria was listening carefully, but she was also glaring out the corner of her eye at Bobby Leone. He'd teased her earlier, using a branch he'd ripped from a struggling sapling in Mrs. M'bituu's outside play yard to poke at the cornrows her precious mother had lovingly and patiently braided the night before. There were eleven perfect rows, woven very close to her scalp and decorated with wooden beads that were more colourful than a rainbow after a summer rainstorm. The rows followed the shape of her small head, their braided ends flowing out from the nape of her neck, hanging low enough that she could feel them brush against her back when she turned her head this way and that. The tight weave of her hair made the broad cheeks of her face stand out so that attention was drawn to the remarkable aqueous blue of her eyes. Those eyes were the colour of the Indian Ocean, a short drive from Cape Town, where Gloria's grandmother had come from, her mother had said. Her eyes were a gift from God, because it meant she was special.

The night before might have been the first moment in her life where she truly began to understand that she was pretty and that being pretty had a sort of power over people.

"Ag shame, ever since you was a baby girl in my arms, you were pretty," her mother had said to Gloria, her deep laugh awash in love.

Her aunties had also sung praises of their niece's beauty, but that evening, as her mother teased her long, thick hair into magnificently tight rows while telling her stories of when her mother had done the same for her, the awareness of her physical self became more fully alive.

I am pretty.

She was thinking of this while wishing all manner of terrible things on Bobby when her vision was filled with a flash of brilliant white light followed by a sharp pain as if someone had stomped on her foot. She wanted to scream out in protest, but Mrs. M'bituu wouldn't like that, so Gloria clamped her teeth and pressed her lips tightly together. Then, in that same moment, as the burst of light briefly robbed her of her sight, she felt in an odd sort of way that she was no longer Gloria, but then she also thought that she was still Gloria. It was a curious feeling that seemed to hurt, like when Bobby yanked on her braids. She wanted to complain loudly, but she didn't. It was story time, and Mrs. M'bituu demanded everyone's rapt attention, and because everyone loved Mrs. M'bituu and loved it when her kind, round face was beaming with happiness, they obeyed her. As her vision slowly returned, Gloria realized no one else had been affected by the bright light. Except for Bobby, every child's eyes were focused on their teacher. He was staring at Gloria, his mouth hanging open like William's when he fell asleep on the couch. She didn't like William, her mother's boyfriend. He looked at her in ways that made her uncomfortable, and she wished he would leave.

Then the voice spoke, sounding very much like her mother's. It was as audible, clear, and present as her teacher's voice, a few metres away.

Hello, it said, sounding more like a question than a greeting.

The voice then laughed, like someone who'd dropped a glass and was relieved it hadn't broken when it hit the floor. Then it spoke again.

How old are you?

Gloria looked around to see who was speaking, but only Mrs. M'bituu was talking. Then she noticed the two flat, round objects in each of her hands. They were almost too warm to hold and had strange pictures, like drawings the children in her kindergarten class made during arts and crafts. She was sure the objects hadn't been in her hands when her mother dropped her off that morning. She caught Bobby Leone also staring at the things, his eyes as large as the saucers her mother would put under the teacups Gloria wasn't allowed to touch when her aunties visited. She didn't know what the objects were or where they had come from, but she was very sure she didn't want Bobby looking at them, so she slipped them into the pockets of the many-coloured dress her mother had sewn for her just for kindergarten. She then very quietly whispered her age. The voice laughed and laughed, only this time it sounded like one of her aunties when they told a funny story that might have been meant for adult ears only. Gloria worried that Mrs. M'bittuu would scold her for making such noise during story time, but no one else heard the voice, not even Bobby.

My name's Gloria, too, the voice then said. *But why don't you call me by our middle name, Adaego?*

Gloria drew her breath in sharply. The voice had the same name as her. She nodded slowly, pulling her mouth shut tight while looking around the room. Her heart was pounding loudly behind the cloth of her pretty dress. A voice inside her head had the same name as hers. This was not normal, her mother might not be happy if she knew this was happening. Gloria might not be very old and might not be a big kid yet, but she knew people shouldn't have voices in their heads.

May I stay for a while inside your body? I won't cause you any trouble, and you can ask me to leave anytime.

"Who are you? I'm not 'posed to talk to strangers," Gloria whispered behind her hand so Mrs. M'bituu would not hear her.

The voice laughed a happy laugh as her mother sometimes did.

I am you, Gloria, but I am much older, like your mama. Don't be afraid, I am here to make your life a happy life.

The voice grew silent then, and a few moments later, when it came time for the children to play outside, Gloria found a quiet corner in Mrs. M'bituu's big backyard and pulled the objects out to look at them.

Then the voice spoke.

Those discs brought me here to you, Gloria.

Gloria was surprised by the voice and jumped, her skin crawling like when a spider would suddenly drop down from the ceiling in front of her. The woman's voice sounded so close, as if inside her head.

"Why?" she asked, looking around to make sure none of the other children were curious about the objects in her hands.

The voice laughed again, only this time it was a sweet-sounding laugh, like when her aunties would hug her and pinch her cheeks between their fingers and thumbs.

They brought me to you so we could live together in your body, and I could help you and our mama and our aunties have lots of happiness and good things in our lives. You want that, don't you, Gloria?

She slid the discs back into the pockets of her dress and looked over at Bobby, who was looking at her with an extraordinary look on his face.

"Will it hurt? Like it did when you first spoke to me?"

No, the voice said reassuringly, *I won't let anyone or anything hurt you or our mama, ever.*

"Okay," Gloria said after a moment, "but I don't think I should tell mama, she might not like having an older lady living inside me."

The voice laughed its singsong sound of joy again.

Thank you, Gloria. Please, call me by our middle name, Adaego.

Gloria nodded happily, her eyes growing with the excitement and wonder of what was happening. Oh, how excited she was. She'd have a friend who lived inside her. She didn't have many friends, especially in the neighbourhood where she lived with her mother. A friend who lived inside her might be fun.

Everything will be okay now, Adaego said.

This time.

This time everything would be different because Adaego knew where the pitfalls and the dangers were hidden, where every evil thing that had shaped her into the person she'd come to despise was waiting for her, like snakes hiding in dark holes in the ground.

From then on, Adaego and Gloria became like sisters to each other, which was exciting, as neither of them had ever had a sister. Adaego, the older Gloria, became the younger Gloria's friend and protector. She told her many things about the world around her, how all creatures were important, from the weakest to the strongest. She said that even the smallest bird deserved a good life, and so did little Gloria. But most importantly, she said, she must protect herself and her mother from people who meant to harm them, including Bobby Leone.

Without telling her mother, the little girl walked the two kilometres to Bobby's house that Saturday and explained to his mother what he'd done to her hair and how it had offended her. Typically Gloria wouldn't have had the courage to undertake such a quest so far from home, much less stand up for herself. Still, the voice encouraged her, telling her that defending herself by demanding the respect she deserved was the best way to stop a bully like Bobby.

You matter, Adaego told her. *Your life matters, and don't ever let anyone tell you differently.*

She could tell Bobby's mother was embarrassed, and Gloria could only imagine what she had said or done to Bobby afterward because he never bothered her again.

Adaego also taught her how to stop her mother's boyfriend, William, from doing unthinkable things to her that would have continued for several years and would have left her damaged and broken and distrustful of men, her mother, and of the many other people she'd meet, who were meant to help her become the best person she could be. Gloria hadn't understood the terrible things William wanted to do to her that night when her mother was away at her job, but Adaego had coached her on kicking him between the legs with her heavy dance shoes when he tried to hold her down on the couch. Adaego helped her be stronger than she was, so when she kicked William between the legs, he fell off the sofa, rolling onto the old coffee table her grandmother had given her mother, and breaking it into pieces. He curled up on the floor and cried and whimpered like a puppy, Gloria thought. Her inner voice also helped her to sound much older than she was when talking to the lovely lady on the telephone.

"9-1-1," the woman had said. "What is the nature of the emergency?"

Gloria told the friendly police officers about the photographs hidden on William's laptop, showing terrible things being done to little children. Gloria had never seen the horrible images, but somehow Adaego knew precisely where they were, so little Gloria told the friendly police people where to look. The police handcuffed and led the man away, who would have done irreparable harm to Gloria and to the heart and mind of the one person who loved her the most in all the world, her mother. Gloria's mother wept and promised no man would ever hurt her baby girl again.

This time.

This time there was no shame for her or her mother and no wrongful sense of guilt for what was and now would never be.

When Gloria turned twelve, she had grown taller than most of her peers, and her body was hinting at the beautiful woman she'd become, a neighbourhood boy, older than her by six years, attempted to sexually assault her. Adaego, who always seemed to know when bad things were going to happen, had prepared her for this moment. The attempted assault was caught on a video camera, hidden in the shed where he'd lure her with the promise of a bicycle pump to fill her flat tire, the video becoming evidence in his conviction. It also showed a young black girl, who had never studied Tae-Kwon Do a day of her short life, expertly landing a deadly back kick, defending her body and self-respect from a would-be assailant.

This time.

This time her sense of self-worth wasn't confused by a young man's twisted need to have control over another human being.

Adaego helped her realize that being pretty didn't mean being silly or a victim. No, it meant accepting who she was as a person. The colour of her skin, her gender, or her crown of intense black hair and striking blue eyes, which often drew unwanted attention and comments, didn't define her value or importance. Adaego told her that she was always a person first, one who could demand respect for her intellect and her accomplishments. You are, Adaego had said many times, a unique and good person, and you will do amazing and good things.

This time.

This time she saw a future that had potential, that wasn't defined by other people's perceptions of her or her skin colour or her gender, but by her perception of herself.

However, it wasn't just Gloria that found help and protection from the events and people who would have hurt her. Adaego began to experience again the joys of being a child, of just being a young girl, of having a mother's love and support, and of what it was like to have a sister to share life with. Even though one person was visible and the other was not, the relationship that grew was one of sisterhood. They laughed together and shared the joys of living, and together they became one young woman consisting of two women, full of imagination and possibilities. On the one hand, Adaego spared Gloria and her beloved mother the trauma of abuse at the hands of those who would have used and harmed them, while on the other, she began to build new memories, new experiences, ones where she was loved, where who she was, a black Canadian girl of South African and Nigerian decent who'd always felt like she didn't belong, finally belonged. Adaego felt like she'd found a home with a mother who hadn't been traumatized by the abuse of the man who'd abused her little girl.

Perhaps even more important was that she'd begun to forgive herself for the terrible person she'd allowed herself to become in the other universe. It wasn't an easy thing, forgiving, for many beings had suffered under her hands, especially as she'd sought the approval and love of Magus and had become even more ruthless, mimicking his cruelty. In time, as her life experiences were replaced with those found in the innocence of this universe's Gloria, she thought less of what she'd been and more of what she was now becoming. However, her enormous power was always present, just at the edge of her new existence, and she felt she needed to tell her host of it.

As this universe's Gloria grew into a confident and intentional teenager, Adaego did something to their shared brain. Sometimes, late in the evening, she'd help her younger self 'see' a universe where beings with immense power ruled the elements. They wore fantastical costumes of many colours emblazoned with emblems meant to inspire or frighten. They could do amazing things, like defy the effects of gravity and fly without experiencing inertia, or controlling matter, manipulating energy to do whatever they desired. Most of these beings were kind and used their powers to help others and to bring justice to all beings, while others were cruel and selfish and took whatever they wanted from whomever they wanted. Many of the stories were sad, filled with Adaego's regrets. She'd told her that some of these beings thought they could rule other sentient beings, but that wasn't good. She said that all beings, whether human or otherwise, should be free to decide their destinies. Adaego explained to her that she had been one of those beings who abused their powers and that this immense power now rested within Gloria.

"No," Gloria had protested at the confession. "You aren't one of those people. You're my friend, my sister."

Yes, she had responded gently, *I am your sister and your friend, but I was not always a good person. I was called Medusa, and I did many terrible things.*

One day, Gloria asked to see those powers, not the evil powers, but the good ones. At first, Adaego said no, but after Gloria had pleaded with her, she agreed and showed her some of the amazing things she could do. They looked through solid objects and listened to conversations hundreds of metres away. One Saturday morning, she instructed Gloria to go behind the small shed in her mother's backyard. When they were sure no one was watching, Adaego asked permission to make her fly.

"Fly, like the super beings you've told me about?" Gloria asked.

Adaego laughed.

Yes, fly like the ones I told you about.

So, they flew, lifting off from the ground behind the shed, shooting straight into the morning sky, before veering suddenly off toward the North Shore Mountains that flanked the City of Vancouver.

It was exhilarating for Gloria and freeing for Adaego. So much of her time in this universe had been focused on not using the full extent of her power, but this, flying, was so peaceful and hinted at a life she could have had, had she not been 'rescued' by Magus. She could have had a life of using her power for something other than hurting people. It made her feel sad about what could have been, but her sadness was quickly replaced with joy as Gloria revelled in the pleasure of Adaego's powers.

So, they laughed together, the young Gloria spotting her shadow far below, racing them along treetops and open rocky areas. They flew several times over the following weeks, but one day, Gloria asked her to show her what else she could do.

No, forgive me, Adaego suddenly said. *We mustn't do this anymore. Power creates its own reality, and to have this much power in a world where we would be the only ones with it, is too dangerous.*

She said it was wise to keep their powers hidden. It would be too tempting to cheat and use them to get what they wanted, so they never flew again, or looked through walls, or listened to other people's private conversations.

Gloria didn't fully understand Adaego's reasons for not wanting to use these fantastic abilities. After all, they could accomplish so many good things in the world. Still, Adaego explained that in a universe with only one super-powered being, people might view her as a god, or rulers of the world might compete for her allegiance and perhaps cause wars over her. No, she was firm about her decision, and after a while, Gloria quit asking, and the stories ended.

It was better that way.

Besides, Gloria realized that using these unique abilities made the sister inside her sad. However, Adaego allowed her power to manipulate Gloria's cells, making them more rigid and stronger, so she never broke a bone, never twisted an ankle, and never cut a finger. Her friends noticed this and called her lucky, and perhaps she was, in a way.

After a while, Adaego directed her power to help her forget who she had been as Medusa and to integrate the two persons, so they became more like one person. And so, after a few years, the two beings living in one body became an everyday experience for both of them. The voice in her head became the reassuring and abiding voice of her conscience. Everyone had a conscience. Everyone had that inner voice of reason, right? By the time Gloria graduated from high school, Adaego was Gloria, and she was Adaego. The two had become one person, and anything that might have happened outside of the accepted laws of physics and the human experience was relegated to her clever imagination, fantastical things she wished might have occurred but hadn't, not really.

When she met the handsome and confident Thomas Stewart at the University of Toronto, Gloria's heart pounded with excitement and surprise and with a bit of confusion. He was tall and intriguing, an American from Philadelphia with a passion for design and business, just like her, but she felt like she knew him already. Her mind grasped at fleeting and strange memories, good and bad, some that she was sure weren't entirely her own, but she'd forgotten why that might be. He was handsome, clever, confident and ambitious in a way that made people want to be near him. He was going to make things happen, he'd say. He was going to be someone you needed to know, and Gloria fell in love, but her conscience, that childhood voice, her inside sister, was hesitant. That voice seemed to say that it was possible that he might be selfish and narcissistic, that he might hurt her and use her strength and confidence to his advantage. It seemed as if her conscience was urging her to run away.

But Gloria also felt pity for him. As peculiar as the thoughts were, she wondered if she could change the course of his life as she'd changed hers, as she'd remade the tragedies of one existence into the possibilities of another. In her thoughts, she had this vague notion of one life where she'd been selfish, ruthless, and blind with anger over what had been and what could have been, and yet she'd changed all that. Hadn't she? Yes, she'd turned her life away from hatred and embraced the rewards of being a loving person. She'd also been able to rewrite many of the bad moments that had shaped the other Gloria, the one that became the feared Medusa. Or, had that just been a strange dream she'd had when she was younger? She couldn't quite remember.

Thomas could be abrupt, but he never threatened her with violence, unlike … unlike whom? Someone she thought she might remember from somewhere else a long time ago, perhaps another life? In time, Gloria and Thomas became a couple and then lovers and then business partners, and Gloria revelled in the excitement of a first great love. Something deep within her, in what might have been memories, seemed to carefully reimagine an old love, one that hadn't really been love at all.

This time, even though this time seemed like the first and only time to Gloria, love too would be different. It would be equal, mutual, something she and Thomas created together. And it was, for a time.

Until that moment in the MajiGrafx meeting room, the morning sun streaming through the windows, bathing the room with hope and potential for the undiscovered future. It had been an exciting week for the new startup. There had been a large Ontario government contract, the prospect of new hires, growth, and plans for the future. But then Thomas was suddenly not Thomas. He was instantly angry, vengeful, a disturbing image of another, ghost-like memory of someone she wasn't sure how she'd known but perhaps had. A Thomas who was quick to exact his form of justice upon those he despised. This wasn't the Thomas she loved, yet it was, and Gloria was confused, uncertain of what was happening and what was real.

It was all so confusing and all so horrifying.

Medusa.

She'd forgotten who she'd once been. She'd commanded her power to hide who she had been from her mind, and the days and experiences of this universe's Gloria had become her only reality. They had become one person, one voice, one conscience. Life was good. Life was defined by love, not hate. Now, Adaego had to remember. Now, she had to believe again. Now, she had to find the person she'd buried from that other universe. She had to turn her mind again upon the frightening power she had used to help her forget who she had once been. She'd accomplished what she'd planned those many years ago. She'd rewritten her story and escaped Magus, but now she had to embrace who she had been, who she had always been.

"You have beautiful eyes," the young Asian girl had said.

The exact words Magus had spoken to her so long ago triggered her memories, striking her like a hard slap to the face. Her power rose to her consciousness and pulled the veil back from her memories. Adaego knew deep within herself that this universe's Thomas Stewart had joined with the mania of that universe's Thomas Stewart, the hateful, vengeful Magus. As horrifying as the thought was, this universe's Thomas Stewart, the man she'd dared to love as Gloria, had chosen to join Magus. He'd willingly participated in the destruction and murders of the previous two days. She knew more than anyone that one Thomas couldn't be the other Thomas without consent, without a tacit agreement, and without full complicity in the merging of the two beings' knowledge and abilities. As this realization stung her consciousness and heart, she was faced with the awakened memories of the buried part of her past, one she'd chosen to forget. Magus had been a horrible, depraved and ruthless being. Yet, Medusa had been a terrible and frightening being as well.

THIRTY-ONE

"I wish to forget who I am and all
I have done."

GLORIA ADAEGO MUSA, CALLED MEDUSA by Magus because of the writhing, shadowy cloud of energy that poured from her ebony skin when she willed her powers to act, had left behind the dehumanizing control Magus had brutally exercised over her. Medusa was far more powerful than Magus, but he was charming, clever in twisting reasoning, a bully, and an abuser.

They met when she'd just turned twenty-two, six years after a blinding light had struck her down, physically paralyzing her and keeping her hospitalized for months until her strange and powerful abilities awakened her. Magus was in his late fifties, though he didn't look much older than thirty and was already known for his ruthless reprisals against anyone who opposed him. Gloria had been an addict, abusing any substance that would make her forget the horrors of her life, when the blast of cosmic energy infused every cell of her body, pushing out the poisons as she lay in a hospital bed, making her body whole, but not her mind and heart. It wasn't what she wanted. Instead, she tried to forget all that had been done to her, and she lashed out, quickly becoming a wanted criminal for the brazen robberies she committed. If she was pretty, as so many men had told her, then she needed pretty things, and nothing and no one could stop her. Invincible, with a penchant for violence fuelled by her anger, she built an empire of one, creating a fortress of sorts in the coastal mountains of the Lower Mainland of British Columbia. The cosmic energy that had infused her body wouldn't allow her to get drunk, and she couldn't find repose from any mind-altering drug. Consequently, the only way to numb the anger she felt for the many ways the black girl with the fantastic blue eyes had been abused was to take whatever she wanted.

The day Magus descended from the sky to her mountainside fortress, Gloria was sure she'd never seen anything so beautiful in all her life. Magus knew how to make an entrance, and his dazzling and brutalist costume, a mosaic of angular surfaces, shades of metallic blue and blood red, with chrome titanium spikes descending incrementally in size down to his elbows from the curves of his shoulders, each one reflecting the fire of the morning sun, immediately drew her awe.

She knew of him, of course. All the world had heard of the villainy of Magus the Terrible and of his furious battles with the equally famous Mighty Titan. Still, when he settled gently to the ground a metre from her, his black cape swaying in the breeze of the mountain air, and smiled reassuringly as he held out one gloved hand, Gloria suddenly saw that her life might finally have some purpose.

"You have beautiful eyes," were the first words he'd ever spoken to her, his voice deep, confident, and calm.

She'd heard those words before, from every scumbag and wannabe pimp that had seen her as a moneymaking opportunity before The Second Event had changed her. Yet the way Magus said it that day as his entire face smiled at her, she felt it was meant as a sign of respect, as a recognition of whom he knew she was beneath all the anger that burned like an unrelenting fire.

"You have beautiful eyes" became an emotional anchor in her mind that kept her bound to Magus over the decades.

That day on the mountain side, she reached out and took his hand, and he promised to take care of her, to guide her, and to help her become all that she could be. He said she was beautiful and should have whatever she wished. He said she was powerful beyond anything in the universe and should take whatever she wanted. Nothing could stop her, he assured her, and she should rule the galaxy with him.

What began as a relationship marked by sexual excitement and the thrill of a partner who understood her power, who was also a mentor in discovering the extent of those powers, slowly transformed into one of master and servant, and lover and abuser. The first time she defied him, early on in their relationship, his retribution was swift and vicious. He hit her so hard and unexpectedly with a blast of energy that she was thrown violently to the ground, gasping for air. He then leapt onto her chest as she lay on the ground and pummelled her head and shoulders with his power-hardened fists, berating her, daring her to defy him again.

"Go ahead," he challenged as he struck her. "Go ahead and defy me. Leave if you want, but I'm the only one who loves you. I'm the only one who takes care of you!"

That first attack made her realize that his love came with a price, not an unfamiliar understanding. Love had always come at a cost. Every man that had ever abused her and every woman that had ever despised her for her beauty had proven that to her. However, this time she felt the price for his love wasn't too high, and she let Magus groom her to feel and need his anger, to find her self-worth in his disdain for anything other than himself. And she embraced it because, in a way, it was the only love she'd ever known as a young adult, and even more importantly, this was the first time in her life that she'd felt secure. As a trade-off for her allegiance, he guided her into the incredible potential of the powers she bore within her body. He loved her, or so she'd thought, and she became enamoured with his arrogance, enthralled by his blood lust, and unable to flee his control, even though she could have crushed him as easily he destroyed his enemies.

If she questioned his decisions concerning her life, he'd threaten her, berate her, and then apologize when he'd seen she'd been pushed too far, but then taunt her for being weak and not using her formidable power against him. Of course, he knew Gloria wouldn't turn on him, and he'd beat her for this sign of weakness. She was weak, useless, he would tell her, and then he'd hit her again, demanding her allegiance, telling her she was nothing without him. She'd always be nothing without the benevolent generosity of Magus. Then he'd bring her a fabulous gift, stolen no doubt, and shower her with praise and declarations of his love for her and adoration of her power. Yes, she could have easily destroyed him. It would have been such a simple act, so great was the power within her, and she'd be free of his cruelty, but then who would love her? Who would ever love Medusa? She'd become Magus's lieutenant, his destroyer, and she'd done much evil in his name. Who could ever see past what she'd become and what she'd done?

Her life caught in the mania of Magus went on, decade after decade, but it was far better than she'd known before, she'd tell herself. She'd resigned herself to live in this broken and destructive relationship until the discovery of the discs.

The existence of the discs was just a rumour, passed around among starship freighter crews and space pirates like a thousand other tales. They were spoken about in cantinas, brothels, and pubs across the galaxy as the ultimate prize to be found, taken, or stolen. Known only as the discs, in Earth English, they were the source of an unimaginable power that could make the one who possessed them invincible and unstoppable. To most, they were just another ancient myth, no different from the countless stories of buried treasure containing fabulous wealth told across a dozen other solar systems. However, for Magus, the tale became an obsession.

He was pillaging precious metals from a mining settlement on a sparsely populated moon in the outer asteroid belt of the B'rinsaf'rius star system when he heard something new about the myth, something more than the tale had already provided. It caught his attention. He was told something that had never been told before, that the discs had a real name. In English, they were called Black Energy. Magus was drawn to ancient artifacts. They were the fodder of stories of glorious times gone by, tales of brutal rulers and galactic conquerors, all of which he envisioned himself to be. The devices, the Black Energy, the miners of the moon had told him, were last seen by a compatriot of theirs more than a half-century earlier, who described them as blacker than the blackest night and holding unimaginable power that would surely make the possessor the most significant being in the universe. They rewrote the laws of science and reality, they said, destroying all matter, a kind of ultimate death one would only reserve for one's worst enemy.

Perhaps they'd only hoped to bargain with him, to retain the meagre profits of their hard-fought livelihood from being stolen. Maybe the story was simply an embellishment upon an already much-embellished fable, but Magus believed them. And when Magus believed something, it was true, even if it wasn't. Soon, he and Medusa were crisscrossing the known galaxy, following the rumours, pursuing the slightest thread of the story, no matter how tenuous. The Black Energy became the one thing Magus wanted above all other things, for the simple reason that he believed it would make him gloriously powerful and enable him to finally destroy the Mighty Titan.

At first, Medusa refused to join him in his quest. She had little desire to strengthen Magus's megalomania further. He was increasingly out of control, often killing wantonly, and destroying without reason, and Medusa was sickened by it all. His response to her refusal was swift and viciously brutal, even by his standards. He attacked her with such ferocity and violence that she fled, hiding out in the furthest corner of the Tzagr'in Empire, hoping to wait it out until his anger had cooled. However, she soon heard that Magus went on a week-long rampage, destroying star freighters, razing mining colonies, and killing thousands of innocent beings. She couldn't bear the thought of so much suffering because of her, so she returned to him, repentant, begging his forgiveness. He laughed and said he knew she'd come crawling back to him.

It was a touch of sweet irony then that it was she who found the location of three of the devices. They had been carefully guarded by a secretive sect of scientist priests on the ocean planet of Rathmus II. Hidden deep below the planet's surface in a temple hewn from stone, its defences were no match for Medusa's power once she'd discovered it. She tore through the Rathmusian's inadequate and antiquated defences and ancient laser weapons, dispersing poorly prepared guards, pushing deep into the edifice until she arrived at a massive and dimly lit chamber with a single ornate stone pedestal the size of a small tree at its centre. On top of this was a large block of stone, upon which sat a small ornate chest. The dozen or so priests guarding it fled as her energy whipped out and around her, lashing out at any creature that didn't move away from her advance. She was slightly disappointed when she pried open the chest and found three smaller and very plain boxes constructed of what appeared to be a woven blend of platinum and carbon. Each box contained two palm-sized hexagonal discs, covered on both sides with hieroglyphs. She'd have brought the entire ancient temple down around the priests to obtain even just one of the objects, hoping, perhaps foolishly, to attain the always elusive favour of Magus. However, there was something unusual about the demeanour of the priests floating several metres away from her, watching her with their large eyes. She could have easily disintegrated their aquatic bodies and the entire temple the objects had been kept in for a thousand of their planet's years. However, there was no malice in these creatures, no sense that they believed they hid the most destructive force in the universe.

She removed the discs from one of the boxes, turning them over in her hands, sensing a warmth that wasn't natural, like they were somehow generating energy. There was something about these objects other than them being an ultimate weapon. She gestured to one of the priests and demanded to know what the devices were. However, the creature could do nothing but beg for its life, its scales flashing in hues of red and blue, until another of the priests, a large female of the species, gently touched its companion's translucent dorsal fin. She propelled herself over to Medusa and levelled large circular eyes at her. In a broken variation of Earth English, its gills quivering slightly, she spoke, the vibrations of her words rippling through the water to Medusa.

"We know who you are, Medusa, lieutenant of Magus. What do you want with these?"

Medusa lifted the box in one hand while pointing to the other two boxes, allowing her energy to swarm around her to frighten the creature.

"Are these a weapon?"

"Not a weapon, but they are very dangerous."

"What are they then?" Medusa demanded, the dark cloud of her energy flashing impatiently around her body.

The two discs in her hand began to glow and emit significant heat. The priest gestured to the discs.

"It is not a weapon. It is a transportation device."

"And you keep a mere transportation device hidden many leagues under your planet?"

"We are its protectors, yes."

Medusa sighed in the protective bubble of her energy.

"I chose not to kill you and your fellow priests, but do not give me a reason to do so now. What do these little pieces of metal do?"

The Rathmusian priest's eyes trembled like jelly in a bowl, but then she gestured to hieroglyphs around the base of the pedestal. Medusa smiled. Magus would have simply killed the creatures and taken the devices. He had no patience for knowledge, but Medusa understood the power of information. The creature began explaining the images, telling a far different story than the myth of a weapon of terrible destruction.

Indeed, the carved glyphs told the tale of an ancient race that had created the technology to communicate between parallel universes. Another grouping of images showed a sun's energy drawn into an oversized, stylized disc that a being was holding in its hands above its head. Other glyphs depicted the same being slowly fading, turning into a cloud of energy, and then superimposing onto another being on another world. The discs were a teleportation device requiring gigawatts, perhaps terawatts, of power to activate its internal hardware and the actual transition.

"These are used to travel between parallel universes?" Medusa asked.

Yes, the priest explained, the being was transported between universes and, as the images showed, the being returned after a time.

She turned the discs over in her hands.

"These will transport the whole of a person between universes?"

The priest shook its large head in an approximation of a no.

"The process is a convergence of mind and soul. It is not meant for the body."

"How does this work? They are so small."

The priest explained. The devices once had companion machinery, which connected them to the plasma of a star to produce the required amount of energy to activate them. Once initialized, the mechanism imprinted the complete neurological identity of one being from this universe down to the quantum level onto both discs. One disc sought out and connected to a parallel universe, linking the user to the corresponding being's DNA. There were many universes so the interaction might be with many different versions of the being. It was an uninvited connection, coming solely and unannounced from this universe, and the originator was encouraged to break the link if the being didn't want it. One disc remained with the originator's body as an anchor to this universe for the neurological identity to return to, while the other acted as a transporter to the different universe, merging them into one being, one mind, and one energy. This meant both beings could occupy the same space and exchange thoughts, knowledge, and skills.

Medusa interrupted the scientist.

"You say these require vast amounts of energy to activate. Energy always produces heat, how can such a small device survive such heat?"

The creature's eyes narrowed as it searched for the words, its scaly sides flashing purple and pink hues. It finally answered.

"They are made of materials that exist simultaneously in the visible universe and within the quantum universe. What sits in your hands is but the visible portion of the device. However, the machinery created to power them has long been lost to time. They are useless without the required energy to activate them."

Medusa nodded, she knew full well that much of the universe was not visible or even perceived by the most delicate sensors many of the galaxy's many civilizations had developed. She also knew that her formidable power would be sufficient to activate the devices.

"What's the point of only the mind going to this other universe?" Medusa asked.

"Oh, not just one, but one of many parallel universes. The point is to learn, to experience the life of the other, it is a convergence of thought, experience, and knowledge. Each universe may be similar, but they are different in many ways."

Medusa lifted the disc and tried to peer into it with her enhanced vision abilities, but the device was inscrutable, dense in a way she had never seen. Suddenly, a thought occurred to her.

"The body stays in this universe?" she asked.

"Yes, it is not meant for the body," the priest responded. "This is very dangerous. Please do not take it."

She ignored the plea.

"So, who has control in the other universe? The one who travels, or the other being?"

The priest made an approximation of a shrug.

"It has not been done in over one hundred centuries, but the stories depicted here," she said, gesturing to the dais, "and sacred writings from the Founders suggest the connections were varied. Sometimes the one from this universe controls the being, while at other times the being in another universe has full control, and at other times it is a sharing of control."

"Would my powers come with me to the other universe?"

"Other universes," the priest corrected.

Medusa's energy flared around her hands.

"Do not anger me, priest. Do my powers come with me?"

The priest shrugged.

"I can only assume your powers would, as tI assume hey are centred in your mind. But control and using your power is not the purpose, learning of the other is."

The priest drifted around the pedestal to other glyphs that detailed centuries of a rich exchange of culture, music, literature, and scientific discovery with parallel beings in parallel universes. Then, the images explained, the ancient civilization had begun to war among itself and scientific interest in the other universes was lost, and the devices, yes, there were many others, were sequestered away in secret locations throughout the galaxy as a way to keep the evil influences of this universe from spreading to the others. Then, like the civilization that created them, they became myths, their proper use forgotten in the tomes of history, except by the few who guarded them.

Medusa lowered her head, her eyes focusing on the device in her hand. The discs, she realized, weren't the instruments of death Magus had hoped for. The machines were something else entirely, something completely unexpected. They were a way for her to alter her miserable existence in this universe. The device was her way out, her route of escape from under the crushing control of the man who claimed to love her but whom she knew only saw her as a weapon to fulfill his increasingly mad ambitions. The discs and what they could do were a way for her to break the emotional and psychological dependence upon the one person who'd shown her any genuine concern in this universe but didn't do so out of compassion. No, Magus only truly loved one person, himself.

"How long can a mind stay in the other universe?" she asked.

"Many sun cycles, ten, maybe more," the priest said. "Too many, you forget you."

Ten solar years was disappointing, but at least it was something.

"How many times could a being return?"

The priest made another approximation of a shrug.

"It has not been done fly any who are alive today and could tell us. History says two, maybe three times, but there are stories of the

Founders going mad. It is very difficult to blend minds together, to coexist for many periods of time, but your unnatural abilities make you different. I do not know the answer."

Medusa's thoughts were drifting, her mind imagining the possibilities, sensing the possibility of hope that lay within her hands. She'd only need the one set of discs, one to carry her away, and the other to remain with her carefully hidden body. As she turned to leave with the case, the scientist priest called after her.

"I can sense that you wish to use the device. You are very powerful. You may be able to activate the device, but if you take and use, have respect for the other you. They may not welcome your presence."

Medusa smiled. She was fairly sure the other Gloria would welcome her, especially if her life had been anything like hers in this universe.

"Hide your body somewhere safe," she heard the priest say. "Somewhere you would wish to return to."

Yes, she thought, that would be the challenge. If she was to flee Magus, he'd come looking for her, and if he found her body without her mind in it, who knew what damage he could inflict.

Then, the Rathmusian priest said something that made her stop.

"I must warn you, if you hold onto the discs together while using your power to initiate the transferring, your entire being will leave. You will be lost to this universe."

"What did you say?" she demanded, spinning around and flashing instantly to within a metre of the creature.

The priest flinched back, her gills and fins rippling as the skin along her sides passed through a spectrum of vibrant colours.

"I can send my entire body to this universe?" she said.

"Yes, yes. It is not advised."

"Why?" Medusa demanded.

The priest quickly propelled itself to the far side of the podium and pointed to a specific set of hieroglyphs, depicting a sad-faced being with two shining discs, one in each hand. The priest's fluted fins rapidly gestured, as it described what they conveyed.

"The discs can be used to send your entire being to the other universe, every molecule, every tiny particle of your being, and you will merge with the other being, body and mind, sharing the same space. The two beings become one complete being. This is not advised. It is impossible to return, and you will experience the forgetting of you."

"No one has ever returned?"

"It is not possible once you embark."

"How do you know this, if no one has ever come back to tell their story?" Medusa asked.

The fish creature blinked rapidly.

"It is simple. The mechanism required to create and maintain the connection between universes comes from one, not both."

It shaped its pectoral fins into a circle.

"The discs are complete within each other. One remains to ensure the return. Take both and you will not return. You will be trapped."

"What happens if I do this and I am trapped, as you say?" Medusa asked.

The priest lifted its fins, bringing them together.

"Two minds and two bodies in one space is too much for one. You forget you, but you are different, you are not like most beings. For you, I do not know."

Medusa glanced down at the box she was holding. Her hands were trembling, and her mind was flooding with an unfamiliar sensation. Hope, hope for a different life, a different future because surely the life she was living now would only end in her violent death one day, whether by the hand of the League or that of Magus.

The scientist made a clicking sound to get her attention. It was pointing to another set of glyphs depicting a carving of two beings, one holding two discs in one hand, while grasping for the disc from the hand of the other being.

"If you take two and travel to that universe, and regret doing so, and take the disc of a fellow traveller to return, you will disperse."

"Disperse?"

The creature struggled to find words but finally spoke.

"If you are with another being from this universe in one of the parallel universes, and you take by force that being's disc in order to return, it is for their body, not yours. You will have no body to connect to here. You will disperse into nothing for there is nothing waiting for you. You will disperse. Understand?"

Medusa tilted her head at the creature.

"If no one has ever returned, how do you know this to be true?"

The creature narrowed its eyes, seemingly exasperated by Medusa's question.

"Such an outcome is determined by the science of the device. Your genetic being is encoded into the devices. If you take another's device to return, the automated process within the stolen device will return your mind and soul, but they will return to nothing. That being's device is encoded with their genetic identity. The automated feature of the device will return the consciousness to this universe, but if the disc does not contain your genetic code, you will return to nothing."

"That doesn't seem like a very safe feature" she responded.

The creature nodded.

"It is how they are made, they are designed to encode to one being."

Medusa nodded slowly. If she did this, there was no coming back. In her hands lay the possibility of escape from who she was and what she'd become. She pulled away from the priest but paused as her eyes cast across the dozen or so wounded and bleeding creatures huddling together in the brine of their sacred temple. She'd caused much grief to these peaceful beings.

She turned back to the priests and suddenly became aware of a familiar feeling within her, sadness. It was a dark companion that had been quietly and relentlessly haunting her for years. She had everything she could want and could take anything she wanted, yet being able to do so had become more and more distasteful to her. These aquatic beings stared back at her, perhaps anticipating another assault. Their deaths, perhaps? Medusa, judge, jury and executioner, had chosen to not kill these beings, yet she'd had no right to hurt them, to begin with. For the first time since arriving in this sacred place, Medusa saw and felt the fear of her in their eyes and bodies, and realized she had been aware of this feeling for some time as she had carried out Magus's bidding. It filled her with revulsion for who she was, and right then, she knew Medusa had to end.

She lowered her head, her voice cracking as she spoke, like it had when she was a child and knew she had disappointed her mother.

"I'm sorry for the pain I've caused you."

She stretched out her hands, sending waves of her energy coursing through the brine and into the wounded, manipulating molecules, causing damaged cells and tissue to be restored.

As the priests chattered excitedly among themselves and examined their healed bodies, bulbous eyes turned to her, and Medusa felt something foreign to her experience, forgiveness. She'd never, ever apologized to any being in all her years as Magus's lieutenant, and neither had she ever repaired any of the damage she'd caused. In a moment of clarity, she saw the chain of abuse that tied the events of her life together. She'd been abused as a child, abused as a young woman, and now she was abused by Magus, and to feel even the smallest sense of control, she became an abuser, using her power to take what she thought would fill the emptiness inside her.

She hated this feeling.

"I promise," she said so all in the chamber could hear, "you'll never be troubled by me again."

"Thank you for healing us," the priest said quickly, its eyes fixed on Medusa's face, "you have shown us great kindness. But, please, do not take the disks, they are dangerous. There is much evil that can be brought to the other universes from ours. That possibility is why they were hidden."

Medusa lifted the box to her armoured chest.

"I promise you, I'll bring no harm to the other me that I connect with. If I'm unwanted, I'll remain silent within this person until I forget who I am, and all I've done."

The priest leaned toward her.

"You wish to end your existence?"

Medusa looked down at the box clasped in her hands.

"My power would not allow it. No, I wish to forget who I am and all I have done."

As she turned away from the podium and the priest near it, she understood more clearly than ever before, that she wanted to undo all that she'd done, and undo the terrible being she'd become in the decades since Magus had found her and brutally shaped her into his weapon of destruction. In the bubble of powerful energy that protected and sustained her from the brine of this watery world, this place she'd so ruthlessly and mercilessly brought fear and chaos to only moments ago,

Medusa wept, crying for perhaps the first time since she was a child hiding in the closet of her small bedroom after her stepfather had done things to her no child should ever experience. As grief over her life overwhelmed her, her powerful body trembled, and her energy lashed out in angry whips, striking blindly out at the memories, then falling back to wrap itself around her, hold her, and comfort her. Eventually, as she let her powers lift her through the misty layers of this blue planet, Medusa drew in a deep breath, letting it escape from between her shuddering lips as if the weight of a thousand suns was lifting from her shoulders.

Her choice was simple then.

She wanted to forget.

It was a way to kill herself, without actually doing it.

THIRTY-TWO

"We've got to do something!"

"CHIKUSHŌ!" SHIMOOKA SWORE as the kid in the Ant-Man mask fell toward the quadrangle, with Thomas Stewart taking swooping victory laps around him as he dropped.

Dupuis had contacted her commander and advised the withdrawal of the incoming F-18 Hornets. They'd veered away from The Hill less than a minute before they would have dropped their air-to-surface ordinance. It would have been one hell of a light show, Shimooka thought, and Gloria Musa and the masked girl would have been casualties, while the Armed Forces and the OPS would have sat before government committees for the next year explaining the decision to bomb the hell out of Parliament Hill. Assuming Stewart was incinerated, that is. Of course, with Ant-Man smacking into the quadrangle like a swatted bug, maybe they shouldn't have called the air strike off. Thomas Stewart seemed to be invincible.

"Why the hell did I listen to you?" Dupuis growled next to her, as she trained her binoculars on the two combatants.

Shimooka shrugged.

"That kid was defying gravity and disappearing things like Stewart. It seemed like a better option than anything the Forces had going on."

Stewart was hovering over the fallen Ant-Man, hitting the kid with another blast of that blue plasma. Terrible cries of anguish could be heard from where she and Dupuis were crouched down in the rubble. The screams were unnerving.

"We've got to do something," she growled.

Dupuis grunted, still looking through the binoculars.

"Like what? Call the Hornets back?"

Shimooka shook her head.

"I don't think that would have worked. We're dealing with something that really is out of this universe."

"There's no such thing, detective," said Dupuis. "There are no wizards, or monsters, or superheroes, just us shitty ol' humans, killing each other."

"Until today, I wouldn't have disagreed with you," Shimooka nodded, turning to cast a derisive look at the soldier, who caught the look. "But it's our job to protect civilians, isn't it?"

"I don't believe that kid for a second," Dupuis responded, as she put the binoculars back to her face. "This is some kind of unknown tech or it's something we just don't understand yet, and maybe—"

She suddenly stood up.

"Merde!"

Shimooka jumped up, scanning the field, her eyes focusing on Stewart, as the Green Lantern Magus guy slammed another blast of blue plasma into the contorting body of Ant-Man.

"What? What do you see?"

Dupuis let the binoculars drop to her chest and pointed above the field.

"Look for yourself."

Shimooka glanced up. Another flying person was dropping down into the fray. The girl with the Wasp mask? No, this person wasn't hiding behind a mask. It was a woman, with a full head of black hair that fanned out around her head and shoulders like a cape.

"Here," she heard Dupuis say.

She'd lifted her binoculars from around her neck and was jerking them in Shimooka's direction.

"You ain't gonna believe this."

Shimooka snatched the binoculars, quickly adjusted their width and pressed them to her eyes. She fidgeted with the focus as she searched in the direction of the newest flying individual. There she was, a tall, young, black woman, black slacks, a dark purple blouse, her dreads floating around her head as if she was laying on her back in a pond of tranquil water. What looked like a dark cloud of gas or mist seemed to be pouring out of every part of her body, flowing out and around her, even through her clothing. The mist was swaying and swooping as if alive.

"No way."

"Yeah," Dupuis replied. "Maybe there are wizards. I'm calling this into my commander. We need to get those F-18s back."

"So, Musa's like him, but is she with him? Why reveal herself now, after so many have died?" Shimooka wondered out loud.

It didn't make sense that she'd be working with Stewart. She'd obviously been his hostage or the hostage of the being inside him.

Suddenly a woman's voice roared impossibly loud as if God had spoken from the Heavens.

"NO!"

It was unnaturally powerful, billowing across The Hill, the wave it created pummelling already broken buildings, knocking over planters, smashing into Shimooka and Dupuis, throwing them to the ground like pieces of paper in a strong wind.

It had come from Gloria Musa.

"Chikushō-me!" Shimooka shouted as she scrambled to get back to her feet while shoving the binoculars hard against her eyes. "How is that even possible?"

She quickly glanced at Dupuis, who was looking, frustrated, at the handset of her comm, clicking the transmit button repeatedly.

"Bloody hell."

Shimooka lifted the glasses back to her eyes. The dark cloud or whatever it was that had been flowing out of Gloria was now becoming a dark and violently roiling thing, billowing and pushing out, becoming denser and growing dramatically. It was unlike anything Shimooka had ever seen. Small flashes of lightning coursed through the expanding cloud, the glare imprinting on Shimooka's retinas. She blinked profusely, demanding that her eyes compensate. She didn't want to miss anything. Then, a sharp crack of thunder pounded her ears as the angry cloud engulfed Musa and Stewart, hiding them from view.

"That bloody scream somehow knocked out my comms," she heard Dupuis complain.

"Here," Shimooka barked.

She tossed the binoculars at the soldier, who snatched them out of the air, then demanded to know what was going on. Shimooka didn't bother answering. She was already bounding over rubble, heading toward the gathered super beings, her pistol in her hand, for whatever good that would do, she thought.

THIRTY-THREE

"I did not sufficiently prepare you
for this battle."

AS HUNTER HIT THE HARD-PACKED grass of the quadrangle, the air exploded from his lungs. Tiny specks danced before his eyes, as he struggled to catch his breath. Panicked, he watched Magus come to a stop with his feet hovering just over his abdomen, the ridiculous Batman cape flapping around his shoulders. Magus's maddening smile and laugh-filled Hunter's head, as he struggled to rise up off the grass. He was sure he shouldn't hurt as much as he did. The knife he tried to plunge into his hand to prove to Mia he was invincible had barely registered as an insignificant tap. However, the blast from Magus had felt like a punch to every part of his body, from every direction at once.

That should not have happened. I did not sufficiently prepare you for this battle.

Hunter moaned.

"What? Really?"

I have understood too late what this transition into your body means. You control my powers, but if you don't know how to use them effectively, you can't fight Magus. If you can't properly imagine what my power can do, you can't counter his ruthlessness.

"What are you saying?" Hunter groaned as he watched Magus lean over to watch his anguish.

Please forgive me, Hunter. My arrogance and pride have brought us to this moment.

"You should have killed him when you had the chance in your universe," Hunter said, the words forced as he struggled to breathe.

Magus laughed.

"Having troubles, Mighty Titan?"

Hunter moaned again, feeling as if every bone in his body was shattered. He focused on Magus.

"What did you do to me?"

Magus leaned in closer and smiled broadly, sneering his pleasure at Hunter's distress, and then drove another blast of the blue energy into his chest.

Hunter screamed.

THIRTY-FOUR

"I'm sorry, eomma."

"WHAT THE HELL?"

When Gloria Musa did the unexpected super being reveal, Mia stood looking off in the direction the woman had disappeared, flying, defying gravity, like Hunter and Magus were doing. How was this possible? Why, if Gloria was super-powered like Hunter, had she waited so long to reveal this? And why did she fly away, instead of towards the battle?

"Stay alive until I return," Gloria had said as she had risen up from the walkway. Return from where?

Hunter's cries pulled Mia back to the immediate situation. She turned around and searched for him on the field. He was laying, crumpled on the grass about thirty metres away, Magus hovering over him, laughing, as he drove another blast of that terrible energy into Hunter's body. She grimaced as she saw him try to pull away from the onslaught, but the blast pinned him to the ground. What should she do? What *could* she do? Her mother, her eomma, had often told her to not just be someone who speaks but to be the person who gives feet to their words. Mia had wanted to come with Hunter, she had insisted on being a part of whatever was happening to him, and now he needed her help.

"Oh, god."

Mia took a deep breath and ran towards Hunter, his cries of agony adding energy to her resolve. She wasn't sure what she was going to do. She was a mere human being after all, compared to the super-powered beings inside Hunter and that evil ae-sae Magus. She was halfway down the steps leading to the quadrangle when Gloria silently swooped down from above, positioning herself behind Magus, out of his line of sight, stopping only a few metres from where he was powering up, or whatever it was he did before striking Hunter with those blasts of energy.

Mia paused on the stairs, unsure of what was about to happen. Gloria, uh, Super Gloria, whatever she was now or had always been, was floating in the air, with some kind of dark, cloud-like vapour flowing out of her, building up like a storm cloud around her. The cloud seemed to be alive like it was part of her, Mia thought. Who was she? Mia took one more step down, as a cry of rage exploded from Gloria's mouth.

"NO!"

The sound seemed to come from everywhere, piercing the air like an explosion, the sonic energy of it knocking Mia back painfully into the hard concrete steps. It was nothing like she had ever heard, and it certainly caught Magus's attention. He spun around in a blur of motion to face the unexpected attacker.

Mia scrambled to her feet, her eyes on what was transpiring on the quadrangle. If she was to reach Hunter and get him out of harm's way, she needed to wait until Gloria and Magus took their fight to the skies. The fierce-looking cloud forming around Gloria was whipping out from her body like wind-blown sheets unfurling from within her. Lightning strikes began to flash outwards from its murky depths, and violent peels of thunder smacked into the air, sending shock waves through Mia's body. Magus's hands began to flare, flashing with that blue energy he'd been hitting Hunter with. Then the two of them began to rise rapidly above the quadrangle, leaving Hunter lying on the ground.

Gloria flickered to within a hairsbreadth of Magus. Things were about to get very bad, Mia thought.

"Oh my god, Hunter," she gasped, as she leapt to the bottom of the steps.

She began running, crouched low, dodging jagged pieces of the damaged East Block, angling toward Hunter, who was unmoving on his back on the grass. Wait, one of his legs moved.

"Hang on, Hunter."

Vicious winds caused by Gloria and her angry cloud slammed into Mia, as she neared her fallen boyfriend. She lifted her arms to shield her eyes, keeping a clear line of sight on him as she leaned her body into the wind and pushed ahead. Lightning slammed into the ground around her, the air crackling with the explosions of super-charged molecules. Both Stewart and Gloria were only about ten metres above her as she threw herself toward Hunter's legs. She hoped neither would see her.

"Hunter?"

Debris from bushes and grass swirled around, driving into her body and striking her face. She tasted blood, but Hunter was her only concern. The roar of the wind and the crashing of thunder were staggering, beating into the depths of her chest, pounding into her ears, and somewhere in all of this Mia heard the tense voices of Gloria Musa and Thomas Stewart. They were arguing, although she couldn't hear what they were arguing about.

Hunter moaned and she called his name again as she clawed her way to his head. The Ant-Man mask was gone. His face was bloodied, his lower lip split and one of his eyes were swollen, but otherwise, he was alive. Mia slid her hands under his head and lifted it onto her lap.

"Hey you, tto-rai, can you hear me?"

His one eye that wasn't swollen like a balloon flickered open, searched for and then focused on Mia.

"Ouch."

"Oh, my god," Mia whispered as she lowered her face to his and gently kissed him on the side of his face. "We have to get out of here, Hunter. Gloria's like Titan and Magus, only maybe worse. She's way more frightening."

Hunter looked past her face to the seething dark cloud and lightning flashes and the two super-beings face-to-face in the fracas above them. He struggled to lift himself up and Mia tried to help, but Hunter was heavy, and he was unable to offer assistance. Suddenly, another pair of hands slipped under his shoulders.

"C'mon kids," Detective Shimooka shouted, over the noise. "Whatever this is, it's getting really nasty,"

She held Hunter by one arm, while Mia grabbed the other.

"No, wait," Hunter cried, as he tried to look up at the warring forces above his head. "Titan says we can't just leave the fight. We have to see it to the end. He says Magus will destroy us all."

"I don't think so, Ant-Man," Shimooka growled. "This is way beyond us now."

"Come on, Hunter," Mia shouted. "Whatever's going on up there is between the two of them. Let's go."

Hunter pulled away and turned to look up. Mia followed his gaze. Gloria and Stewart were literally face-to-face, and the thick dark cloud that writhed around the two of them flashed and thundered like something angry, splitting the air with shocking peels, casting violent shadows across the quadrangle. The swirling mass of cloud, like Gloria's hair, seemed alive. She placed her hand against Magus's chest, and then Gloria screamed.

Magus pulled Gloria's hand away and violently pushed her back. He looked down, and Mia could sense the flashing rage emanating from his eyes, as they sought her out. He then drove a blast of his energy into Gloria, sending her spinning away. Mia blinked and Magus was in front of her, appearing terrifying and unbalanced in the Green Lantern costume.

"Oh, shut it. You won't die today," he growled, forcefully.

For a moment Mia thought maybe he was talking to them and wouldn't harm them, but then with a flick of a hand, he knocked the detective away without touching her, before the same hand reached out for Mia. His fingers wrapped around her neck, cold and thin, and terribly strong. As she suddenly struggled for air, Mia caught a glimpse of Magus's other hand also snaking around Hunter's neck. She felt her feet leave the ground. She wrapped her hands around Magus's forearms, trying to save herself as he slowly squeezed, choking her. Panic exploded across Mia's mind. She didn't want to die. Out of the corner of her eye, just as dark spots began to dance like flies across her vision, she saw Detective Shimooka pull a gun from somewhere in her jacket and fire point-blank at the side of Stewart's head. He laughed, as he turned his face to hers. A blast of orange and yellow fire erupted from his eyes, engulfing the detective's head.

The detective barely had time to scream as she fell over, out of sight. Mia let go of her attacker's arm and reached out for then found Hunter's limp hand beside her. She grasped for it desperately, stitching their fingers together. Don't let go of my hand, he'd said earlier. I don't want to die, she thought, as a blinding light began to crowd her vision and thought became increasingly difficult.

She couldn't breathe.

"I don't want to die," she gasped feebly.

"You won't," a voice said, breaking through the roar of death in her head.

Suddenly, she was falling backward, her vision wrenched from the twisted mix of rage and glee on Stewart's face to the turbulent sky above. Brilliant flashes of blue and white lightning that seemed oddly close stung her eyes. Rapidly flowing clouds, like storm clouds she'd seen coursing over the tops of mountains in Banff, swooped around her arms and head. A storm's coming, her mind suggested, trying to understand what she was seeing. It looks like it might rain.

She hit the ground, hard. Her breath exploded from her lungs, what little of it was left. She sucked air back in, hard, desperate, every cell gasping for oxidation, for energy to continue existing. But it wasn't enough. Magus's plasma energy that flowed from his hand into her body had broken her deep inside and Mia could feel it.

Hunter.

She was still holding his hand. He lay on the grass beside her, his body unmoving. She knew he was dead.

Then her eyes filled with a brilliant, white light, so complete, so all-encompassing that she saw nothing else, just the blinding light. She jammed her eyes shut as her retinas protested.

I'm dying, she thought. This is how it really happens?

She could feel the light growing. It was like a living thing, caressing her body, touching her like a feather, then violently, dramatically probing, invading every pore of her skin, pushing down into muscle, sinew, dancing along her nerves, her veins, her bones, expanding into her brain, bounding across her cerebrum, the brainstem and the cerebellum. Her eyes popped open, her eyelids stretching with the intensity, and light brighter than the sun filled her vision.

She screamed and screamed and then thought of how much she was going to miss her mother.

"I'm sorry, eomma," she sobbed. "I'm sorry."

THIRTY-FIVE

"Aw, c'mon. Give me a break, I really hurt."

HUNTER COULDN'T BELIEVE HOW MUCH he was hurting. The pain pulsated throughout his entire body, hitting every nerve, and shocking every muscle. Even his eyes ached with an otherworldly agony. It was like he was hurting not only inside himself but outside of his body.

I am sorry.

Hunter couldn't answer. He simply couldn't find the neurological pathway from his brain to his mouth to say what he wanted to say.

He wanted to say that it was okay, that he'd agreed to do this, that they'd get away, recover, and then carry on to fight another day.

His mouth never voiced the words, but he felt the Mighty Titan agreeing. As long as Mia was safe, then it had been worth it. She was leading Thomas's girlfriend, Gloria, away from this not-so-epic battle. They'd be safe. It was okay, then. It was all okay.

He opened his eyes and realized the screaming he'd been hearing was coming from his own mouth. It seemed to fit, a part of his brain surmised, considering how much pain he was in. With Maggots hitting him over and over with that blue energy, of course, it made sense he'd be the one doing the screaming.

"NO!" a voice somewhere else screamed.

It was loud and so full of commanding energy that it reverberated deep in his chest.

"Was that me?" he vaguely heard himself ask, his own voice tiny, cracked, and weak.

Get up! He has stopped his attack. We must attack.

Hunter forced his one eye that hadn't swollen shut to open and search the immediate surroundings. He couldn't see Maggots, but there was a lot of wind and thunder. Had a storm rolled in while they'd been fighting? Were the pilots in those jets safe?

We must attack, Hunter. Get up!

He closed his eye and blew out his breath, feeling his lips rattle against his teeth. They hurt, too.

Hunter, go!

"All right, all right, jeez, you're so bossy," he muttered, trying to roll over onto his side.

Not much happened. One leg stirred, but that was the best he could do.

"I'm sorry," he said, weakly. "I can't feel anything."

You are the Mighty Titan. Your entire being is infused with all of my power. Get up!

"Hunter!"

"Aw, c'mon. Give me a break, I really hurt."

"Hunter!"

Mia? Why was he hearing Mia's voice? She should be down by the Ottawa River with that poor woman. What was her name?

"Hunter?"

He tried to open his eyes, to look for the voice that was being swallowed by the violent storm that had suddenly appeared over The Hill. That happens back home, he thought. Sunny in the morning, storming like crazy by evening. Stupid Alberta weather.

"Hey you, tto-rai, can you hear me?" Mia said from far, far away.

"Ouch," he managed to reply as he forced one eye open. Mia was holding his head in her hands.

He was confused that she was here, but was also happy that she was. Maybe he wouldn't hurt so much now. She started talking about Gloria and Titan as she cradled his throbbing and fractured head, but he didn't understand. How was this going to make him feel better? Then she was suddenly pulling on his shoulder, and then the detective was helping her, and he couldn't really focus his eyes to see either of them clearly. He wanted to say he was fine, and that the Mighty Titan would make him better if they could get away from Maggots. His feet were moving, taking involuntary steps, but at least he was getting away.

We cannot leave. We have to see this through to the end, or he will kill everyone.

"No, wait," Hunter cried. "Titan says we can't just leave the fight. We have to see it through to the end."

He tried to look up to where both Mia and the detective were looking, as they dragged him away toward the Centre Block.

"He says Magus will destroy us all."

Then, almost as quickly as he'd left, Maggots returned. Out of the slit of his good eye, Hunter saw the man in the silly costume sweep the detective away with a wave of his hand like she'd been nothing but a speck of dust. Mia screamed and his heart began to pound with anger.

"Leave her alone," he wanted to yell, but the messages still weren't quite making it from his brain to his lips.

Hunter, we have to fight back. You must believe in the power within you.

Mia screamed again, but the sound was pinched off.

Hunter, fight!

Then he felt Maggot's hand flow around his neck like a slithering snake, circling the coils of his hard, cold fingers around his flesh, his vertebrae, his trachea, choking him, lifting him off the grass so that his feet hung beneath him, useless, like a rag doll.

Mia, she came back. Why?

He couldn't breathe. He tried to struggle, to resist, but he couldn't get his body to move. He felt something brush his right hand, twice, no, more, until finally, a hand gripped his, squeezing. Mia. Reaching for his hand like they always had, reaching for each other's hands, their silent gesture of affection. He tried to squeeze it back, but nothing happened. He wanted to cry, but couldn't. He wanted to kiss Mia one last time, wanted to tell her how much he loved her and would always love her, but his life was being crushed from him by this madman from another universe.

Hunter, if you pass out, maybe I can control your body like I did when I made you float while you were sleeping.

Can I pass out on command? Hunter asked himself. Is that one of Titan's powers? Passing out on demand?

He was falling. Mia was still holding his hand, but gravity was clawing them both down into the grass of the quadrangle, like the bony fingers of death, pulling them mercilessly down into the darkness of the Earth. He felt his body impact the ground, felt his breath leave his body, sucked away into the universe, fleeing away from him like a helium-filled balloon cut loose from its tether.

He was dying.

It was unfair, really. He was only nineteen. He had his whole life ahead of him. He had a life with Mia ahead of him, ahead of them.

I am sorry, Hunter. I have made a grave mistake.

He wanted to say it wasn't a problem, but then a bright and powerful light pierced through his closed eyes.

This was death, he thought, this is how it ends. I'm sorry, Mia, I failed you. I failed the world.

THIRTY-SIX

"I can't let what happened in your universe
happen in this one."

MOMENTS AGO —

When the young Asian girl had reached her hand out to her at the arch of the Peace Tower on Parliament Hill and said that she had beautiful eyes, the memories of Medusa, all the days and moments from the long life she'd chosen to forget in Gloria's universe, suddenly returned in a crushing wave. Instantly, every memory, every event in her life, both before her transition to this universe and after her arrival, was splayed open before her. She recalled who both of her selves, Adaego and Gloria, were in relation to each other, and to the past she'd hoped to forever forget. The sudden deluge of memories caused a spike of blinding pain in her head, but it was nothing compared to the agony of the unwanted memories themselves. She'd come to this universe to forget. It was the price she'd been willing to pay, and now every memory, every horrible action she'd taken in her alliance with Magus, every terrible deed she'd done in her quest for his love, was crashing through her mind.

"You have beautiful eyes."

These were the first words Magus had said to her, so long ago. Four simple words, spoken offhandedly by someone who knew that charm was almost as powerful as the cosmic energy coursing through his body. That day and those words marked the beginning of her descent into decades of hell managing Magus's mania and drive for domination. She'd escaped that life. Now, it all came flooding back. Gloria, who'd been a four-year-old girl and Medusa, who'd been troubled and abused, and an aging villain, had merged together to become one being. The technological wizardry of the discs, that the Rathmusian scientist-priests had kept hidden, had fused their minds and bodies into one space in time, and because she hadn't left one of the discs in her own universe, she was forever bound to this one. That was twenty-two years ago.

Her power had enabled her to forget all that the older Gloria had done as Medusa. Forgetting is what she'd wanted, and so she forgot all she'd been, and this new life, the two Glorias in one body, became the most normal and carefree years of her short, but long, long life.

Until Magus appeared.

Magus. Thomas Stewart. She remembered everything. Her power had always magnified her natural ability to recall events and even minor details that may have happened decades earlier. Now, as those four words connected her to the beginning of her painful and terrible relationship with Magus, her power was jolted awake within her, and she remembered every horrific detail of who she'd once been. She also recalled how she'd escaped from Magus, and where she'd buried the two discs that had given her a second chance so long ago when she had merged with the four-year-old Gloria of this universe.

The discs were buried in the backyard of what used to be her mother's house in Surrey, BC. When she'd seen Magus and Titan attacking each other above the quadrangle on Parliament Hill as Mia led her away, Adaego knew she could no longer hide from who and what she was. When she'd asked Gloria if she could take charge of their shared body, and her kind-hearted host had said yes, she'd suddenly felt the need to retrieve her discs. She wasn't sure why she needed them, but the power flowing within her seemed to be prompting her to retrieve them. In the past, her power had sometimes acted as if it had thoughts of its own, and this was one of those moments. She'd learned to listen to its silent voice.

After leaving Parliament Hill, it had taken her less than four seconds to cross the country to the West Coast and land in the backyard that had entertained her as a child, especially as a child with a much older, and much more experienced version of herself as a mentor. The yard appeared considerably smaller of course, as childhood memories are often shaped by the perspective and perception of the young mind. She waited for a moment, letting her vision peer through the walls of her old home, her mind filling with the memories of many wonderful moments here. In Adaego's universe, this home had been demolished many decades ago and the neighbourhood, once alive with families, had been reduced to poorly-built apartment blocks and crime-ridden strip malls.

This universe's mother no longer lived here. She'd sold this house a few years earlier and purchased a condo apartment in the west end of the city, overlooking the Nicomekl River. Her mother's partner, a kind and gentle man who made her mother feel safe and loved, was probably with her. The two of them worried for Gloria, the young, black woman that the murderer Thomas Stewart was holding hostage on Parliament Hill.

Adaego's mother had died decades earlier in the other universe, a victim of abuse by her own hand and by the hands of many abusers. Gloria's mother, the one that Adaego embraced as her own, was similar to her mother in personality and temperament, but her life had been much more joyous, in large part because of Adaego's intervention. Because of those life-altering moments, where she kept Gloria and her mother safe with her foreknowledge of what could happen, this woman had been given a chance to live a life of loving and caring for her daughter and family. Adaego smiled at the memories of this mother braiding her, or rather Gloria's, hair, helping her with schoolwork, singing sweetly to her when she was troubled, and telling her stories of other black women who'd fought hard to make a way for dignity and love in a world that didn't always accept them.

Gloria sensed her older self's thoughts and spoke within their mind.

Our mother will be fine. She is a strong woman.

Adaego nodded, feeling a swell of emotion in her chest. Yes, their mother was strong. She was soft of heart, graceful, but hard in her resolve. She'd believed in her daughter and had struggled and worked and studied to become a registered nurse to make sure Gloria was able to go to university. She was a strong and amazing woman, one of the countless mothers who believed in their daughters and their sons.

"She's been the mother I couldn't save in my own universe," she whispered. "I have to make this right, for all of us. I have to destroy Magus."

Was it fair, though, she asked herself, to bring this world's Gloria into her hatred of Magus? She'd been an innocent child, and she hadn't asked for any of this. She'd merely been the vessel that gave the troubled Medusa a way out of the abuse and trauma caused by Magus and by her own selfish choices. Gloria's life lay before her, filled with potential and promise.

Gloria spoke to Adaego.

I can hear your thoughts. I'd forgotten who you were, but now I remember who we are. I remember how powerful you are and what you've done for me. You saved my life from the hell you knew might be waiting for me in this universe. You gave my mother, our mother, a better life by putting a stop to the things that would have crushed her spirit and made her feel like she wasn't worth anything to anyone, least of all to herself.

"But it's not fair to you," Adaego pleaded. "I entered your body when you were just a little girl."

I said yes, didn't I?

"I asked permission of a four-year-old child. I used you to escape the life I'd helped to create for myself. The life I hated."

I understand, Adaego, but you also saved us. I also know you're powerful enough to kill Magus, but I'd rather not kill anyone, not even him. Why did your power lead us back to the discs? There must be a reason.

Adaego thought carefully, using her reawakened memories to replay the words of the scientist from long ago and on another world in another universe.

"The scientist told me that if I take a fellow traveller's disc and try to use it to return to my universe, my consciousness will return, but not to my body. My body isn't there, it's here, merged with yours."

Adaego took a slow, deep breath as she plunged her hand deep into the hard-packed dirt in the back corner of her old yard, pushing into the soil up to her elbow, her fingers finding the old coffee can that held the two discs. Then, as she pulled it loose from the ground and pried the rusted lid open, she let the discs tumble out into her palm. When she saw them, the meaning of the words became clear again.

They seem smaller than I remember.

Adaego smiled and nodded.

"It was many years ago, you were just a child."

Do you believe these can help us defeat Magus?

"Yes, I believe they might be the only way to rid ourselves of him without actually killing him by our hand."

Really? How?

"Magus will have the disc that brought him to this universe. He saw them as a source of ultimate power, so it's likely he would have it on him at all times."

Ah, I think I know what you are planning.

Adaego laughed, as she turned the almost non-reflective discs over in her hands, recalling the first time she'd seen them and how hope for a new life had given birth within her.

"If I can somehow switch discs with Magus, and if we can frighten him just enough that his cowardly ass will want to flee this universe, then he'll use the disc I've switched for his. Even if he only used one disc to come to our universe and his body is over there, he won't go back into it because he won't have the right disc.

They both laughed, one inside, one outside, a feeling of joy and relief rising in their consciousnesses.

You're so clever. This would mean Thomas would be back to who he was before Magus came here. He alone will be responsible for what Magus has done. Can we live with that?

Adaego sighed.

"He abused me in my universe, but I loved him in this one, he wasn't completely the same damaged person. I think when you and I first met him at U of T, there was a part of me that thought the relationship could work this time. It was very confusing then, I remember."

Yes, Gloria said, *it was as if I knew him. I suppose I did because you felt like you did, but there was a part of me that believed he could be a different person than the one you'd known. You made a choice to not be Medusa. I guess I thought he'd be able to do the same, especially without the power that turned him into Magus in your universe.*

"I did make a choice leaving that life behind, and a part of me must have thought he might be different without the power. It's clear what Thomas wants though, and that's Magus's power."

If we do this, Magus will go back to your universe and die or disperse as that priest told you, right? And Thomas will pay the price for what the two of them have done here in our universe?

"Yes, I'm sure of that."

Gloria fell silent for a moment.

"We can try and find another way," Adaego suggested. "If not for your beautiful and compassionate soul, my sister, I would have no regrets about killing him."

Gloria's reply came swiftly.

No, Thomas made his choice, and we've made ours. I guess he was already cheating on me, on us. He has let Magus do whatever he wanted with his body. We saw that in what he did in the boardroom, and when he killed that security officer in the bathroom, and now, all these poor people on Parliament Hill. He's made no attempt to stop Magus. He could have, right? He could've stopped Magus, right?

Adaego nodded, as she looked back over the yard that had given the two of them so much pleasure when Gloria was a child.

"I think so. He's not the Thomas of my universe, but he's very much like Magus. He loves the opportunity that the power gives him to take whatever he wants, just like Magus. He's seen how easy it is now, he'll do whatever he wants, no matter the cost to anyone else."

She could feel the heat of the discs burning patiently against her palm, the technology of them reacting to the power that coursed through her body. She slipped them separately into the pockets of the slacks she'd taken from the Goodwill in Nepean a day earlier. It felt like it was a year ago now.

Then, this is what we have to do. I'm okay with this decision. Are you?

Adaego nodded slowly.

"I guess so. Yes, I have to be. There's a part of me that would rather see him torn to pieces."

I know, my sister. Justice doesn't always give us what we want. Sometimes we have to take the more difficult road. Magus will take the easy road of escape. This is the way, we can't let what happened in your universe happen in this one. Mama wouldn't like that.

Adaego chuckled, knowing her sister was right in her reasoning.

"Damn straight. Mama would be pissed."

Damn straight.

"Gloria, how about you and I go save this universe from a couple of evil assholes?"

THIRTY-SEVEN

"I am Adaego, I am not Medusa."

HAPPENING NOW —

The violence and strength of her power at this moment were almost comforting to Adaego. Its rage and torrent of elemental expressions had always impressed and even frightened her at times, and, she knew, those her formidable power had terrorized. As her hands grabbed the thin costume material over Magus's chest and she pulled him close to her, she could feel the compassionless rage of her power. The power felt her anger and begged to consume him, to separate every last molecule of his being and disperse it into nothingness. The intense emotion was familiar, like an old coat she'd worn many years ago, and now she'd found it again and was trying it on, feeling how it hung from her shoulders and wrapped around her body like a comforting hug from an old friend.

It would be so easy to kill him, she thought, so very easy.

No, please, Adaego. We aren't killers.

Adaego groaned, replying in her mind, the conversation with her younger self transpiring much faster than normal human thought.

"But he's done so much harm to me. You of all people know that."

Gloria replied.

Yes, I know what he's done to you, but we're not like him. Killing him won't fix what he's done, not ever. Let him destroy himself, while we continue making a better life here and for our mother.

Adaego screamed in her mind, her frustration clouding her earlier resolve.

"Ah, but I hate him! I hate him! He doesn't deserve to live!"

Gloria agreed with her.

Oh, yes, I've seen things that I wish I hadn't seen, but if we kill him, what then? What does that make us, not just you, Adaego, but us? You came to this universe to break the cycle of abuse. You're no longer Medusa. We can't become the abuser.

Adaego answered in her mind again.

"Yes, yes, that's not who we are, not this time."

Gloria sighed with hope.

You're no longer the person known as Medusa. You're Adaego, you're kind, and your power is meant to help, not destroy.

"Yes, I am Adaego, I am not Medusa, she is gone. Thank you, my little sister."

So, despite what she longed to do, Adaego used the power of her senses to search for Magus's disc, to feel for its power, until, yes, there it was, in the front left pocket of the jeans taken from Goodwill. When one of his hands moved stealthily down and began to rip apart the thin material of his silly costume to gain access to his pants beneath, she gave Magus a shake, small, but abrupt, just enough to make him pull his hand away. In that moment, her hand moved faster than light itself, time slowing to an almost imperceptible flow as she moved one of her discs, the one that would have been used to return her to her home universe, had she not brought the anchor disc with her. She slid this into his pocket while removing his disc, just before Magus grew brave enough to push his hand back toward his pocket. He never noticed the switch, so afraid was he of Adaego's power and his need to have the upper hand. She let her heart smile. Magus had never been a great thinker, had never really used the full potential of his mind. He just craved power, and to him, the discs represented that power.

As he pushed the disc, her disc, against her skin, she feigned an overreaction to the pain and pulled away from him. She wanted him to clasp it between his hands and use it to return, but to return to nothing.

Gloria anticipated what was to come.

We're not killers, but this will be merciful.

Magus paused and then suddenly slid the disc back into his pocket. He looked down. Adaego followed his gaze, where she could see the girl called Mia and the prone younger Titan, along with an older woman she didn't recognize.

What's he doing? Why isn't he using the disc?

Adaego groaned, her teeth clenching in frustration.

"He's going to try to hurt the ones he knows we're protecting before he makes his grand escape."

Without warning, Magus drove a blast of intense energy at Adaego. The strike was point blank, and smashed violently into her chest, sending her twisting and twirling back toward Wellington Street like a leaf in a wind. Just as she was about to hurl past the Centennial Flame, she reached out and grabbed ahold of an overturned and burning military vehicle that had flipped on top of it from Magus's initial attack, using the gutted hulk to stop her momentum. She quickly searched for Magus with her vision. He'd dropped down to where the two teens and the older woman were. The woman was firing a small weapon straight at Magus's head. He laughed and responded by engulfing the woman with a blast of plasma from his eyes. Adaego felt a stab of anger pierce her heart, as the detective fell to the grass. She'd failed this woman who, despite not being a powered person, was willing to fight an impossible battle to save the lives of Hunter and Mia. Magus continued to laugh, as he picked up the two young people by their necks, lifting them off the ground, their backs turned to her. Energy from his hands erupted like fiery blue blossoms around their heads. Adaego quickly crossed the space between them and pushed her way between the two young people. She could feel the girl's fear, saw her reach out for and grasp Hunter's hand and heard her whispering over and over.

"I don't want to die."

"You won't," Adaego said as Magus reacted to her sudden appearance and darted back, dropping his victims.

Anger enflamed his face, as he plunged a hand into his pocket, grasping for the disc. He triumphantly displayed it, laughing maniacally as he clasped the ancient object between his hands. Adaego reached out and enveloped his hands with her own.

He screamed over the angry roar of her power, as he struggled to pull away.

"You can't have it. It's mine!"

"Oh, yes, it's all yours!" Adaego sneered, as she squeezed his hands together, and stared fiercely into her abuser's eyes.

She'd been afraid of those eyes, of how they could transform in an instant from a look of love to a crushing look of disdain whenever she'd displeased him. At that moment, she again wished him dead, wished for an end to all he'd done to her, an end to every fear, to every abuse, an end to the shame that had trampled her self-worth again and again, because she hadn't stood up to him when she could have. She was far more powerful than he, but she hadn't been able to bring herself to kill him, so she simply ran away. Even then, after so many years in this universe, it was too late. She couldn't escape what she was, what Magus had already turned her into, a beast like himself.

An abuser.

A taker.

A destroyer.

She wanted the torment to end.

It was at that moment that something began to move within Adaego's chest. She could feel it as the device struggled between the two competing forces fighting for control of its technology. The magnificent energy of the dark cloud that poured from every cell of her body, that energy that had been with her since a young woman in that other universe, that had protected her, defended her, struck down enemies for her, now abruptly expanded, a bubble growing, stretching, pulsing, and pushing outward like someone trying to escape from the inside of a giant balloon. It was as if it was alive and wanted out. Then Adaego began to feel a presence, mysterious, vague, untouchable, one she knew had always been present, yet didn't really know. She could feel her own heart beating, her breath flowing in, flowing out, in and out, in and out.

And then the universe froze.

THIRTY-EIGHT

"We won't die today."

MEDUSA'S APPEARANCE WAS DEFINITELY UNEXPECTED. The rage and the threat of her power was also unexpected. She was dangerous and had always been so, but never to him, not really. Magus had found her when she was a young broken woman, and almost mad with not knowing who or what she was or could become. She was reckless and out of control, lashing out at anything and anyone that hurt her. He'd sensed the formidable power lying untapped and unexplored within her, and had carefully exploited her fears and her pathetic need for belonging and her weakness for love. It didn't take long for him to groom her into his most impressive and compliant weapon. She so desperately craved the need to be loved that Magus had been able to use that as a weapon itself. If she misbehaved, he withdrew his affection and then, after a sufficient time, would physically lash out, beating her, pounding her with not just his plasma, but his power-hardened fists, until she'd cower and promise to be better, to do better. She was, most likely, his greatest creation, and, to be honest, she'd been the reason he'd been so successful at his villainy. If he couldn't achieve something or felt it might be too dangerous for him, then Gloria would make it happen. She was brilliant at creating terror and at achieving his goals. It was her, after all, who'd first found the Black Energy.

He'd assumed that Titan had killed her and disposed of the discs she'd retrieved from the ocean planet and its weird fish people, but no, Medusa hadn't been killed. She'd transported into this universe's Gloria like he and Titan had into their respective counterparts. Perhaps the ultimate power of the discs was that it carried you into other universes, providing other realms to pillage, to rule over. Magus had no idea how this was possible, and he didn't care. He only cared about power, and he felt the power he needed sitting in a pocket of the jeans under his flimsy Green Lantern costume.

The pathetic voice of Thomas Stewart in his head was whimpering, blathering on about not wanting to die, and begging his Gloria for forgiveness. Yes, he'd cheated on her. Yes, he was sorry and promised to never do that again. But, the power, he was muttering between sobs, the power is so wonderful, so, so me, so who I am. Magus smiled slightly, ignoring the searing pain of Medusa's energy sizzling the flesh of his chest where she had grabbed hold of him, and wished for a way to kill the weak, snivelling Thomas within him. As Gloria breathed her need for vengeance into Magus's ear, and Stewart cried and sobbed inside him, Magus slowly tore through the thin fabric of his unworthy costume and slid his hand into the front pocket of the jeans underneath.

The disc was there, hot, burning, almost unbearable to touch, even with his near-invincible skin. He wished for his platinum gloves, but he now understood why his skin needed to feel it, and what it could do for him. He clasped it and quickly pulled it out, feeling the mysterious material reacting to the explosive energy that was growling around them. He heard voices beneath him, Titan and maybe that masked girl he'd seen earlier with him, and a plan came to his mind. He'd push the disruptive energy of the disc against Gloria's skin. That should distract her long enough for him to blast her away, giving him the moment he needed to kill Titan and the girl. Then, he'd clasp the burning disc between his hands, like it had been clasped between the hands of he and Titan over Scotland, and let it take only him somewhere else, to another universe, or perhaps back into his body. There was no shame in running, not when the odds were stacked against him.

"I never thought I'd have the chance to end your miserable life, but I've learned to take the opportunities life gives," Gloria said to him, the narrow slits of her angry eyes flashing hues of orange and yellow and red.

I don't want to die. I don't want to die.

Magus groaned with the annoyance of the moment and quickly raised his hand, driving the flat of the disc into Gloria's cheek. The object flared and flashed, and Gloria pulled back with the sudden pain of it. He shoved her away, and Magus slid the device back into his pocket and looked down, spotting three individuals through the swirling wind of debris. Medusa had followed his gaze. Her attention on him distracted, he quickly drove a blast of his energy at her, hitting her square in the chest, and sending her spinning away with the impact.

He dropped. There was an older woman supporting one arm of the injured Titan. There was also the younger woman holding onto him, she no longer had a mask on, but he was sure it was the woman he'd seen earlier. It didn't matter, he'd kill them all. They seemed surprised to see him. Magus laughed, as he flicked the older woman away with a burst of his power. She grunted as she was thrown hard backward, onto the ground.

No, no, I don't want to die.

"Oh, shut it. We won't die today," he barked at the pathetic version of himself in his head.

Magus reached out and grasped the slumping Titan and the startled girl by their necks, lifting them off the ground. This was his moment. He knew he only had a few seconds before Gloria recovered and would be upon him, so he squeezed their silly youthful necks with his powerful youthful hands, letting his energy build and arc around those hands. He'd dissolve the flesh from their bones and then destroy them completely down to the molecular level. He wanted to relish this moment, to take all the time in the universe, to taste their deaths at his hands, but he knew he didn't have much time.

Suddenly that woman, whom he now assumed must have been some sort of police authority, had pulled a tiny weapon from somewhere out of her clothing and was unloading its ordinance at the side of his head. The little bits of metal were absorbed into the energy that protected him. He laughed and commanded fire to erupt from his eyes, something he hadn't done in many years. The power of flame pouring from his retinas would leave them stinging for a few moments afterward, but for this particular annoying cretin, he'd make an exception.

Oh, my god, I didn't know we could do that!

"You have much to learn," Magus hissed, not bothering to mask the annoyance he was feeling toward the inner Thomas.

The detective's body convulsed back in shock, as flames flowed like water around her. She staggered, stumbling, horror filling her face, the weapon she'd fired falling as she slumped to her knees and then toppled over backward onto the grass. Magus laughed, as the woman's voice was choked off by the searing heat. He turned his attention back to Titan and the girl, willing every bit of power in his being to course through his body, down his arms, across his hands, and into their pathetic, little necks. Blue energy splashed across their heads, lighting their teeth, searing their wide, terrified eyes and Magus laughed, his victory nearing completion.

Once more, he was ending the sad, useless life of his nemesis, the Mighty Titan. He laughed raucously, letting the moment fill him with the same glee he'd felt in their battle over Scotland just days earlier. How magnificent, he thought, how appropriate, to kill Titan again.

Kill them! Crush them! Squeeze the life out of them!

Magus laughed again, feeling his younger self's excitement for the kill.

Suddenly, Gloria appeared behind his two victims, her dreads swirling and whipping around her head, her body emanating huge ribbons of her power. Lightning flashed and drove violently into the ground at Magus's feet, kicking up tufts of grass. The air reverberated with the pulse of thunderclaps and Magus dropped Titan and the girl and stepped back, desperately reaching for the disc in his pocket. He'd escape, he'd get away, he'd fight another day. Gloria's teeth flashed brilliantly white, as she smiled.

Get us out of here.

Magus felt the disc burning the flesh of his hand as he pressed it into the palm of his other hand. He would get away.

What are you doing? Will that thing take us to your universe?

"Yes!" Magus barked.

What about me? Will that thing take me with you?

Gloria crossed the space between them in a blink and covered his hands with hers. Magus gasped in pain and focused his mind to will whatever he needed to happen with the disc to happen.

"You can't have it. It's mine!"

"Oh, yes, it's all yours," he heard Gloria say, through clenched teeth.

Her entire face embraced the sneer that played across her broad lips. Her eyes were narrowing, focusing on whatever she thought would happen. And happen it did. Her power began to pour into the disc in Magus's hands, flashing out and around them, through them, spiking out in lightning flashes that struck the grass around Mia and Hunter as they lay motionless on the ground.

Sparks, like tiny shooting stars, began to erupt between Gloria's and Magus's hands, finding spaces of release from around their fingers where her hand enfolded the disc pressed against Magus's skin. The smell of burning flesh enveloped them both, as the device reacted to this sudden convergence of powerful energies. A light as intense as Sol flashed and rapidly expanded, consuming both, flashing out to envelope Titan, Mia, and Detective Shimooka, who lay on her side on the ground, her smouldering body in a fetal position.

Magus screamed. The pain was so complete, so thorough, that he could no longer resist, and anguish poured from him in shocking torrents. He could feel every molecule of his powerful body rend itself apart. Somewhere in his mind, his brain registered Gloria's screams, matching his own. Then he felt her hands pull away, and he gloated. She couldn't handle the violent pain. She was never his match. Magus held the disc even more tightly in his hands. It was his. He was the master of his fate, not this pathetic woman, not this treacherous vile traitor.

He was the victor.

What's happening? I'm coming with you, right? To your universe?

"God, I hope not," Magus managed to gasp between clenched teeth.

Yet he had very little idea what was about to happen. He hoped the snivelling Thomas would remain. To have this insufferable, whiny wretch remain inside his head would surely drive him mad. He could feel something familiar, a sense of disconnection from the physical realm, like what he'd experienced when he first arrived in this pitiful excuse for a universe. He screamed, he laughed, his emotions torn between anguish and exaltation. He'd return to his reality and embark on such a reign of vengeance and violence that none would ever forget. The Magnificent Magus would wreak such terrifying retribution against the League and any who opposed him, that the tale of it would be echoed throughout the Milky Way for eons.

What's happening? I think I can feel my hands.

"Shut it!" Magus growled as he flashed a smile at the woman he'd called Medusa.

He could feel his essence leaving this body, leaving this universe.

He'd won.

THIRTY-NINE

"Thomas could have been so much

more than this."

THE UNIVERSE FROZE.

Everything stopped, the wind, the lightning, the peels of thunder, every torn piece of sod and dirt and twig and shattered glass and twisted metal and debris from the damaged buildings. Magus, Gloria-Adaego, Hunter, Mia, and the dead detective, were frozen, suspended in the moment of their movement or in their deathly stillness as if caught in a digital snapshot.

Her hands were over Magus's hands, her disc clasped between his.

His face was paralyzed in the moment of frozen time, his eyes filled with fear and rage and a hint of the belief that he was about to escape.

She couldn't move.

Her power.

Her power was a living thing. All of the many beings changed by the energy spoke of its presence like this.

Gloria spoke apprehensively within their shared body.

What's happening?

"It's my power," Adaego thought, in the moment of unmoving time. "It's a living thing. I believe it's stopped the flow of time around us."

Your power's a living thing?

"Yes," Adaego said within herself. "It's always been a part of me, but also apart from me."

I don't understand.

"I was sixteen when I and others in my universe were struck by what scientists said was a massive energy pulse, which appeared from out of the black hole at the centre of the Milky Way galaxy. It was called The Second Event, after the First Event that changed Thomas and Hunter and others in my universe. It was immensely powerful, and many were transformed, changed on a genetic level into beings with extraordinary abilities. Many became heroes, and some, like me, followed the example of villains like Magus. When I was hit by the pulse, all I remember is this horrible, blinding pain. My body was already so damaged from substance abuse that the energy put me in a coma while it repaired what I'd done to myself. I woke up in a hospital almost three months later, as I am now, changed."

Yes, I understand, you've shared that with me before. I didn't know that you thought it was a living being.

"I don't think it's alive, as we think of aliveness. It's ambivalent to ethics, and to concepts of right and wrong. It's always responded to what I wanted it to do, or whatever I could imagine I wanted it to do, whether that thing would bring good or harm to another being. However, I don't believe it's just a thing, like a stone. If I was struck unconscious in battle, it would remove me to safety, it would somehow know where to take me. I think it's an entity, like a virus, neither living nor dead, but committed to preserving itself."

What does it want? Can it even want?

Adaego looked at the unblinking eyes of Magus across from her, so filled with rage and a belief in his pending victory, and then at her hands covering his.

"Perhaps it senses what I'm now doing will kill it and non-existence isn't within its scope of hoped-for experience."

I don't understand. What do you mean?

"If I don't let go of Magus, I'll be ripped from your body and pulled back to the other universe, the same way Titan was brought here by him. Only I'll be pulled back into nothing. If I don't let go of his hands, I'll die."

That was it, wasn't it? She still wanted Medusa to end. Medusa, and everything she'd been and done, had to end. She was holding onto Magus's hands. She didn't need to hold them for him to transition back to their universe, but she had reached out and grasped them between hers. She'd come to this universe to escape who she'd been, and yet the terror and evil of that other life had followed her. Her past was inescapable and unforgivable. She wanted to die with Magus, and her power had somehow sensed that.

You, you wish to die?

Adaego thought for a moment, letting her thoughts and reasons play out.

"Yes," she admitted in her mind, causing Gloria to cry out.

No!

"My dear little sister, you're the only sister I've ever had," Adaego said. "But I remember all I've done before we became sisters. I've done terrible things, and I've hurt many people."

No! You're not that person. You've changed.

"That may be, but it doesn't change what I've done, I've killed many beings who didn't deserve to die by my hand."

No. You use the word done. That's past tense, Adaego. This isn't who you are anymore.

"But, is that true? Haven't I been a killer?"

No! You haven't been that person here. You've changed!

Adaego fell silent.

I don't know that person. I only know you, my sweet Adaego, my precious sister.

Adaego looked again at the eyes of her old mentor and saw the hatred, the callousness and disregard for other beings, his lack of empathy that his need for power had created in him, and then she thought of the previous twenty-two years. Medusa, the terrible enforcer for Magus, had come to an end in that other universe when she'd left. In this one, the feared Medusa hadn't been known, hadn't been seen, not until today. Perhaps she had indeed changed. Perhaps she was no longer the terrible Medusa.

"Magus showing up in this universe has forced me to remember who I am and to reveal who I am to a world that doesn't have super-beings," she said. "I can't hide any longer, Gloria. This moment is making a choice for us. If I stay, our lives will change forever. If I stay, I can't be what I once was. I can no longer be Medusa and we can no longer just be Gloria Adaego Musa."

Adaego, I don't know this person you call Medusa, she is gone. I know the stories you've told me, and I've cried with you over the regret and sorrow you've felt for who that person was, but you are and have always been Adaego to me. We're both Gloria Adaego Musa, that's who we are, sisters, one inside, and one outside. Stay, and together we'll make a difference in this world. We'll do what you wished you'd done in your universe. We'll make a difference.

Adaego suddenly felt hope, similar to the moment when she'd first asked Gloria if she could stay in her four-year-old body. There was a chance to make a difference then, a chance to make Gloria's and her mother's lives better, and that same opportunity was reaching out to her now. Her power was awakened from its slumber, it ached to be used, and this time she'd use it for good. They'd make a difference in this universe.

"Oh, Gloria, I do love you," said Adaego. "You've always managed to help me feel like I'm worth more than I believe I am. I am Adaego. I've called myself by our middle name since the day I arrived here, this is who I am."

Her heart sighed with the growing sense of hope and a future as she gazed into Magus's angry eyes, waiting for her power to unfreeze time now that she had chosen to live. But, nothing was changing, they were still frozen, still caught in this moment.

"I don't understand." Adaego finally said, "I thought we had figured out what my power wants, but I don't know what to do now."

It must want something from you, from us. It can't keep us frozen in time forever, can it?

"I don't know. Honestly, I didn't know any of us affected by the events could do something like this. We all have varying degrees of powers and abilities, reproduced within us from the same energy pulse."

Oh, Adaego, that gives me an idea. You said your power was like a virus, right?

"Yes, I guess it seems like one. A virus is not really alive, and it's not really dead. I remember that from the high school biology classes we took. Why?"

Well, if your power's like a virus, other than infecting its host, it really only has one purpose, doesn't it? Its purpose is to replicate itself.

Adaego thought about this for a moment, and then, if she'd been able to move, she'd have thrown her head back and laughed loudly.

"I'm so proud of you, Gloria. You're the best part of both of us."

Do you think I'm right, then? That instead of letting you kill yourself along with it, it would rather replicate in this universe. That would make other super beings, right?

"I guess it would, as the two Events in my universe did."

And that way, it wouldn't just be us, there would be others like us who could help make a difference. Right?

"Yes!"

What's it waiting for then?

"I don't know. I've already decided to let go of Magus's hands, surely it senses that, but here we are, staring at his ugly face."

Gloria laughed.

"Now what? Or are we just making wild guesses here?"

I don't know, but if it wants to replicate, what does it need from us? Your permission?

"I'm not sure," Adaego said, as the silence of interrupted time hung heavily over them. "But if it's something it wants to do, I'm not opposed to it. Those that chose to do good in my universe, with the abilities that came from the two Events, have made a significant difference to many worlds and to many civilizations. They've done so much good, and would have been able to do so much more, if not for those like Magus and Medusa"

As she said the last words, she suddenly began to sense another stirring similar to what she'd felt just before the universe came to a stop. It was something deep within her cells, her power, stirring on a molecular level. She'd felt her remarkable power countless times before, a thing apart but a part of her, but this time it was shifting and stretching, pushing out like a child struggling to be born, tearing against the metaphoric uterus walls of the body it had inhabited for seven decades in that other universe, and for only a few in this one. At first, the tearing tickled, like an insect crawling across her arm, but then it began to rip and rend, sending waves of pain across her unmoving body, searing, burning, until suddenly a white light exploded across her field of vision, as bright and as violent as a thousand supernovas.

Adaego screamed.

Gloria screamed.

Time unfroze, and the wind and roar of her power danced around her, and lightning struck, and thunder pealed. Adaego pulled her hands away from Magus's, the heat from the embrace fading as quickly as her power began expanding outward. The pain she'd felt was swept aside, forgotten, a distant memory, as something newborn and extraordinary filled the void it left. It was a feeling of release, of an unburdening of heaviness. She could imagine no other way to describe it. Then a brilliant irregular bubble of light pushed out from her body, as she floated further away from Magus. He looked at it, curious about the expanding bubble, but not inquisitive enough to reason its purpose. He laughed, not understanding what he was seeing. The bubble of energy, her energy, continued to expand, enveloping Mia and Hunter and the woman Magus had killed with fire from his eyes. It rippled out across the quadrangle in ribbons, in streamers, in darts of ecstatic energy, moving faster and faster, flickering and dancing, seeking out new hosts, hungry to make itself known in this universe, replicating.

Replicating.

Replicating itself.

Thomas Stewart's arms fell to his sides, as he took a shuddering step backward. He seemed to tremble, then slumped slowly to the ground, dropping first to his knees and then falling over onto his side, a look of utter surprise filling his wide-open and terrified eyes.

"How?" he managed to utter, as the presence of the Magnificent Magus, the Scourge of the Universe, the Destroyer of the Worlds within him began to fade from this universe like a morning mist vaporized by the heat of the rising sun.

As his head flopped to the soft earth, Adaego's disc tumbled from Thomas's hand, flipping over onto a patch of grass that was still green, freshly cut that morning by maintenance crews, and miraculously undamaged by the fierce battle that had taken place all around it.

She walked over to the disc and picked it up, holding it tightly in her hand. It was extremely hot, but she could feel the heat quickly dissipating.

We didn't kill him, sister, not directly anyway. He was the engineer of his own death.

"Yes," she said quietly, gazing down at the unconscious man who'd been their lover and business partner. "I feel sad for him. Thomas could have been so much more than this."

We tried. We gave him the opportunity to take a different path, just like you did for us when you came to this universe.

Adaego nodded in agreement, as she lifted her eyes and slowly surveyed the damage caused by Magus and the battle between him and the Mighty Titan.

"Yes, we have a chance to take a different path."

FORTY

"I think I damaged the Peace Tower."

HUNTER FELT OFF BALANCE.

He couldn't describe the feeling any other way. He was floating, but not in a body of water, just floating, unattached from and untethered to anything. Perhaps this is what it would be like to be in outer space. Wait, he had been to space, and he'd even vomited in space. He, Hunter MacKenzie, had been to space and had left the contents of his stomach floating somewhere in orbit around Earth, endlessly circling the planet forever.

He laughed.

Then he was slammed back into Earth's gravity. It hurt for a brief moment, like jumping off something just a little too high from the ground, where his knees would complain from the sudden impact, but then he was floating again, and his mind returned to the vast expanse and of the mysteries of the universe. Could he call himself an astronaut now? Would that be fair?

Once, when he'd been about seven, he'd been on a rollercoaster with his grandfather at the Pacific National Exhibition in Vancouver. It was a ride that he was too young to be allowed on, but he'd been deceptively tall at that age. His grandfather had falsely assured the pimple-faced youth eyeballing the younger riders that Hunter was over ten, so he and his grandfather had stepped into a narrow car emblazoned with bright flames, the kind of flames you'd see after a fiery crash. The attendant had pushed the safety bar down across their laps, and Hunter wrapped his fingers around the hot and worn metal of the bar, where countless others had before him, squeezing so hard his little knuckles had turned white.

"Hey," his grandfather had said, patting his hands, leaning so close that Hunter could smell the pleasant sharpness of his aftershave. "Don't worry, it's the most incredible experience in the entire world. It's like riding a rocket ship to the moon."

He was thrilled, of course. Doing anything with his grandfather, who lived more than a day's drive away from Calgary, was always an exciting adventure. What he hadn't realized, and why would he at such a young age, was that the ride included two consecutive loops. By the time the various ups and downs and curves and corners had pushed the train of rollercoaster cars to the appropriate speed, they hit the loops at such a furious speed that all he would remember was the momentary feeling of floating, followed by that of being slammed into the hard plastic seat of the car they were locked into, and then of floating again.

This feeling was like that.

Floating.

Then, boom, his entire body hits something hard.

Then floating.

Then, boom, hitting that hard something again.

He opened his eyes and immediately squinted at the blast of light assaulting his retinas.

Mia. She was looking down at him, her face the most worried he'd ever seen it. In her beautiful hands, with their long fingers, she held an impossibly large chunk of masonry above her head. It looked like she was about to smash him with it.

"Mia?" he asked incredulously. "Are you hitting me with that?"

"Oh my, god, Hunter," she burst out, tossing the masonry away like it was a small stone. "You're alive."

She threw her arms around him, pulled him up then kissed him hard. He tried to return the kiss, but his mind was scattered, struggling to understand what was happening.

"Hey, let's give him some air," a voice said.

Mia pulled back and laughed, her beautiful almond-shaped eyes crinkled around the edges with a relief he couldn't quite understand. Hunter could see the detective leaning over them, one hand on Mia's shoulder, the other holding their masks. The detective appeared to be in good health, though her clothes looked like they'd been scorched with fire. Her jacket was hanging in blackened pieces from her shoulders and had large, melted spots where the flames had consumed the fabric. He'd seen her collapse to the ground, engulfed by the orange fire that had shot out of Magus's eyes, hadn't he? That had happened, right?

"Here," Mia said, grabbing Hunter under both arms and lifting him effortlessly to his feet.

Stars danced before his eyes from the sudden movement, but Mia quickly steadied him.

"What?" he managed to grunt. "How did you—?"

Mia laughed.

"I know! Crazy, eh?" she said, stepping back and placing her hands on her hips. It was an unusual pose, and Hunter wondered at it.

He looked from her to the detective and then thought to look down at his body. His t-shirt was torn, shredded, and definitely wouldn't be worn again. His jeans would require the heavy soil setting on his parent's washing machine, but otherwise, there didn't appear to be a mark anywhere on his body, at least that he could see. He should have been in pain, considering the horrific energy blasts Magus had been pummelling him with, but, well, he no longer hurt, not even a little.

"What happened? I thought we were—" he started pointing at the detective. "Magus burned you with his eyes. I saw that. You were on fire. I thought you were—"

"Dead?" Shimooka interjected, her eyes staring unblinkingly at Hunter, her face deadly serious.

"Uh, yeah."

Her gaze drifted past his shoulder as she pulled the tattered remains of her jacket from her shoulders, tossing them aside.

"I think I was."

Hunter frowned, uncertain of the meaning of what she'd just said. He turned to Mia.

"I think I damaged the Peace Tower. What happened? I thought Magus was about to kill us?"

Mia laughed again and grabbed Hunter's hand, turning him in the direction the detective was looking.

"It was Gloria or Adaego, or both of them. She's like you and Titan, there are two people in her body. One of them uses Gloria's name, and the other uses their middle name, Adaego. They saved us."

Gloria Adaego Musa was standing a few metres away, her arms wrapped tightly around her shoulders, her eyes fixed on the handcuffed Thomas Stewart, who was lying on his side at her feet.

"Is he, is he dead?" Hunter asked Mia.

Mia shook her head.

"No, he's unconscious. Detective Shimooka tried to rouse him, but he's really out."

She shrugged.

"Magus has returned to their universe and left Thomas behind to face the consequences for what they've done."

Gloria's head lifted as she heard Mia's explanation. She smiled at them both, sadness hovering at the corners of her blue eyes.

"Hello, Hunter," she said as she approached them.

She seemed far more confident than the frightened, crying woman he'd observed sitting at the edge of the portico earlier.

"I never knew you at this age," Gloria said.

"Knew me?"

She nodded, stopping near them.

"The other you, I mean, the Mighty Titan, the other Hunter MacKenzie. The first time we met, you were much older."

Hunter smiled, but he wasn't sure what to say.

"Thank you for fighting Magus," Gloria continued. "I know you weren't ready for this, but he's gone now."

"Magus is gone?"

Gloria smiled softly.

"Yes," she replied, nodding. "Magus is gone. He's the reason I came to your universe in the first place, the reason Gloria and I share this body."

Hunter looked between Gloria and Mia.

"You came to our universe, too? What do you mean?"

Mia laughed and slipped an arm around his.

"She's like Titan. She called herself Medusa in the other universe but insists she's not to be called by that name anymore."

"Medusa?" said Hunter. "You mean like the Greek mythological Gorgon?"

Gloria lightly touched Hunter's arm.

"Yes, it was a silly name Magus gave me. I came from the same universe as he and Titan, but many years ago, when this Gloria," she said, as she placed a hand over her chest, "was a child."

Hunter frowned.

"So, uh, what do I call you? Am I talking to this universe's Gloria, or is it like Titan and me, where I'm like the person on the outside, and he's on the inside?"

Gloria smiled.

"It's a little hard to wrap your head around, as I'm sure you've been experiencing since Titan entered your body,"

She briefly placed her left hand over her heart.

"We've been together for twenty-two years in this body, and because of that, we've become indistinguishable. We share this body, and our thoughts are often the same. Sometimes I, who used to be called Medusa," she explained, as she briefly touched her right hand to her chest, opposite the one over her heart, "and I, the Gloria that Medusa came to when I was only four, speak within the same sentence."

Hunter frowned again.

"You both just spoke? That's really weird."

Gloria laughed, her broad smile playing into her eyes.

"How about this, since the day we were born, in both our universes, we've been Gloria Adaego Musa. You may simply call us Gloria to our face, and we'll let you know which one of us is talking to you if need be."

Hunter smiled and shrugged.

"All right, Gloria, it is."

Hunter looked past her at the unconscious Thomas Stewart.

"So, it's over?" he asked.

He let his gaze fall on the debris littered across the quadrangle, the smoking pile of the partially destroyed East Block, and the smouldering remnants of an impossibly one-sided battle.

"Yes," Mia said. "We won, thanks to you and Gloria."

Hunter turned to her.

"Wow, I thought for sure I was going to die, like the detective, uh, did."

Shimooka grimaced as her gaze was pulled away from them.

"The people with guns are moving in now that Stewart's down."

Mia leaned into him and pointed toward Wellington Street.

"I think we need to leave."

Hunter followed her gaze. A growing group of soldiers and police were coming out of hiding along Wellington Street.

Hunter suddenly gasped. His brain was silent.

"Wait, I think Titan's gone, too."

"What?" Mia gasped. "He's not talking to you?"

Hunter shook his head.

"No, I mean, I don't know. I can't hear him. He usually never shuts up."

Gloria peered into his face.

"May I touch you?"

"Why?" Mia asked. "Will you be able to sense if he's there?"

"Yes," she said. "Those of us affected by the Events can sense each other, even from a great distance. May I touch you, Hunter?"

Hunter shrugged.

"Sure."

Gloria gently pressed a hand against the side of his face and closed her eyes. Images and sounds began to flash through Hunter's mind as clear and focused as if they were happening before his opened eyes. He saw heroes and villains dressed in striking costumes that resembled ones he'd only ever seen in comic books and movies, but he understood that these were real in that universe. He saw Magus and Titan fighting in a hundred different locales, driving blast after blast of energy into one another or grappling and driving their fists into each other. He saw Medusa, her power coursing out from her, striking other super-powered beings, some with shields of energy, others with flaming swords that spat multi-coloured streams of destructive energy and some with amulets and helmets that glowed with the colours of burning coals. He saw horrific battles, violent and explosive, some in the vastness of outer space, some on moons that circled Jupiter-sized planets, and others over vast bodies of water, rolling fields, and on jagged otherworldly mountain peaks. It was as if he was watching a video streaming service that only offered all the fight scenes from superhero movies, spliced together into one never-ending sequence of furious back and forth battles. The explosive noise and violent clashes overwhelmed him, and he began to feel the pain of all this fighting, all this warring between these powerful beings, good and evil, heroes and villains, and then suddenly it stopped.

"Oh, there you are," Gloria's voice said out loud, but also from inside Hunter's head.

Medusa?

"Yes."

You are alive. How?

"Titan?" Hunter asked slowly.

Hunter, listen carefully. We must leave immediately. Medusa is extremely dangerous, and I am not sure we can withstand an attack from her in our present condition.

"Whoa! Wait!" Hunter sputtered as Gloria's eyes opened wide. "She saved us from Magus. She's one of the good ones."

Medusa saved us from Magus? Do not be fooled by her treachery. She is ruthless, like Magus.

"I don't know about any of that, but she's the Gloria from your universe, and, just like you paired with my body, she says she paired with the Gloria from this universe."

But I do not understand. I watched her die years ago.

"Yes, I suppose it might be difficult to understand," Gloria said, a sadness sweeping across her eyes as she continued to touch Hunter's face. "We were enemies, after all."

Yes, we were, but not by my choice.

"You're right, and it was by my choosing. I regret that we were enemies. I wasn't my best self in our universe."

The Gloria of this universe interjected.

It's true, my sister isn't that person.

Titan spoke to her.

Ah, the other Gloria. I presume you are the one from this universe?

She answered.

Yes, and she isn't the person you say she is. The Medusa you know hasn't existed in this universe.

Titan was skeptical.

So, what now? She wishes to be good and forget all that has transpired in our universe. You have committed many crimes, Medusa. Hiding out in this universe does not absolve you of the harm you have done.

Gloria sighed, her eyes fixed on the young face of the one who, in her universe, had been her enemy for many years. Hunter smiled uncomfortably as he returned her gaze. Then she closed her eyes and answered.

"I came here to this universe because I had to remove myself from everything I felt I was incapable of changing. I may be powerful, Titan, but I'm a very weak person. The substance abuse I inflicted on my body before the Second Event was merely replaced by the power that allowed me to try and fill that hole by taking whatever I wanted. Magus offered me structure and discipline, but he was also violently abusive to me, and I couldn't seem to free myself of him, nor was I able to destroy myself. The power within me wouldn't allow it, so the discs provided a way to leave, and this Gloria and I have lived a life of peace.

Titan argued.

But you have done so much harm, justice must prevail. Your deeds cannot go unanswered.

Tears pressed out from Gloria's shut eyes, and Hunter could sense the intense sorrow that resided deep within her.

"I'm sorry, I would return to my universe if I could and present myself to the League and the United Planetary Nations for judgment, but I brought both discs with me, and I can't return. Please, forgive me."

Hunter could hear the Mighty Titan sigh within his head. It was a long awkward moment for him, with Gloria's hand on the side of his face and the emotions of a difficult conversation between two longtime foes lingering in his mind before titan responded.

The last few days have been challenging for young Hunter and me, but I believe I can understand. Life is not as black and white as I have made it in my quest to be altruistic in using this power. I too feel I must apologize. I should have found you before Magus did. I knew of your existence and had heard of how powerful you were, but there were so many who were changed by the Second Event who needed our help. I searched for you, but you were very good at hiding.

"Yes," she said, laughing softly, relief slipping into her voice. "Hurting people don't trust people, so I hid."

I could have made a difference in your life. I am sorry.

"He's there?" Mia asked, touching Hunter's arm.

"Yes," Hunter whispered out of the corner of his mouth, turning his eyes to Mia. "You can hear, uh, Gloria, but all three of them are talking it out, inside my head. This is really weird and awkward."

"All three inside your head?" Mia said, her eyebrows rising.

Hunter grimaced.

"Yeah, Titan, this universe's Gloria and the other Gloria whom we're not supposed to call Medusa."

"That's freaky."

Hunter raised his eyebrows and then turned his eyes to the woman in front of him.

You remained hidden here. Why? You could have ruled this universe with your power. You could have had whatever you wished for with none capable of stopping you.

Gloria lowered her head, her eyes still shut.

"Yes, I could have, but that's why I came here. I could no longer be that horrible person. My lack of courage in choosing a better path for my life was the cause of much harm and sorrow for so many beings who didn't deserve what my existence brought to them, and this seemed to be the only way to remove what I was from our universe. This was my sentence, my punishment, to trap myself here and to have my power make me forget who Medusa had been and that I even had abilities.

I would not call coming to this universe punishment.

"No, it certainly is not, but I found everything I'd ever genuinely wished for in this universe."

And that was?

Gloria pulled in a long, slow breath, tears streaming down her face

"Love. I found a way to make love happen."

The other Gloria agreed.

I have known nothing but love from my sister, to me and to our mother and aunties.

Titan was silent for a moment, and Hunter wondered if the conversation was over, but then he spoke.

Your mother, you were able to save her in this universe?

Gloria frowned.

"Yes. I, I saved us both."

I am happy for both of you.

"You knew my mother?"

Yes, she contacted the League not too long before she died and asked us to find you. What the Second Event did to you only made you even angrier, and she wanted us to befriend you and help you before anything terrible happened. But, there were so many like you who were suddenly transformed by the energy pulse and who needed our help. I am sorry I failed you.

Gloria shook her head.

"No, Titan, I failed myself. It was always my choice. The day you thought you saw me die, I made a choice. At the time, it seemed like the only one left to me. I got away from Magus."

She paused, then continued.

"As far away from him as one could go, I started over. I made retribution of sorts for my crimes by keeping this Gloria safe from the things that would have damaged her life as they had mine. I can't repair all I've done or restore the lives I've taken, but I've lived every day here as if Medusa were dead."

The other Gloria interrupted.

It's true. My sister has only shown goodness and kindness all the years we've shared this body. I only know of this Medusa from what she told me before her power made us forget, but I've never seen this person she says she used to be. She's changed.

Titan chuckled.

You certainly have a champion in this universe's Gloria.

Gloria agreed.

"Yes, she's the best part of us. She's become what I once could have been."

Titan was silent for a few seconds before he responded.

So, here we are, at this remarkable juncture in our journey.

"Yes, here we are. I will do whatever you ask of me, Titan. I would even use the disc I tricked Magus into using, to return to our universe and experience the same fate as him."

No. Titan said quickly and firmly, *That will not be necessary. I have always been rigid in my views of right and wrong, but I always wished for a better life for you. I believe you have found it here. Thank you for saving us, for saving me. As my younger self has said, you are one of the good ones.*

Gloria opened her glistening eyes and looked into Hunter's.

"Thank you, Titan. I don't deserve your mercy."

No, I suppose not, but I know Magus. He did not have an ounce of compassion or mercy for anyone, least of all you.

"Thank you," she said, sobs slipping from her throat, her shoulders dropping, tears glimmering along the edges of her eyes.

Titan was curious.

Something is different within this body, I feel it. What have you done to us?

"I've separated you from your younger self," Gloria replied.

What? Why? I must protect him with my power. He knows so little.

Gloria chuckled.

"It isn't necessary. My power has replicated, it's expanded outward. It's within him now and others. It is, I suppose, like what happened to me and the others many years ago. I guess you could say this is the Third Event. You may return to our universe. You're needed more there than you are here."

Hunter frowned, squinting into the woman's eyes before him. Were they Gloria's, or were they Adaego's? This was very confusing.

"Wait? What? Your power's inside me, not Titan's?"

Yes, it appears so. I feel a form of her energy within us. It is rather stirring, I must confess, Titan said.

Shimooka interrupted them.

"Hey, I hate to break up the family reunion, but the people with the really big guns are moving in."

She turned and pointed toward Wellington Street, where a squad of heavily armed soldiers were slowly approaching where they were on the quadrangle. Gloria pulled her hand away from Hunter's face and turned to look where the detective was pointing.

"I'll stay with you, detective. I'm a witness to Thomas's actions. There will be quite the media circus, but these two need to leave," she said, reaching into a pocket and pulling out the disc she'd taken from Magus's hand earlier, the one he'd thought he was using to return to his universe. Hunter glanced at it, and Titan immediately recognized it.

She has the disc!

"What disc?" Hunter said.

The disc that brought Magus and me here. She has it.

Gloria reached out and took Hunter's hand, placing the disc into his palm.

"Here, this is for Titan. Adaego says his entity was imprinted on it when he and Magus travelled here. It will allow him to return to their universe, to his body."

Hunter clasped his hands around the disc, "Uh, so you're Gloria? Adaego is on the inside now?"

Gloria laughed, "Yes, I'm sorry. We're getting used to this, too. No one ever knew there were two of us before today, and, of course, Adaego had instructed her power to make us forget this fact."

"But what about you, uh, the you from the other universe? Titan wants to know what you're planning to do."

"May I touch your face again?"

Hunter nodded, and Gloria placed her hand against Hunter's face and spoke as Adaego.

"This has been my home. It's time I quit hiding and make a difference for good, beyond the difference I was able to make for this universe's Gloria."

You are right. Titan agreed. *This is where you belong. If I understand what has happened, your power replicating in this universe, you will be needed here as I was needed when The Second Event occurred in our universe.*

Gloria nodded and continued, "I can do the same for the people affected by my power replicating, as you did for so many in our universe after the Second Event. I can help them."

They will need your help. I can see that you have learned that this power must be used for the good of all.

Gloria inside spoke, her voice strong and confident.

They will have both of our help, Titan. We have an advantage, there are two of us.

Gloria, her eyes still moist with tears, pulled her hand away from Hunter's head.

"We shall have to start with you and your amazing girlfriend."

Hunter wasn't sure what she meant, but he turned to Mia as he slid the disc into a pocket.

"So, the bad guys are gone, the other good guys are," he paused in mid-speech as he turned to look at the approaching group, "are heading our way. I guess we should get out of here. I'll fly us back to Calgary."

Mia laughed as she stepped back and slowly floated up off the ground.

"You don't have to."

Hunter's mouth dropped open.

"What? How?"

Mia dropped lightly down to the grass.

"Gloria, or, I guess, Adaego's power did this. The detective has superpowers as well."

Hunter turned to Shimooka, who frowned and shrugged.

"Sorry, I'm not showboating for anybody, not that you were doing that," she said, gesturing at Mia, "but I'm not doing anything until I figure out what the hell this means."

Mia laughed and tugged on Hunter's arm.

"I'll explain later," she said. "We really do need to get out of here if we're to protect our identities."

Shimooka handed them the damaged Ant-Man and Wasp masks.

"Here," she said. "Gloria, or one of the Gloria's, assures me that her power has been generating a wobble or some such thing in the space continuum thing around us, so no one's been able to see any of this clearly. She says every electronic device within a two or three-kilometre radius of here is fried, so there won't be a record of what happened, at least for the last twenty minutes. Is that correct?"

Gloria, who'd been gazing at the unmoving form of Thomas Stewart, turned her face to the detective and nodded.

"Yes, your death by the hand of Magus, detective, won't have been recorded on any device, and the identities of the individuals who stopped Thomas, including mine, should be safe for now." She let her gaze turn to the approaching group of military, then to Hunter and Mia, "However, the world knows that something extraordinary happened here today. I'll need to go with the detective and see this through, but we need to talk about what has happened here and soon."

"You'll find us?" Mia asked.

Gloria nodded.

"Yes. I would suggest you both don't do anything outside of what is normal for your lives. Don't draw attention to what has happened within you."

Shimooka groaned and looked down at the black screen of the cellphone she'd pulled from her pocket. She was tapping it over and over with her thumb.

"Damn. Okaa-san won't believe this."

"You can't—" Gloria began.

"I know the superhero routine," the detective interrupted. She slid the dead phone into the back pocket of her slacks.

"I can't tell her."

Hunter was still stuck on the latest revelation.

"Wait. So, we're all super-powered now?"

Shimooka shrugged and walked over to Gloria.

"We can meet up later, like, on the moon or something," she said over her shoulder, laughing in a not-too-serious way.

"And, as the Glorias said, we can discuss what this means."

Mia grabbed his arm.

"Hunter, we should go."

Hunter slipped the mask over his head and let Mia guide him up into the overcast sky, the quadrangle and Parliament Hill shrinking rapidly beneath them as he looked down. Detective Shimooka was checking Stewart's handcuffs, he was still unmoving, and Adaego was standing next to her as dozens of armed personnel poured toward them from multiple directions. Hunter zoomed in with his vision to watch the detective turning Stewart over onto his back. His head was moving slightly, and Hunter could see his eyes fluttering open. He seemed alarmed.

I did not expect this.

"You didn't expect this? I was stocking shelves at Earls two days ago," Hunter said as they sped west.

"What?" Mia asked.

Hunter shrugged as they soared high above Lake Superior, holding onto each other.

"Titan's having a moment," he said.

EPILOGUE

THE MIGHTY TITAN COULD HEAR a faraway voice, and it was making a terrifying sound as if the owner of the voice had just had a limb violently ripped from their body. He'd heard that disturbing cry once before, just before he was slammed into his younger self in the other universe.

Then it struck him, it was he who was doing the screaming.

Then he wasn't.

He opened his eyes and immediately shrunk back. Magus's face was a hands breadth from his, one eye shut, the other partially open and lifeless, the pupil in full dilation. Titan had seen that look before, far too many times over the years. He realized his hands were still clasped over his enemy's, locked in that furious last-desperate-act grip from three days earlier. He pulled his hands away, revealing the disc that had brought both he and Magus to Hunter's universe now gripped again in Magus's ungloved hand, as it had been days earlier. Titan wrestled the object from the clenched hand, quickly examining it. It looked like the one Gloria had taken from Magus and given Hunter, the one they'd used to return him to his universe. It was.

He pulled away, rolling over to look down at the planet beneath them. This was Earth, somewhere over the Pacific Ocean. He zoomed in with his vision, scanning, searching. They were over Polynesia. Yes, there was Samoa, the tiny island vibrant with vegetation and alive with civilization. He pulled his vision back and turned around to examine Magus, his lifeless body stiff, frozen in postmortem rigidity. No, wait, his lifelong enemy was breathing ever so slightly. Titan glided over to the body, resting a hand on its chest. The slight rise was barely discernible, the breathing shallow but steady. Ah, yes, his body was alive, but the very thing that made Magus who Magus was, his consciousness, his soul, whatever one would choose to call it, was not present. Gloria had explained what she'd done to him, tricking the not-so-clever Magus into using her disc to return to their universe, to return to nothing, because her body and entity were wholly in the other universe, fused in an inexplicable way to her other self there.

Titan looked down at the disc in his hand, the device Magus had used in his ignorance, believing he was destroying Titan when, instead, it had brought them both to the parallel universe. Now, it had brought Titan back to his body, which he supposed had been orbiting around the planet along with the soulless body of Magus since the moment they'd left, believing, he reminded himself, that his life was at an end. Titan laughed softly and searched for the wounds that Magus had inflicted upon his body during their battle high above the night sky over Scotland. There were none. His suit was torn and ripped in places, stained with dried blood and plasma burns, but his formidable power had healed his body while he and his power had been in the other universe. How was that possible? A portion of his powerful essence must have remained here, keeping him alive and safe from the unforgiving environment around them.

He rose above Magus's body, positioning himself to look into the one open eye. Gloria's ploy had worked. Magus's essence had returned to this universe, but not to his body. He pushed the eyelid shut with a finger, wondering how long the cosmic energy infused in this empty shell would allow it to live without the full power of its former occupant. It could be a long time, he mused. He'd never fully understood the energy that had transformed their bodies over a hundred years earlier, but he'd understood that he could do tremendous good with what had happened to him. Thomas Stewart, on the other hand, had chosen to do immense evil. Many others had experienced that instantaneous transformation long ago, but sadly Thomas and a few dozen like him had decided to pursue a selfish existence with their gifts. When the second wave of transformative energy coursed through the galaxy, when Gloria and still others had been transformed in various ways, he and Magus had already been pummelling each other across the universe for almost three decades, the never-ending battle between good and evil.

We have all made choices, Titan thought. The gift of the power, from wherever it had come from, had forced each being affected by it to make a choice. He looked into the face of his foe. They hadn't always been the best choices, but now it was over, at least between him and Magus.

He remembered that there should be a second disc that matched the one that brought him back from the other universe. He searched through the various pockets and folds of Magus's suit until he found a hidden pouch that held two thin, rectangular cases. Each case was made from a soft, silver material, platinum, he guessed, based on what he remembered Magus had said to him. He opened one, discovering that it contained two discs similar to the one in his hand. He opened the second, which had one disc and an indentation next to it in the case, designed to hold the one he held. He slid his disc into the container alongside that one and then placed the cases into the only pocket along his thigh that hadn't been ripped during their battle.

Where was the mind and soul of Magus? Floating somewhere in the vastness of space as indefinable energy, no body, no way to inflict further pain and violence on the beings of this universe? Titan smiled and wondered if his old enemy was conscious of this fact. If there were any mercy in the vast chaos of the galaxy, the sociopath would be aware of every moment, for however long he continued to exist.

Titan huffed.

"That was not very charitable of me."

He gazed at the scarred, placid face of the being who had once simply been Thomas Alexander Stewart.

"Maybe Hunter is right. Maybe I should have ended your reign of terror long ago."

He looked away to the sliver of the Moon playing with the Earth's edge. So much loss and sorrow could have been avoided if he'd made that choice. There had been many times he could have ended Magus's life, he'd wanted to do it, and had even on occasion tried to convince himself that he could live with the choice, but it hadn't been a line he felt he could cross. Still, the Gloria Musa of this universe may have had a different life if he'd crossed his ethical boundary.

"Perhaps," Titan said out loud, letting his gaze fall to the oddly tranquil face of Magus. "But what would separate us then? How would your death by my hand be any different from the many deaths caused by your hand? I will not be that person."

Titan sighed, letting the emotion of his return and the end of Magus wash over him. He grabbed a strip of the tattered cape still fixed to the costume that clothed the empty shell of his enemy and turned his mind toward the Fortress and the League, who kept the universe safe from the madness of villains such as Magus and, at one time, Medusa.

Gloria.

She'd found a way to make another choice, another life.

She should have been brought to justice, but he'd give her this one chance. As far as this universe was concerned, she'd killed herself in a moment of contrition and regret for the decades of terror she and Magus had brought upon so many. In a sense, she did kill herself by removing her influence from this universe. Now, she'd found a new path, a new life, and ironically, she would make a positive difference in that universe, especially now that her power had, what did she say, replicated?

That should be interesting, he thought, as he focused his will on the northern hemisphere and the northern tip of Greenland, on the Fortress and the powerful group of multi-species and super-powered beings who called themselves the League. These were his friends, his family, and those who worked together to better every known civilization throughout the known galaxy. They didn't just fight villainy, they also fought against famine, poverty, and disease, bringing relief and hope to the trillions of beings that populated their universe.

He arrived at the Fortress's giant shielded doors in the millisecond it took to think of them.

About the Author

Wyatt Tremblay is perhaps best known for his 30 years of political cartooning for the Yukon News. Born in Jasper, Alberta, he spent much of his life in the Yukon but now lives in Airdrie, Alberta. His short story collection, *iDead and Other Short Stories* is available everywhere through Raspberry Press. He is a regular arts feature writer for AirdrieLife Magazine.

Medusa Gone is his first published novel.

Look for his second novel, *The Key to Enniskillen*, coming out in 2023 through Raspberry Press.

Acknowledgements

I owe a huge thank you to Cheryl Fountain and Raspberry Press for taking a chance on this novel and to Simon Rose, who took on the task of doing the professional edit.

I am greatly indebted to the many writers I have had the privilege to know who have encouraged me to keep writing. Patricia Robertson (The Goldfish Dancer, Hour of the Crab), Erling Friis-Baastad (Wood Spoken, Fossil Light), and my longtime friend Josephine Holmes, who was my first editor many years ago, all deserve credit for what you hold in your hands.

Most of all, I wish to thank my best friend and partner in life, Bonnie Woelk, for believing in me and encouraging me not to stop until *Medusa Gone* saw the light of day.

Thanks for reading! Please add a short review on Amazon.ca, or write me at wyattsworld@me.com and let me know what you think!